NORA ROBERTS

A DAY AWAY

Published by Silhouette Books

America's Publisher of Contemporary Romance

SILHOUETTE BOOKS

A DAY AWAY

ISBN-13: 978-0-373-28162-6

Copyright © 2012 by Harlequin Books S.A.

The publisher acknowledges the copyright holder of the individual works as follows:

ONE SUMMER
Copyright © 1986 by Nora Roberts

TEMPTATION
Copyright © 1987 by Nora Roberts

Recycling programs for this product may not exist in your area.

CONTENTS

ONE SUMMER

Chapter 1

The room was dark. Pitch-dark. But the man named Shade was used to the dark. Sometimes he preferred it. It wasn't always necessary to see with your eyes. His fingers were both clever and competent, his inner eye as keen as a knife blade.

There were times, even when he wasn't working, when he'd sit in a dark room and simply let images form in his mind. Shapes, textures, colors. Sometimes they came clearer when you shut your eyes and just let your thoughts flow. He courted darkness, shadows, just as relentlessly as he courted the light. It was all part of life, and life—its images—was his profession.

He didn't always see life as others did. At times it was harsher, colder, than the naked eye could see—or wanted to. Other times it was softer, more lovely, than the busy world imagined. Shade observed it, grouped the elements, manipulated time and shape, then recorded it his way. Always his way.

Now, with the room dark and the sound of recorded jazz coming quiet and disembodied from the corner, he worked with his hands and his mind. Care and timing. He used them both in every aspect of his work. Slowly, smoothly, he opened the capsule and transferred the undeveloped film onto the reel. When the light-tight lid was on the developing tank, he set the timer with his free hand, then pulled the chain that added the amber light to the room.

Shade enjoyed developing the negative and making the print as much as, sometimes more than, he enjoyed taking the photograph. Darkroom work required precision and accuracy. He needed both in his life. Making the print allowed for creativity and experimentation. He needed those as well. What he saw, what he felt about what he saw, could be translated exactly or left as an enigma. Above all, he needed the satisfaction of creating something himself, alone. He always worked alone.

Now, as he went through each precise step of developing—temperature, chemicals, agitation, timing—the amber light cast his face into shadows. If Shade had been looking to create the image of photographer at work, he'd never have found a clearer statement than himself.

His eyes were dark, intense now as he added the stop bath to the tank. His hair was dark as well, too long for the convention he cared nothing about. It brushed over his ears, the back of his T-shirt, and fell over his forehead nearly to his eyebrows. He never gave much thought to style. His was cool, almost cold, and rough around the edges.

His face was deeply tanned, lean and hard, with strong bones dominating. His mouth was taut as he concentrated. There were lines spreading out finely from his eyes, etched there by what he'd seen and what he'd felt about it. Some would say there'd already been too much of both.

The nose was out of alignment, a result of a professional hazard. Not everyone liked to have his picture taken. The Cambodian soldier had broken Shade's nose, but Shade had gotten a telling picture of the city's devastation, of the waste. He still considered it an even exchange.

In the amber light, his movements were brisk. He had a rangy, athletic body, the result of years in the field—often a foreign, unfriendly field—miles of legwork and missed meals.

Even now, years after his last staff assignment for *International View,* Shade remained lean and agile. His work wasn't as grueling as it had been in his early years in Lebanon, Laos, Central America, but his pattern hadn't changed. He worked long hours, sometimes waiting endlessly for just the right shot, sometimes using a roll of film within minutes. If his style and manner were aggressive, it could be said that they'd kept him alive and whole during the wars he'd recorded.

The awards he'd won, the fee he now commanded, remained secondary to the picture. If no one had paid him or recognized his work, Shade would still have been in the darkroom, developing his film. He was respected, successful and rich. Yet he had no assistant and continued to work out of the same darkroom he'd set up ten years before.

When Shade hung his negatives up to dry, he already had an idea which ones he'd print. Still, he barely glanced at them, leaving them hanging as he unlocked the darkroom door and stepped out. Tomorrow his outlook would be fresher. Waiting was an advantage he hadn't always had. Right now he wanted a beer. He had some thinking to do.

He headed straight for the kitchen and grabbed a cold bottle. Popping off the lid, he tossed it into the can his once-a-week housekeeper lined with plastic. The room was clean, not particularly cheerful with the hard whites and blacks, but then it wasn't dull.

After he tilted the bottle back, he chugged the beer down, draining half. He lit a cigarette, then took the beer to the kitchen table where he leaned back in a chair and propped his feet on the scrubbed wood surface.

The view out the kitchen window was of a not-so-glamorous L.A. It was a little seamy, rough, sturdy and tough. The early-evening light couldn't make it pretty. He could've moved to a glossier part of town, or out to the hills, where the lights of the city at night looked like a fairy tale. Shade preferred the small apartment that looked out over the unpampered streets of a city known for glitz. He didn't have much patience with glitz.

Bryan Mitchell. She specialized in it.

He couldn't deny that her portraits of the rich, famous and beautiful were well done—even excellent ones of their kind. There was compassion in her photographs, humor and a smooth sensuality. He wouldn't even deny that there was a place for her kind of work in the field. It just wasn't his angle. She reflected culture, he went straight for life.

Her work for *Celebrity* magazine had been professional, slick and often searing in its way. The larger-than-life people she'd photographed had often been cut down to size in a way that made them human and approachable. Since she'd decided to freelance, the stars, near-stars and starmakers she'd photographed for the glossy came to her. Over the years, she'd developed a reputation and style that had made her one of them, part of the inner, select circle.

It could happen to a photographer, he knew. They could come to resemble their own themes, their own studies. Sometimes what they tried to project became a part of them. Too much a part. No, he didn't begrudge Bryan Mitchell her state of the art. Shade simply had doubts about working with her.

He didn't care for partnerships.

Yet those were the terms. When he'd been approached by *Life-style* to do a pictorial study of America, he'd been intrigued. Photo essays could make a strong, lasting statement that could rock and jar or soothe and amuse. As a photographer, he had sought to do that. *Life-style* wanted him, wanted the strong, sometimes concise, sometimes ambiguous emotions his pictures could portray. But they also wanted a counterbalance. A woman's view.

He wasn't so stubborn that he didn't see the point and the possibilities. Yet it irked him to think that the assignment hinged on his willingness to share the summer, his van and the credit with a celebrity photographer. And with a woman at that. Three months on the

road with a female who spent her time perfecting snap-
shots of rock stars and personalities. For a man who'd
cut his professional teeth in war-torn Lebanon, it didn't
sound like a picnic.

But he wanted to do it. He wanted the chance to
capture an American summer from L.A. to New York,
showing the joy, the pathos, the sweat, the cheers and
disappointments. He wanted to show the heart, even
while he stripped it to the bone.

All he had to do was say yes, and share the summer
with Bryan Mitchell.

"Don't think about the camera, Maria. Dance."
Bryan lined up the forty-year-old ballet superstar in
her viewfinder. She liked what she saw. Age? Touches
of it, but years meant nothing. Grit, style, elegance. Endurance—most of all, endurance. Bryan knew how to
catch them all and meld them.

Maria Natravidova had been photographed countless
times over her phenomenal twenty-five-year career. But
never with sweat running down her arms and dampen-
ing her leotard. Never with the strain showing. Bryan
wasn't looking for the illusions dancers live with, but
the exhaustion, the aches that were the price of triumph.

She caught Maria in a leap, legs stretched parallel to
the floor, arms flung wide in perfect alignment. Drops
of moisture danced from her face and shoulders; muscles bunched and held. Bryan pressed the shutter, then
moved the camera slightly to blur the motion.

That would be the one. She knew it even as she finished off the roll of film.

"You make me work," the dancer complained as

she slid into a chair, blotting her streaming face with a towel.

Bryan took two more shots, then lowered her camera. "I could've dressed you in costume, backlit you and had you hold an arabesque. That would show that you're beautiful, graceful. Instead I'm going to show that you're a strong woman."

"And you're a clever one." Maria sighed as she let the towel drop. "Why else do I come to you for the pictures for my book?"

"Because I'm the best." Bryan crossed the studio and disappeared into a back room. Maria systematically worked a cramp out of her calf. "Because I understand you, admire you. And—" she brought out a tray, two glasses and a pitcher clinking with ice "—because I squeeze oranges for you."

"Darling." With a laugh, Maria reached for the first glass. For a moment, she held it to her high forehead, then drank deeply. Her dark hair was pulled back severely in a style only good bones and flawless skin could tolerate. Stretching out her long, thin body in the chair, she studied Bryan over the rim of her glass.

Maria had known Bryan for seven years, since the photographer had started at *Celebrity* with the assignment to take pictures of the dancer backstage. The dancer had been a star, but Bryan hadn't shown awe. Maria could still remember the young woman with the thick honey-colored braid and bib overalls. The elegant prima ballerina had found herself confronted with candid eyes the color of pewter, an elegant face with slanting cheekbones and a full mouth. The tall, athletic body had nearly been lost inside the baggy clothes. She'd worn ragged sneakers and long, dangling earrings.

Maria glanced down at the dingy Nikes Bryan wore. Some things didn't change. At first glance, you'd categorize the tall, tanned blonde in sneakers and shorts as typically California. Looks could be deceiving. There was nothing typical about Bryan Mitchell.

Bryan accepted the stare as she drank. "What do you see, Maria?" It interested her to know. Conceptions and preconceptions were part of her trade.

"A strong, smart woman with talent and ambition." Maria smiled as she leaned back in the chair. "Myself, nearly."

Bryan smiled. "A tremendous compliment."

Maria acknowledged this with a sweeping gesture. "There aren't many women I like. Myself I like, and so, you. I hear rumors, my love, about you and that pretty young actor."

"Matt Perkins." Bryan didn't believe in evading or pretending. She lived, by choice, in a town fueled by rumors, fed by gossip. "I took his picture, had a few dinners."

"Nothing serious?"

"As you said, he's pretty." Bryan smiled and chewed on a piece of ice. "But there's barely room enough for his ego and mine in his Mercedes."

"Men." Maria leaned forward to pour herself a second glass.

"Now you're going to be profound."

"Who better?" Maria countered. "Men." She said the word again, savoring it. "I find them tedious, childish, foolish and indispensable. Being loved…sexually, you understand?"

Bryan managed to keep her lips from curving. "I understand."

"Being loved is exhilarating, exhausting. Like Christmas. Sometimes I feel like the child who doesn't understand why Christmas ends. But it does. And you wait for the next time."

It always fascinated Bryan how people felt about love, how they dealt with it, groped for it and avoided it. "Is that why you never married, Maria? You're waiting for the next time?"

"I married dance. To marry a man, I would have to divorce dance. There's no room for two for a woman like me. And you?"

Bryan stared into her drink, no longer amused. She understood the words too well. "No room for two," she murmured. "But I don't wait for the next time."

"You're young. If you could have Christmas every day, would you turn away from it?"

Bryan moved her shoulders. "I'm too lazy for Christmas every day."

"Still, it's a pretty fantasy." Maria rose and stretched. "You've made me work long enough. I have to shower and change. Dinner with my choreographer."

Alone, Bryan absently ran a finger over the back of her camera. She didn't often think about love and marriage. She'd been there already. Once a fantasy was exposed to reality, it faded, like a photo improperly fixed. Permanent relationships rarely worked, and still more rarely worked well.

She thought of Lee Radcliffe, married to Hunter

Brown for nearly a year, helping to raise his daughter and pregnant with her first child. Lee was happy, but then she'd found an extraordinary man, one who wanted her to be what she was, even encouraged her to explore herself. Bryan's own experience had taught her that what's said and what's felt can be two opposing things.

Your career's as important to me as it is to you. How many times had Rob said that *before* they'd been married? *Get your degree. Go for it.*

So they'd gotten married, young, eager, idealistic. Within six months he'd been unhappy with the time she'd put into her classes and her job at a local studio. He'd wanted his dinner hot and his socks washed. Not so much to ask, Bryan mused. To be fair, she had to say that Rob had asked for little of her. Just too much at the time.

They'd cared for each other, and both had tried to make adjustments. Both had discovered they'd wanted different things for themselves—different things from each other, things neither could be, neither could give.

It would've been called an amicable divorce—no fury, no bitterness. No passion. A signature on a legal document, and the dream had been over. It had hurt more than anything Bryan had ever known. The taint of failure had stayed with her a long, long time.

She knew Rob had remarried. He was living in the suburbs with his wife and their two children. He'd gotten what he'd wanted.

And so, Bryan told herself as she looked around her studio, had she. She didn't just want to be a photographer. She was a photographer. The hours she spent in the field, in her studio, in the darkroom, were as essential to her as sleep. And what she'd done in the six years since the end of her marriage, she'd done on her own. She didn't have to share it. She didn't have to share her time. Perhaps she was a great deal like Maria. She was a woman who ran her own life, made her own decisions, personally and professionally. Some people weren't made for partnerships.

Shade Colby. Bryan propped her feet on Maria's chair. She might just have to make a concession there. She admired his work. So much so, in fact, that she'd plunked down a heady amount for his print of an L.A. street scene at a time when money had been a large concern. She'd studied it, trying to analyze and guess at the techniques he'd used for setting the shot and making the print. It was a moody piece, so much gray, so little light. And yet, Bryan had sensed a certain grit in it, not hopelessness, but ruthlessness. Still, admiring his work and working with him were two different things.

They were based in the same town, but they moved in different circles. For the most part, Shade Colby didn't move in any circles. He kept to himself. She'd seen him at a handful of photography functions, but they'd never met.

He'd be an interesting subject, she reflected. Given enough time, she could capture that air of aloofness and earthiness on film. Perhaps if they agreed to take the assignment she'd have the chance.

Three months of travel. There was so much of the country she hadn't seen, so many pictures she hadn't taken. Thoughtfully, she pulled a candy bar out of her back pocket and unwrapped it. She liked the idea of taking a slice of America, a season, and pulling the images together. So much could be said.

Bryan enjoyed doing her portraits. Taking a face, a personality, especially a well-known one, and finding out what lay behind it was fascinating. Some might find it limited, but she found it endlessly varied. She could take the tough female rock star and show her vulnerabilities, or pull the humor from the cool, regal megastar. Capturing the unexpected, the fresh—that was the purpose of photography to her.

Now she was being offered the opportunity to do the same thing with a country. The people, she thought. So many people.

She wanted to do it. If it meant sharing the work, the discoveries, the fun, with Shade Colby, she still wanted to do it. She bit into the chocolate. So what if he had a reputation for being cranky and remote? She could get along with anyone for three months.

"Chocolate makes you fat and ugly."

Bryan glanced up as Maria swirled back into the room. The sweat was gone. She looked now as people expected a prima ballerina to look. Draped in silk, studded with diamonds. Cool, composed, beautiful.

"It makes me happy," Bryan countered. "You look fantastic, Maria."

"Yes." Maria brushed a hand down the draping silk at her hip. "But then it's my job to do so. Will you work late?"

"I want to develop the film. I'll send you some test proofs tomorrow."

"And that's your dinner?"

"Just a start." Bryan took a huge bite of chocolate. "I'm sending out for pizza."

"With pepperoni?"

Bryan grinned. "With everything."

Maria pressed a hand to her stomach. "And I eat with my choreographer, the tyrant, which means I eat next to nothing."

"And I'll have a soda instead of a glass of Taittinger. We all have our price to pay."

"If I like your proofs, I'll send you a case."

"Of Taittinger?"

"Of soda." With a laugh, Maria swept out.

An hour later, Bryan hung her negatives up to dry. She'd need to make the proofs to be certain, but out of more than forty shots, she'd probably print no more than five.

When her stomach rumbled, she checked her watch. She'd ordered the pizza for seven-thirty. Well timed, she decided as she left the darkroom. She'd eat and go over the prints of Matt she'd shot for a layout in a glossy. Then she could work on the one she chose until the negatives of Maria were dry. She began rummaging through the two dozen folders on her desk—her personal method of filing—when someone knocked at the studio door.

"Pizza," she breathed, greedy. "Come on in. I'm starving." Plopping her enormous canvas bag on the desk, Bryan began to hunt for her wallet. "This is great timing. Another five minutes and I might've just faded away. Shouldn't miss lunch." She dropped a fat, ragged notebook, a clear plastic bag filled with cosmetics, a key ring and five candy bars on the desk. "Just set it down anywhere, I'll find the money in a minute." She dug deeper into the bag. "How much do you need?"

"As much as I can get."

"Don't we all." Bryan pulled out a worn man's bill-fold. "And I'm desperate enough to clean out the safe for you, but…" She trailed off as she looked up and saw Shade Colby.

He gave her face a quick glance, then concentrated on her eyes. "What would you like to pay me for?"

"Pizza." Bryan dropped the wallet onto the desk with half the contents of her purse. "A case of starvation and mistaken identity. Shade Colby." She held out her hand, curious and, to her surprise, nervous. He looked more formidable when he wasn't in a crowd. "I recognize you," she continued, "but I don't think we've met."

"No, we haven't." He took her hand and held it while he studied her face a second time. Stronger than he'd expected. He always looked for the strength first, then the weaknesses. And younger. Though he knew she was only twenty-eight, Shade had expected her to look harder, more aggressive, glossier. Instead, she looked like someone who'd just come in from the beach.

Her T-shirt was snug, but she was slim enough to warrant it. The braid came nearly to her waist and made him speculate on how her hair would look loose and free. Her eyes interested him—gray edging toward silver, and almond-shaped. They were eyes he'd like to photograph with the rest of her face in shadow. She might carry a bag of cosmetics, but it didn't look as if she used any of them.

Not vain about her appearance, he decided. That would make things simpler if he decided to work with her. He didn't have the patience to wait while a woman painted and groomed and fussed. This one wouldn't. And she was assessing him even as he assessed her. Shade accepted that. A photographer, like any artist, looked for angles.

"Am I interrupting your work?"

"No, I was just taking a break. Sit down."

They were both cautious. He'd come on impulse. She wasn't certain how to handle him. Each decided to bide their time before they went beyond the polite, impersonal stage. Bryan remained behind her desk. Her turf, his move, she decided.

Shade didn't sit immediately. Instead, he tucked his hands in his pockets and looked around her studio. It was wide, well lit from the ribbon of windows. There were baby spots and a blue backdrop still set up from an earlier session in one section. Reflectors and umbrellas stood in another, with a camera still on a tripod. He didn't have to look closely to see that the equipment was first-class. But then, first-class equipment didn't make a first-class photographer.

She liked the way he stood, not quite at ease, but ready, remote. If she had to choose now, she'd have photographed him in shadows, alone. But Bryan insisted on knowing the person before she made a portrait.

How old was he? she wondered. Thirty-three, thirty-five. He'd already been nominated for a Pulitzer when she'd still been in college. It didn't occur to her to be intimidated.

"Nice place," he commented before he dropped into the chair opposite the desk.

"Thanks." She tilted her chair so that she could study

him from another angle. "You don't use a studio of your own, do you?"

"I work in the field." He drew out a cigarette. "On the rare occasion I need a studio, I can borrow or rent one easily enough."

Automatically she hunted for an ashtray under the chaos on her desk. "You make all your own prints?"

"That's right."

Bryan nodded. On the few occasions at *Celebrity* when she'd been forced to entrust her film to someone else, she hadn't been satisfied. That had been one of the major reasons she'd decided to open her own business. "I love darkroom work."

She smiled for the first time, causing him to narrow his eyes and focus on her face. What kind of power was that? he wondered. A curving of lips, easy and relaxed. It packed one hell of a punch.

Bryan sprang up at the knock on the door. "At last."

Shade watched her cross the room. He hadn't known she was so tall. Five-ten, he estimated, and most of it leg. Long, slender, bronzed leg. It wasn't easy to ignore the smile, but it was next to impossible to ignore those legs.

Nor had he noticed her scent until she moved by him. Lazy sex. He couldn't think of another way to describe it. It wasn't floral, it wasn't sophisticated. It was basic. Shade drew on his cigarette and watched her laugh with the delivery boy.

Photographers were known for their preconceptions; it was part of the trade. He'd expected her to be sleek and cool. That was what he'd nearly resigned himself to working with. Now it was a matter of rearranging his thinking. Did he want to work with a woman who smelled like twilight and looked like a beach bunny?

Turning away from her, Shade opened a folder at random. He recognized the subject—a box-office queen with two Oscars and three husbands under her belt. Bryan had dressed her in glitters and sparkles. Royal trappings for royalty. But she hadn't shot the traditional picture.

The actress was sitting at a table jumbled with pots and tubes of lotions and creams, looking at her own reflection in a mirror and laughing. Not the poised, careful smile that didn't make wrinkles, but a full, robust laugh that could nearly be heard. It was up to the viewer to speculate whether she laughed at her reflection or an image she'd created over the years.

"Like it?" Carrying the cardboard box, Bryan stopped beside him.

"Yeah. Did she?"

Too hungry for formalities, Bryan opened the lid and dug out the first piece. "She ordered a sixteen-by-twenty-four for her fiancé. Want a piece?"

Shade looked inside the box. "They miss putting anything on here?"

"Nope." Bryan searched in a drawer of her desk for napkins and came up with a box of tissues. "I'm a firm believer in overindulgence. So…" With the box opened on the desk between them, Bryan leaned back in her chair and propped up her feet. It was time, she decided, to get beyond the fencing stage. "You want to talk about the assignment?"

Shade took a piece of pizza and a handful of tissues. "Got a beer?"

"Soda—diet or regular." Bryan took a huge, satisfying bite. "I don't keep liquor in the studio. You end up having buzzed clients."

"We'll skip it for now." They ate in silence a moment, still weighing each other. "I've been giving a lot of thought to doing this photo essay."

"It'd be a change for you." When he only lifted a brow, Bryan wadded a tissue and tossed it into the trash can. "Your stuff overseas—it hit hard. There was sensitivity and compassion, but for the most part, it was grim."

"It was a grim time. Everything I shoot doesn't have to be pretty."

This time she lifted a brow. Obviously he didn't think much of the path she'd taken in her career. "Everything I shoot doesn't have to be raw. There's room for fun in art."

He acknowledged this with a shrug. "We'd see different things if we looked through the same lens."

"That's what makes each picture unique." Bryan leaned forward and took another piece.

"I like working alone."

She ate thoughtfully. If he was trying to annoy her, he was right on target. If it was just an overflow of his personality, it still wouldn't make things any easier. Either way, she wanted the assignment, and he was part of it. "I prefer it that way myself," she said slowly. "Sometimes there has to be compromise. You've heard of compromise, Shade. You give, I give. We meet somewhere close to the middle."

She wasn't as laid-back as she looked. Good. The last thing he needed was to go on the road with someone so mellow she threatened to mold. Three months, he thought again. Maybe. Once the ground rules were set. "I map out the route," he began briskly. "We start here in L.A. in two weeks. Each of us is responsible for their own equipment. Once we're on the road, each of us goes our own way. You shoot your pictures, I shoot mine. No questions."

Bryan licked sauce from her finger. "Anyone ever question you, Colby?"

"It's more to the point whether I answer." It was said simply, as it was meant. "The publisher wants both views, so he'll have them. We'll be stopping off and on to rent a darkroom. I'll look over your negatives."

Bryan wadded more tissue. "No, you won't." Lazily, she crossed one ankle over the other. Her eyes had gone to slate, the only outward show of a steadily growing anger.

"I'm not interested in having my name attached to a series of pop-culture shots."

To keep herself in control, Bryan continued to eat. There were things, so many clear, concise things, she'd like to say to him. Temper took a great deal of energy, she reminded herself. It usually accomplished nothing. "The first thing I'll want written into the contract is that each of our pictures carries our own bylines. That way neither of us will be embarrassed by the other's work. I'm not interested in having the public think I have no sense of humor. Want another piece?"

"No." She wasn't soft. The skin on the inside of her elbow might look soft as butter, but the lady wasn't. It might annoy him to be so casually insulted, but he preferred it to spineless agreement. "We'll be gone from

June fifteenth until after Labor Day." He watched her scoop up a third piece of pizza. "Since I've seen you eat, we'll each keep track of our own expenses."

"Fine. Now, in case you have any odd ideas, I don't cook and I won't pick up after you. I'll drive my share, but I won't drive with you if you've been drinking. When we rent a darkroom, we trade off as to who uses it first. From June fifteenth to after Labor Day, we're partners. Fifty-fifty. If you have any problems with that, we'll hash it out now, before we sign on the dotted line."

He thought about it. She had a good voice, smooth, quiet, nearly soothing. They might handle the close quarters well enough—as long as she didn't smile at him too often and he kept his mind off her legs. At the moment, he considered that the least of his problems. The assignment came first, and what he wanted for it, and from it.

"Do you have a lover?"

Bryan managed not to choke on her pizza. "If that's an offer," she began smoothly, "I'll have to decline. Rude, brooding men just aren't my type."

Inwardly he acknowledged another hit; outwardly his face remained expressionless. "We're going to be living in each other's pockets for three months." She'd challenged him, whether she realized it or not. Whether he realized it or not, Shade had accepted. He leaned closer. "I don't want to hassle with a jealous lover chasing along after us or constantly calling while I'm trying to work."

Just who did he think she was? Some bimbo who couldn't handle her personal life? She made herself pause a moment. Perhaps he'd had some uncomfortable experiences in his relationships. His problem, Bryan decided.

"I'll worry about my lovers, Shade." Bryan bit into her crust with a vengeance. "You worry about yours." She wiped her fingers on the last of the tissue and smiled. "Sorry to break up the party, but I've got to get back to work."

He rose, letting his gaze skim up her legs before he met her eyes. He was going to take the assignment. And he'd have three months to figure out just how he felt about Bryan Mitchell. "I'll be in touch."

"Do that."

Bryan waited until he'd crossed the room and shut the studio door behind him. With uncommon energy, and a speed she usually reserved for work, she jumped up and tossed the empty cardboard box at the door.

It promised to be a long three months.

Chapter 2

She knew exactly what she wanted. Bryan might've been a bit ahead of the scheduled starting date for the American Summer project for *Life-style*, but she enjoyed the idea of being a step ahead of Shade Colby. Petty, perhaps, but she did enjoy it.

In any case, she doubted a man like him would appreciate the timeless joy of the last day of school. When else did summer really start, but with that one wild burst of freedom?

She chose an elementary school because she wanted innocence. She chose an inner-city school because she wanted realism. Children who would step out the door and into a limo weren't the image she wanted to project. This school could've been in any city across the country. The kids who'd bolt out the door would be all kids.

People who looked at the photograph, no matter what their age, would see something of themselves.

Bryan gave herself plenty of time to set up, choosing and rejecting half a dozen vantage points before she settled on one. It wasn't possible or even advisable to stage the shoot. Only random shots would give her what she wanted—the spontaneity and the rush.

When the bell rang and the doors burst open, she got exactly that. It was well worth nearly being trampled under flying sneakers. With shouts and yells and whistles, kids poured out into the sunshine.

Stampede. That was the thought that went through her mind. Crouching quickly, Bryan shot up, catching the first rush of children at an angle that would convey speed, mass and total confusion.

Let's go, let's go! It's summer and every day's Saturday. September was years away. She could read it on the face of every child.

Turning, she shot the next group of children head-on. In the finished spot, they'd appear to be charging right out of the page of the magazine. On impulse, she shifted her camera for a vertical shot. And she got it. A boy of eight or nine leaped down the flight of steps, hands flung high, a grin splitting his face. Bryan shot him in midair while he hung head and shoulders above the scattering children. She'd captured the boy filled with the triumph of that magic, golden road of freedom spreading out in all directions.

Though she was dead sure which shot she'd print for the assignment, Bryan continued to work. Within ten minutes, it was over.

Satisfied, she changed lenses and angles. The school

was empty now, and she wanted to record it that way. She didn't want the feel of bright sunlight here, she decided as she added a low-contrast filter. When she developed the print, Bryan would "dodge" the light in the sky by holding something over that section of the paper to keep it from being overexposed. She wanted the sense of emptiness, of waiting, as a contrast to the life and energy that had just poured out of the building. She'd exhausted a roll of film before she straightened and let the camera hang by its strap.

School's out, she thought with a grin. She felt that charismatic pull of freedom herself. Summer was just beginning.

Since resigning from the staff of *Celebrity*, Bryan had found her work load hadn't eased. If anything, she'd found herself to be a tougher employer than the magazine. She loved her work and was likely to give it all of her day and most of her evenings. Her ex-husband had once accused her of being obsessed not with her camera, but by it. It was something she'd neither been able to deny nor defend. After two days of working with Shade, Bryan had discovered she wasn't alone.

She'd always considered herself a meticulous craftsman. Compared to Shade, she was lackadaisical. He had a patience in his work that she admired even as it set her teeth on edge. They worked from entirely different perspectives. Bryan shot a scene and conveyed her personal viewpoint—her emotions, her feelings about the image. Shade deliberately courted ambiguity. While his photographs might spark off a dozen varied reactions, his personal view almost always remained his secret. Just as everything about him remained half shadowed.

He didn't chat, but Bryan didn't mind working in silence. It was nearly like working alone. His long, quiet looks could be unnerving, however. She didn't care to be dissected as though she were in a viewfinder.

They'd met twice since their first encounter in her studio, both times to argue out their basic route and the themes for the assignment. She hadn't found him any easier, but she had found him sharp. The project meant enough to both of them to make it possible for them to do as she'd suggested—meet somewhere in the middle.

After her initial annoyance with him had worn off, Bryan had decided they could become friends over the next months—professional friends, in any case. Then, after two days of working with him, she'd known it would never happen. Shade didn't induce simple emotions like friendship. He'd either dazzle or infuriate. She didn't choose to be dazzled.

Bryan had researched him thoroughly, telling herself her reason was routine. You didn't go on the road with a man you knew virtually nothing about. Yet the more she'd found out—rather, the more she hadn't found out—the deeper her curiosity had become.

He'd been married and divorced in his early twenties. That was it—no anecdotes, no gossip, no right and wrong. He covered his tracks well. As a photographer for *International View,* Shade had spent a total of five years overseas. Not in pretty Paris, London and Madrid, but in Laos, Lebanon, Cambodia. His work there had earned him a Pulitzer nomination and the Overseas Press Club Award.

His photographs were available for study and dissection, but his personal life remained obscure. He socialized rarely. What friends he had were unswervingly loyal and frustratingly closedmouthed. If she wanted to learn more about him, Bryan would have to do it on the job.

Bryan considered the fact that they'd agreed to spend their last day in L.A. working at the beach a good sign. They'd decided on the location without any argument. Beach scenes would be an ongoing theme throughout the essay—California to Cape Cod.

At first they walked along the sand together, like friends or lovers, not touching but in step with each other. They didn't talk, but Bryan had already learned that Shade didn't make idle conversation unless he was in the mood.

It was barely ten, but the sun was bright and hot. Because it was a weekday morning, most of the sun- and water-seekers were the young or the old. When Bryan stopped, Shade kept walking without either of them saying a word.

It was the contrast that had caught her eye. The old woman was bundled in a wide, floppy sun hat, a long beach dress and a crocheted shawl. She sat under an umbrella and watched her granddaughter—dressed only in frilly pink panties—dig a hole in the sand beside her. Sun poured over the little girl. Shadow blanketed the old woman.

She'd need the woman to sign a release form. Invariably, asking someone if you could take her picture stiffened her up, and Bryan avoided it whenever it was possible. In this case it wasn't, so she was patient enough to chat and wait until the woman had relaxed again.

Her name was Sadie, and so was her granddaughter's. Before she'd clicked the shutter the first time, Bryan knew she'd title the print *Two Sadies*. All she had to do was get that dreamy, faraway look back in the woman's eyes.

It took twenty minutes. Bryan forgot she was uncomfortably warm as she listened, thought and reasoned out the angles. She knew what she wanted. The old woman's careful self-preservation, the little girl's total lack of it, and the bond between them that came with blood and time.

Lost in reminiscence, Sadie forgot about the camera, not noticing when Bryan began to release the shutter. She wanted the poignancy—that's what she'd seen. When she printed it, Bryan would be merciless with the lines and creases in the grandmother's face, just as she'd highlight the flawlessness of the toddler's skin.

Grateful, Bryan chatted a few more minutes, then noted the woman's address with the promise of a print. She walked on, waiting for the next scene to unfold.

Shade had his first subject as well, but he didn't chat. The man lay facedown on a faded beach towel. He was red, flabby and anonymous. A businessman taking the morning off, a salesman from Iowa—it didn't matter. Unlike Bryan, he wasn't looking for personality, but for the sameness of those who grilled their bodies under the sun. There was a plastic bottle of tanning lotion stuck in the sand beside him and a pair of rubber beach thongs.

Shade chose two angles and shot six times without exchanging a word with the snoring sunbather. Satisfied, he scanned the beach. Three yards away, Bryan was casually stripping out of her shorts and shirt. The sleek red maillot rose tantalizing high at the thighs. Her profile was to him as she stepped out of her shorts. It was sharp, well defined, like something sculpted with a meticulous hand.

Shade didn't hesitate. He focused her in his view-finder, set the aperture, adjusted the angle no more than a fraction and waited. At the moment when she reached down for the hem of her T-shirt, he began to shoot.

She was so easy, so unaffected. He'd forgotten any-one could be so totally unselfconscious in a world where self-absorption had become a religion. Her body was one long lean line, with more and more exposed as she drew the shirt over her head. For a moment, she tilted her face up to the sun, inviting the heat. Something crawled into his stomach and began to twist, slowly.

Desire. He recognized it. He didn't care for it.

It was, he could tell himself, what was known in the trade as a decisive moment. The photographer thinks, then shoots, while watching the unfolding scene. When the visual and the emotional elements come to-gether—as they had in this case, with a punch—there was success. There were no replays here, no reshoot-ing. Decisive moment meant exactly that, all or nothing. If he'd been shaken for an instant, it only proved he'd been successful in capturing that easy, lazy sexuality.

Years before, he'd trained himself not to become overly emotional about his subjects. They could eat you alive. Bryan Mitchell might not look as though she'd take a bite out of a man, but Shade didn't take chances. He turned away from her and forgot her. Almost.

It was more than four hours later before their paths crossed again. Bryan sat in the sun near a concession stand, eating a hot dog buried under mounds of mustard and relish. On one side of her she'd set her camera bag, on the other a can of soda. Her narrow red sunglasses shot his reflection back at him.

"How'd it go?" she asked with her mouth full.

"All right. Is there a hot dog under that?"

"Mmm." She swallowed and gestured toward the stand. "Terrific."

"I'll pass." Reaching down, Shade picked up her warming soda and took a long pull. It was orange and sweet. "How the hell do you drink this stuff?"

"I need a lot of sugar. I got some shots I'm pretty pleased with." She held out a hand for the can. "I want to make prints before we leave tomorrow."

"As long as you're ready at seven."

Bryan wrinkled her nose as she finished off her hot dog. She'd rather work until 7:00 A.M. than get up that early. One of the first things they'd have to iron out on the road was the difference in their biological schedules. She understood the beauty and power of a sunrise shot. She just happened to prefer the mystery and color of sunset.

"I'll be ready." Rising, she brushed sand off her bottom, then pulled her T-shirt over her suit. Shade could've told her she was more modest without it. The way the hem skimmed along her thighs and drew the eyes to them was nearly criminal. "As long as you drive the first shift," she continued. "By ten I'll be functional."

He didn't know why he did it. Shade was a man who

analyzed each movement, every texture, shape, color. He cut everything into patterns, then reassembled them. That was his way. Impulse wasn't. Yet he reached out and curled his fingers around her braid without thinking of the act or the consequences. He just wanted to touch.

She was surprised, he could see. But she didn't pull away. Nor did she give him that small half smile women used when a man couldn't resist touching what attracted him.

Her hair was soft; his eyes had told him that, but now his fingers confirmed it. Still, it was frustrating not to feel it loose and free, not to be able to let it play between his fingers.

He didn't understand her. Yet. She made her living recording the elite, the glamorous, the ostentatious, yet she seemed to have no pretensions. Her only jewelry was a thin gold chain that fell to her breasts. On the end was a tiny ankh. Again, she wore no makeup, but her scent was there to tantalize. She could, with a few basic female touches, have turned herself into something breathtaking, but she seemed to ignore the possibilities and rely on simplicity. That in itself was stunning.

Hours before, Bryan had decided she didn't want to be dazzled. Shade was deciding at that moment that he didn't care to be stunned. Without a word, he let her braid fall back to her shoulder.

"Do you want me to take you back to your apartment or your studio?"

So that was it? He'd managed to tie her up in knots in a matter of seconds, and now he only wanted to know where to dump her off. "The studio." Bryan reached down and picked up her camera bag. Her throat was dry, but she tossed the half-full can of soda into the trash. She wasn't certain she could swallow. Before they'd reached Shade's car, she was certain she'd explode if she didn't say something.

"Do you enjoy that cool, remote image you've perfected, Shade?"

He didn't look at her, but he nearly smiled. "It's comfortable."

"Except for the people who get within five feet of you." Damned if she wouldn't get a rise out of him. "Maybe you take your own press too seriously," she suggested. "Shade Colby, as mysterious and intriguing as his name, as dangerous and as compelling as his photographs."

This time he did smile, surprising her. Abruptly he looked like someone she'd want to link hands with, laugh with. "Where in hell did you read that?"

"*Celebrity,*" she muttered. "April, five years ago. They did an article on the photo sales in New York. One of your prints sold for seventy-five hundred at Sotheby's."

"Did it?" His gaze slid over her profile. "You've a better memory than I."

Stopping, she turned to face him. "Damn it, I bought it. It's a moody, depressing, fascinating street scene that I wouldn't have given ten cents for if I'd met you first. And if I wasn't so hooked on it, I'd pitch it out the minute I get home. As it is, I'll probably have to turn it to face the wall for six months until I forget that the artist behind it is a jerk."

Shade watched her soberly, then nodded. "You make quite a speech once you're rolling."

With one short, rude word, Bryan turned and started toward the car again. As she reached the passenger side and yanked open the door, Shade stopped her. "Since we're essentially going to be living together for the next three months, you might want to get the rest of it out now."

Though she tried to speak casually, it came out between her teeth. "The rest of what?"

"Whatever griping you have to do."

She took a deep breath first. She hated to be angry. Invariably it exhausted her. Resigned to it, Bryan curled her hands around the top of the door and leaned toward him. "I don't like you. I'd say it's just that simple, but I can't think of anyone else I don't like."

"No one?"

"No one."

For some reason, he believed her. He nodded, then dropped his hands over hers on top of the door. "I'd rather not be lumped in a group in any case. Why should we have to like each other?"

"It'd make the assignment easier."

He considered this while holding her hands beneath his. The tops of hers were soft, the palms of his hard. He liked the contrast, perhaps too much. "You like things easy?"

He made it sound like an insult, and she straightened. Her eyes were on a level with his mouth, and she shifted slightly. "Yes. Complications are just that. They get in the way and muck things up. I'd rather shovel them aside and deal with what's important."

"We've had a major complication before we started."

She might've concentrated on keeping her eyes on his, but that didn't prevent her from feeling the light, firm pressure of his hands. It didn't prevent her from understanding his meaning. Since it was something they'd meticulously avoided mentioning from the beginning, Bryan lunged at it, straight on.

"You're a man and I'm a woman."

He couldn't help but enjoy the way she snarled it at him. "Exactly. We can say we're both photographers and that's a sexless term." He gave her the barest hint of a smile. "It's also bullshit."

"That may be," she said evenly. "But I intend to handle it, because the assignment comes first. It helps a great deal that I don't like you."

"Liking doesn't have anything to do with chemistry."

She gave him an easy smile because her pulse was beginning to pound. "Is that a polite word for lust?"

She wasn't one to dance around an issue once she'd opened it up. Fair enough, he decided. "Whatever you call it, it goes right back to your complication. We'd better take a good look at it, then shove it aside."

When his fingers tightened on hers, she dropped her gaze to them. She understood his meaning, but not his reason.

"Wondering what it would be like's going to distract both of us," Shade continued. She looked up again, wary. He could feel her pulse throb where his fingers brushed her wrist, yet she'd made no move to pull back. If she had... There was no use speculating; it was better to move ahead. "We'll find out. Then we'll file it, forget it and get on with our job."

It sounded logical. Bryan had a basic distrust of any-thing that sounded quite so logical. Still, he'd been right on target when he'd said that wondering would be dis-tracting. She'd been wondering for days. His mouth seemed to be the softest thing about him, yet even that looked hard, firm and unyielding. How would it feel? How would it taste?

She let her gaze wander back to it, and the lips curved. She wasn't certain if it was amusement or sar-casm, but it made up her mind.

"All right." How intimate could a kiss be when a car door separated them?

They leaned toward each other slowly, as if each waited for the other to draw back at the last moment. Their lips met lightly, passionlessly. It could've ended then, with each of them shrugging the other off in dis-interest. It was the basic definition of a kiss. Two pairs of lips meeting. Nothing more.

Neither one would be able to say who changed it, whether it was calculated or accidental. They were both curious people, and curiosity might have been the fac-tor. Or it might have been inevitable. The texture of the kiss changed so slowly that it wasn't possible to stop it until it was too late for regrets.

Lips opened, invited, accepted. Their fingers clung. His head tilted, and hers, so that the kiss deepened. Bryan found herself pressing against the hard, unyield-ing door, searching for more, demanding it, as her teeth nipped at his bottom lip. She'd been right. His mouth was the softest thing about him. Impossibly soft, un-reasonably luxurious as it heated on hers.

She wasn't used to wild swings of mood. She'd never

experienced anything like it. It wasn't possible to lie back and enjoy. Wasn't that what kisses were for? Up to now, she'd believed so. This one demanded all her strength, all her energy. Even as it went on, she knew when it ended she'd be drained. Wonderfully, totally drained. While she reveled in the excitement, she could anticipate the glory of the aftermath.

He should've known. Damn it, he should've known she wasn't as easy and uncomplicated as she looked. Hadn't he looked at her and ached? Tasting her wasn't going to alleviate any of it, only heighten it. She could undermine his control, and control was essential to his art, his life, his sanity. He'd developed and perfected it over years of sweat, fear and expectations. Shade had learned that the same calculated control he used in the darkroom, the same careful logic he used to set up a shot, could be applied to a woman successfully. Painlessly. One taste of Bryan and he realized just how tenuous control could be.

To prove to himself, perhaps to her, that he could deal with it, he allowed the kiss to deepen, grow darker, moister. Danger hovered, and perhaps he courted it.

He might lose himself in the kiss, but when it was over, it would be over, and nothing would be changed.

She tasted hot, sweet, strong. She made him burn. He had to hold back, or the burn would leave a scar. He had enough of them. Life wasn't as lovely as a first kiss on a hot afternoon. He knew better than most.

Shade drew away, satisfying himself that his control was still in place. Perhaps his pulse wasn't steady, his mind not perfectly clear, but he had control.

Bryan was reeling. If he'd asked her a question, any

question, she'd have had no answer. Bracing herself against the car door, she waited for her equilibrium to return. She'd known the kiss would drain her. Even now, she could feel her energy flag.

He saw the look in her eyes, the soft look any man would have to struggle to resist. Shade turned away from it. "I'll drop you at the studio."

As he walked around the car to his side, Bryan dropped down on the seat. File it and forget it, she thought. Fat chance.

She tried. Bryan put so much effort into forgetting what Shade had made her feel that she worked until 3:00 a.m. By the time she'd dragged herself back to her apartment, she'd developed the film from the school and the beach, chosen the negatives she wanted to print and perfected two of them into what she considered some of her best work.

Now she had four hours to eat, pack and sleep. After building herself an enormous sandwich, Bryan took out the one suitcase she'd been allotted for the trip and tossed in the essentials. Groggy with fatigue, she washed down bread, meat and cheese with a great gulp of milk. None of it felt too steady on her stomach, so she left her partially eaten dinner on the bedside table and went back to her packing.

She rummaged in the top of her closet for the box with the prim man-tailored pajamas her mother had given her for Christmas. Definitely essential, she decided as she dropped them on the disordered pile of lingerie and jeans. They were sexless, Bryan mused. She could only hope she felt sexless in them. That afternoon she'd been forcibly reminded that she was a woman, and a woman had some vulnerabilities that couldn't always be defended.

She didn't want to feel like a woman around Shade again. It was too perilous, and she avoided perilous situations. Since she wasn't the type to make a point of her femininity, there should be no problem.

She told herself.

Once they were started on the assignment, they'd be so wound up in it that they wouldn't notice if the other had two heads and four thumbs.

She told herself.

What had happened that afternoon was simply one of those fleeting moments the photographer sometimes came across when the moment dictated the scene. It wouldn't happen again, because the circumstances would never be the same.

She told herself.

And then she was finished thinking of Shade Colby. It was nearly four, and the next three hours were all hers, the last she had left to herself for a long time. She'd spend them the way she liked best. Asleep. Stripping, Bryan let her clothes fall in a heap, then crawled into bed without remembering to turn off the light.

Across town, Shade lay in the dark. He hadn't slept, although he'd been packed for hours. His bag and his equipment were neatly stacked at the door. He was organized, prepared and wide-awake.

He'd lost sleep before. The fact didn't concern him, but the reason did. Bryan Mitchell. Though he'd managed to push her to the side, to the back, to the corner of his mind throughout the evening, he couldn't quite get her out.

He could dissect what had happened between them that afternoon point by point, but it didn't change one essential thing. He'd been vulnerable. Perhaps only for an instant, only a heartbeat, but he'd been vulnerable. That was something he couldn't afford. It was something he wouldn't allow to happen a second time.

Bryan Mitchell was one of the complications she claimed she liked to avoid. He, on the other hand, was used to them. He'd never had any problem dealing with complications. She'd be no different.

He told himself.

For the next three months, they'd be deep into a project that should totally involve all their time and energy. When he worked, he was well able to channel his concentration on one point and ignore everything else. That was no problem.

He told himself.

What had happened had happened. He still believed it was best done away with before they started out—best that they did away with the speculation and the tension it could cause. They'd eliminated the tension.

He told himself.

But he couldn't sleep. The ache in his stomach had nothing to do with the dinner that had grown cold on his plate, untouched.

He had three hours to himself, then he'd have three months of Bryan. Closing his eyes, Shade did what he was always capable of doing under stress. He willed himself to sleep.

Chapter 3

Bryan was up and dressed by seven, but she wasn't ready to talk to anyone. She had her suitcase and tripod in one hand, with two camera bags and her purse slung crosswise over her shoulders. As Shade pulled up to the curb, she was walking down the stairs and onto the sidewalk. She believed in being prompt, but not necessarily cheerful.

She grunted to Shade; it was as close to a greeting as she could manage at that hour. In silence, she loaded her gear into his van, then kicked back in the passenger seat, stretched out her legs and closed her eyes.

Shade looked at what he could see of her face behind round, amber-lensed sunglasses and under a battered straw hat. "Rough night?" he asked, but she was already asleep. Shaking his head, he released the brake and pulled out into the street. They were on their way.

Shade didn't mind long drives. They gave him a chance to think or not think, as he chose. In less than an hour, he was out of L.A. traffic and heading northeast on the interstate. He liked riding into the rising sun with a clear road ahead. Light bounced off the chrome on the van, shimmered on the hood and sliced down on the road signs.

He planned to cover five or six hundred miles that day, leading up toward Utah, unless something interesting caught his eye and they stopped for a shoot. After this first day, he saw no reason for them to be mileage-crazy. It would hamper the point of the assignment. They'd drive as they needed to, working toward and around the definite destinations they'd ultimately agreed on.

He had a route that could easily be altered, and no itinerary. Their only time frame was to be on the East Coast by Labor Day. He turned the radio on low and found some gritty country music as he drove at a steady, mile-eating pace. Beside him, Bryan slept.

If this was her routine, he mused, they wouldn't have any problems. As long as she was asleep, they couldn't grate on each other's nerves. Or stir each other's passion. Even now he wondered why thoughts of her had kept him restless throughout the night. What was it about her that had worried him? He didn't know, and that was a worry in itself.

Shade liked to be able to put his finger on things and pick a problem apart until the pieces were small enough to rearrange to his preference. Even though she was quiet, almost unobtrusive, at the moment, he didn't believe he'd be able to do that with Bryan Mitchell.

After his decision to take the assignment, he'd made it his business to find out more about her. Shade might guard his personal life and snarl over his privacy, but he wasn't at a loss for contacts. He'd known of her work for *Celebrity*, and her more inventive and personalized work for magazines like *Vanity* and *In Touch*. She'd developed into something of a cult artist over the years with her offbeat, often radical photographs of the famous.

What he hadn't known was that she was the daughter of a painter and a poet, both eccentric and semisuccessful residents of Carmel. She'd been married to an accountant before she was twenty, and divorced him three years later. She dated with an almost studied casualness, and she had vague plans about buying a beach house at Malibu. She was well liked, respected and, by all accounts, dependable. She was often slow in doing things—a combination of her need for perfection and her belief that rushing was a waste of energy.

He'd found nothing surprising in his research, and no clue as to his attraction to her. But a photographer, a successful one, was patient. Sometimes it was necessary to come back to a subject again and again until you understood your own emotion toward it.

As they crossed the border into Nevada, Shade lit a cigarette and rolled down his window. Bryan stirred, grumbled, then groped for her bag.

"Morning." Shade sent her a brief, sidelong look.

"Mmm-hmm." Bryan rooted through the bag, then gripped the chocolate bar in relief. With two quick rips, she unwrapped it and tossed the trash in her purse. She usually cleaned it out before it overflowed.

"You always eat candy for breakfast?"

"Caffeine." She took a huge bite and sighed. "I prefer mine this way." Slowly, she stretched, torso, shoulders, arms, in one long, sinuous move that was completely unplanned. It was, Shade thought ironically, one definitive clue as to the attraction. "So where are we?"

"Nevada." He blew out a stream of smoke that whipped out the open window. "Just."

Bryan folded her legs under her as she nibbled on the candy bar. "It must be about my shift."

"I'll let you know."

"Okay." She was content to ride as long as he was content to drive. She did, however, give a meaningful glance at the radio. Country music wasn't her style. "Driver picks the tunes."

He shrugged his acceptance. "If you want to wash that candy down with something, there's some juice in a jug in the back."

"Yeah?" Always interested in putting something into her stomach, Bryan unfolded herself and worked her way into the back of the van.

She hadn't paid any attention to the van that morning, except for a bleary scan that told her it was black and well cared-for. There were padded benches along each side that could, if you weren't too choosy, be suitable for beds. Bryan thought the pewter carpet might be the better choice.

Shade's equipment was neatly secured, and hers was loaded haphazardly into a corner. Above, glossy ebony cabinets held some essentials. Coffee, a hot plate, a small teakettle. They'd come in handy, she thought, if they stopped in any campgrounds with electric hookups. In the meantime, she settled for the insulated jug of juice.

"Want some?"

He glanced in the rearview mirror to see her standing, legs spread for balance, one hand resting on the cabinet. "Yeah."

Bryan took two jumbo plastic cups and the jug back to her seat. "All the comforts of home," she commented with a jerk of her head toward the back. "Do you travel in this much?"

"When it's necessary." He heard the ice thump against the cup and held out his hand. "I don't like to fly. You lose any chance you'd have at getting a shot at something on the way." After flipping his cigarette out the window, he drank his juice. "If it's an assignment within five hundred miles or so, I drive."

"I hate to fly." Bryan propped herself in the V between the seat and the door. "It seems I'm forever having to fly to New York to photograph someone who can't or won't come to me. I take a bottle of Dramamine, a supply of chocolate bars, a rabbit's foot and a socially significant, educational book. It covers all the bases."

"The Dramamine and the rabbit's foot, maybe."

"The chocolate's for my nerves. I like to eat when I'm tense. The book's a bargaining point." She shook her cup so the ice clinked. "I feel like I'm saying—see, I'm doing something worthwhile here. Let's not mess it up by crashing the plane. Then, too, the book usually puts me to sleep within twenty minutes."

The corner of Shade's mouth lifted, something Bryan took as a hopeful sign for the several thousand miles they had to go. "That explains it."

"I have a phobia about flying at thirty thousand feet in a heavy tube of metal with two hundred strangers, many of whom like to tell the intimate details of their lives to the person next to them." Propping her feet on the dash, she grinned. "I'd rather drive across country with one cranky photographer who makes it a point to tell me as little as possible."

Shade sent her a sidelong look and decided there was no harm in playing the game as long as they both knew the rules. "You haven't asked me anything."

"Okay, we'll start with something basic. Where'd Shade come from? The name, I mean."

He slowed down, veering off toward a rest stop. "Shadrach."

Her eyes widened in appreciation. "As in Meshach and Abednego in the Book of Daniel?"

"That's right. My mother decided to give each of her offspring a name that would roll around a bit. I've a sister named Cassiopeia. Why Bryan?"

"My parents wanted to show they weren't sexist."

The minute the van stopped in a parking space, Bryan hopped out, bent from the waist and touched her palms to the asphalt—much to the interest of the man climbing into the Pontiac next to her. With the view fuddling his concentration, it took him a full thirty seconds to fit his key in the ignition.

"God, I get so stiff!" She stretched up, standing on her toes, then dropped down again. "Look, there's a snack bar over there. I'm going to get some fries. Want some?"

"It's ten o'clock in the morning."

"Almost ten-thirty," she corrected. "Besides, people eat hash browns for breakfast. What's the difference?"

He was certain there was one, but didn't feel like a debate. "You go ahead. I want to buy a paper."

"Fine." As an afterthought, Bryan climbed back inside and grabbed her camera. "I'll meet you back here in ten minutes."

Her intentions were good, but she took nearly twenty. Even as she approached the snack bar, the formation of the line of people waiting for fast food caught her imagination. There were perhaps ten people wound out like a snake in front of a sign that read Eat Qwik.

They were dressed in baggy Bermudas, wrinkled sundresses and cotton pants. A curvy teenager had on a pair of leather shorts that looked as though they'd been painted on. A woman six back from the stand fanned herself with a wide-brimmed hat banded with a floaty ribbon.

They were all going somewhere, all waiting to get there, and none of them paid any attention to anyone else. Bryan couldn't resist. She walked up the line one way, down it another, until she found her angle.

She shot them from the back so that the line seemed elongated and disjointed and the sign loomed promisingly. The man behind the counter serving food was nothing more than a vague shadow that might or might not have been there. She'd taken more than her allotted ten minutes before she joined the line herself.

Shade was leaning against the van reading the paper when she returned. He'd already taken three calculated shots of the parking lot, focusing on a line of cars with license plates from five different states. When he glanced up, Bryan had her camera slung over her shoulder, a giant chocolate shake in one hand and a jumbo order of fries smothered in ketchup in the other.

"Sorry." She dipped into the box of fries as she walked. "I got a couple of good shots of the line at the snack bar. Half of summer's hurry up and wait, isn't it?"

"Can you drive with all that?"

"Sure." She swung into the driver's side. "I'm used to it." She balanced the shake between her thighs, settled the fries just ahead of it and reached out a hand for the keys.

Shade glanced down at the breakfast snuggled between very smooth, very brown legs. "Still willing to share?"

Bryan turned her head to check the rearview as she backed out. "Nope." She gave the wheel a quick turn and headed toward the exit. "You had your chance." With one competent hand steering, she dug into the fries again.

"You eat like that, you should have acne down to your navel."

"Myths," she announced, and zoomed past a slower-moving sedan. With a few quick adjustments, she had an old Simon and Garfunkel tune pouring out of the radio. "That's music," she told him. "I like songs that give me a visual. Country music's usually about hurting and cheating and drinking."

"And life."

Bryan picked up her shake and drew on the straw. "Maybe. I guess I get tired of too much reality. Your work depends on it."

"And yours often skirts around it."

Her brows knit, then she deliberately relaxed. In his way, he was right. "Mine gives options. Why'd you take this assignment, Shade?" she asked suddenly. "Summer in America exemplifies fun. That's not your style."

"It also equals sweat, crops dying from too much sun and frazzled nerves." He lit another cigarette. "More my style?"

"You said it, I didn't." She swirled the chocolate in her mouth. "You smoke like that, you're going to die."

"Sooner or later." Shade opened the paper again and ended the conversation.

Who the hell was he? Bryan asked herself as she leveled the speed at sixty. What factors in his life had brought out the cynicism as well as the genius? There was humor in him—she'd seen it once or twice. But he seemed to allow himself only a certain degree and no more.

Passion? She could attest firsthand that there was a powder keg inside him. What might set it off? If she was certain of one thing about Shade Colby, it was that he held himself in rigid control. The passion, the power, the fury—whatever label you gave it—escaped into his work, but not, she was certain, into his personal life. Not often, in any case.

She knew she should be careful and distant; it would be the smartest way to come out of this long-term assignment without scars. Yet she wanted to dig into his character, and she knew she'd have to give in to the temptation. She'd have to press the buttons and watch the results, probably because she didn't like him and was attracted to him at the same time.

She'd told him the truth when she'd said that she

couldn't think of anyone else she didn't like. It went hand in hand with her approach to her art—she looked into a person and found qualities, not all of them admirable, not all of them likable, but something, always something, that she could understand. She needed to do that with Shade, for herself. And because, though she'd bide her time telling him, she wanted very badly to photograph him.

"Shade, I want to ask you something else."

He didn't glance up from the paper. "Hmm?"

"What's your favorite movie?"

Half annoyed at the interruption, half puzzled at the question, he looked up and found himself wondering yet again what her hair would look like out of that thick, untidy braid. "What?"

"Your favorite movie," she repeated. "I need a clue, a starting point."

"For what?"

"To find out why I find you interesting, attractive and unlikable."

"You're an odd woman, Bryan."

"No, not really, though I have every right to be." She stopped speaking a moment as she switched lanes. "Come on, Shade, it's going to be a long trip. Let's humor each other on the small points. Give me a movie."

"*To Have and Have Not.*"

"Bogart and Bacall's first together." It made her smile at him in the way he'd already decided was dangerous. "Good. If you'd named some obscure French film, I'd have had to find something else. Why that one?"

He set the paper aside. So she wanted to play games.

It was harmless, he decided. And they still had a long day ahead of them. "On-screen chemistry, tight plotting and camera work that made Bogart look like the consummate hero and Bacall the only woman who could stand up to him."

She nodded, pleased. He wasn't above enjoying heroes, fantasies and bubbling relationships. It might've been a small point, but she could like him for it. "Movies fascinate me, and the people who make them. I suppose that was one of the reasons I jumped at the chance to work for *Celebrity*. I've lost count of the number of actors I've shot, but when I see them up on the screen, I'm still fascinated."

He knew it was dangerous to ask questions, not because of the answers, but because of the questions you'd be asked in return. Still, he wanted to know. "Is that why you photograph the beautiful people? Because you want to get close to the glamour?"

Because she considered it a fair question, Bryan decided not to be annoyed. Besides, it made her think about something that had simply seemed to evolve, almost unplanned. "I might've started out with something like that in mind. Before long, you come to see them as ordinary people with extraordinary jobs. I like finding that spark that's made them the chosen few."

"Yet for the next three months you're going to be photographing the everyday. Why?"

"Because there's a spark in all of us. I'd like to find it in a farmer in Iowa, too."

So he had his answer. "You're an idealist, Bryan."

"Yes." She gave him a frankly interested look. "Should I be ashamed of it?"

He didn't like the way the calm, reasonable question affected him. He'd had ideals of his own once, and he knew how much it hurt to have them rudely taken away. "Not ashamed," he said after a moment. "Careful."

They drove for hours. In midafternoon, they switched positions and Bryan skimmed through Shade's discarded paper. By mutual consent, they left the freeway and began to travel over back roads. The pattern became sporadic conversations and long silences. It was early evening when they crossed the border into Idaho.

"Skiing and potatoes," Bryan commented. "That's all I can think of when I think of Idaho." With a shiver, she rolled up her window. Summer came slower in the north, especially when the sun was low. She gazed out the glass at the deepening twilight.

Sheep, hundreds of them, in what seemed like miles of gray or white bundles, were grazing lazily on the tough grass that bordered the road. She was a woman of the city, of freeways and office buildings. It might've surprised Shade to know she'd never been this far north, nor this far east except by plane.

The acres of placid sheep fascinated her. She was reaching for her camera when Shade swore and hit the brakes. Bryan landed on the floor with a plop.

"What was that for?"

He saw at a glance that she wasn't hurt, not even annoyed, but simply curious. He didn't bother to apologize. "Damn sheep in the road."

Bryan hauled herself up and looked out the windshield. There were three of them lined unconcernedly across the road, nearly head to tail. One of them turned its head and glanced up at the van, then looked away again.

"They look like they're waiting for a bus," she decided, then grabbed Shade's wrist before he could lean on the horn. "No, wait a minute. I've never touched one."

Before Shade could comment, she was out of the van and walking toward them. One of them shied a few inches away as she approached, but for the most part, the sheep couldn't have cared less. Shade's annoyance began to fade as she leaned over and touched one. He thought another woman might look the same as she stroked a sable at a furrier. Pleased, tentative and oddly sexual. And the light was good. Taking his camera, he selected a filter.

"How do they feel?"

"Soft—not as soft as I'd thought. Alive. Nothing like a lamb's-wool coat." Still bent over, one hand on the sheep, Bryan looked up. It surprised her to be facing a camera. "What's that for?"

"Discovery." He'd already taken two shots, but he wanted more. "Discovery has a lot to do with summer. How do they smell?"

Intrigued, Bryan leaned closer to the sheep. He framed her when her face was all but buried in the wool. "Like sheep," she said with a laugh, and straightened. "Want to play with the sheep and I'll take your picture?"

"Maybe next time."

She looked as if she belonged there, on the long deserted road surrounded by stretches of empty land, and it puzzled him. He'd thought she set well in L.A., in the center of the glitz and illusions.

"Something wrong?" She knew he was thinking of her, only of her, when he looked at her like that. She wished she could've taken it a step further, yet was oddly relieved that she couldn't.

"You acclimate well."

Her smile was hesitant. "It's simpler that way. I told you I don't like complications."

He turned back to the truck, deciding he was thinking about her too much. "Let's see if we can get these sheep to move."

"But, Shade, you can't just leave them on the side of the road." She jogged back to the van. "They'll wander right back out. They might get run over."

He gave her a look that said he clearly wasn't interested. "What do you expect me to do? Round 'em up?"

"The least we can do is get them back over the fence." As if he'd agreed wholeheartedly, Bryan turned around and started back to the sheep. As he watched, she reached down, hauled one up and nearly toppled over. The other two bleated and scattered.

"Heavier than they look," she managed, and began to stagger toward the fence strung along the shoulder of the road while the sheep she carried bleated, kicked and struggled. It wasn't easy, but after a test of wills and brute strength, she dropped the sheep over the fence. With one hand, she swiped at the sweat on her forehead as she turned to scowl at Shade. "Well, are you going to help or not?"

He'd enjoyed the show, but he didn't smile as he leaned against the van. "They'll probably find the hole in the fence again and be back on the road in ten minutes."

"Maybe they will," Bryan said between her teeth as she headed for the second sheep. "But I'll have done what should be done."

"Idealist," he said again.

With her hands on her hips, she whirled around. "Cynic."

"As long as we understand each other." Shade straightened. "I'll give you a hand."

The others weren't as easily duped as the first. It took Shade several exhausting minutes to catch number two, with Bryan running herd. Twice he lost his concentration and his quarry because her sudden husky laughter distracted him.

"Two down and one to go," he announced as he set the sheep free in pasture.

"But this one looks stubborn." From opposite sides of the road, the rescuers and the rescuee studied each other. "Shifty eyes," Bryan murmured. "I think he's the leader."

"She."

"Whatever. Look, just be nonchalant. You walk around that side, I'll walk around this side. When we have her in the middle, wham!"

Shade sent her a cautious look. "Wham?"

"Just follow my lead." Tucking her thumbs in her back pockets, she strolled across the road, whistling.

"Bryan, you're trying to outthink a sheep."

She sent him a bland look over her shoulder. "Maybe between the two of us we can manage to."

He wasn't at all sure she was joking. His first urge was to simply get back in the van and wait until she'd finished making a fool of herself. Then again, they'd already wasted enough time. Shade circled around to the left as Bryan moved to the right. The sheep eyed them both, swiveling her head from side to side.

"Now!" Bryan shouted, and dived.

Without giving himself the chance to consider the absurdity, Shade lunged from the other side. The sheep danced delicately away. Momentum carrying them both, Shade and Bryan collided, then rolled together onto the soft shoulder of the road. Shade felt the rush of air as they slammed into each other, and the soft give of her body as they tumbled together.

With the breath knocked out of her, Bryan lay on her back, half under Shade. His body was very hard and very male. She might not have had her wind, but Bryan had her wit. She knew if they stayed like this, things were going to get complicated. Drawing in air, she stared up into his face just above her.

His look was contemplative, considering and not altogether friendly. He wouldn't be a friendly lover, that she knew instinctively. It was in his eyes—those dark, deepset eyes. He was definitely a man to avoid having a personal involvement with. He'd overwhelm quickly, completely, and there'd be no turning back. She had to remind herself that she preferred easy relationships, as her heart started a strong, steady rhythm.

"Missed," she managed to say, but didn't try to move away.

"Yeah." She had a stunning face, all sharp angles and soft skin. Shade could nearly convince himself that his interest in it was purely professional. She'd photograph wonderfully from any angle, in any light. He could make her look like a queen or a peasant, but she'd always look like a woman a man would want. The lazy sexuality he could sense in her would come across in the photograph.

Just looking at her, he could plot half a dozen settings he'd like to shoot her in. And he could think of dozens of ways he'd like to make love to her. Here was first, on the cool grass along the roadside with the sun setting behind them and no sound.

She saw the decision in his eyes, saw it in time to avoid the outcome. But she didn't. She had only to shift away, only to protest with one word or a negative movement. But she didn't. Her mind told her to, arguing with an urge that was unarguably physical. Later, Bryan would wonder why she hadn't listened. Now, with the air growing cool and the sky darkening, she wanted the experience. She couldn't admit that she wanted him.

When he lowered his mouth to hers, there wasn't any of the light experimentation of the first time. Now he knew her and wanted the full impact of her passion. Their mouths met greedily, as if each one were racing the other to delirium.

Her body heated so quickly that the grass seemed to shimmer like ice beneath her. She wondered it didn't melt. It was a jolt that left her bewildered. With a small sound in her throat, Bryan reached for more. His fingers were in her hair, tangled in the restriction of her braid as if he didn't choose, or didn't dare, to touch her yet. She moved under him, not in retreat but in advance. Hold me, she seemed to demand. Give me more. But he continued to make love only to her mouth. Devastatingly.

She could hear the breeze; it tickled through the grass beside her ear and taunted her. He'd give sparingly of himself. She could feel it in the tenseness of his body. He'd hold back. While his mouth stripped away her defenses, one by one, he held himself apart. Frustrated, Bryan ran her hands up his back. She'd seduce.

Shade wasn't used to the pressure to give, to the desire to. She drew from him a need for merging he'd thought he'd beaten down years before. There seemed to be no pretenses in her—her mouth was warm and eager, tasting of generosity. Her body was soft and agile, tempting. Her scent drifted around him, sexual, uncomplicated. When she said his name, there seemed to be no hidden meaning. For the first time in too long for him to remember, he wanted to give, unheedingly, boundlessly.

He held himself back. Pretenses, he knew, could be well hidden. But he was losing to her. Even though Shade was fully aware of it, he couldn't stop it. She drew and drew from him, with a simplicity that couldn't be blocked. He might've sworn against it, cursed her, cursed himself, but his mind was beginning to swim. His body was throbbing.

They both felt the ground tremble, but it didn't occur to either of them that it was anything but their own passion. They heard the noise, the rumble, growing louder and louder, and each thought it was inside his or her own head. Then the wind rocketed by them and the truck driver gave one long, rude blast of the horn. It was enough to jolt them back to sanity. Feeling real panic for the first time, Bryan scrambled to her feet.

"We'd better take care of that sheep and get going." She swore at the breathiness of her own voice and wrapped her arms protectively around herself. There was a chill in the air, she thought desperately. That was all. "It's nearly dark."

Shade hadn't realized how deep the twilight had become. He'd lost track of his surroundings—something he never allowed to happen. He'd forgotten that they were on the side of the road, rolling in the grass like a couple of brainless teenagers. He felt the lick of anger, but stemmed it. He'd nearly lost control once. He wouldn't lose it now.

She caught the sheep on the other side of the road, where it grazed, certain that both humans had lost interest. It bleated in surprised protest as she scooped it up. Swearing under his breath, Shade stalked over and grabbed the sheep from her before Bryan could take another tumble. He dumped it unceremoniously in the pasture.

"Satisfied now?" he demanded.

She could see the anger in him, no matter how tightly he reined it in. Her own bubbled. She'd had her share of frustrations as well. Her body was pulsing, her legs were unsteady. Temper helped her to forget them.

"No," she tossed back. "And neither are you. It seems to me that should prove to both of us that we'd better keep a nice, clean distance."

He grabbed her arm as she started to swing past. "I didn't force you into anything, Bryan."

"Nor I you," she reminded him. "I'm responsible for my own actions, Shade." She glanced down at the hand that was curled around her arm. "And my own mistakes. If you like to shift blame, it's your prerogative."

His fingers tightened on her arm, briefly, but long enough for her eyes to widen in surprise at the strength and the depth of his anger. No, she wasn't used to wild swings of mood in herself or to causing them in others.

Slowly, and with obvious effort, Shade loosened his grip. She'd hit it right on the mark. He couldn't argue with honesty.

"No," he said a great deal more calmly. "I'll take my share, Bryan. It'll be easier on both of us if we agree to that nice, clean distance."

She nodded, steadier. Her lips curved into a slight smile. "Okay." Lighten up, she warned herself, for everyone's sake. "It'd have been easier from the beginning if you'd been fat and ugly."

He'd grinned before he'd realized it. "You too."

"Well, since I don't suppose either of us is willing to do anything about that particular problem, we just have to work around it. Agreed?" She held out her hand.

"Agreed."

Their hands joined. A mistake. Neither of them had recovered from the jolt to their systems. The contact, however casual, only served to accentuate it. Bryan linked her hands behind her back. Shade dipped his into his pockets.

"Well..." Bryan began, with no idea where to go.

"Let's find a diner before we head into camp. Tomorrow's going to start early."

She wrinkled her nose at that but started toward her side of the truck. "I'm starving," she announced, and pretended she was in control by propping her feet on the dash. "Think we'll find something decent to eat soon, or should I fortify myself with a candy bar?"

"There's a town about ten miles down this road." Shade turned on the ignition. His hand was steady, he told himself. Or nearly. "Bound to be a restaurant of some kind. Probably serve great lamb chops."

Bryan looked at the sheep grazing beside them, then sent Shade a narrowed-eyed glance. "That's disgusting."

"Yeah, and it'll keep your mind off your stomach until we eat."

They bumped back onto the road and drove in silence. They'd made it over a hump, but each of them knew there'd be mountains yet to struggle over. Steep, rocky mountains.

Chapter 4

Bryan recorded vacationers floating like corks in the Great Salt Lake. When the shot called for it, she used a long or a wide-angle lens to bring in some unusual part of the landscape. But for the most part, Bryan concentrated on the people.

In the salt flats to the west, Shade framed race car enthusiasts. He angled for the speed, the dust, the grit. More often than not, the people included in his pictures would be anonymous, blurred, shadowy. He wanted only the essence.

Trips to large cities and through tidy suburbs used up rolls of film. There were summer gardens, hot, sweaty traffic jams, young girls in thin dresses, shirtless men, and babies in strollers being pushed along sidewalks and in shopping malls.

Their route through Idaho and Utah had been winding, but steady. Neither was displeased with the pace or the subjects. For a time, after the turbulent detour on the country road in Idaho, Bryan and Shade worked side by side in relative harmony. They concentrated on their own subjects, but they did little as a team.

They'd already taken hundreds of pictures, a fraction of which would be printed and still a smaller fraction published. Once it occurred to Bryan that the pictures they'd taken far outnumbered the words they'd spoken to each other.

They drove together up to eight hours a day, stopping along the way whenever it was necessary or desirable to work. And they worked as much as they drove. Out of each twenty-four hours, they were together an average of twenty. But they grew no closer. It was something either of them might have accomplished with the ease of a friendly gesture or a few casual words. It was something both of them avoided.

Bryan learned it was possible to keep an almost obsessive emotional distance from someone while sharing a limited space. She also learned a limited space made it very difficult to ignore what Shade had once termed chemistry. To balance the two, Bryan kept her conversations light and brief and almost exclusively centered on the assignment. She asked no more questions. Shade volunteered no more information.

By the time they crossed the border into Arizona, at the end of the first week, she was already finding it an uncomfortable way to work.

It was hot. The sun was merciless. The van's air-conditioning helped, but just looking out at the endless desert and faded sage made the mouth dry. Bryan had an enormous paper cup filled with soda and ice. Shade drank bottled iced tea as he drove.

She estimated that they hadn't exchanged a word for fifty-seven miles. Nor had they spoken much that morning when they'd set up to shoot, each in separate territory, at Glen Canyon in Utah. Bryan might be pleased with the study she'd done of the cars lined up at the park's entrance, but she was growing weary of their unspoken agreement of segregation.

The magazine had hired them as a team, she reminded herself. Each of them would take individual pictures, naturally, but there had to be some communication if the photo essay were to have any cohesion. There had to be some blending if the final result was the success both of them wanted. Compromise, she remembered with a sigh. They'd forgotten the operative word.

Bryan thought she knew Shade well enough at this point to be certain he'd never make the first move. He was perfectly capable of driving thousands of miles around the country without saying her name more than once a day. As in, Pass the salt, Bryan.

She could be stubborn. Bryan thought about it as she brooded out the window at the wide stretches of Arizona. She could be just as aloof as he. And, she admitted with a grimace, she could bore herself to death within another twenty-four hours.

Contact, she decided. She simply couldn't survive without some kind of contact. Even if it was with a hard-edged, casually rude cynic. Her only choice was to swallow her pride and make the first move herself. She gritted her teeth, gnawed on ice and thought about it for another ten minutes.

"Ever been to Arizona?"

Shade tossed his empty bottle into the plastic can they used for trash. "No."

Bryan pried off one sneaker with the toe of the other. If at first you don't succeed, she told herself. "They filmed *Outcast* in Sedona. Now that was a tough, thinking-man's Western," she mused, and received no response. "I spent three days there covering the filming for *Celebrity*." After adjusting her sun visor, she sat back again. "I was lucky enough to miss my plane and get another day. I spent it in Oak Creek Canyon. I've never forgotten it—the colors, the rock formations."

It was the longest speech she'd made in days. Shade negotiated the van around a curve and waited for the rest.

Okay, she thought, she'd get more than one word out of him if she had to use a crowbar. "A friend of mine settled there. Lee used to work for *Celebrity*. Now she's a novelist with her first book due out in the fall. She married Hunter Brown last year."

"The writer?"

Two words, she thought, smug. "Yes, have you read his stuff?"

This time Shade merely nodded and pulled a cigarette out of his pocket. Bryan began to sympathize with dentists who had to coax a patient to open wide.

"I've read everything he's written, then I hate myself for letting his books give me nightmares."

"Good horror fiction's supposed to make you wake up at 3:00 a.m. and wonder if you've locked your doors."

This time she grinned. "That sounds like something Hunter would say. You'll like him."

Shade merely moved his shoulders. He'd agreed to the stop in Sedona already, but he wasn't interested in taking flattering, commercial pictures of the occult king and his family. It would, however, give Shade the break he needed. If he could dump Bryan off for a day or two with her friends, he could take the time to get his system back to normal.

He hadn't had an easy moment since the day they'd started out of L.A. Every day that went by only tightened his nerves and played havoc with his libido. He'd tried, but it wasn't possible to forget she was there within arm's reach at night, separated from him only by the width of the van and the dark.

Yes, he could use a day away from her, and that natural, easy sexuality she didn't even seem aware of.

"You haven't seen them for a while?" he asked her.

"Not in months." Bryan relaxed, more at ease now that they'd actually begun a two-way conversation. "Lee's a good friend. I've missed her. She'll have a baby about the same time her book comes out."

The change in her voice had him glancing over. There was something softer about her now. Almost wistful.

"A year ago, we were both still with *Celebrity*, and now…" She turned to him, but the shaded glasses hid her eyes. "It's odd thinking of Lee settled down with a family. She was always more ambitious than me. It used to drive her crazy that I took everything with such a lack of intensity."

"Do you?"

"Just about everything," she murmured. Not you, she thought to herself. I don't seem to be able to take you easily. "It's simpler to relax and live," she went on, "than to worry about how you'll be living next month."

"Some people have to worry *if* they'll be living next month."

"Do you think the fact they worry about it changes things?" Bryan forgot her plan to make contact, forgot the fact that she'd been groping for some sort of compromise from him. He'd seen more than she'd seen of the world, of life. She had to admit that he'd seen more than she wanted to see. But how did he feel about it?

"Being aware can change things. Looking out for yourself's a priority some of us haven't a choice about."

Some of us. She noted the phrase but decided not to pounce on it. If he had scars, he was entitled to keep them covered until they'd faded a bit more.

"Everyone worries from time to time," she decided. "I'm just not very good at it. I suppose it comes from my parents. They're..." She trailed off and laughed. It occurred to him he hadn't heard her laugh in days, and that he'd missed it. "I guess they're what's termed bohemians. We lived in this little house in Carmel that was always in varying states of disrepair. My father would get a notion to take out a wall or put in a window, then in the middle of the project, he'd get an inspiration, go back to his canvases and leave the mess where it lay."

She settled back, no longer aware that she was doing all the talking and Shade all the listening. "My mother liked to cook. Trouble was, you'd never know what mood she'd be in. You might have grilled rattlesnake one day, cheeseburgers the next. Then, when you least expected it, there'd be gooseneck stew."

"Gooseneck stew?"

"I ate at the neighbors' a lot." The memory brought on her appetite. Taking out two candy bars, she offered one to Shade. "How about your parents?"

He unwrapped the candy absently while he paced his speed to the state police car in the next lane. "They retired to Florida. My father fishes and my mother runs a craft shop. Not as colorful as yours, I'm afraid."

"Colorful." She thought about it, and approved. "I never knew they were unusual until I'd gone away to college and realized that most kids' parents were grown-up and sensible. I guess I never realized how much I'd been influenced by them until Rob pointed out things like most people preferring to eat dinner at six, rather than scrounging for popcorn or peanut butter at ten o'clock at night."

"Rob?"

She glanced over quickly, then straight ahead. Shade listened too well, she decided. It made it too easy to say more than you intended. "My ex-husband." She knew she shouldn't still see the "ex" as a stigma; these days it was nearly a status symbol. For Bryan, it was the symbol that proved she hadn't done what was necessary to keep a promise.

"Still sore?" He'd asked before he could stop himself. She made him want to offer comfort, when he'd schooled himself not to become involved in anyone's life, anyone's problem.

"No, it was years ago." After a quick shrug, she nibbled on her candy bar. Sore? she thought again. No, not sore, but perhaps she'd always be just a little tender. "Just sorry it didn't work out, I suppose."

"Regrets are more a waste of time than worrying."

"Maybe. You were married once, too."

"That's right." His tone couldn't have been more dismissive. Bryan gave him a long, steady look.

"Sacred territory?"

"I don't believe in rehashing the past."

This wound was covered with scar tissue, she mused. She wondered if it troubled him much, or if he'd truly filed it away. In either case, it wasn't her business, nor was it the way to keep the ball rolling between them.

"When did you decide to become a photographer?" That was a safe topic, she reflected. There shouldn't be any tender points.

"When I was five and got my hands on my father's new thirty-five-millimeter. When he had the film developed, he discovered three close-ups of the family dog. I'm told he didn't know whether to congratulate me or give me solitary confinement when they turned out to be better than any of his shots."

Bryan grinned. "What'd he do?"

"He bought me a camera of my own."

"You were way ahead of me," she commented. "I didn't have any interest in cameras until high school. Just sort of fell into it. Up until then, I'd wanted to be a star."

"An actress?"

"No." She grinned again. "A star. Any kind of a star, as long as I had a Rolls, a gold lamé dress and a big tacky diamond."

He had to grin. She seemed to have the talent for forcing it out of him. "An unassuming child."

"No, materialistic." She offered him her drink, but he shook his head. "That stage coincided with my parents' return-to-the-earth period. I guess it was my way of rebelling against people who were almost impossible to rebel against."

He glanced down at her ringless hands and her faded jeans. "Guess you got over it."

"I wasn't made to be a star. Anyway, they needed someone to take pictures of the football team." Bryan finished off the candy bar and wondered how soon they could stop for lunch. "I volunteered because I had a crush on one of the players." Draining her soda, she dumped the cup in with Shade's bottle. "After the first day, I fell in love with the camera and forgot all about the defensive lineman."

"His loss."

Bryan glanced over, surprised by the offhand compliment. "That was a nice thing to say, Colby. I didn't think you had it in you."

He didn't quite defeat the smile. "Don't get used to it."

"Heaven forbid." But she was a great deal more pleased than his casual words warranted. "Anyway, my parents were thrilled when I became an obsessive photographer. They'd lived with this deadly fear that I had no creative drives and would end up being a smashing business success instead of an artist."

"So now you're both."

She thought about it a moment. Odd how easy it was to forget about one aspect of her work when she concentrated so hard on the other. "I suppose you're right. Just don't mention it to Mom and Dad."

"They won't hear it from me."

They both saw the construction sign at the same time. Whether either of them realized it, their minds followed the same path. Bryan was already reaching for her camera when Shade slowed and eased off the road. Ahead of them, a road crew patched, graded and sweated under the high Arizona sun.

Shade walked off to consider the angle that would show the team and machinery battling against the erosion of the road. A battle that would be waged on roads across the country each summer as long as roads existed. Bryan homed in on one man.

He was bald and had a yellow bandanna tied around his head to protect the vulnerable dome of his scalp. His face and neck were reddened and damp, his belly sagging over the belt of his work pants. He wore a plain white T-shirt, pristine compared to the colorful ones slashed with sayings and pictures the workmen around him had chosen.

To get in close she had to talk to him and deal with the comments and grins from the rest of the crew. She did so with an aplomb and charm that would've caused a public relations expert to rub his hands together. Bryan was a firm believer that the relationship between the photographer and the subject showed through in the final print. So first, in her own way, she had to develop one.

Shade kept his distance. He saw the men as a team—the sunburned, faceless team that worked roads across the country and had done so for decades. He wanted no relationship with any of them, nothing that would color the way he saw them as they stood, bent and dug.

He took a telling shot of the grime, dust and sweat. Bryan learned that the foreman's name was Al and he'd worked for the road commission for twenty-two years.

It took her a while to ease her way around his self-consciousness, but once she got him talking about what the miserable winter had done to his road, everything clicked. Sweat dribbled down his temple. When he reached up with one beefy arm to swipe at it, Bryan had her picture.

The impulsive detour took them thirty minutes. By the time they piled back in the van, they were sweating as freely as the laborers.

"Are you always so personal with strangers?" Shade asked her as he switched on the engine and the air-conditioning.

"When I want their picture, sure." Bryan opened the cooler and pulled out one of the cold cans she'd stocked, and another bottle of iced tea for Shade. "You get what you wanted?"

"Yeah."

He'd watched her at work. Normally they separated, but this time he'd been close enough to see just how she went about her job. She'd treated the road man with more respect and good humor than many photographers showed their hundred-dollar-an-hour models. And she hadn't done it just for the picture, though Shade wasn't sure she realized it. She'd been interested in the man— who he was, what he was and why.

Once, a long time before, Shade had had that kind of curiosity. Now he strapped it down. Knowing involved you. But it wasn't easy, he was discovering, to strap down his curiosity about Bryan. Already she'd told him more than he'd have asked. Not more than he wanted to know, but more than he'd have asked. It still wasn't enough.

For nearly a week he'd backed off from her—just as far as it was possible under the circumstances. He hadn't stopped wanting her. He might not like to rehash the past, but it wasn't possible to forget that last molten encounter on the roadside.

He'd closed himself off, but now she was opening him up again. He wondered if it was foolish to try to fight it, and the attraction they had for each other. It might be better, simpler, more logical, to just let things progress to the only possible conclusion.

They'd sleep together, burn the passion out and get back to the assignment.

Cold? Calculated? Perhaps, but he'd do nothing except follow the already routed course. He knew it was important to keep the emotions cool and the mind sharp.

He'd let his emotions fuddle his logic and his perception before. In Cambodia, a sweet face and a generous smile had blinded him to treachery. Shade's fingers tightened on the wheel without his realizing it. He'd learned a lesson about trust then—it was only the flip side of betrayal.

"Where've you gone?" Bryan asked quietly. A look had come into his eyes that she didn't understand, and wasn't certain she wanted to understand.

He turned his head. For an instant she was caught in the turmoil, in the dark place he remembered too well and she knew nothing about. Then it was over. His eyes were remote and calm. His fingers eased on the wheel.

"We'll stop in Page," he said briefly. "Get some shots of the boats and tourists on Lake Powell before we go down to the canyon."

"All right."

He hadn't been thinking of her. Bryan could comfort herself with that. She hoped the look that had come into his eyes would never be applied to her. Even so, she was determined that sooner or later she'd discover the reason for it.

She could've gotten some good technical shots of the dam. But as they passed through the tiny town of Page, heading for the lake, Bryan saw the high golden arches shimmering behind waves of heat. It made her grin. Cheeseburgers and fries weren't just summer pastimes. They'd become a way of life. Food for all seasons. But she couldn't resist the sight of the familiar building settled low below the town, almost isolated, like a mirage in the middle of the desert.

She rolled down her window and waited for the right angle. "Gotta eat," she said as she framed the building. "Just gotta." She clicked the shutter.

Resigned, Shade pulled into the lot. "Get it to go," he ordered as Bryan started to hop out. "I want to get to the marina."

Swinging her purse over her shoulder, she disappeared inside. Shade didn't have the chance to become impatient before she bounded back out again with two white bags. "Cheap, fast and wonderful," she told him as she slid back into her seat. "I don't know how I'd make it through life if I couldn't get a cheeseburger on demand."

She pulled out a wrapped burger and handed it to him.

"I got extra salt," she said over her first taste of fries. "Mmm, I'm starving."

"You wouldn't be if you'd eat something besides a candy bar for breakfast."

"I'd rather be awake when I eat," she mumbled, involved in unwrapping her burger.

Shade unwrapped his own. He hadn't asked her to bring him anything. He'd already learned it was typical of her to be carelessly considerate. Perhaps the better word was *naturally*. But it wasn't typical of him to be moved by the simple offer of a piece of meat in a bun. He reached in a bag and brought out a paper napkin. "You're going to need this."

Bryan grinned, took it, folded her legs under her and dug in. Amused, Shade drove leisurely to the marina.

They rented a boat, what Bryan termed a putt-putt. It was narrow, open and about the size of a canoe. It would, however, carry them, and what equipment they chose, out on the lake.

She liked the little marina, with its food stands and general stores with displays of suntan oil and bathing suits. The season was in full swing; people strolled by dressed in shorts and cover-ups, in hats and sunglasses. She spotted a teenage couple, brown and gleaming, on a bench, licking at dripping ice-cream cones. Because they were so involved with each other, Bryan was able to take some candid shots before the paperwork on the rental was completed.

Ice cream and suntans. It was a simple, cheerful way to look at summer. Satisfied, she secured her camera in its bag and went back to Shade.

"Do you know how to drive a boat?"

He sent her a mild look as they walked down the dock. "I'll manage."

A woman in a neat white shirt and shorts gave them a rundown, pointing out the life jackets and explaining the engine before she handed them a glossy map of the lake. Bryan settled herself in the bow and prepared to enjoy herself.

"The nice thing about this," she called over the engine, "is it's so unexpected." She swept one arm out to indicate the wide expanse of blue.

Red-hued mesas and sheer rock walls rose up steeply to cradle the lake, settled placidly where man had put it. The combination was fascinating to her. Another time, she might've done a study on the harmony and power that could result in a working relationship between human imagination and nature.

It wasn't necessary to know all the technical details of the dam, of the labor force that built it. It was enough that it was, that they were here—cutting through water that had once been desert, sending up a spray that had once been sand.

Shade spotted a tidy cabin cruiser and veered in its direction. For the moment, he'd navigate and leave the camera work to Bryan. It'd been a long time since he'd spent a hot afternoon on the water. His muscles began to relax even as his perception sharpened.

Before he was done, he'd have to take some pictures of the rocks. The texture in them was incredible, even in their reflection on the water. Their colors, slashed against the blue lake, made them look surreal. He'd make the prints sharp and crisp to accent the incongruity. He edged a bit closer to the cabin cruiser as he planned the shot for later.

Bryan took out her camera without any definite plan.

She hoped there'd be a party of people, perhaps greased up against the sun. Children maybe, giddy with the wind and water. As Shade steered, she glanced toward the stern and lifted the camera quickly. It was too good to be true.

Poised at the stern of the cruiser was a hound— Bryan couldn't think of any other description for the floppy dog. His big ears were blowing back, and his tongue was lolling as he stared down at the water. Over his chestnut fur was a bright orange life vest.

"Go around again!" she yelled to Shade.

She waited impatiently for the angle to come to her again. There were people on the boat, at least five of them, but they no longer interested her. Just the dog, she thought, as she gnawed on her lip and waited. She wanted nothing but the dog in the life jacket leaning out and staring down at the water.

There were towering mesas just behind the boat. Bryan had to decide quickly whether to work them in or frame them out. If she'd had more time to think... She opted against the drama and settled on the fun. Shade had circled the trim little cruiser three times before she was satisfied.

"Wonderful!" With a laugh, Bryan lowered her camera. "That one print's going to be worth the whole trip."

He veered off to the right. "Why don't we see what else we can dig up, anyway?"

They worked for two hours, shifting positions after the first. Stripped to the waist as defense against the heat, Shade knelt at the bow and focused in on a tour boat. The rock wall rose in the background, the water shimmered cool and blue. Along the rail the people were no more than a blur of color. That's what he wanted. The anonymity of tours, and the power of what drew the masses to them.

While Shade worked, Bryan kept the speed low and looked at everything. She'd decided after one glimpse of his lean, tanned torso that it'd be wiser for her to concentrate on the scenery. If she hadn't, she might've missed the cove and the rock island that curved over it.

"Look." Without hesitating, she steered toward it, then cut the engines until the boat drifted in its own wake. "Come on, let's take a swim." Before he could comment, she'd hopped out in the ankle-deep water and was securing the lines with rocks.

Wearing a snug tank top and drawstring shorts, Bryan dashed down to the cove and sank in over her head. When she surfaced, laughing, Shade was standing on the island above her. "Fabulous," she called out. "Come on, Shade, we haven't taken an hour to play since we started."

She was right about that. He'd seen to it. Not that he hadn't needed to relax, but he'd thought it best not to around her. He knew, even as he watched her smoothly treading in the rock-shadowed water, that it was a mistake. Yet he'd told himself it was logical to stop fighting what would happen between them. Following the logic, he walked down to the water.

"It's like opening a present," she decided, shifting onto her back to float briefly. "I had no idea I was being slowly boiled until I stepped in here." With a sigh, she dipped under the water and rose again so that it flowed from her face. "There was a pond a few miles away from home when I was a kid. I practically lived there in the summer."

The water was seductive, almost painfully so. As Shade lowered himself into it, he felt the heat drain, but not the tension. Sooner or later, he knew, he'd have to find an outlet for it.

"We did a lot better here than I expected to." Lazily she let the water play through her fingers. "I can't wait to get to Sedona and start developing." She tossed her dripping braid behind her back. "And sleep in a real bed."

"You don't seem to have any trouble sleeping." One of the first things he'd noticed was that she could fall asleep anywhere, anytime, and within seconds of shutting her eyes.

"Oh, it's not the sleeping, it's the waking up." And waking up only a few feet away from him, morning after morning—seeing his face shadowed by a night's growth of beard, dangerously attractive, seeing his muscles ripple as he stretched, dangerously strong. No, she couldn't deny that the accommodations occasionally gave her a few twinges.

"You know," she began casually, "the budget could handle a couple of motel rooms every week or so—nothing outrageous. A real mattress and a private shower, you know. Some of those campgrounds we've stopped in advertise hot water with their tongues in their cheeks."

He had to smile. It hadn't given him much pleasure to settle for tepid water after a long day on the road. But there was no reason to make it too easy on her. "Can't handle roughing it, Bryan?"

She stretched out on her back again, deliberately kicking water up and over him. "Oh, I don't mind roughing it," she said blandly. "I just like to do it on my own time. And I'm not ashamed to say I'd rather spend the weekend at the Beverly Wilshire than rubbing two sticks together in the wilderness." She closed her eyes and let her body drift. "Wouldn't you?"

"Yeah." With the admission, he reached out, grabbed her braid and tugged her head under.

The move surprised her, but it pleased her as well, even as she came up sputtering. So he was capable of a frivolous move from time to time. It was something else she could like him for.

"I'm an expert on water games," she warned him as she began to tread again.

"Water suits you." When had he relaxed? He couldn't pinpoint the moment when the tension began to ease from him. There was something about her—laziness? No, that wasn't true. She worked every bit as hard as he, though in her own fashion. *Easiness* was a better word, he decided. She was an easy woman, comfortable with herself and whatever surroundings she found herself in.

"It looks pretty good on you, too." Narrowing her eyes, Bryan focused on him—something she'd avoided for several days. If she didn't allow herself a clear look, it helped bank down on the feelings he brought out in her. Many of them weren't comfortable, and Shade had been right. She was a woman who liked to be comfortable. But now, with the water lapping cool around her and the only sound that of boats putting in the distance, she wanted to enjoy him.

His hair was damp and tangled around his face,

which was as relaxed as she'd ever seen it. There didn't seem to be any secrets in his eyes just now. He was nearly too lean, but there were muscles in his forearms, in his back. She already knew just how strong his hands were. She smiled at him because she wasn't sure just how many quiet moments they'd share.

"You don't let up on yourself enough, Shade."

"No?"

"No. You know…" She floated again, because treading took too much effort. "I think deep down, really deep down, there's a nice person in you."

"No, there isn't."

But she heard the humor in his voice. "Oh, it's buried in there somewhere. If you let me do your portrait, I'd find it."

He liked the way she floated in the water; there was absolutely no energy expended. She lay there, trusting buoyancy. He was nearly certain that if she lay quietly for five minutes, she'd be asleep. "Would you?" he murmured. "I think we can both do without that."

She opened her eyes again, but had to squint against the sun to see him. It was at his back, glaring. "Maybe you can, but I've already decided to do it—once I know you better."

He circled her ankle with his finger, lightly. "You have to have my cooperation to do both."

"I'll get it." The contact was more potent than she could handle. She'd tensed before she could stop it. And so, she realized after a long ten seconds, had he. Casually, she let her legs drop. "The water's getting cold." She swam toward the boat with smooth strokes and a racing heart.

Shade waited a moment. No matter what direction he took with her, he always ended up in the same place. He wanted her, but wasn't certain he could handle the consequences of acting on that desire. Worse now, she was perilously close to becoming his friend. That wouldn't make things any easier on either of them.

Slowly, he swam out of the cove and toward the boat, but she wasn't there. Puzzled, he looked around and started to call, but then he saw her perched high on the rock.

She'd unbraided her hair and was brushing it dry in the sun. Her legs were folded under her, her face tilted up. The thin summer clothes she wore were drenched and clung to every curve. She obviously didn't care. It was the sun she sought, the heat, just as she'd sought the cool water only moments before.

Shade reached in his camera bag and attached his long lens. He wanted her to fill the viewfinder. He focused and framed her. For the second time, her careless sexuality gave him a staggering roundhouse punch. He was a professional, Shade reminded himself as he set the depth of field. He was shooting a subject, that was all.

But when she turned her head and her eyes met his through the lens, he felt the passion sizzle—from himself and from her. They held each other there a moment, separated, yet irrevocably joined. He took the picture, and as he did, Shade knew he was recording a great deal more than a subject.

A bit steadier, Bryan rose and worked her way down the curve of the rock. She had to remind herself to play it lightly—something that had always come easily to her. "You didn't get a release form, Colby," she reminded him as she dropped her brush into her over-size bag.

Reaching out, he touched her hair. It was damp, hanging rich and heavy to her waist. His fingers curled into it, his eyes locked on hers. "I want you."

She felt her legs liquefy, and heat started somewhere in the pit of her stomach and spread out to her finger-tips. He was a hard man, Bryan reminded herself. He wouldn't give, but take. In the end, she'd need him to do both.

"That's not good enough for me," she said steadily. "People want all the time—a new car, a color TV. I have to have more than that."

She stepped around him and into the boat. Without a word, Shade joined her and they drifted away from the cove. As the boat picked up speed, both of them wondered if Shade could give any more than what he'd offered.

Chapter 5

Bryan had romanticized Oak Creek Canyon over the years since she'd been there. When she saw it again, she wasn't disappointed. It had all the rich strength, all the colors, she'd remembered.

Campers would be pocketed through it, she knew. They'd be worth some time and some film. Amateur and serious fishermen by the creek, she mused, with their intense expressions and colorful lures. Evening campfires with roasting marshmallows. Coffee in tin cups. Yes, it would be well worth the stop.

They planned to stay for three days, working, developing and printing. Bryan was itching to begin. But before they drove into town to handle the details, they'd agreed to stop in the canyon where Bryan could see Lee and her family.

"According to the directions, there should be a little dirt road leading off to the right just beyond a trading post."

Shade watched for it. He, too, was anxious to begin. Some of the shots he'd taken were pulling at him to bring them to life. He needed the concentration and quiet of a darkroom, the solitude of it. He needed to let his creativity flow, and hold in his hands the results.

The picture of Bryan sitting on the island of rock. He didn't like to dwell on that one, but he knew it would be the first roll he developed.

The important thing was that he'd have the time and the distance he'd promised himself. Once he dropped her at her friends'—and he was certain they'd want her to stay with them—he could go into Sedona, rent a darkroom and a motel room for himself. After living with her for twenty-four hours a day, he was counting on a few days apart to steady his system.

They'd each work on whatever they chose—the town, the canyon, the landscape. That gave him room. He'd work out a schedule for the darkroom. With luck, they wouldn't so much as see each other for the next three days.

"There it is," Bryan told him, though he'd already seen the narrow road and slowed for it. She looked at the steep, tree-lined road and shook her head. "God, I'd never have pictured Lee here. It's so wild and rough and she's...well, elegant."

He'd known a few elegant women in his life. He'd lived with one. Shade glanced at the terrain. "What's she doing here, then?"

"She fell in love," Bryan said simply, and leaned forward. "There's the house. Fabulous."

Glass and style. That's what she thought of it. It wasn't the distinguished town house she would have imagined for Lee, but Bryan could see how it would suit her friend. There were flowers blooming, bright red-orange blossoms she couldn't identify. The grass was thick, the trees leafy.

In the driveway were two vehicles, a dusty late-model Jeep and a shiny cream-colored sedan. As they pulled up behind the Jeep, a huge silver-gray form bounded around the side of the house. Shade swore in sheer astonishment.

"That must be Santanas." Bryan laughed, but gave the dog a wary once-over with her door firmly closed.

Fascinated, Shade watched the muscles bunch as the dog moved. But the tail was wagging, the tongue lolling. Some pet, he decided. "It looks like a wolf."

"Yeah." She continued to look out the window as the dog paced up and down the side of the van. "Lee tells me he's friendly."

"Fine. You go first."

Bryan shot him a look that he returned with a casual smile. Letting out a deep breath, Bryan opened the door. "Nice dog," she told him as she stepped out, keeping one hand on the handle of the door. "Nice Santanas."

"I read somewhere that Brown raised wolves," Shade said carelessly as he stepped out of the opposite side.

"Cute," Bryan mumbled, and cautiously offered her hand for the dog to sniff.

He did so, and obviously liked her, because he knocked her to the ground in one bounding leap. Shade was around the van before Bryan had a chance to draw a breath. Fear and fury had carried him, but whatever he might've done was stopped by the sound of a high whistle.

"Santanas!" A young girl darted around the house, braids flying. "Cut it out right now. You're not supposed to knock people down."

Caught in the act, the huge dog plopped down on his belly and somehow managed to look innocent. "He's sorry." The girl looked at the tense man looming over the dog and the breathless woman sprawled beside him. "He just gets excited when company comes. Are you Bryan?"

Bryan managed a nod as the dog dropped his head on her arm and looked up at her.

"It's a funny name. I thought you'd look funny too, but you don't. I'm Sarah."

"Hello, Sarah." Catching her wind, Bryan looked up at Shade. "This is Shade Colby."

"Is that a real name?" Sarah demanded.

"Yeah." Shade looked down as the girl frowned up at him. He wanted to scold her for not handling her dog, but found he couldn't. She had dark, serious eyes that made him want to crouch down and look into them from her level. A heartbreaker, he decided. Give her ten years, and she'll break them all.

"Sounds like something from one of my dad's books. I guess it's okay." She grinned down at Bryan and shuffled her sneakers in the dirt. Both she and her dog looked embarrassed. "I'm really sorry Santanas knocked you down. You're not hurt or anything, are you?"

Since it was the first time anyone had bothered to ask, Bryan thought about it. "No."

"Well, maybe you won't say anything to my dad." Sarah flashed a quick smile and showed her braces. "He gets mad when Santanas forgets his manners."

Santanas swiped an enormous pink tongue over Bryan's shoulder.

"No harm done," she decided.

"Great. We'll go tell them you're here." She was off in a bound. The dog clambered up and raced after her without giving Bryan a backward look.

"Well, it doesn't look like Lee's settled for a dull life," Bryan commented.

Shade reached down and hauled her to her feet. He'd been frightened, he realized. Seriously frightened for the first time in years, and all because a little girl's pet had knocked down his partner.

"You okay?"

"Yeah." With quick swipes, she began to brush the dirt off her jeans. Shade ran his hands up her arms, stopping her cold.

"Sure?"

"Yes, I..." She trailed off as her thoughts twisted into something incoherent. He wasn't supposed to look at her like that, she thought. As though he really cared. She wished he'd look at her like that again, and again. His fingers were barely touching her arms. She wished he'd touch her like that again. And again.

"I'm fine," she managed finally. But it was hardly more than a whisper, and her eyes never left his.

He kept his hands on her arms. "That dog had to weigh a hundred and twenty."

"He didn't mean any harm." Why, she wondered

vaguely, were they talking about a dog, when there really wasn't anything important but him and her?

"I'm sorry." His thumb skimmed over the inside of her elbow, where the skin was as soft as he'd once imagined. Her pulse beat like an engine. "I should've gotten out first instead of playing around." If she'd been hurt... He wanted to kiss her now, right now, when he was thinking only of her and not the reasons that he shouldn't.

"It doesn't matter," she murmured, and found that her hands were resting on his shoulders. Their bodies were close, just brushing. Who had moved? "It doesn't matter," she said again, half to herself, as she leaned closer. Their lips hovered, hesitated, then barely touched. From the house came the deep, frantic sound of barking. They drew back from each other with something close to a jerk.

"Bryan!" Lee let the door slam behind her as she came onto the porch. It wasn't until she'd already called out that she noticed how intent the two people in her driveway were on each other.

With a quick shudder, Bryan took another step back before she turned. Too many feelings, was all she could think. Too many feelings, too quickly.

"Lee." She ran over, or ran away—she wasn't certain. All she knew was, at that moment she needed someone. Grateful, she felt herself closed in Lee's arms. "Oh, God, it's so good to see you."

The greeting was just a little desperate. Lee took a long look over Bryan's shoulder at the man who remained several paces back. Her first impression was that he wanted to stay that way. Separate. What had

Bryan gotten herself into? she wondered, and gave her friend a fierce hug.

"I've got to look at you," Bryan insisted, laughing now as the tension drained. The elegant face, the carefully styled hair—they were the same. But the woman wasn't. Bryan could feel it before she glanced down to the rounded swell beneath Lee's crisp summer dress.

"You're happy." Bryan gripped Lee's hands. "It shows. No regrets?"

"No regrets." Lee took a long, hard study. Bryan looked the same, she decided. Healthy, easy, lovely in a way that seemed exclusively her own. The same, she thought, but for the slightest hint of trouble in her eyes. "And you?"

"Things are good. I've missed you, but I feel better about it after seeing you here."

With a laugh, Lee slipped her arm around Bryan's waist. If there was trouble, she'd find the source. Bryan was hopeless at hiding anything for long. "Come inside. Sarah and Hunter are making iced tea." She sent a significant look in Shade's direction and felt Bryan tense. Just a little, but Lee felt it and knew she'd already found the source.

Bryan cleared her throat. "Shade."

He moved forward, Lee thought, like a man who was used to testing the way.

"Lee Radcliffe—Lee Radcliffe Brown," Bryan corrected, and relaxed a bit. "Shade Colby. You remember when I spent the money I'd saved for a new car on one of his prints."

"Yes, I told you you were crazy." Lee extended her

hand and smiled, but her voice was cool. "It's nice to meet you. Bryan's always admired your work."

"But you haven't," he returned, with more interest and respect than he'd intended to feel.

"I often find it harsh, but always compelling," Lee said simply. "Bryan's the expert, not me."

"Then she'd tell you that we don't take pictures for experts."

Lee nodded. His handshake had been firm—not gentle, but far from cruel. His eyes were precisely the same. She'd have to reserve judgment for now. "Come inside, Mr. Colby."

He'd intended to simply drop Bryan off and move along, but he found himself accepting. It wouldn't hurt, he rationalized, to cool off a bit before he drove into town. He followed the women inside.

"Dad, if you don't put more sugar in it, it tastes terrible."

As they walked into the kitchen, they saw Sarah with her hands on her hips, watching her father mop up around a pitcher of tea.

"Not everyone wants to pour sugar into their system the way you do."

"I do." Bryan grinned when Hunter turned. She thought his work brilliant—often cursing him for it in the middle of the night, when it kept her awake. She thought he looked like a man one of the Brontë sisters would have written about—strong, dark, brooding. But more, he was the man who loved her closest friend. Bryan opened her arms to him.

"It's good to see you again." Hunter held her close, chuckling when he felt her reach behind him to the plate of cookies Sarah had set out. "Why don't you gain weight?"

"I keep trying," Bryan claimed, and bit into the chocolate chip cookie. "Mmm, still warm. Hunter, this is Shade Colby."

Hunter put down his dishcloth. "I've followed your work," he told Shade as they shook hands. "It's powerful."

"That's the word I'd use to describe yours."

"Your latest had me too paranoid to go down to the basement laundry room for weeks," Bryan accused Hunter. "I nearly ran out of clothes."

Hunter grinned, pleased. "Thanks."

She glanced around the sunlit kitchen. "I guess I expected your house to have cobwebs and creaking boards."

"Disappointed?" Lee asked.

"Relieved."

With a laugh, Lee settled at the kitchen table with Sarah on her left and Bryan across from her. "So how's the project going?"

"Good." But Lee noticed she didn't look at Shade as she spoke. "Maybe terrific. We'll know more once we develop the film. We've made arrangements with one of the local papers for the use of a darkroom. All we have to do is drive into Sedona, check in and get a couple of rooms. Tomorrow, we work."

"Rooms?" Lee set down the glass Hunter handed her. "But you're staying here."

"Lee." Bryan gave Hunter a quick smile as he offered the plate of cookies. "I wanted to see you, not drop in bag and baggage. I know both you and Hunter are working on new books. Shade and I'll be up to our ears in developing fluid."

"How are we supposed to visit if you're in Sedona?" Lee countered. "Damn it, Bryan, I've missed you. You're staying here." She laid a hand on her rounded stomach. "Pregnant women have to be pampered."

"You should stay," Shade put in before Bryan could comment. "It might be the last chance for quite a while for a little free time."

"We've a lot of work to do," Bryan reminded him.

"It's a short drive into town from here. That won't make any difference. We're going to need to rent a car, in any case, so we can both be mobile."

Hunter studied the man across the room. Tense, he thought. Intense. Not the sort of man he'd have picked for the free-rolling, slow-moving Bryan, but it wasn't his place to judge. It was his place, and his talent, to observe. What was between them was obvious to see. Their reluctance to accept it was just as obvious. Calmly, he picked up his tea and drank.

"The invitation applies to both of you."

Shade glanced over with an automatic polite refusal on the tip of his tongue. His eyes met Hunter's. They were both intense, internalized men. Perhaps that's why they understood each other so quickly.

I've been there before, Hunter seemed to say to him with a hint of a smile. *You can run fast but only so far.*

Shade sensed something of the understanding, and something of the challenge. He glanced down to see Bryan giving him a long, cool look.

"I'd love to stay," he heard himself say. Shade crossed to the table and sat.

* * *

Lee looked over the prints in her precise, deliberate way. Bryan paced up and down the terrace, ready to explode.

"Well?" she demanded. "What do you think?"

"I haven't finished looking through them yet."

Bryan opened her mouth, then shut it again. It wasn't like her to be nervous over her work. She knew the prints were good. Hadn't she put her sweat and her heart into each of them?

More than good, she told herself as she yanked a chocolate bar out of her pocket. These prints ranked with her best work. It might've been the competition with Shade that had pushed her to produce them. It might've been the need to feel a bit smug after some of the comments he'd made on her particular style of work. Bryan didn't like to think she was base enough to resort to petty rivalry, but she had to admit that now she was. And she wanted to win.

She and Shade had lived in the same house, worked in the same darkroom for days, but had managed to see almost nothing of each other. A neat trick, Bryan thought ruefully. Perhaps it had worked so well because they'd both played the same game. Hide and don't seek. Tomorrow they'd be back on the road.

Bryan found that she was anxious to go even while she dreaded it. And she wasn't a contrary person, Bryan reminded herself almost fiercely. She was basically straightforward and...well, yes, she was amiable. It was simply her nature to be. So why wasn't she with Shade?

"Well."

Bryan whirled around as Lee spoke. "Well?" she echoed, waiting.

"I've always admired your work, Bryan. You know that." In her tidy way, Lee folded her hands on the wrought-iron table.

"But?" Bryan prompted.

"But these are the best." Lee smiled. "The very best you've ever done."

Bryan let out the breath she'd been holding and crossed to the table. Nerves? Yes, she had them. She didn't care for them. "Why?"

"I'm sure there're a lot of technical reasons—the light and the shading, the cropping."

Impatiently, Bryan shook her head. "Why?"

Understanding, Lee chose a print. "This one of the old woman and the little girl on the beach. Maybe it's my condition," she said slowly as she studied it again, "but it makes me think of the child I'll have. It also makes me remember I'll grow old, but not too old to dream. This picture's powerful because it's so basically simple, so straightforward and so incredibly full of emotion. And this one…"

She shuffled the prints until she came to the one of the road worker. "Sweat, determination, honesty. You know when you look at this face that the man believes in hard work and paying his bills on time. And here, these teenagers. I see youth just before those inevitable changes of adulthood. And this dog." Lee laughed as she looked at it. "The first time I looked, it just struck me as cute and funny, but he looks so proud, so, well, human. You could almost believe the boat was his."

While Bryan remained silent, Lee tidied the prints

again. "I could go over each one of them with you, but the point is, each one of them tells a story. It's only one scene, one instant of time, yet the story's there. The feelings are there. Isn't that the purpose?"

"Yes." Bryan smiled as her shoulders relaxed. "That's the purpose."

"If Shade's pictures are half as good, you'll have a wonderful essay."

"They will be," Bryan murmured. "I saw some of his negatives in the darkroom. They're incredible."

Lee lifted a brow and watched Bryan devour chocolate. "Does that bother you?"

"What? Oh, no, no, of course not. His work is his work—and in this case it'll be part of mine. I'd never have agreed to work with him if I hadn't admired him."

"But?" This time Lee prompted with a raised brow and half smile.

"I don't know, Lee, he's just so—so perfect."

"Really?"

"He never fumbles," Bryan complained. "He always knows exactly what he wants. When he wakes up in the morning, he's perfectly coherent, he never misses a turn on the road. He even makes decent coffee."

"Anyone would detest him for that," Lee said dryly.

"It's frustrating, that's all."

"Love often is. You are in love with him, aren't you?"

"No." Genuinely surprised, Bryan stared over at Lee. "Good God, I hope I've more sense than that. I have to work hard at even liking him."

"Bryan, you're my friend. Otherwise what I'm calling concern would be called prying."

"Which means you're going to pry," Bryan put in.

"Exactly. I've seen the way the two of you tiptoe around each other as if you're terrified that if you happened to brush up against each other there'd be spontaneous combustion."

"Something like that."

Lee reached out and touched her hand. "Bryan, tell me."

Evasions weren't possible. Bryan looked down at the joined hands and sighed. "I'm attracted," she admitted slowly. "He's different from anyone I've known, mostly because he's just not the type of man I'd normally socialize with. He's very remote, very serious. I like to have fun. Just fun."

"Relationships have to be made up of more than just fun."

"I'm not looking for a relationship." On this point she was perfectly clear. "I date so I can go dancing, go to a party, listen to music or see a movie. That's it. The last thing I want is all the tension and work that goes into a relationship."

"If someone didn't know you, they'd say that was a pretty shallow sentiment."

"Maybe it is," Bryan tossed back. "Maybe I am."

Lee said nothing, just tapped a finger on the prints.

"That's my work," Bryan began, then gave up. A lot of people might take what she said at face value, not Lee. "I don't want a relationship," she repeated, but in a quieter tone. "Lee, I've been there before, and I'm lousy at it."

"Relationship equals two," Lee pointed out. "Are you still taking the blame?"

"Most of the blame was mine. I was no good at being a wife."

"At being a certain kind of wife," Lee corrected.

"I imagine there's only a handful of definitions in the dictionary."

Lee only raised a brow. "Sarah has a friend whose mother is wonderful. She keeps not just a clean house, but an interesting one. She makes jelly, takes the minutes at the P.T.A. and runs a Girl Scout troop. The woman can take colored paper and some glue and create a work of art. She's lovely and helps herself stay that way with exercise classes three times a week. I admire her a great deal, but if Hunter had wanted those things from me, I wouldn't have his ring on my finger."

"Hunter's special," Bryan murmured.

"I can't argue with that. And you know why I nearly ruined it with him—because I was afraid I'd fail at building and maintaining a relationship."

"It's not a matter of being afraid." Bryan shrugged her shoulders. "It's more a matter of not having the energy for it."

"Remember who you're talking to," Lee said mildly.

With a half laugh, Bryan shook her head. "All right, maybe it's a matter of being cautious. *Relationship*'s a very weighty word. *Affair*'s lighter," she said consideringly. "But an affair with a man like Shade's bound to have tremendous repercussions."

That sounded so cool, Bryan mused. When had she started to think in such logical terms? "He's not an easy man, Lee. He has his own demons and his own way of dealing with them. I don't know whether he'd share them with me, or if I'd want him to."

"He works at being cold," Lee commented. "But I've seen him with Sarah. I admit the basic kindness in him surprised me, but it's there."

"It's there," Bryan agreed. "It's just hard to get to."

"Dinner's ready!" Sarah yanked open the screen door and let it hit the wall with a bang. "Shade and I made spaghetti, and it's terrific."

It was. During the meal, Bryan watched Shade. Like Lee, she'd noticed his easy relationship with Sarah. It was more than tolerance, she decided as she watched him laugh with the girl. It was affection. It hadn't occurred to her that Shade could give his affection so quickly or with so few restrictions.

Maybe I should be a twelve-year-old with braces, she decided, then shook her head at her own thought pattern. She didn't want Shade's affection. His respect, yes.

It wasn't until after dinner that she realized she was wrong. She wanted a great deal more.

It was the last leisurely evening before the group separated. On the front porch they watched the first stars come out and listened to the first night sounds begin. By that time the next evening, Shade and Bryan would be in Colorado.

Lee and Hunter sat on the porch swing with Sarah nestled between them. Shade stretched out in a chair just to the side, relaxed, a little tired, and mentally satisfied after his long hours in the darkroom. Still, as he sat talking easily to the Browns, he realized that he'd needed this visit as much as, perhaps more than, Bryan.

He'd had a simple childhood. Until these past days, he'd nearly forgotten just how simple, and just how solid. The things that had happened to him as an adult had blocked a great deal of it out. Now, without consciously realizing it, Shade was drawing some of it back.

Bryan sat on the first step, leaning back against a post. She joined in the conversation or distanced herself from it as she chose. There was nothing important being said, and the easiness of the conversation made the scene that much more appealing. A moth battered itself against the porch light, crickets called, and the breeze rippled through the full leaves of the surrounding trees. The sounds made a soothing conversation of their own.

She liked the way Hunter had his arm across the back of the swing. Though he spoke to Shade, his fingers ran lightly over his wife's hair. His daughter's head rested against his chest, but once in a while, she'd reach a hand over to Lee's stomach as if to test for movement. Though she hadn't been consciously setting the scene, it grew in front of her eyes. Unable to resist, Bryan slipped inside.

When she returned a few moments later, she had her camera, tripod and light stand.

"Oh, boy." Sarah took one look and straightened primly. "Bryan's going to take our picture."

"No posing," Bryan told her with a grin. "Just keep talking," she continued before anyone could protest. "Pretend I'm not even here. It's so perfect," she began to mutter to herself as she set up. "I don't know why I didn't see it before."

"Let me give you a hand."

Bryan glanced up at Shade in surprise, and nearly refused before she stopped the words. It was the first time he'd made any attempt to work with her. Whether it was a gesture to her or to the affection he'd come to feel for her friends, she wouldn't toss it back at him. Instead, she smiled and handed him her light meter.

"Give me a reading, will you?"

They worked together as though they'd been doing so for years. Another surprise, for both of them. She adjusted her light, already calculating her exposure as Shade gave her the readings. Satisfied, Bryan checked the angle and framing through the viewfinder, then stepped back and let Shade take her place.

"Perfect." If she was looking for a lazy summer evening and a family content with it and one another, she could've done no better. Stepping back, Shade leaned against the wall of the house. Without thinking about it, he continued to help by distracting the trio on the swing.

"What do you want, Sarah?" he began as Bryan moved behind the camera again. "A baby brother or a sister?"

As she considered, Sarah forgot her enchantment with being photographed. "Well…" Her hand moved to Lee's stomach again. Lee's hand closed over it spontaneously. Bryan clicked the shutter. "Maybe a brother," she decided. "My cousin says a little sister can be a real pain."

As Sarah spoke Lee leaned her head back, just slightly, until it rested on Hunter's arm. His fingers brushed her hair again. Bryan felt the emotion well up in her and blur her vision. She took the next shot blindly.

Had she always wanted that? she wondered as she continued to shoot. The closeness, the contentment that came with commitment and intimacy? Why had it waited to slam into her now, when her feelings toward

Shade were already tangled and much too complicated? She blinked her eyes clear and opened the shutter just as Lee turned her head to laugh at something Hunter said.

Relationship, she thought as the longing rose up in her. Not the easy, careless friendships she'd permitted herself, but a solid, demanding, sharing relationship. That was what she saw through the viewfinder. That was what she discovered she needed for herself. When she straightened from the camera, Shade was beside her.

"Something wrong?"

She shook her head and reached over to switch off the light. "Perfect," she announced with a casualness that cost her. She gave the family on the swing a smile. "I'll send you a print as soon as we stop and develop again."

She was trembling. Shade was close enough to see it. He turned and dealt with the camera and tripod himself. "I'll take this up for you."

She turned to tell him no, but he was already carrying it inside. "I'd better pack my gear," she said to Hunter and Lee. "Shade likes to leave at uncivilized hours."

When she went inside, Lee leaned her head against Hunter's arm again. "They'll be fine," he told her. "She'll be fine."

Lee glanced toward the doorway. "Maybe."

Shade carried Bryan's equipment up to the bedroom she'd been using and waited. The moment she came in with the light, he turned to her. "What's wrong?"

Bryan opened the case and packed her stand and light. "Nothing. Why?"

"You were trembling." Impatient, Shade took her arm and turned her around. "You're still trembling."

"I'm tired." In its way, it was true. She was tired of having her emotions sneak up on her.

"Don't play games with me, Bryan. I'm better at it than you."

God, could he have any idea just how much she wanted to be held at that moment? Would he have any way of understanding how much she'd give if only he'd hold her now? "Don't push it, Shade."

She should've known he wouldn't listen. With one hand, he cupped her chin and held her face steady. The eyes that saw a great deal more than he was entitled to looked into hers. "Tell me."

"No." She said it quietly. If she'd been angry, insulted, cold, he'd have dug until he'd had it all. He couldn't fight her this way.

"All right." He backed off, dipping his hands into his pockets. He'd felt something out on the porch, something that had pulled at him, offered itself to him. If she'd made one move, the slightest move, he might have given her more at that moment than either of them could imagine. "Maybe you should get some sleep. We'll leave at seven."

"Okay." Deliberately she turned away to pack up the rest of her gear. "I'll be ready."

He was at the door before he felt compelled to turn around again. "Bryan, I saw your prints. They're exceptional."

She felt the first tears stream down her face and was appalled. Since when did she cry because someone acknowledged her talent? Since when did she tremble because a picture she was taking spoke to her personally?

She pressed her lips together for a moment and continued to pack without turning around. "Thanks."

Shade didn't linger any longer. He closed the door soundlessly on his way out.

Chapter 6

By the time they'd passed through New Mexico and into Colorado, Bryan felt more in tune with herself. In part, she thought that the break in Oak Creek Canyon had given her too much time for introspection. Though she often relied heavily on just that in her work, there were times when it could be self-defeating.

At least that's what she'd been able to convince herself of after she and Shade had picked up the routine of drive and shoot and drive some more.

They weren't looking for cities and major events on this leg. They sought out small, unrecognizable towns and struggling ranches. Families that worked with the land and one another to make ends meet. For them, summer was a time of hard, endless work to prepare for the rigors of winter. It wasn't all fun, all games, all sun and sand. It was migrant workers waiting to pick

August peaches, and gardens being weeded and tended to offset the expense of winter vegetables.

They didn't consider Denver, but chose instead places like Antonito. They didn't go after the big, sprawling cattle spreads, but the smaller, more personal operations.

Bryan had her first contact with a cattle branding on a dusty little ranch called the Bar T. Her preconception of sweaty, loose-limbed cowboys rounding 'em up and heading 'em out wasn't completely wrong. It just didn't include the more basic aspects of branding—such as the smell of burned flesh and the splash of blood as potential bulls were turned into little steers.

She was, she discovered as her stomach heaved, a city girl at heart.

But they got their pictures. Cowboys with bandannas over their faces and spurs on their boots. Some of them laughed, some of them swore. All of them worked.

She learned the true meaning of *workhorse* as she watched the men push their mounts through their paces. The sweat of a horse was a heavy, rich smell. It hung thickly in the air with the sweat of men.

Bryan considered her best shot a near-classic study of a man taking hold of his leisure time with both hands. The young cowboy was rangy and ruddy, which made him perfect for what she was after. His chambray shirt was dark with patches of sweat down the front, down the back and spreading from under the arms. More sweat mixed with dust ran down his face. His work boots were creased and caked with grime. The back pocket of his jeans was worn from the constant rub against a round can of chewing tobacco. With his hat tilted back and his bandanna tied loosely around his throat, he straddled the fence and lifted an icy can of beer to his lips.

Bryan thought when the picture was printed you'd almost be able to see his Adam's apple move as he swallowed. And every woman who looked at it, she was certain, would be half in love. He was the mystic, the swashbuckler, the last of the knights. Having that picture in her camera nearly made up for almost losing her lunch over the branding.

She'd seen Shade home right in on it and known his pictures would be gritty, hard and detailed. Yet she'd also seen him focusing in on a young boy of eleven or twelve as he'd ridden in his first roundup with all the joy and innocence peculiar to a boy of that age. His choice had surprised her, because he rarely went for the lighter touch. It was also, unfortunately for her state of mind, something else she could like him for. There were others.

He hadn't made any comment when she'd turned green and distanced herself for a time from what was going on in the small enclosed corral where calves bawled for their mothers and let out long, surprised wails when knife and iron were applied. He hadn't said a word when she'd sat down in the shade until she was certain her stomach would stay calm. Nor had he said a word when he'd handed her a cold drink. Neither had she.

That night they camped on Bar T land. Shade had given her space since they'd left Arizona, because she suddenly seemed to need it. Oddly, he found he didn't. In the beginning, it had always been Bryan who'd all but forced him into conversations when he'd have been content to drive in silence for hours. Now he wanted to talk to her, to hear her laugh, to watch the way her hands moved when she became enthusiastic about a certain point. Or to watch the way she stretched, easily, degree by inching degree, as her voice slowed.

Something undefinable had shifted in both of them during their time in Oak Creek. Bryan had become remote, when she'd always been almost too open for his comfort. He found he wanted her company, when he'd always been solitary. He wanted, though he didn't fully comprehend why, her friendship. It was a shift he wasn't certain he cared for, or even understood. In any case, because the opposing shifts had happened in both of them simultaneously, it brought them no closer.

Shade had chosen the open space near a fast-running creek for a campsite for no reason other than that it appealed to him. Bryan immediately saw other possibilities.

"Look, I'm going down to wash off." She was as dusty as the cowboys she'd focused on all afternoon. It occurred to her, not altogether pleasantly, that she might smell a bit too much like the horses she'd watched. "It's probably freezing, so I'll make it fast and you can have a turn."

Shade pried the top off a beer. Perhaps they hadn't rounded up cattle, but they'd been on their feet and in the sun for almost eight hours. "Take your time."

Bryan grabbed a towel and a cake of soap and dashed off. The sun was steadily dropping behind the mountains to the west. She knew enough of camping by now to know how quickly the air would cool once the sun went down. She didn't want to be wet and naked when it did.

She didn't bother to glance around before she stripped off her shirt. They were far enough away from the ranch house that none of the men would wander out that way at sunset. Shade and she had already established the sanctity of privacy without exchanging a word on the subject.

Right now, she thought as she wiggled out of her jeans, the cowboys they'd come to shoot were probably sitting down to an enormous meal—red meat and potatoes, she mused. Hot biscuits with plenty of butter. Lord knows they deserved it, after the day they'd put in. And me, too, she decided, though she and Shade were making do with cold sandwiches and a bag of chips.

Slim, tall and naked, Bryan took a deep breath of the pine-scented air. Even a city girl, she thought as she paused a moment to watch the sunset, could appreciate all this.

Gingerly she stepped into the cold knee-high water and began to rinse off the dust. Strange, she didn't mind the chill as much as she once had. The drive across America was bound to leave its mark. She was glad of it.

No one really wanted to stay exactly the same throughout life. If her outlook changed and shifted as they traveled, she was fortunate. The assignment was giving her more than the chance for professional exposure and creative expression. It was giving her experiences. Why else had she become a photographer, but to see things and understand them?

Yet she didn't understand Shade any better now than when they'd started out. Had she tried? In some ways, she thought, as she glided the soap over her arms. Until what she saw and understood began to affect her too deeply and too personally. Then she'd backed off fast.

She didn't like to admit it. Bryan shivered and began to wash more swiftly. The sun was nearly set. Self-preservation, she reminded herself. Perhaps her image was one of take what comes and make the best of it, but she had her phobias as well. And she was entitled to them.

It had been a long time since she'd been hurt, and that was because of her own deceptively simple maneuvering. If she stood at a crossroads and had two routes, one smooth, the other rocky, with a few pits, she'd take the smooth one. Maybe it was less admirable, but she'd always felt you ended up in the same place with less energy expended. Shade Colby was a rocky road.

In any case, it wasn't just a matter of her choice. They could have an affair—a physically satisfying, emotionally shallow affair. It worked well for a great many people. But...

He didn't want to be involved with her any more than she did with him. He was attracted, just as she was, but he wasn't offering her any more than that. If he ever did... She dropped that line of thought like a stone. Speculation wasn't always healthy.

The important thing was that she felt more like herself again. She was pleased with the work she'd done since they'd left Arizona, and was looking forward to crossing over into Kansas the next day. The assignment, as they'd both agreed from the outset, was the first priority.

Wheat fields and tornadoes, she thought with a grin. Follow the yellow brick road. That was what Kansas brought to her mind. She knew better now, and looked forward to finding the reality. Bryan was beginning to enjoy having her preconceptions both confirmed and blown to bits.

That was for tomorrow. Right now it was dusk and she was freezing.

Agile, she scrambled up the small bank and reached for the towel. Shade could wash up while she stuffed herself with whatever was handy in the cupboards. She pulled on a long-sleeved oversize shirt and reached up to button it. That's when she saw the eyes.

For a moment she only stared with her hands poised at the top button. Then she saw there was more to it than a pair of narrow yellow eyes peering out of the lowering light. There was a sleek, muscled body and a set of sharp, white teeth only a narrow creek bed away.

Bryan took two steps back, tripped over her own tangled jeans and let out a scream that might've been heard in the next county.

Shade was stretched out in a folding chair beside the small campfire he'd built on impulse. He'd enjoyed himself that day—the rough-and-ready atmosphere, the baking sun and cold beer. He'd always admired the camaraderie that went hand in hand with people who work outdoors.

He needed the city—it was in his blood. For the most part, he preferred the impersonal aspects of people rushing to their own places, in their own time. But it helped to touch base with other aspects of life from time to time.

He could see now, even after only a few weeks on the road, that he'd been getting stale. He hadn't had the

challenge of his early years. That get-the-shot-and-stay-
alive sort of challenge. He didn't want it. But he'd let
himself become too complacent with what he'd been
doing.

This assignment had given him the chance to explore himself as well as his country. He thought of his
partner with varying degrees of puzzlement and interest. She wasn't nearly as simple or laid-back as he'd
originally believed. Still, she was nearly 180 degrees
removed from him. He was beginning to understand
her. Slowly, but he was beginning to.

She was sensitive, emotional and inherently kind. He
was rarely kind, because he was careful not to be. She
was comfortable with herself, easily amused and candid. He'd learned long ago that candor can jump back
on you with teeth.

But he wanted her—because she was different or in
spite of it, he wanted her. Forcing himself to keep his
hands off her in all the days and nights that had passed
since that light, interrupted kiss in Hunter Brown's
driveway was beginning to wear on him. He had his
control to thank for the fact that he'd been able to, the
control that he honed so well that it was nearly a prison.

Shade tossed his cigarette into the fire and leaned
back. He wouldn't lose that control, or break out of that
prison, but that didn't mean that sooner or later he and
Bryan wouldn't be lovers. He meant it to happen. He
would simply bide his time until it happened his way.
As long as he was holding the reins, he wouldn't steer
himself into the mire.

When he heard her scream, a dozen agonizing images rushed into his head, images that he'd seen and

lived through, images that only someone who had could conjure up. He was out of the chair and running before he'd fully realized they were only memories.

When he got to her, Bryan was scrambling up from the tumble she'd taken. The last thing she expected was to be hauled up and crushed against Shade. The last thing she expected was exactly what she needed. Gasping for air, she clung to him.

"What happened?" Her own panic muffled her ears to the thread of panic in his voice. "Bryan, are you hurt?"

"No, no. It scared me, but it ran away." She pushed her face against his shoulder and just breathed. "Oh, God, Shade."

"What?" Gripping her by the elbows, he pulled her back far enough to see her face. "What scared you?"

"A cat."

He wasn't amused. His fear turned to fury, tangibly enough that Bryan could see the latter even before he cursed her. "Damn it! What kind of fool are you?" he demanded. "Letting out a scream like that over a cat."

She drew air in and out, in and out, and concentrated on her anger—genuine fear was something she didn't care for. "Not a house cat," she snapped. She was still shaken, but not enough to sit back and be called a fool. "It was one of those…I don't know." She lifted a hand to push at her hair and dropped it again when it trembled. "I have to sit down." She did so with a plop on the grass.

"A bobcat?" Calmer, Shade crouched down beside her.

"I don't know. Bobcat, cougar—I wouldn't know the difference. It was a hell of a lot bigger than any tabby." She lowered her head to her knees. Maybe she'd been frightened before in her life, but she couldn't remember anything to compare with this. "He just stood over there, staring at me. I thought—I thought he was going to jump over the creek. His teeth…" She shuddered and shut her eyes. "Big," she managed, no longer caring if she sounded like a simpleminded fool. "Real big."

"He's gone now." His fury turned inward. He should've known she wasn't the kind of woman who jumped at shadows. He knew what it was to be afraid and to feel helpless with it. This time he cursed himself as he slipped an arm around her. "The way you screamed, he's ten miles away and still running."

Bryan nodded but kept her face buried against her knees. "I guess he wasn't that big, but they look different out of the zoo. I just need a minute to pull myself together."

"Take your time."

He found he didn't mind offering comfort, though it was something he hadn't done in a long time. The air was cool, the night still. He could hear the sound of the water rushing by in the creek. For a moment he had a quick flash of the Browns' porch, of the easy family portrait on the swing. He felt a touch of the same contentment here, with his arm around Bryan and night closing in.

Overhead a hawk screeched, out for its first flight of the night. Bryan jolted.

"Easy," Shade murmured. He didn't laugh at her reaction, or even smile. He soothed.

"I guess I'm a little jumpy." With a nervous laugh, she lifted her hand to push at her hair again. It wasn't until then that Shade realized she was naked beneath the open, billowing shirt.

The sight of her slim, supple body beneath the thin, fluttering material sent the contentment he'd felt skyrocketing into need. A need, he discovered only in that instant, that was somehow exclusively for her—not just for a woman with a lovely face, a desirable body, but for Bryan.

"Maybe we should get back and…" She turned her head and found her eyes only inches from his. In his, she saw everything he felt. When she started to speak again, he shook his head.

No words. No words now. Only needs, only feelings. He wanted that with her. As his mouth closed over hers, he gave her no choice but to want it as well.

Sweetness? Where had it come from and how could she possibly turn away from it? They'd been together nearly a month, but she'd never suspected he had sweetness in him. Nor had she known just how badly she'd needed to find it there.

His mouth demanded, but so slowly, so subtly, that she was giving before she was aware of it. Once she'd given, she couldn't take away again. She felt his hand, warm and firm on her bare skin, but she sighed in pleasure, not in protest. She'd wanted him to touch her, had waited for it, had denied her waiting. Now she leaned closer. There'd be no denying.

He'd known she'd feel like this—slim, strong, smooth. A hundred times, he'd imagined it. He hadn't forgotten that she'd taste like this—warm, tempting, generous. A hundred times, he'd tried not to remember.

This time she smelled of the creek, fresh and cool. He could bury his face in her throat and smell the summer night on her. He kissed her slowly, leaving her lips for her throat, her throat for her shoulder. As he lingered there, he gave himself the pleasure of discovering her body with his fingertips.

It was torture. Exquisite. Agonizing. Irresistible. Bryan wanted it to go on, and on and on. She drew him closer, loving the hard, lean feel of his body against hers, the brush of his clothes against her skin, the whisper of his breath across it. And through it all, the quick, steady beat of his heart near hers.

She could smell the work of the day on him, the faint tang of healthy sweat, the traces of dust he hadn't yet washed off. It excited her with memories of the way his muscles had bunched beneath his shirt when he'd climbed onto a fence for a better angle. She could remember exactly how he'd looked then, though she'd pretended to herself that she hadn't seen, hadn't needed to.

She wanted his strength. Not the muscles, but the inner strength she'd sensed in him from the start. The strength that had carried him through what he'd seen, what he'd lived with.

Yet wasn't it that strength that helped to harden him, to separate him emotionally from the people around him? With her mind whirling, her body pulsing, she struggled to find the answer she needed.

Wants weren't enough. Hadn't she told him so herself? God, she wanted him. Her bones were melting from the desire for him. But it wasn't enough. She only wished she knew what was.

"Shade…" Even when she tried to speak, he cut her off with another long, draining kiss.

She wanted him to drain her. Mind, body, soul. If he did, there'd be no question and no need for answers.

But the questions were there. Even as she held him to her, they were there.

"Shade," she began again.

"I want to make love with you." He lifted his head, and his eyes were so dark, so intense, it was almost impossible to believe his hands were so gentle. "I want to feel your skin under my hand, feel your heart race, watch your eyes."

The words were quiet, incredibly calm when his eyes were so passionate. More than the passion and demand in his eyes, the words frightened her.

"I'm not ready for this." She barely managed the words as she drew away from him.

He felt the needs rise and the anger begin. It took all his skill to control both. "Are you saying you don't want me?"

"No." She shook her head as she drew her shirt together. When had it become so cold? she wondered. "No, lying's foolish."

"So's backing away from something we both want to happen."

"I'm not sure I do. I can't be logical about this, Shade." She gathered her clothes quickly and hugged them against her as she stood. "I can't think something like this through step-by-step the way you do. If I could, it'd be different, but I can only go with my feelings, my instincts."

There was a deadly calm around him when he rose. The control he'd nearly forfeited to her was back in place. Once more he accepted the prison he'd built for himself. "And?"

She shivered without knowing if it was from the cold without or the cold within. "And my feelings tell me

I need more time." When she looked up at him again, her face was honest, her eyes were eloquent. "Maybe I do want this to happen. Maybe I'm just a little afraid of how much I want you."

He didn't like her use of the word *afraid*. She made him feel responsible, obliged. Defensive. "I've no intention of hurting you."

She gave herself a moment. Her breathing was easier, even if her pulse was still unsteady. Whether he knew it or not, Shade had already given her the distance she needed to resist him. Now she could look at him, calmer. Now she could think more clearly.

"No, I don't think you do, but you could, and I have a basic fear of bruises. Maybe I'm an emotional coward. It's not a pretty thought, but it might be true." With a sigh, she lifted both hands to her hair and pushed it back. "Shade, we've a bit more than two months left on the road. I can't afford to spend it being torn up inside because of you. My instincts tell me you could very easily do that to me, whether you planned on it or not."

She knew how to back a man into a corner, he thought in frustration. He could press, relieve the knot she'd tightened in his stomach. And by doing so, he'd run the risk of having her words echo back at him for a long time to come. It'd only taken a few words from her to remind him what it felt like to be responsible for someone else.

"Go back to the van," he told her, turning away to strip off his shirt. "I have to clean up."

She started to speak, then realized there was nothing more she could say. Instead, she left him to follow the thin, moonlit trail back to the van.

Chapter 7

Wheat fields. Bryan's preconception wasn't slashed as they drove through the Midwest, but reinforced. Kansas was wheat fields.

Whatever else Bryan saw as they crossed the state, it was the endless, rippling gold grass that captivated her, first and last. Color, texture, shape, form. Emotion. There were towns, of course, cities with modern buildings and plush homes, but in seeing basic Americana, grain against sky, Bryan saw it all.

Some might have found the continuous spread of sun-ripened grain waving, acre after acre, monotonous. Not Bryan. This was a new experience for a woman of the city. There were no jutting mountains, no glossy towering buildings, no looping freeways, to break the lines. Here was space, just as awesome as the terrain of Arizona, but lusher, and somehow calmer. She could look at it and wonder.

In the fields of wheat and acres of corn, Bryan saw the heart and the sweat of the country. It wasn't always an idyllic scene. There were insects, dirt, grimy machinery. People worked here with their hands, with their backs.

In the cities, she saw the pace and energy. On the farms, she saw a schedule that would have made a corporate executive wilt. Year after year, the farmer gave himself to the land and waited for the land to give back.

With the right angle, the proper light, she could photograph a wheat field and make it seem endless, powerful. With evening shadows, she could give a sense of serenity and continuity. It was only grass, after all, only stalks growing to be cut down, processed, used. But the grain had a life and a beauty of its own. She wanted to show it as she saw it.

Shade saw the tenuous, inescapable dependence of man on nature. The planter, keeper and harvester of the wheat, was irrevocably tied to the land. It was both his freedom and his prison. The man riding the tractor in the Kansas sunlight, damp with healthy sweat, lean from years of labor, was as dependent on the land as the land was on him. Without man, the wheat might grow wild, it might flourish, but then it would wither and die. It was the tie Shade sensed, and the tie he meant to record.

Still, perhaps for the first time since they'd left L.A., he and Bryan weren't shooting as separate entities. They might not have realized it yet, but their feelings, perceptions and needs were drawing them closer to the same mark.

They made each other think. How did she see this

cene? How did he feel about this setting? Where before each of them had considered their photographs separately, now subtly, unconsciously, they began to do two things that would improve the final result: compete and consult.

They'd spent a day and a night in Dodge City for the Fourth of July celebrations in what had once been a Wild West town. Bryan thought of Wyatt Earp, of Doc Holliday and the desperadoes who had once ridden through town, but she'd been drawn to the street parade that might've been in Anytown, U.S.A.

It was here, caught up in the pageantry and the flavor, that she'd asked Shade his opinion of the right angle for shooting a horse and rider, and he in turn had taken her advice on capturing a tiny, bespangled majorette.

The step they'd taken had been lost in the moment to both of them. But they'd stood side by side on the curb as the parade had passed, music blaring, batons flying. Their pictures had been different—Shade had looked for the overview of holiday parades while Bryan had wanted individual reactions. But they'd stood side by side.

Bryan's feelings for Shade had become more complex, more personal. When the change had begun or how, she couldn't say. But because her work was most often a direct result of her emotions, the pictures she took began to reflect both the complexity and the intimacy. Their view of the same wheat field might be radically different, but Bryan was determined that when their prints were set side by side, hers would have equal impact.

She'd never been an aggressive person. It just wasn't

her style. But Shade had tapped a need in her to compete—as a photographer, and as a woman. If she had to travel in close quarters for weeks with a man who ruffled her professional feathers and stirred her feminine needs, she had to deal with him directly—on both counts. Directly, she decided, but in her own fashion and her own time. As the days went on, Bryan wondered if it would be possible to have both success and Shade without losing something vital.

She was so damn calm! It drove him crazy. Every day, every hour, they spent together pushed Shade closer to the edge. He wasn't used to wanting anyone so badly. He didn't enjoy finding out he could, and that there was nothing he could do about it. Bryan put him in the position of needing, then having to deny himself. There were times he nearly believed she did so purposely. But he'd never known anyone less likely to scheme than Bryan. She wouldn't think of it—and if she did, she'd consider it too much bother.

Even now, as they drove through the Kansas twilight, she was stretched out in the seat beside him, sound asleep. It was one of the rare times she'd left her hair loose. Full, wavy and lush, it was muted to a dull gold in the lowering light. The sun had given her skin all the color it needed. Her body was relaxed, loose like her hair. Shade wondered if he'd ever had the capability to let his mind and body go so enviably limp. Was it that that tempted him, that drove at him? Was he simply pushed to find that spark of energy she could turn on and off at will? He wanted to set it to life. For himself.

Temptation. The longer he held himself back, the

more intense it became. To have her. To explore her. To absorb her. When he did—he no longer used the word *if*—what cost would there be? Nothing was free.

Once, he thought as she sighed in sleep. Just once. His way. Perhaps the cost would be high, but he wouldn't be the one to pay it. His emotions were trained and disciplined. They wouldn't be touched. There wasn't a woman alive who could make him hurt.

His body and his mind tensed as Bryan slowly woke. Groggy and content to be so, she yawned. The scent of smoke and tobacco stung the air. On the radio was low, mellow jazz. The windows were half open, so that when she shifted, the slap of wind woke her more quickly than she'd have liked.

It was fully dark now. Surprised, Bryan stretched and stared out the window at a moon half covered by clouds. "It's late," she said on another yawn. The first thing she remembered as her mind cleared of sleep was that they hadn't eaten. She pressed a hand to her stomach. "Dinner?"

He glanced at her just long enough to see her shake back her hair. It rippled off her shoulders and down her back. As he watched, he had to fight back the urge to touch it. "I want to get over the border tonight."

She heard it in his voice—the tension, the annoyance. Bryan didn't know what had prompted it, nor at the moment did she want to. Instead, she lifted a brow. If he was in a hurry to get to Oklahoma and was willing to drive into the night to get there, it was his business. She'd stocked a cabinet in the back of the van with a few essentials just for moments like this. Bryan started to haul herself out of her seat when she heard the long blare of a horn and the rev of an engine.

The scarred old Pontiac had a hole in the muffler you could've tossed a baseball through. The sound of the engine clattered like a badly tuned plane. It swerved around the van at a dangerous speed, fishtailed, then bolted ahead, radio blaring. As Shade swore, Bryan got a glimpse that revealed the dilapidated car was packed with kids.

"Saturday night in July," she commented.

"Idiots," he said between his teeth as he watched the taillights weave.

"Yeah." She frowned as she watched the car barrel ahead, smoke streaming. "They were just kids, I hope they don't..."

Even as she thought it, it happened. The driver decided to press his luck by passing another car over the double yellow lines. The truck coming toward him laid on the horn and swerved. Bryan felt her blood freeze.

Shade was already hitting the brakes as the Pontiac screeched back into its own lane. But it was out of control. Skidding sideways, the Pontiac kissed the fender of the car it had tried to pass, then flipped into a telephone pole.

The sound of screaming tires, breaking glass and smashing metal whirled in her head. Bryan was up and out of the van before Shade had brought it to a complete stop. She could hear a girl screaming, others weeping. Even as the sounds shuddered through her, she told herself it meant they were alive.

The door on the passenger's side was crushed against the telephone pole. Bryan rushed to the driver's side and wrenched at the handle. She smelled the blood before she saw it. "Good God," she whispered as she managed to yank the door open on the second try. Then Shade was beside her, shoving her aside.

"Get some blankets out of the van," he ordered without looking at her. It had only taken him one glance at the driver to tell him it wasn't going to be pretty. He shifted enough to block Bryan's view, then reached in to check the pulse in the driver's throat as he heard her run back to the van. Alive, he thought, then blocked out everything but what had to be done. He worked quickly.

The driver was unconscious. The gash on his head was serious, but it didn't worry Shade as much as the probability of internal injuries. And nothing worried him as much as the smell of gas that was beginning to sweeten the air. Under other circumstances, Shade would've been reluctant to move the boy. Now there was no choice. Locking his arms under the boy's arms, Shade hauled him out. Even as Shade began to drag him, the driver of the truck ran over and took the boy's legs.

"Got a CB in the truck," he told Shade breathlessly. "Called for an ambulance."

With a nod, Shade laid the boy down. Bryan was already there with the first blanket.

"Stay here. The car's going to go up." He said it calmly. Without a backward glance, he went back to the crippled Pontiac.

Terror jolted through her. Within seconds, Bryan was at the car beside him, helping to pull the others out of the wreck.

"Get back to the van!" Shade shouted at her as Bryan half carried a sobbing girl. "Stay there!"

Bryan spoke soothingly, covered the girl with a blanket, then rushed back to the car. The last passenger was also unconscious. A boy, Bryan saw, of no more than sixteen. She had to half crawl into the car to reach him. By the time she'd dragged him to the open door, she was drenched and exhausted. Both Shade and the truck driver carried the other injured passengers. Shade had just set a young girl on the grass when he turned and saw Bryan struggling with the last victim.

Fear was instant and staggering. Even as he started to run, his imagination worked on him. In his mind, Shade could see the flash of the explosion, hear the sound of bursting metal and shattering, flying glass. He knew exactly what it would smell like the moment the gas ignited. When he reached Bryan, Shade scooped up the unconscious boy as though he were weightless.

"Run!" he shouted at her. Together, they raced away from the Pontiac.

Bryan didn't see the explosion. She heard it, but more, she felt it. The whoosh of hot air slammed into her back and sent her sprawling onto the grassy shoulder of the road. There was a whistle of metal as something hot and twisted and lethal flew overhead. One of the teenagers screamed and buried her face in her hands.

Stunned, Bryan lay prone a moment, waiting to catch her breath. Over the sound of fire, she could hear the whine of sirens.

"Are you hurt?" Shade half dragged her up to her knees. He'd seen the flying slice of metal whiz by her head. Hands that had been rock steady moments before trembled as they gripped her.

"No." Bryan shook her head and, finding her balance, turned to the whimpering girl beside her. A broken arm, she realized as she tucked the blanket under the girl's chin. And the cut on her temple would need stitches. "Take it easy," Bryan murmured, pulling out a piece of gauze from the first-aid box she'd brought from the van. "You're going to be fine. The ambulance is coming. Can you hear it?"

As she spoke, she pressed the gauze against the wound to stop the bleeding. Her voice was calm, but her fingers trembled.

"Bobby." Tears ran down the girl's face as she clung to Bryan. "Is Bobby all right? He was driving."

Bryan glanced over and looked directly at Shade before she lowered her gaze to the unconscious boy. "He's going to be fine," she said, and felt helpless.

Six young, careless children, she thought as she scanned those sitting or lying on the grass. The driver of the other car sat dazedly across from them, holding a rag to the cut on his own head. For a moment, a long, still moment, the night was quiet—warm, almost balmy. Stars were brilliant overhead. Moonlight was strong and lovely. Thirty feet away, what was left of the Pontiac crackled with flame. Bryan slipped her arm around the shoulders of the girl and watched the lights of the ambulance speed up the road.

As the paramedics began to work, another ambulance and the fire department were called. For twenty minutes, Bryan sat by the young girl, talking to her, holding her hand while her injuries were examined and tended to.

Her name was Robin. She was seventeen. Of the six teenagers in the car, her boyfriend, Bobby, was the oldest at nineteen. They'd only been celebrating summer vacation.

As Bryan listened and soothed, she glanced up to see Shade calmly setting his camera. Astonished, she watched as he carefully focused and framed in the injured. Dispassionately, he recorded the scene of the accident, the victims and what was left of the car. As astonishment faded, Bryan felt the fury bubble inside her. When Robin was carried to the second ambulance, Bryan sprang up.

"What the hell are you doing?" She grabbed his shoulder, spoiling a shot. Still calm, Shade turned to her and gave her one quick study.

She was pale. Her eyes showed both strain and fury. And, he thought, a dull sheen of shock. For the first time since he'd known her, Shade saw how tense her body could be. "I'm doing my job," he said simply, and lifted the camera again.

"Those kids are bleeding!" Bryan grabbed his shoulder again, swinging herself around until she was face-to-face with him. "They've got broken bones. They're hurt and they're frightened. Since when is your job taking pictures of their pain?"

"Since I picked up a camera for pay." Shade let the camera swing by its strap. He'd gotten enough, in any case. He didn't like the feeling in his own stomach, the tension behind his eyes. Most of all, he didn't like the look in Bryan's as she stared at him. Disgust. He shrugged it off.

"You're only willing to take pictures of fun in the sun for this assignment, Bryan. You saw the car, those kids. That's part of it too. Part of life. If you can't handle it, you'd better stick to your celebrity shots and leave the real world alone."

He'd taken two steps toward the van when Bryan was on him again. She might avoid confrontations as a matter of habit, take the line of least resistance as often as possible, but there were times when she'd fight. When she did, she used everything.

"I can handle it." She wasn't pale any longer; her face glowed with anger. Her eyes gleamed with it. "What I can't handle are the vultures who love picking at bones, making a profit off misery in the name of art. There were six people in that car. *People,*" she repeated, hissing at him. "Maybe they were foolish, maybe they deserved what happened, but I'll be damned if I'm going to judge. Do you think it makes you a better photographer, a better artist, because you're cold enough, you're *professional* enough, to freeze their pain on printing paper? Is this the way you look for another Pulitzer nomination?"

She was crying now, too angry, too churned up by what she'd seen, to be aware of the tears streaming down her cheeks. Yet somehow the tears made her look stronger. They thickened her voice and gave it impact. "I'll tell you what it makes you," she went on when Shade remained silent. "It makes you empty. Whatever compassion you were born with died somewhere along the way, Shade. I'm sorry for you."

She left him standing in the middle of the road by the shell of the car.

* * *

It was nearly 3:00 a.m. Shade had learned that the mind was at its most helpless in those early hours of the morning. The van was dark and quiet, parked in a small campground just over the Oklahoma border. He and Bryan hadn't exchanged a word since the accident. Each had prepared for bed in silence, and though both of them had lain awake for some time, neither had spoken. Now they slept, but only Bryan slept dreamlessly.

There'd been a time, during the first months after his return from Cambodia, that Shade had had the dream regularly. Over the years it had come to him less and less. Often he could force himself awake and fight the dream off before it really took hold. But now, in the tiny Oklahoma campground, he was powerless.

He knew he was dreaming. The moment the figures and shapes began to form in his mind, Shade understood it wasn't real—that it wasn't real any longer. It didn't stop the panic or the pain. The Shade Colby in the dream would go through the same motions he'd gone through all those years ago, leading to the same end. And in the dream there were no soft lines, no mists to lessen the impact. He saw it as it had happened, in strong sunlight.

Shade came out of the hotel and onto the street with Dave, his assistant. Between them, they carried all their luggage and equipment. They were going home. After four months of hard, often dangerous work in a city torn, ravaged and smoldering, they were going home. It had occurred to Shade that they were calling it close—but he'd called it close before. Every day they stayed on added to the risk of getting out at all. But there'd always been one more picture to take, one more statement to make. And there'd been Sung Lee.

She'd been so young, so eager, so wise. As a contact in the city, she'd been invaluable. She'd been just as invaluable to Shade personally. After a bumpy, unpleasant divorce from a wife who'd wanted more glamour and less reality, Shade had needed the long, demanding assignment. And he'd needed Sung Lee.

She was devoted, sweet, undemanding. When he'd taken her to bed, Shade had finally been able to block out the rest of the world and relax. His only regret in going back home was that she wouldn't leave her country.

As they'd stepped out on the street, Shade had been thinking of her. They'd said their goodbyes the night before, but he was thinking of her. Perhaps if he hadn't been, he'd have sensed something. He'd asked himself that hundreds of times in the months that followed.

The city was quiet, but it wasn't peaceful. The tension in the air could erupt at any time. Those who were getting out were doing so in a hurry. Tomorrow, the next day, the doors might be closed. Shade took one last look around as they started toward their car. One last picture, he'd thought, of the calm before the storm.

A few careless words to Dave and he was alone, standing on the curb pulling his camera out of its case. He laughed as Dave swore and struggled with the luggage on his way to the car. Just one last picture. The next time he lifted his camera to shoot, it would be on American soil.

"Hey, Colby!" Young, grinning, Dave stood beside the car. He looked like a college student on spring break.

"How about taking one of a future award-winning photographer on his way out of Cambodia?"

With a laugh, Shade lifted his camera and framed in his assistant. He remembered exactly the way he'd looked. Blond, tanned, a bit gangly, with a crooked front tooth and a faded USC T-shirt.

He took the shot. Dave turned the key in the lock.

"Let's go home," his assistant yelled the instant before the car exploded.

"Shade. Shade!" Heart pounding, Bryan shook him. "Shade, wake up, it's a dream." He grabbed her hard enough to make bruises, but she kept talking. "It's Bryan, Shade. You're having a dream. Just a dream. We're in Oklahoma, in your van. Shade." She took his face in her hands and felt the skin cold and damp. "Just a dream," she said quietly. "Try to relax. I'm right here."

He was breathing too quickly. Shade felt himself straining for air and forced himself to calm. God, he was cold. He felt the warmth of Bryan's skin under his hands, heard her voice, calm, low, soothing. With an oath, he dropped back down again and waited for the shuddering to stop.

"I'll get you some water."

"Scotch."

"All right." The moonlight was bright enough. She found the plastic cup and the bottle and poured. Behind her, she heard the flare of his lighter and the hiss as it caught paper and tobacco. When Bryan turned, he was sitting up on the bunk, resting back against the side of the van. She had no experience with whatever trauma haunted Shade, but she did know how to soothe nerves.

She handed him the drink, then, without asking, sat beside him. She waited until he'd taken the first sip.

"Better?"

He took another sip, a deeper one. "Yeah."

She touched his arm lightly, but the contact was made. "Tell me."

He didn't want to speak of it, not to anyone, not to her. Even as the refusal formed on his lips, she increased the grip on his arm.

"We'll both feel better if you do. Shade…" She had to wait again, this time for him to turn and look at her. Her heartbeat was steadier now, and so, as her fingers lay over his wrist, was his. But there was still a thin sheen of sweat drying on his skin. "Nothing gets better and goes away if you hold it in."

He'd held it in for years. It'd never gone away. Perhaps it never would. Maybe it was the quiet understanding in her voice, or the late hour, but he found himself talking.

He told her of Cambodia, and though his voice was flat, she could see it as he had. Ripe for explosion, crumbling, angry. Long, monotonous days punctuated by moments of terror. He told her how he'd reluctantly taken on an assistant and then learned to appreciate and enjoy the young man fresh out of college. And Sung Lee.

"We ran across her in a bar where most of the journalists hung out. It wasn't until a long time later that I put together just how convenient the meeting was. She was twenty, beautiful, sad. For nearly three months, she gave us leads she supposedly learned from a cousin who worked at the embassy."

"Were you in love with her?"

"No." He drew on his cigarette until there was nothing left but filter. "But I cared. I wanted to help her. And I trusted her."

He dropped his cigarette into an ashtray and concentrated on his drink. The panic was gone. He'd never realized he could talk about it calmly, think about it calmly. "Things were heating up, and the magazine decided to pull its people out. We were going home. We were coming out of the hotel, and I stopped to take a couple of shots. Like a tourist." He swore and drained the rest of the Scotch. "Dave got to the car first. It'd been booby-trapped."

"Oh, my God." Without realizing it, she moved closer to him.

"He was twenty-three. Carried a picture of the girl he was going to marry."

"I'm sorry." She laid her head against his shoulder, wound her arm around him. "I'm so sorry."

He braced himself against the flood of sympathy. He wasn't ready for it. "I tried to find Sung Lee. She was gone; her apartment was empty. It turned out that I'd been her assignment. The group she'd worked for had let things leak through so I'd relax and trust her. They'd intended to make a statement by blowing away an important American reporter. They'd missed me. An assistant photographer on his first overseas assignment didn't make any impact. The kid died for nothing."

And he'd watched the car explode, she thought. Just as he'd watched the car explode tonight. What had it done to him—then and now? Was that why, she wondered, he'd coolly taken out his camera and recorded it all? He was so determined not to feel.

"You blame yourself," she murmured. "You can't."

"He was a kid. I should've looked out for him."

"How?" She shifted so that they were face-to-face again. His eyes were dark, full of cold anger and frustration. She'd never forget just how they looked at that moment. "How?" she repeated. "If you hadn't stopped to take those pictures, you'd have gotten into the car with him. He'd still be dead."

"Yeah." Suddenly weary, Shade ran his hands over his face. The tension was gone, but not the bitterness. Perhaps that's what he was weary of.

"Shade, after the accident—"

"Forget it."

"No." This time she had his hand caught in hers. "You were doing what you had to, for your own reasons. I said I wouldn't judge those kids, but I was judging you. I'm sorry."

He didn't want her apology, but she gave it. He didn't want her to cleanse him, but she was washing away the guilt. He'd seen so much—too much—of the dark side of human nature. She was offering him the light. It tempted him and it terrified him.

"I'll never see things as you do," he murmured. After a moment's hesitation, he laced his fingers with hers. "I'll never be as tolerant."

Puzzled, she frowned as they stared at each other. "No, I don't think you will. I don't think you have to."

"You were right earlier when you said my compassion was dead. I haven't any." She started to speak, but he shook his head. "I haven't any patience, very little sympathy."

Did he look at his own pictures? she wondered. Didn't he see the carefully harnessed emotion in them? But she said nothing, letting him make whatever point he needed to.

"I stopped believing in intimacy, genuine intimacy, permanency, between two people a long time ago. But I do believe in honesty."

She might've drawn away from him. There was something in his voice that warned her, but she stayed where she was. Their bodies were close. She could feel his heartbeat steady as hers began to race. "I think permanency works for some people." Was that her voice? she wondered, so calm, so practical. "I stopped looking for it for myself."

Isn't that what he'd wanted to hear? Shade looked down at their joined hands and wondered why her words left him dissatisfied. "Then it's understood that neither of us wants or needs promises."

Bryan opened her mouth, amazed that she wanted to object. She swallowed. "No promises," she managed. She had to think, had to have the distance to manage it. Deliberately she smiled. "I think we both could use some sleep, though."

He tightened his grip on her hand as she started to move. Honesty, he'd said. Though the words weren't easy for him, he'd say what he meant. He looked at her a long time. What was left of the moonlight showered her face and shadowed her eyes. Caught in his, her hand was steady. Her pulse wasn't.

"I need you, Bryan."

There were so many things he could have said, and to any of them she'd have had an answer. Wants—no, wants weren't enough. She'd already told him. Demands could be refused or shrugged off.

Needs. Needs were deeper, warmer, stronger. A need was enough.

He didn't move. He waited. Watching him, Bryan knew he'd let her take the step toward or away. Choices. He was a man who demanded them for himself, yet he was also capable of giving them. How could he know she'd had none the moment he'd spoken?

Slowly, she drew her hand from his. Just as slowly, she lifted both hands to his face and brought her mouth to his. With their eyes open, they shared a long, quiet kiss. It was a move that both offered and took.

She offered, with her hands light on his skin. She took, with her mouth warm and certain. He accepted. He gave. And then in the same instant, they both forgot the rules.

Her lashes fluttered down, her lips parted. Mindlessly he pulled her against him until their bodies were crushed close. She didn't resist, but went with him as they slid from the bunk and onto the rug.

She'd wanted this—the triumph and the weakness of being touched by him. She'd wanted the glory of letting herself go, of allowing her longings freedom. With his mouth hungry on hers, there was no need to think, no need to hold back what she'd wanted so desperately to give him. Only to him.

Take more. Her mind was reeling from the demands of her body. Take all. She could feel him tug at the wide neck of her sleep shirt until her shoulder was bare and vulnerable to his mouth. Still more. She skimmed her hands up his back, naked and warm from the night breeze flowing in the windows.

He wasn't easy as a lover. Hadn't she known it? There was no patience in him. Hadn't he told her? She'd known it before, but she was already aware that she'd never know relaxation with Shade. He drove her quickly, thoroughly. While she experienced all, she had no time to luxuriate in separate sensations. Masses of them swirled around, inside her.

Tastes…his lips, his skin—dark flavor. Scents… flowers, flesh—sweet and pungent. Textures…the nap of the rug rubbing against her legs, the hard brush of his palm, the soft warmth of his mouth. Sounds…her heartbeat pounding in her head, the murmur of her name in his whisper. She could see shadows, moonlight, the gleam of his eyes before his mouth took hers again. Everything merged and mixed together until they were one overpowering sensation. Passion.

He pulled the shirt lower until her arms were pinned. For a moment, she was helpless as he trailed his lips down her breast, pausing to taste, taste thoroughly, with lips, tongue, teeth. Some women would've found him merciless.

Perhaps it was the sound of her moan that made him linger when he was driven to hurry on. She was so slender, so smooth. The moonlight filtered in so that he could see where her tan gave way to paler, more vulnerable skin. Once he'd have turned away from vulnerability, knowing the dangers of it. Now it drew him—the softness of it. Her scent was there, clinging to the underside of her breast where he could taste as well as smell it. Sexy, tempting, subtle. It was as she was, and he was lost.

He felt his control slip, skid away from him. Ruthlessly, he brought it back. They would make love once—a hundred times that night—but he'd stay in control. As he was now, he thought as she arched under him. As he'd promised himself he would be, always. He would drive her, but he would not, could not, be driven by her.

Pulling the material down, he explored every inch of her mercilessly. He would show no mercy to either of them. Already she was beyond thought and he knew it. Her skin was hot, and somehow softer with the heat; her scent intensified with it. He could run those hungry, openmouthed kisses wherever he chose.

Her hands were free. Energy and passion raced together inside her. She tumbled over the first peak, breathless and strong. Now she could touch, now she could enrage him, entice him, weaken him. She moved quickly, demanding when he'd expected surrender. It was too sudden, too frantic, to allow him to brace himself against it. Even as she raced to the next peak, she felt the change in him.

He couldn't stop it. She wouldn't permit him to take without giving. His mind swam. Though he tried to clear it, fought to hold himself back, she seduced. Not his body, he'd have given that freely. She seduced his mind until it reeled with her. Emotion raged through him. Clean, hot, strong.

Tangled together, body and mind, they drove each other higher. They took each other over.

Chapter 8

They were both very careful. Neither Bryan nor Shade wanted to say anything the other could misunderstand. They'd made love, and for each of them it had been more intense, more vital, than anything they'd ever experienced. They'd set rules, and for each of them the need to abide by them was paramount.

What had happened between them had left them both more than a little stunned, and more wary than ever.

For a woman like Bryan, who was used to saying what she wanted, doing as she pleased, it wasn't easy to walk on eggshells twenty-four hours a day. But they'd made themselves clear before making love, she reminded herself. No complications, no commitments. No promises. They'd both failed once at the most important of relationships, marriage. Why should either of them risk failure again?

They traveled in Oklahoma, giving an entire day to a small-town rodeo. Bryan hadn't enjoyed anything as much since the Fourth of July celebrations they'd seen in Kansas. She enjoyed watching the heat of competition, the pitting of man against animal and man against man and the clock. Every man who'd lowered himself onto a bronc or a bull had been determined to make it to the bell.

Some had been young, others had been seasoned, but all had had one goal. To win, and then to go on to the next round. She'd liked seeing that a game could be turned into a way of life.

Unable to resist, she bought a pair of boots with fancy stitching and a stubby heel. Since the van was too small to permit indiscriminate souvenir buying, she'd restrained herself this far. But there wasn't any point in being a martyr about it. The boots made her happy, but she resisted buying a leather belt with an oversize silver buckle for Shade. It was just the sort of gesture he might misunderstand. No, they wouldn't give each other flowers or trinkets or pretty words.

She drove south toward Texas while Shade read the paper in the seat beside her. On the radio was a raspy Tina Turner number that was unapologetically sexy.

Summer had reached the point when the heat began to simmer. Bryan didn't need the radio announcer to tell her it was ninety-seven and climbing, but both she and Shade had agreed to use the air-conditioning sparingly on the long trips. On the open highway, the breeze was almost enough. In defense, she was wearing a skimpy tank top and shorts while she drove in her bare feet. She thought of Dallas and an air-conditioned hotel room with cool sheets on a soft mattress.

"I've never been to Texas," she said idly. "I can't imagine any place that has cities fifty and sixty miles across. A cab ride across town could cost you a week's pay."

The paper crackled as he flipped the page. "You live in Dallas or Houston, you own a car."

It was like him to give a brief practical answer, and she'd come to accept it. "I'm glad we're taking a couple of days in Dallas to print. Ever spent any time there?"

"A little." He shrugged as he turned the next section of the paper. "Dallas, Houston—those cities are Texas. Big, sprawling, wealthy. Plenty of Tex-Mex restaurants, luxury hotels and a freeway system that leaves the out-of-towner reeling. That's why I routed in San Antonio as well. It's something apart from the rest of Texas. It's elegant, serene, more European."

She nodded, glancing out at the road signs. "Did you have an assignment in Texas?"

"I tried living in Dallas for a couple of years in between the overseas work."

It surprised her. She just couldn't picture him anywhere but L.A. "How'd you like it?"

"Not my style," he said simply. "My ex-wife stayed on and married oil."

It was the first time he'd made any sort of reference to his marriage. Bryan wiped her damp hands on her shorts and wondered how to handle it. "You don't mind going back?"

"No."

"Does it…" She trailed off, wondering if she was getting in deeper than she should.

Shade tossed the paper aside. "What?"

"Well, does it bother you that she's remarried and settled? Don't you ever think back and try to figure out what messed things up?"

"I know what messed things up. There's no use dwelling on it. After you admit you've made a mistake, you've got to go on."

"I know." She pushed at her sunglasses. "I just sometimes wonder why some people can be so happy together, and others so miserable."

"Some people don't belong with each other."

"And yet it often seems like they do before they walk up the aisle."

"Marriage doesn't work for certain kinds of people."

Like us? Bryan wondered. After all, they'd both failed at it. Perhaps he was right, and it was as simple as that. "I made a mess out of mine," she commented.

"All by yourself?"

"Seems that way."

"Then you screwed up and married Mr. Perfect."

"Well, I…" She glanced over and saw him looking at her, one brow raised and a bland look of anticipation on his face. She'd forgotten he could make her laugh as well as ache. "Mr. Nearly Perfect, anyway." She grinned. "I'd have been smarter to look for someone with flaws."

After lighting a cigarette, he rested his feet on the dash as Bryan was prone to do. "Why didn't you?"

"I was too young to realize flaws were easier to deal with. And I loved him." She hadn't realized it would be so painless to say it, to put it in the past tense. "I really did," she murmured. "In a naive, rose-tinted way. At the time I didn't realize I'd have to make a choice between his conception of marriage and my work."

He understood exactly. His wife hadn't been cruel, she hadn't been vindictive. She'd simply wanted things he couldn't give. "So you married Mr. Nearly Perfect and I married Ms. Socially Ambitious. I wanted to take important pictures, and she wanted to join the country club. Nothing wrong with either goal—they just don't mesh."

"But sometimes don't you regret that you couldn't make it fit?"

"Yeah." It came out unexpectedly, surprising him a great deal more than it surprised her. He hadn't realized he had regrets. He hadn't allowed himself to. "You're getting low on gas," he said abruptly. "We'll stop in the next town and fill up."

Bryan had heard of one-horse towns, but nothing fitted the phrase more perfectly than the huddle of houses just over the Oklahoma-Texas border. Everything seemed to be dusty and faded by the heat. Even the buildings looked tired. Perhaps the state was enriched by oil and growth, but this little corner had slept through it.

As a matter of habit, Bryan took her camera as she stepped from the van to stretch her legs. As she walked around the side of the van, the skinny young attendant goggled at her. Shade saw the boy gape and Bryan smile before he walked into the little fan-cooled store behind the pumps.

Bryan found a small, fenced yard just across the

street. A woman in a cotton housedress and a faded apron watered the one colorful spot—a splash of pansies along the edge of the house. The grass was yellow, burned by the sun, but the flowers were lush and thriving. Perhaps they were all the woman needed to keep her content. The fence needed painting badly and the screen door to the house had several small holes, but the flowers were a bright, cheerful slash. The woman smiled as she watered them.

Grateful she'd picked up the camera she'd loaded with color film, Bryan tried several angles. She wanted to catch the tired, sun-faded wood of the house and the parched lawn, both a contrast to that bouquet of hope.

Dissatisfied, she shifted again. The light was good, the colors perfect, but the picture was wrong. Why? Stepping back, she took it all in again and asked herself the all-important question. What do I feel?

Then she had it. The woman wasn't necessary, just the illusion of her. Her hand holding the watering can, no more. She could be any woman, anywhere, who needed flowers to complete her home. It was the flowers and the hope they symbolized that were important, and that was what Bryan finally recorded.

Shade came out of the store with a paper bag. He saw Bryan across the street, experimenting with angles. Content to wait, he set the bag in the van, drawing out the first cold can before he turned to pay the attendant for the gas. The attendant, Shade noticed, who was so busy watching Bryan he could hardly screw on the gas cap.

"Nice van," he commented, but Shade didn't think he'd even looked at it.

"Thanks." He allowed his own gaze to follow the boy's until it rested on Bryan's. He had to smile. She was a very distracting sight in the swatch of material she called shorts. Those legs, he mused. They seemed to start at the waist and just kept going. Now he knew just how sensitive they could be—on the inside of the knee, just above the ankle, on the warm, smooth skin high on the thigh.

"You and your wife going far?"

"Hmm?" Shade lost track of the attendant as he became just as fascinated by Bryan.

"You and the missus," the boy repeated, sighing a little as he counted out Shade's change. "Going far?"

"Dallas," he murmured. "She's not…" He started to correct the boy's mistake about their relationship, then found himself stopping. The *missus*. It was a quaint word, and somehow appealing. It hardly mattered if a boy in a border town thought Bryan belonged to him. "Thanks," he said absently and, stuffing the change in his pocket, walked to her.

"Good timing," she told him as she crossed toward him. They met in the middle of the road.

"Find something?"

"Flowers." She smiled, forgetting the unmerciful sun. If she breathed deeply enough, she could just smell them over the dust. "Flowers where they didn't belong. I think it's…" She felt the rest of the words slide back down her throat as he reached out and touched her hair.

He never touched her, not in the most casual of ways. Unless they were making love, and then it was never casual. There was never any easy brush of hands, no gentle squeeze. Nothing. Until now, in the center of the road, between a parched yard and a grimy gas station.

"You're beautiful. Sometimes it stuns me."

What could she say? He never spoke soft words. Now they flowed over her as his fingers trailed to her cheek. His eyes were so dark. She had no idea what he saw when he looked at her, what he felt. She'd never have asked. Perhaps for the first time, he was giving her the opportunity, but she couldn't speak, only stare.

He might have told her that he saw honesty, kindness, strength. He might have told her he felt needs that were growing far beyond the borders he'd set up between him and the rest of the world. If she'd asked, he might have told her that she was making a difference in his life he hadn't foreseen but could no longer prevent.

For the first time, he bent toward her and kissed her, with an uncharacteristic gentleness. The moment demanded it, though he wasn't sure why. The sun was hot and hard, the road dusty, and the smell of gasoline was strong. But the moment demanded tenderness from him. He gave it, surprised that it was in him to offer.

"I'll drive," he murmured as he slipped her hand into his. "It's a long way to Dallas."

His feelings had changed. Not for the city they drove into, but for the woman beside him. Dallas had changed since he'd lived there, but Shade knew from experience that it seemed to change constantly. Even though he'd only lived there briefly, it had seemed as though a new building would grow up overnight. Hotels, office buildings, popped up wherever they could find room, and there seemed to be an endless supply of room in Dallas.

The architecture leaned toward the futuristic—glass, spirals, pinnacles. But you never had to look far to find that unique southwestern flavor. Men wore cowboy hats as easily as they wore three-piece suits.

They'd agreed on a midtown hotel because it was within walking distance of the darkroom they'd rented for two days. While one worked in the field, the other would have use of the equipment to develop and print. Then they'd switch.

Bryan looked up at the hotel with something like reverence as they pulled up in front of it. Hot running water, feather pillows. Room service. Stepping out, she began to unload her share of the luggage and gear.

"I can't wait," she said as she hauled out another case and felt sweat bead down her back. "I'm going to wallow in the bathtub. I might even sleep there."

Shade pulled out his tripod, then hers. "Do you want your own?"

"My own?" She swung the first camera bag strap over her shoulder.

"Tub."

She looked up and met his calm, questioning glance. He wouldn't assume, she realized, that they'd share a hotel room as they shared the van. They might be lovers, but the lack of strings was still very, very clear. Yes, they'd agreed there'd be no promises, but maybe it was time she took the first step. Tilting her head, she smiled.

"That depends."

"On?"

"Whether you agree to wash my back."

He gave her one of his rare spontaneous smiles as he lifted the rest of the luggage. "Sounds reasonable."

Fifteen minutes later, Bryan dropped her cases inside their hotel room. With equal negligence, she tossed down her shoes. She didn't bother to go to the window and check out the view. There'd be time for that later. There was one vital aspect of the room that demanded immediate attention. She flopped lengthwise on the bed.

"Heaven," she decided, and closed her eyes on a sigh. "Absolute heaven."

"Something wrong with your bunk in the van?" Shade stacked his gear in a corner before pulling open the drapes.

"Not a thing. But there's a world of difference between bunk and bed." Rolling onto her back, she stretched across the spread diagonally. "See? It's just not possible to do this on a bunk."

He gave her a mild look as he opened his suitcase. "You won't be able to do that on a bed, either, when you're sharing it with me."

True enough, she thought as she watched him methodically unpack. She gave her own suitcase an absent glance. It could wait. With the same enthusiasm as she'd had when she'd plopped down, Bryan sprang up. "Hot bath," she said, and disappeared into the bathroom.

Shade dropped his shaving kit onto the dresser as he heard the water begin to run. He stopped for a moment, listening. Already, Bryan was beginning to hum. The combination of sounds was oddly intimate—a woman's low voice, the splash of water. Strange that something so simple could make him burn.

Perhaps it'd been a mistake to take only one room in the hotel. It wasn't quite like sharing the van in a campground. Here, they'd had a choice, a chance for privacy and distance. Before the day was over, he mused, her things would be spread around the room, tossed here, flung there. It wasn't like him to freely invite disorder. And yet he had.

Glancing up, he saw himself in the mirror, a dark man with a lean body and a lean face. Eyes a bit too hard, mouth a bit too sensitive. He was too used to his own reflection to wonder what Bryan saw when she looked at him. He saw a man who looked a bit weary and needed a shave. And he didn't want to wonder, though he stared at himself as an artist stares at his subject, if he saw a man who'd already taken one irrevocable step toward change.

Shade looked at his face, reflected against the hotel room behind him. Just inside the door were Bryan's cases and the shoes she'd carried into the room. Fleetingly, he wondered if he took his camera and set the shot to take in his reflection, and that of the room and cases behind, just what kind of picture he'd have. He wondered if he'd be able to understand it. Shaking off the mood, he crossed the room and walked into the bath.

Her head moved, but that was all. Though her breath caught when he strolled into the room, Bryan kept her body still and submerged. This kind of intimacy was new and left her vulnerable. Foolishly, she wished she'd poured in a layer of bubbles so that she'd have some mystique.

Shade leaned against the sink and watched her. If she had plans to wash, she was taking her time about it. The little cake of soap sat wrapped in its dish while she lay naked in the tub. It struck him that it was the first time he'd seen her, really seen her, in the light. Her body was one long, alluring line. The room was small and steamy. He wanted her. Shade wondered if a man could die from wanting.

"How's the water?" he asked her.

"Hot." Bryan told herself to relax, be natural. The water that had soothed her now began to arouse.

"Good." Calmly, he began to strip.

Bryan opened her mouth, but shut it again. She'd never seen him undress. Always they'd held to their own unspoken, strict code of ethics. When they camped, each of them changed in the showers. Since they'd become lovers, they'd fallen into a sense of urgency at the end of the day, undressing themselves and each other in the dark van while they made love. Now, for the first time, she could watch her lover casually reveal his body to her.

She knew how it looked. Her hands had shown her. But it was a far different experience to see the slopes, the contours. Athletic, she thought, in the way of a runner or a hurdler. She supposed it was apt enough. Shade would always expect the next hurdle and be prepared to leap over it.

He left his clothes on the sink but made no comment when he had to step over hers where she'd dropped them.

"You said something about washing your back," he commented as he eased in behind her. Then he swore lightly at the temperature of the water. "You like to take off a couple layers of skin when you bathe?"

She laughed, relaxed and shifted to accommodate him. When his body rubbed and slid against hers, she decided there was something to be said for small tubs.

Content, she snuggled back against him, a move that at first surprised him, then pleased.

"We're both a little long," she said as she adjusted her legs. "But it helps that we're on the slim side."

"Keep eating." He gave in to the urge to kiss the top of her head. "It's bound to stick sooner or later."

"Never has." She ran her hand along his thigh, trailing from the knee. It was a light, casual stroke that made his insides churn. "I like to believe I burn up calories just thinking. But you..."

"Me?"

On a quiet sigh, Bryan closed her eyes. He was so complex, so...driven. How could she explain it? She knew so little of what he'd seen and been through. Just one isolated incident, she thought. Just one scar. She didn't have to be told there were others.

"You're very physical," she said at length. "Even your thought pattern has a kind of physical force to it. You don't relax. It's like—" She hesitated for another moment, then plunged. "It's like you're a boxer in the ring. Even between rounds you're tensed and waiting for the bell to ring."

"That's life, isn't it?" But he found himself tracing the line of her neck with his finger. "One long match. A quick breather, then you're up and dancing."

"I've never looked at it that way. It's an adventure," she said slowly. "Sometimes I don't have the energy for it, so I can sit back and watch everyone else go through the moves. Maybe that's why I wanted to be a photographer, so I could pull in little pieces of life and keep them. Think of it, Shade."

Shifting slightly, she turned her head so that she

could look at him. "Think of the people we've met, the places we've been and seen. And we're only halfway done. Those rodeo cowboys," she began, eyes brightening. "All they wanted was a plug of tobacco, a bad-tempered horse and a handful of sky. The farmer in Kansas, riding his tractor in the heat of the day, sweating and aching and looking out over acres of his own land. Children playing hopscotch, old men weeding kitchen gardens or playing checkers in the park. That's what life is. It's women with babies on their hips, young girls sunning at the beach and kids splashing in little rubber swimming pools in the side yard."

He touched her cheek. "Do you believe that?"

Did she? It sounded so simplistic.... Idealistic? She wondered. Frowning, she watched the steam rise from the water. "I believe that you have to take what good there is, what beauty there is, and go with it. The rest has to be dealt with, but not every minute of every day. That woman today..."

Bryan settled back again, not sure why it was so important for her to tell him. "The one in the house just across from where we stopped for gas. Her yard was burning up in the sun, the paint was peeling on the fence. I saw arthritis in her hands. But she was watering her pansies. Maybe she's lived in that tiny little house all her life. Maybe she'll never know what it's like to sit in a new car and smell the leather or fly first-class or shop at Saks. But she was watering her pansies. She'd planted, weeded and tended them because they gave her pleasure. Something of value, one bright foolish spot she can look at, smile at. Maybe it's enough."

"Flowers can't grow everywhere."

"Yes, they can. You only have to want them to."

It sounded true when she said it. It sounded like something he'd like to believe. Unconsciously, he rested his cheek against her hair. It was damp from the steam, warm, soft. She made him relax. Just being with her, listening to her, uncurled something in him. But he remembered the rules, those they'd both agreed on. Keep it easy, he reminded himself. Keep it light.

"Do you always have philosophical discussions in the tub?"

Her lips curved. It was so rare and so rewarding to hear that touch of humor in his voice. "I figure if you're going to have one, you might as well be comfortable. Now, about my back…"

Shade picked up the soap and unwrapped it. "Do you want the first shift in the darkroom tomorrow?"

"Mmm." She leaned forward, stretching as he rubbed the dampened soap over her back. Tomorrow was too far away to worry about. "Okay."

"You can have it from eight to twelve."

She started to object to the early hour, then subsided. Some things didn't change. "What're you…" The question trailed off into a sigh as he skimmed the soap around her waist and up to her throat. "I like being pampered."

Her voice was sleepy, but he traced a soapy finger over her nipple and felt the quick shudder. He ran the soap over her in steady circles, lower, still lower, until all thought of relaxation was over. Abruptly, she twisted until he was trapped beneath her, her mouth fixed on his. Her hands raced over him, taking him to the edge before he had a chance to brace himself.

"Bryan—"

"I love to touch you." She slid down until her mouth could skim over his chest, tasting flesh and water. She nibbled, listening to the thunder of his heart, then rubbed her cheek against his damp flesh just to feel, just to experience. She felt him tremble and lie still a moment. When was the last time he'd let himself be made love to? she wondered. Perhaps this time she'd give him no choice.

"Shade." She let her hands roam where they pleased. "Come to bed with me." Before he could answer, she rose. While the water streamed from her, she smiled down at him and slowly pulled the pins from her hair. As it fell, she shook it back, then reached for a towel. It seemed they were through with words.

She waited until he stepped from the tub, then took another towel and rubbed it over him herself. He made no objection, but she could sense him building up the emotional defense. Not this time, she thought. This time it would be different.

As she dried him, she watched his eyes. She couldn't read his thoughts, she couldn't see beneath the desire. For now, it was enough. Taking his hand, she walked toward the bed.

She would love him this time. No matter how strong, how urgent, the need, she would show him what he made her feel. Slowly, her arms already around him, she lowered herself to the bed. As the mattress gave, her mouth found his.

The need was no less. It tore through him. But this time, Shade found himself unable to demand, unable to pull her to his pace. She was satiating him with the luxury of being enjoyed. Her lips took him deep, deeper, but lazily. He learned that with her, passion could be built, layer by finite layer, until there was nothing else. They smelled of the bath they'd shared, of the soap that had rubbed from his skin to hers. She seemed content to breathe it in, to breathe it out, while slowly driving him mad.

It was pleasure enough to see him in the late-afternoon sunlight. No darkness now, no shadows. To make love in the light, freely and without barriers, was something she hadn't even known she craved. His shoulders were still damp. She could see the sheen of water on them, taste it. When their mouths met, she could watch his eyes and see the desire there that echoed what pulsed inside her. In this they were the same, she told herself. In this, if nothing else, they understood each other.

And when he touched her, when she saw his gaze follow the trail of his hand, she trembled. Needs, his and hers, collided, shuddered, then merged together.

There was more here than they'd allowed themselves or each other before. At last this was intimacy, shared knowledge, shared pleasure. No one led, no one held back. For the first time, Shade dropped all pretenses of keeping that thin emotional barrier between them. She filled him, completed him. This time he wanted her— all of her—more than he'd ever wanted anything. He wanted the fun of her, the joy, the kindness. He wanted to believe it could make a difference.

The sun slanted in across the deep, vivid gray of her eyes, highlighting them as he'd once imagined. Her mouth was soft, yielding. Above him, her hair flowed down, wild, free. The lowering sun seemed trapped in her skin, making it gleam gold. She might have been something he'd only imagined—woman, lean, agile and primitive, woman without restraints, accepting her own passions. If he photographed her this way, would he recognize her? Would he be able to recapture the emotions she could push into him?

Then she tossed back her head and she was young, vibrant, reachable. This woman he'd know, this feeling he'd recognize, if he went away alone for decades. He'd need no photograph to remind him of that one astonishing instant of give and take.

Shade drew her closer, needing her. You, he thought dizzily as their bodies merged and their thoughts twined. Only you. He watched her eyes slowly close as she gave herself to him.

Chapter 9

"I could get used to this."

With her camera settled comfortably in her lap, Bryan stretched back in the pirogue, the trim little dugout canoe they'd borrowed from a family who lived on the bayou. A few miles away was the bustling city of Lafayette, Louisiana, but here was a more slumberous view of summer.

Bees humming, shade spreading, birds trilling. Dragonflies. One whisked by, too fast for her camera, but slow enough to appreciate. Spanish moss hung overhead, shading and dipping toward the river as the water moved slowly. Why hurry? It was summer, fish were there for catching, flowers were there for picking. Cypress trees thrust their way out of the water, and an occasional frog stirred himself enough to plop from his pad and take a swim.

Why hurry, indeed? Life was there to be enjoyed.

As Shade had once pointed out, Bryan was adaptable. In the rush of Dallas, she'd worked long hours in the darkroom and on the street. All business. When the moment called for it, she could be efficient, quick and energetic. But here, where the air was heavy and the living slow, she was content to lie back, cross her ankles and wait for whatever came.

"We're supposed to be working," he pointed out.

She smiled. "Aren't we?" While she swung one foot in lazy circles, she wished they'd thought to borrow a fishing pole as well. What did it feel like to catch a catfish? "We took dozens of pictures before we got in the boat," she reminded him.

It'd been her idea to detour into the bayou, though she was all but certain Shade had topped her with his pictures of the family who'd welcomed them. She might've charmed them into the use of their boat, but Shade had won hands down with camera work.

"The one you took of Mrs. Bienville shelling beans has to be fabulous. Her hands." Bryan shook her head and relaxed. "I've never seen such hands on a woman. I imagine she could make the most elegant of soufflés right before she went out and cut down a tree."

"Cajuns have their own way of life, their own rules." She tilted her head as she studied him. "You like that."

"Yeah." He rowed, not because they needed to get anywhere, but because it felt so good. It warmed his muscles and relaxed his mind. He nearly smiled, thinking that being with Bryan accomplished almost the same thing. "I like the independence and the fact that it works."

Bryan lay back, listening to the buzz and hum of insects, the sounds of the river. They'd walked along another river in San Antonio, but the sounds had been different there. Soft Spanish music from musicians, the clink of silver on china from the outdoor cafés. It had been fabulous at night, she remembered. The lights had glowed on the water, the water had rippled from the river taxis, the taxis had been full of people content with the Texas version of a gondola. She'd taken a picture of two young lovers, newlyweds perhaps, huddled together on one of the arched stone bridges above the water.

When they'd driven into Galveston, she'd seen yet another kind of Texas, one with white sand beaches, ferries and bicycle surreys. It'd been easier to talk Shade into renting one than she'd imagined. With a smile, she thought of just how far they'd come, and not only in miles. They were working together, and when he could be distracted, they played.

In Malibu, they'd gone their separate ways on the beach. In Galveston, after two hours of work, they'd walked hand in hand along the shore. A small thing for many people, Bryan mused, but not for either of them.

Each time they made love, there seemed to be something more. She didn't know what it was, but she didn't question it. It was Shade she wanted to be with, laugh with, talk with. Every day she discovered something new, something different, about the country and the people. She discovered it with Shade. Perhaps that was all the answer she needed.

What was it about him? Whether she chose to or

not, there were times she wondered. What was it about Shade Colby that made her happy? He wasn't always patient. One moment he might be generous and something close to sweet, and the next he could be as cool and aloof as a stranger. Being with him wasn't without its frustrations for a woman accustomed to less fluctuating moods. But being with him was exactly what she wanted.

At the moment, he was relaxed. He wasn't often, she knew, but the mood of the river seemed to have seeped into him. Still, he was watching. Someone else might have floated down the river, glancing at the scenery, appreciating the overall effect. Shade dissected it.

This she understood, because it was her way as well. A tree might be studied for the texture of its leaves, the grain in the wood, the pattern of shade and light it allowed to fall on the ground. A layman might take a perfectly competent picture of the tree, but it would be only that. When Bryan took the picture, she wanted it to pull feelings out of the viewer.

She specialized in people, Bryan remembered as she watched Shade draw the oars through the water. Landscapes, still lifes, she considered a change of pace. It was the human element that fascinated her, and always would. If she wanted to understand her feelings about Shade, maybe it was time to treat him as she would any other subject.

Under half-lowered lashes, she studied and dissected. He had very dominating physical looks, she mused. Being dominated was definitely not her ambition in life. Perhaps that was why she was so often drawn to his mouth, because it was sensitive, vulnerable.

She knew his image—cool, distant, pragmatic. Part of it was true, she thought, but part of it was illusion. Once she'd thought to photograph him in shadows. Now she wondered what sort of study she'd get if she photographed him in quiet sunlight. Without giving herself a chance to think, she lifted her camera, framed him in and shot.

"Just testing," she said lightly when he arched a brow. "And after all, you've already taken a couple of me."

"So I have." He remembered the picture he'd taken of her brushing her hair on the rock in Arizona. He hadn't told her that he'd sent the print back to the magazine, even though he had no doubt it would be used in the final essay. Nor had he told her it was a print he intended to keep in his private collection.

"Hold it a minute." With brisk, professional movements, she changed her lens, adjusted for distance and depth and focused on a heron perched on top of a cypress knee. "A place like this," she murmured as she took two more insurance shots, "makes you think summer just goes on and on."

"Maybe we should take another three months traveling back and do autumn."

"It's tempting." She stretched back again. "Very tempting. A study on all seasons."

"Your clients might get testy."

"Unfortunately true. Still…" She let her fingers dip into the water. "We miss the seasons in L.A. I'd like to see spring in Virginia and winter in Montana." Tossing her braid back, she sat up. "Have you ever thought of chucking it, Shade? Just packing up and moving to, oh, say, Nebraska, and setting up a little studio. Wedding and graduation pictures, you know."

He gave her a long steady look. "No."

With a laugh, she flopped back. "Me either."

"You wouldn't find many megastars in Nebraska."

She narrowed her eyes but spoke mildly. "Is that another subtle shot at my work?"

"Your work," he began as he gently turned the boat back, "is uniformly excellent. Otherwise, we wouldn't be working together."

"Thank you very much. I think."

"And because of the quality of your work," he continued, "I wonder why you limit yourself to the pretty people."

"It's my specialty." She saw a clump of wildflowers on the mossy, muddy edge of the river. Carefully she adjusted her camera again. "And a great many of my subjects are far from pretty—physically or emotionally. They interest me," she said before he could comment. "I like to find out what's under the image and give a glimpse of it."

And she was well skilled at it, he decided. In truth, he'd discovered he admired her for it—not only for her skill, but for her perception. He simply couldn't rationalize her following the glitz trail. "Culture art?"

If he'd meant it as an insult, however mild, it missed its mark. "Yes. And if you asked, I'd say Shakespeare wrote culture art. Are you hungry?"

"No." Fascinating woman, he thought, as reluctant as ever to be fascinated. He craved her, it was true. Her body, her company. But he couldn't resolve the constant fascination she held for him, mind to mind. "You had a bowl of shrimp and rice big enough to feed a family of four before we started out."

"That was hours ago."

"Two, to be exact."

"Picky," she mumbled, and stared up at the sky. So peaceful, she mused. So simple. Moments like this were meant to be savored. Lowering her gaze, she smiled at him. "Ever made love in a pirogue?"

He had to grin. She made it impossible to do otherwise. "No, but I don't think we should ever refuse a new experience."

Bryan touched her tongue to her top lip. "Come here."

They left the lazy, insect-humming air of the bayou behind and landed in bustling, raucous New Orleans. Sweating trumpet players on Bourbon Street, merchants fanning themselves in the Farmers Market, artists and tourists around Jackson Square—it was a taste of the South, they both agreed, that was as far apart from the South as San Antonio had been apart from Texas.

From there, they traveled north to Mississippi for a touch of July in the Deep South. Heat and humidity. Tall, cool drinks and precious shade. Life was different here. In the cities, men sweated in white shirts and loosened ties. In the rural districts, farmers worked under the sweltering sun. But they moved more slowly than their counterparts to the north and west. Perhaps temperatures soaring to a hundred and more caused it, or perhaps it was just a way of life.

Children exercised the privilege of youth and wore next to nothing. Their bodies were browned and damp and dusty. In a city park, Bryan took a close-up of a grinning boy with mahogany skin cooling himself in a fountain.

The camera didn't intimidate him. As she homed in, he laughed at her, squealing as the water cascaded over him, white and cool, until he looked encased in glass.

In a small town just northwest of Jackson, they stumbled across a Little League game. It wasn't much of a field, and the bleachers looked as if they'd object to more than fifty people at a time, but they pulled off and parked between a pickup and a rusted-out sedan.

"This is great." Bryan grabbed her camera bag.

"You just smell hot dogs."

"That too," she agreed easily. "But this *is* summer. We might get to a Yankee game in New York, but we'll get better pictures here today." She hooked her arm through his before he could get too far away. "I'll reserve judgment on the hot dogs."

Shade took a long, sweeping view. The crowd was spread out, on the grass, in folding chairs, on the bleachers. They cheered, complained, gossiped and gulped iced drinks. He was all but certain everyone there knew one another by name or by sight. He watched an old man in a baseball cap casually spit out a plug of tobacco before he berated the umpire.

"I'm going to wander around a bit," he decided, considering a seat on the bleachers too limiting for the moment.

"Okay." Bryan had taken her own scan and considered the bleachers the focal point for what she wanted.

They separated, Shade moving toward the old man who'd already captured his attention. Bryan walked to the bleachers, where she and the onlookers would have a solid view of the game.

The players wore white pants, already grass-stained and dusty, with bright red or blue shirts emblazoned with team names. A good many of them were too small for the uniforms, and the mitts looked enormous on the ends of gangling arms. Some wore spikes, some wore sneakers. A few had batting gloves hung professionally from their back pocket.

It was the hats, she decided, that told of the individual's personality. One might wear it snug or tipped back, another tilted rakishly over the eyes. She wanted an action shot, something that would bring the color and the personalities together with the sport itself. Until something formed for her, Bryan contented herself with taking a shot of the second baseman, who passed the time until the batter stepped into the box by kicking his spikes against the bag and blowing bubbles with his wad of gum.

Scooting up another step, she tried her long lens. Better, she decided, and was pleased to see that her second baseman had a face full of freckles. Above her, someone snapped gum and whistled when the umpire called a strike.

Bryan lowered her camera and allowed herself to become involved in the game. If she wanted to portray the atmosphere, she had to let herself feel it. It was more than the game, she thought, it was the feeling of community. As the batters came up, people in the crowd called them by name, tossing out casual remarks that indicated a personal knowledge. But the sides were definitely drawn.

Parents had come to the game from work, grand-parents had pushed away from an early dinner, and neighbors had chosen the game against an evening by the TV. They had their favorites, and they weren't shy about rooting for them.

The next batter interested Bryan mainly because she was a strikingly pretty girl of about twelve. At a glance, Bryan would've set her more easily at a ballet bar than home plate. But when she watched the way the girl gripped the bat and bent into her stance, Bryan lifted her camera. This was one to watch.

Bryan caught her in the first swing on a strike. Though the crowd moaned, Bryan was thrilled with the flow of movement. She might be shooting a Little League game in a half-forgotten town in Mississippi, but she thought of her studio work with the prima ballerina. The batter poised for the pitch, and Bryan poised for the next shot. She had to wait, growing impatient, through two balls.

"Low and outside," she heard someone mumble beside her. All she could think was, if the girl walked, she'd lose the picture she wanted.

Then it came over, too fast for Bryan to judge the placement of the ball, but the girl connected with a solid swing. The batter took off, and using the motor drive, Bryan followed her around the bases. When she rounded second, Bryan homed in on her face. Yes, Maria would understand that look, Bryan thought. Strain, determination and just plain guts. Bryan had her as she slid into third with a storm of dust and a swing of body.

"Wonderful!" She lowered the camera, so thrilled

that she didn't even realize she'd spoken out loud. "Just wonderful!"

"That's our girl."

Distracted, Bryan glanced over to the couple beside her. The woman was her own age, perhaps a year or two older. She was beaming. The man beside her was grinning over a wad of gum.

Perhaps she hadn't heard properly. They were so young. "She's your daughter?"

"Our oldest." The woman slipped a hand into her husband's. Bryan saw the plain twin wedding bands. "We've got three others running around here, but they're more interested in the concession stand than the game."

"Not our Carey." The father looked out to where his daughter took a short lead on third. "She's all business."

"I hope you don't mind my taking her picture."

"No." The woman smiled again. "Do you live in town?"

It was a polite way to find out who she was. Bryan hadn't a doubt the woman knew everyone within ten miles. "No, I'm traveling." She paused as the next batter blooped to right field and brought Carey home. "Actually, I'm a freelance photographer on assignment for *Life-style*. Perhaps you've heard of it."

"Sure." The man jerked a head at his wife as he kept his eyes on the game. "She picks it up every month."

Pulling a release form out of her bag, she explained her interest in using Carey's picture. Though she kept it short and her voice low, word spread throughout the bleachers. Bryan found herself answering questions and dealing with curiosity. In order to handle it all in the simplest fashion, she climbed down from the bleachers, changed to a wide-angle lens and took a group shot. Not a bad study, she decided, but she didn't want to spend the next hour having people pose for her. To give the baseball fans time to shift their attention back to the game, she wandered to the concession stand.

"Any luck?"

She swiveled her head around to see Shade fall into step beside her. "Yeah. You?"

He nodded, then leaned on the counter of the stand. There was no relief from the heat, though the sun was lowering. It promised to be as sweltering a night as it had a day. He ordered two large drinks and two hot dogs.

"Know what I'd love?" she asked as she began to bury her hot dog under relish.

"A shovel?"

Ignoring him, she piled on mustard. "A long, cool dip in an enormous pool, followed closely by an iced margarita."

"For now you'll have to settle for the driver's seat of the van. It's your turn."

She shrugged. A job was a job. "Did you see the girl who hit the triple?" They walked over the uneven grass toward the van.

"Kid that ran like a bullet?"

"Yes. I sat next to her parents in the stands. They have four kids."

"So?"

"Four kids," she repeated. "And I'd swear she wasn't more than thirty. How do people do it?"

"Ask me later and I'll show you."

With a laugh, she jabbed him with her elbow. "That's

not what I meant—though I like the idea. What I mean is, here's this couple—young, attractive. You could tell they even liked each other."

"Amazing."

"Don't be cynical," she ordered as she pulled open the door to the van. "A great many couples don't, especially when they've got four kids, a mortgage and ten or twelve years of marriage under their belts."

"Now who's being cynical?"

She started to speak and frowned instead. "I guess I am," she mused as she turned on the engine. "Maybe I've picked a world that's tilted my outlook, but when I see a happily married couple with a track record, I'm impressed."

"It is impressive." Carefully, he stored his camera bag under the dash before he sat back. "When it really works."

"Yeah."

She fell silent, remembering the jolt of envy and longing she'd felt when she'd framed the Browns in her viewfinder. Now, weeks and miles later, it was another jolt for Bryan to realize she hadn't brushed off that peculiar feeling. She had managed to put it aside, somewhere to the back of her mind, but it popped out again now as she thought of the couple in the bleachers of a small-town park.

Family, cohesion. Bonding. Did some people just keep promises better than others? she wondered. Or were some people simply unable to blend their lives with someone else's, make those adjustments, the compromises?

When she looked back, she believed both she and

Rob had tried, but in their own ways. There'd been no meeting of the minds, but two separate thought patterns making decisions that never melded with each other. Did that mean that a successful marriage depended on the mating of two people who thought along the same lines?

With a sigh, she turned onto the highway that would lead them into Tennessee. If it was true, she decided, she was much better off single. Though she'd met a great many people she liked and could have fun with, she'd never met anyone who thought the way she did. Especially the man seated next to her with his nose already buried in the newspaper. There alone they were radically different.

He'd read that paper and every paper in every town they stopped in from cover to cover, devouring the words. She'd skim the headlines, glance over the style or society pages and go straight for the comics. If she wanted news, she'd rather have it in spurts on the radio or blurbs on televisions. Reading was for relaxation, and relaxation was not an analysis of détente.

Relationships. She thought back on the discussion she'd had with Lee just weeks before. No, she simply wasn't cut out for relationships on a long-term basis. Shade himself had pointed out that some people just weren't capable of permanency. She'd agreed, hadn't she? Why should the truth suddenly depress her?

Whatever her feelings were for Shade, and she'd yet to define them satisfactorily, she wasn't going to start smelling orange blossoms. Maybe she had a few twinges when she saw couples together who seemed to complete each other rather than compete, but that was only natural. After all, she didn't want to start making adjustments in her lifestyle to accommodate someone else at this stage. She was perfectly content the way things were.

If she was in love... Bryan felt the twinge again and ignored it. *If* she was, it would complicate things. The fact was, she was very happy with a successful career, her freedom and an attractive, interesting lover. She'd be crazy if she wasn't happy. She'd be insane to change one single thing.

"And it doesn't have anything to do with being afraid," she said aloud.

"What?"

She turned to Shade and, to his astonishment and hers, blushed. "Nothing," she muttered. "Thinking out loud."

He gave her a long, quiet look. Her expression came very close to a baffled sort of pout. Giving in to the urge, he leaned over and touched a hand to her cheek. "You're not eating your hot dog."

She could have wept. For some absurd reason, she wanted to stop the van, drop her head on the steering wheel and drown herself in hot, violent tears. "Not hungry," she managed.

"Bryan." He watched her snatch her sunglasses from the dash and push them on, though the sun was riding low. "Are you all right?"

"Fine." She took a deep breath and kept her eyes straight ahead. "I'm fine."

No, she wasn't. Though strain in her voice was rare, he recognized it. Only a few weeks before, he'd have shrugged and turned back to his reading. Deliberately, he dropped the paper on the floor at his feet. "What is it?"

"Nothing." She cursed herself and turned up the radio. Shade simply switched it off.

"Pull over."

"What for?"

"Just pull over."

With more violence than necessary, Bryan swung the van toward the shoulder, slowed and stopped. "We won't make very good time if we stop ten minutes after we start."

"We won't be making any time at all until you tell me what's wrong."

"Nothing's wrong!" Then she gritted her teeth and sat back. It wasn't any use saying nothing was wrong if you snarled at the same time. "I don't know," she evaded. "I'm edgy, that's all."

"You?"

She turned on him with a vengeance. "I've a right to foul moods, Colby. You don't have a patent on them."

"You certainly have," he said mildly. "Since it's the first one I've witnessed, I'm interested."

"Don't be so damn patronizing."

"Wanna fight?"

She stared through the windshield. "Maybe."

"Okay." Willing to oblige, he made himself comfortable. "About anything in particular?"

She swung her head around, ready to pounce on anything. "Do you have to bury your face in a paper every time I get behind the wheel?"

He smiled maddeningly. "Yes, dear."

A low sound came from her throat as she stared through the windshield again. "Never mind."

"I could point out that you have a habit of falling asleep when you sit in this seat."

"I said never mind." She reached for the key. "Just never mind. You make me sound like a fool."

He put his hand over hers before she could turn the key. "You sound foolish skirting around whatever's bothering you." He wanted to reach her. Without being aware when, he'd passed the point where he could tell himself not to get involved and follow the advice. Whether he wanted it or not, whether she accepted it or not, he was involved. Slowly, he lifted her hand to his lips. "Bryan, I care."

She sat there stunned that a simple statement could spin through her with such force. *I care.* He'd used the same word when he'd spoken about the woman who'd caused his nightmare. Along with the pleasure his words brought her came an inescapable sense of responsibility. He wouldn't allow himself to care indiscriminately. Glancing up, she met his eyes, patient, puzzled, as they studied her face.

"I care too," she said quietly. She twined her fingers with his, only briefly, but it unsettled them both.

Shade took the next step carefully, not certain of her, or himself. "Is that what's bothering you?"

She let out a long breath, as wary as he now. "Some. I'm not used to it...not like this."

"Neither am I."

She nodded, watching the cars breeze by. "I guess we'd both better take it easy then."

"Sounds logical." And next to impossible, he thought.

Right now he wanted to gather her close, forget where they were. Just hold her, he realized. It was all he wanted to do. With an effort, he drew back. "No complications?"

She managed to smile. Rule number one was the most important, after all. "No complications," she agreed. Again she reached for the key. "Read your paper, Colby," she said lightly. "I'll drive until dark."

Chapter 10

They took a slice out of Tennessee—Nashville, Chatta-nooga—caught the eastern corner of Arkansas—mountains and legends—and headed up through Twain's Missouri to Kentucky. There they found tobacco leaves, mountain laurel, Fort Knox and Mammoth Cave, but when Bryan thought of Kentucky, she thought of horses. Kentucky was sleek, glossy Thoroughbreds grazing on rich grass. It made her think of long-legged foals running in wide pastures and wide-chested colts pounding the track at Churchill Downs.

As they crossed the state toward Louisville, she saw much more. Tidy suburban homes bordered the larger cities and smaller towns as they did in every state across the country. Farms spread acre after acre—tobacco, horses, grain. Cities rose with their busy office buildings and harried streets. So much was the same as it had been to the west and to the south, and yet so much was different.

"Daniel Boone and the Cherokees," Bryan murmured as they traveled down another long, monotonous highway.

"What?" Slade glanced up from the map he'd been checking. When Bryan was driving, it didn't hurt to keep an eye on the navigation.

"Daniel Boone and the Cherokees," Bryan repeated. She increased the speed to pass a camper loaded down with bikes on the back bumper and fishing poles on the front. And where were they going? she wondered. Where had they come from? "I was thinking maybe it's the history of a place that makes it different from another. Maybe it's the climate, the topography."

Shade glanced back down at the map, idly figuring the time and mileage. He didn't give the camper rolling along behind them more than a passing thought. "Yes."

Bryan shot him an exasperated smile. One and one always added up to two for Shade. "But people are basically the same, don't you think? I imagine if you took a cross section of the country and polled, you'd find out that most people want the same things. A roof over their heads, a good job, a couple weeks off a year to play."

"Flowers in the garden?"

"All right, yes." She gave a careless little shrug and refused to believe it sounded foolish. "I think most peoples' wants are fairly simple. Italian shoes and a trip to Barbados might add in, but it's the basic things that touch everyone. Healthy children, a nest egg, a steak on the grill."

"You've a way of simplifying things, Bryan."

"Maybe, but I don't see any reason to complicate them."

Interested, he set down the map and turned to her. Perhaps he'd avoided digging too deeply into her, leery of what he might find. But now, behind his sunglasses, his eyes were direct. So was his question. "What do you want?"

"I…" She faltered a moment, frowning as she took the van around a long curve. "I don't know what you mean."

He thought she did, but they always seemed to end up fencing. "A roof over your head, a good job? Are those the most important things to you?"

Two months before, she might've shrugged and agreed. Her job came first, and gave her whatever she needed. That was the way she'd planned it, the way she'd wanted it. She wasn't sure any longer. Since she'd left L.A., she'd seen too much, felt too much. "I have those things," she said evasively. "Of course I want them."

"And?"

Uncomfortable, she shifted. She hadn't meant to have her idle speculation turned back on her. "I wouldn't turn down a trip to Barbados."

He didn't smile as she'd hoped he would, but continued to watch her from behind the protection of tinted glasses. "You're still simplifying."

"I'm a simple person."

Her hands were light and competent on the wheel, and her hair was scooped back in its habitual braid. She wore no makeup, a pair of faded cut-offs and a T-shirt two sizes too large for her. "No," he decided after a moment, "you're not. You only pretend to be."

Abruptly wary, she shook her head. Since her outburst in Mississippi, Bryan had managed to keep herself level, and to keep herself, she admitted, from thinking too deeply. "You're a complicated person, Shade, and you see complications where there aren't any."

She wished she could see his eyes. She wished she could see the thoughts behind them.

"I know what I see when I look at you, and it isn't simple."

She shrugged carelessly, but her body had begun to tense. "I'm easily read."

He corrected her with a short, concise word calmly spoken. Bryan blinked once, then gave her attention to the road. "Well, I'm certainly not full of mysteries."

Wasn't she? Shade watched the thin gold loops sway at her ears. "I wonder what you're thinking when you lie beside me after we've made love—in those minutes after passion and before sleep. I often wonder."

She wondered, too. "After we've made love," she said in a tolerably steady voice, "I have a hard time thinking at all."

This time he did smile. "You're always soft and sleepy," he murmured, making her tremble. "And I wonder what you might say, what I might hear if you spoke your thoughts aloud."

That I might be falling in love with you. That every day we have together takes us a day closer to the end. That I can't imagine what my life will be like when I don't have you there to touch, to talk to. Those were her thoughts, but she said nothing.

She had her secrets, Shade thought. Just as he did. "One day, before we're finished, you'll tell me."

He was easing her into a corner; Bryan felt it, but she didn't know why. "Haven't I told you enough already?"

"No." Giving in to the urge that came over him more and more often, he touched her cheek. "Not nearly."

She tried to smile, but she had to clear her throat to speak. "This is a dangerous conversation to have when I'm driving on an interstate at sixty miles an hour."

"It's a dangerous conversation in any case." Slowly, he drew his hand away. "I want you, Bryan. I can't look at you and not want you."

She fell silent, not because he was saying things she didn't want to hear, but because she no longer knew how to deal with them, and with him. If she spoke, she might say too much and break whatever bond had begun to form. She couldn't tell him so, but it was a bond she wanted.

He waited for her to speak, needing her to say something after he'd all but crossed over the line they'd drawn in the beginning. Risk. He'd taken one. Couldn't she see it? Needs. He needed her. Couldn't she feel it? But she remained silent, and the step forward became a step back.

"Your exit's coming up," he told her. Picking up the map, he folded it carefully. Bryan switched lanes, slowed down and left the highway.

Kentucky had made her think of horses; horses led them to Louisville, and Louisville to Churchill Downs. The Derby was long over, but there were races and there were crowds. If they were going to include in their glimpse of summer those who spent an afternoon watching races and betting, where else would they go?

The moment Bryan saw it, she thought of a dozen angles. There were cathedrallike domes and clean white buildings that gave a quiet elegance to the frenzy. The track was the focal point, a long oval of packed dirt. Stands rose around it. Bryan walked about, wondering just what kind of person would come there, or to any track, to plop down two dollars—or two hundred—on a race that would take only minutes. Again, she saw the variety.

There was the man with reddened arms and a sweaty T-shirt who pored over a racing form, and another in casually elegant slacks who sipped something long and cool. She saw women in quietly expensive dresses holding field glasses and families treating their children to the sport of kings. There was a man in a gray hat with tattoos snaking up both arms and a boy laughing on top of his father's shoulders.

They'd been to baseball games, tennis matches, drag races across the country. Always she saw faces in the crowd that seemed to have nothing in common except the game. The games had been invented, Bryan mused, and turned into industries. It was an interesting aspect of human nature. But people kept the games alive; they wanted to be amused, they wanted to compete.

She spotted one man leaning against the rail, watching a race as though his life depended on the outcome. His body was coiled, his face damp. She caught him in profile.

A quick scan showed her a woman in a pale rose dress and summer hat. She watched the race idly, distanced from it the way an empress might've been from a contest in a coliseum. Bryan framed her as the crowd roared the horses down the stretch.

Shade rested a hip on the rail and shot the horses in varying positions around the track, ending with the final lunge across the finish line. Before, he'd framed in the odds board, where numbers flashed and tempted. Now he waited until the results were posted and focused on it again.

Before the races were over, Shade saw Bryan standing at the two-dollar window. With her camera hanging around her neck and her ticket in her hand, she walked back toward the stands.

"Haven't you got any willpower?" he asked her.

"No." She'd found a vending machine, and she offered Shade a candy bar that was already softening in the heat. "Besides, there's a horse in the next race called Made in the Shade." When his eyebrow lifted up, she grinned. "How could I resist?"

He wanted to tell her she was foolish. He wanted to tell her she was unbearably sweet. Instead, he drew her sunglasses down her nose until he could see her eyes. "What's his number?"

"Seven."

Shade glanced over at the odds board and shook his head. "Thirty-five to one. How'd you bet?"

"To win, of course."

Taking her arm, he led her down to the rail again. "You can kiss your two bucks goodbye, hotshot."

"Or I can win seventy." Bryan pushed her glasses back in place. "Then I'll take you out to dinner. If I lose," she continued as the horses were led to the starting gate, "I've always got plastic. I can still take you out to dinner."

"Deal," Shade told her as the bell rang.

Bryan watched the horses lunge forward. They were nearly to the first turn before she managed to find number 7, third from the back. She glanced up to see Shade shake his head.

"Don't give up on him yet."

"When you bet on a long shot, love, you've got to be ready to lose."

A bit flustered by his absent use of the endearment, she turned back to the race. Shade rarely called her by name, much less one of those sweetly intimate terms. A long shot, she agreed silently. But she wasn't altogether sure she was as prepared to lose as she might've been.

"He's moving up," she said quickly as number 7 passed three horses with long, hard-driving strides. Forgetting herself, she leaned on the rail and laughed. "Look at him! He's moving up." Lifting her camera, she used the telephoto lens like a field glass. "God, he's beautiful," she murmured. "I didn't know he was so beautiful."

Watching the horse, she forgot the race, the competition. He was beautiful. She could see the jockey riding low in a blur of color that had a style of its own, but it was the horse, muscles bunching, legs pounding, that held her fascinated. He wanted to win; she could feel it. No matter how many races he'd lost, how many times he'd been led back to the stables sweating, he wanted to win.

Hope. She sensed it, but she no longer heard the call of the crowd around her. The horse straining to overtake the leaders hadn't lost hope. He believed he could win, and if you believed hard enough... With a last burst of speed, he nipped by the leader and crossed the wire like a champion.

"I'll be damned," Shade murmured. He found he had his arm around Bryan's shoulders as they watched the winner take his victory lap in long, steady strides.

"Beautiful." Her voice was low and thick.

"Hey." Shade tipped up her chin when he heard the tears. "It was only a two-dollar bet."

She shook her head. "He did it. He wanted to win, and he just didn't give up until he did."

Shade ran a finger down her nose. "Ever hear of luck?"

"Yeah." More composed, she took his hand in hers. "And this had nothing to do with it."

For a moment, he studied her. Then, with a shake of his head, he lowered his mouth to hers lightly, sweetly. "And this from a woman who claims to be simple."

And happy, she thought as her fingers laced with his. Ridiculously happy. "Let's go collect my winnings."

"There was a rumor," he began as they worked their way through the stands, "about you buying dinner."

"Yeah. I heard something about it myself."

She was a woman of her word. That evening, as the sky flashed with lightning and echoed with the thunder of a summer storm, they stepped into a quiet, low-lighted restaurant.

"Linen napkins," Bryan murmured to Shade as they were led to a table.

He laughed in her ear as he pulled out her chair. "You're easily impressed."

"True enough," she agreed, "but I haven't seen a linen napkin since June." Picking it off her plate, she ran it through her hands. It was smooth and rich. "There isn't a vinyl seat or a plastic light in this place. There won't be any little plastic containers of ketchup either." With a wink, she knocked a finger against a plate and let it ring. "Try that with paper and all you get is a thump."

Shade watched her experiment with the water glass next. "All this from the queen of fast food?"

"A steady diet of hamburgers is all right, but I like a change of pace. Let's have champagne," she decided as their waiter came over. She glanced at the list, made her choice and turned back to Shade again.

"You just blew your winnings on a bottle of wine."

"Easy come, easy go." Cupping her chin on her hands, she smiled at him. "Did I mention you look wonderful by candlelight?"

"No." Amused, he leaned forward as well. "Shouldn't that be my line?"

"Maybe, but you didn't seem in a rush to come out with it. Besides, I'm buying. However..." She sent him a slow, simmering look. "If you'd like to say something flattering, I wouldn't be offended."

Lazily, she ran a finger along the back of his hand, making him wonder why any man would object to the benefits of women's liberation. It wasn't a hardship to be wined and dined. Nor would it be a hardship to relax and be seduced. All the same, Shade decided as he lifted her hand to his lips, there was something to be said for partnership.

"I might say that you always look lovely, but tonight..." He let his gaze wander over her face. "Tonight, you take my breath away."

Momentarily flustered, she allowed her hand to stay in his. How was it he could say such things so calmly, so unexpectedly? And how could she, when she was used to casual, inconsequential compliments from men, deal with one that seemed so serious? Carefully, she warned herself. Very carefully.

"In that case I'll have to remember to use lipstick more often."

With a quick smile, he kissed her fingers again. "You forgot to put any on."

"Oh." Stuck, Bryan stared at him.

"Madame?" The wine steward held out the bottle of champagne, label up.

"Yes." She let out a quiet breath. "Yes, that's fine."

Still watching Shade, she heard the cork give in to pressure and the wine bubble into her glass. She sipped, closing her eyes to enjoy it. Then, with a nod, she waited until the steward filled both glasses. Steadier, Bryan lifted her glass and smiled at Shade.

"To?"

"One summer," he said, and touched his rim to hers. "One fascinating summer."

It made her lips curve again, so that her eyes reflected the smile as she sipped. "I expected you to be a terrible bore to work with."

"Really." Shade let the champagne rest on his tongue a moment. Like Bryan, it was smooth and quiet, with energy bubbling underneath. "I expected you to be a pain in the—"

"However," she interrupted dryly. "I've been pleased

that my preconception didn't hold true." She waited a moment. "And yours?"

"Did," he said easily, then laughed when she narrowed her eyes at him. "But I wouldn't have enjoyed you nearly as much if it'd been otherwise."

"I liked your other compliment better," she mumbled, and picked up her menu. "But I suppose since you're stingy with them, I have to take what I get."

"I only say what I mean."

"I know." She pushed back her hair as she skimmed the menu. "But I— Oh look, they've got chocolate mousse."

"Most people start at the appetizers."

"I'd rather work backward, then I can gauge how much I want to eat and still have room for dessert."

"I can't imagine you turning down anything chocolate."

"Right you are."

"What I can't understand is how you can shovel it in the way you do and not be fat."

"Just lucky, I guess." With the menu open over her plate, she smiled at him. "Don't you have any weaknesses, Shade?"

"Yeah." He looked at her until she was baffled and flustered again. "A few." And one of them, he thought as he watched her eyes, was becoming more and more acute.

"Are you ready to order?"

Distracted, Bryan looked up at the well-mannered waiter. "What?"

"Are you ready to order?" he repeated. "Or would you like more time?"

"The lady'll have the chocolate mousse," Shade said smoothly.

"Yes, sir." Unflappable, the waiter marked it down. "Will that be all?"

"Not by a long shot," Shade told him, and picked up his wine again.

With a laugh, Bryan worked her way through the menu.

"Stuffed," Bryan decided over an hour later, as they drove through a hard, driving rain. "Absolutely stuffed."

Shade cruised through an amber light. "Watching you eat is an amazing way to pass the time."

"We're here to entertain," she said lightly. Snuggled back in her seat with champagne swimming in her head and thunder grumbling in a bad-tempered sky, she was content to ride along wherever he chose to go. "It was sweet of you to let me have a bite of your cheesecake."

"Half," Shade corrected her. Deliberately he turned away from the campground they'd decided on that afternoon. The wipers made quick swishing sounds against the windshield. "But you're welcome."

"It was lovely." She let out a sigh, quiet and sleepy. "I like being pampered. Tonight should get me through another month of fast-food chains and diners with stale doughnuts." Content, she glanced around at the dark, wet streets, the puddles at the curbs. She liked the rain, especially at night, when it made everything glisten. Watching it, she fell to dreaming, rousing herself only when he turned into the lot of a small motel.

"No campground tonight," he said before she could question. "Wait here while I get a room."

She didn't have time to comment before he was out of the van and dashing through the rain. No campground, she thought, looking over her shoulder at the narrow twin bunks on either side of the van. No skinny, make-shift beds and trickling showers.

With a grin, she jumped up and began to gather his equipment and hers. She never gave the suitcases a thought.

"Champagne, linen napkins and now a bed." She laughed as he climbed back into the van, soaking wet. "I'm going to get spoiled."

He wanted to spoil her. There was no logic to it, only fact. Tonight, if only for tonight, he wanted to spoil her. "Room's around the back." When Bryan dragged the equipment forward, he drove slowly around, checking numbers on the lines of doors. "Here." He strapped camera bags over his shoulder. "Wait a minute." She'd grabbed another bag and her purse by the time he'd pulled open her door from the outside. To her astonishment, she found herself lifted into his arms.

"Shade!" But the rain slapped into her face, making her gasp as he dashed across the lot to an outside door.

"Least I could do after you sprang for dinner," he told her as he maneuvered the oversize key into the lock. Bryan was laughing as he struggled to open the door holding her, the camera bags and tripods.

Kicking the door closed with his foot, he fastened his mouth on hers. Still laughing, Bryan clung to him.

"Now we're both wet," she murmured, running a hand through his hair.

"We'll dry off in bed." Before she knew his intention,

Bryan was falling through the air and landing with two bounces full-length onto the mattress.

"So romantic," she said dryly, but her body stayed limp. She lay there, smiling, because he'd made a rare frivolous gesture and she intended to enjoy it.

Her dress clung to her, her hair fanned out. He'd seen her change for dinner and knew she wore a thin teddy cut high at the thigh, low over her breasts, and sheer, sheer stockings. He could love her now, love her for hours. It wouldn't be enough. He knew how relaxed, how pliant, her body could be. How full of fire, strength, vibrancy. He could want all of it, have all of it. It wouldn't be enough.

He was an expert at capturing the moment, the emotions, the message. Letting his own feelings hum, he reached for his camera bag.

"What're you doing?"

When she started to sit up, Shade turned back. "Stay there a minute."

Intrigued and wary, she watched him set his camera. "I don't—"

"Just lie back like you were," he interrupted. "Relaxed and rather pleased with yourself."

His intention was obvious enough now. Bryan lifted a brow. An obsession, she thought, amused. The camera was an obsession for both of them. "Shade, I'm a photographer, not a model."

"Humor me." Gently, he pushed her back on the bed.

"I've too much champagne in my system to argue with you." She smiled up at him as he held the camera over his face. "You can play if you like, or take serious pictures if you must. As long as I don't have to do anything."

She did nothing but smile, and he began to throb. So often he'd used the camera as a barrier between himself and his subject, other times as a conductor for his emotion, emotion he refused to let loose any other way. Now, it was neither. The emotion was already in him, and barriers weren't possible.

He framed her quickly and shot, but was unsatisfied. "That's not what I want." He was so businesslike that Bryan didn't see it as a defense, only as his manner. But when he came over, pulled her into a sitting position and unzipped her dress, her mouth fell open.

"Shade!"

"It's that lazy sex," he murmured as he slipped the dress down over one shoulder. "Those incredible waves of sensuality that take no effort at all, but just are. It's the way your eyes look." But when his came back to hers, she forgot the joke she'd been about to make. "The way they look when I touch you—like this." Slowly, he ran a hand over her naked shoulder. "The way they look just after I kiss you—like this." He kissed her, lingering over it while her mind emptied of thought and her body filled with sensation.

"Like this," he whispered, more determined than ever to capture that moment, make it tangible so that he could hold it in his hands and see it. "Just like this," he said again, backing off one step, then two. "The way you look just before we make love. The way you look just after."

Helplessly aroused, Bryan stared into the lens of the camera as he lifted it. He caught her there, like a quarry in the crosshairs of a scope, empty of thoughts, jumbled with feeling. At the same time, he caught himself.

For an instant her heart was in her eyes. The shutter opened, closed and captured it. When he printed the photograph, he thought as he carefully set down his camera, would he see what she felt? Would he be certain of his own feelings?

Now she sat on the bed, her dress disarrayed, her hair tumbled, her eyes clouded. Secrets, Shade thought again. They both had them. Was it possible he'd locked a share of each of their secrets on film inside his camera?

When he looked at her now, he saw a woman aroused, a woman who aroused. He could see passion and pliancy and acceptance. He could see a woman whom he'd come to know better than anyone else. Yet he saw a woman he'd yet to reach—one he'd avoided reaching.

He went to her in silence. Her skin was damp but warm, as he'd known it would be. Raindrops clung to her hair. He touched one, then it was gone. Her arms lifted.

While the storm raged outside, he took her and himself where there was no need for answers.

Chapter 11

If they had more time…

As August began to slip by, that was the thought
that continued to run through Bryan's mind. With more
time, they could have stayed longer at each stop. With
more time, they might have passed through more states,
more towns, more communities. There was so much to
see, so much to record, but time was running out.

In less than a month, the school she'd photographed
empty and waiting in the afternoon light would be filled
again. Leaves that were full and green would take on
those vibrant colors before they fell. She would be back
in L.A., back in her studio, back to the routine she'd
established. For the first time in years, the word *alone*
had a hollow ring.

How had it happened? Shade Colby had become her
partner, her lover, her friend. He'd become, though it

was frightening to admit, the most important person in her life. Somehow she'd become dependent on him, for his opinion, his company, for the nights they spent involved only with each other.

She could imagine how it would be when they returned to L.A. and went their separate ways. Separate parts of the city, she thought, separate lives, separate outlooks.

The closeness that had so slowly, almost painfully, developed between them would dissolve. Wasn't that what they'd both intended from the start? They'd made a bargain with each other, just as they'd made the bargain to work together. If her feelings had changed, she was responsible for them, for dealing with them. As the odometer turned over on the next mile, as the next state was left behind, she wondered how to begin.

Shade had his own thoughts to deal with. When they'd crossed into Maryland, they'd crossed into the East. The Atlantic was close, as close as the end of summer. It was the end that disturbed him. The word no longer seemed to mean finished, but over. He began to realize he was far from ready to draw that last line. There were ways to rationalize it. He tried them all.

They'd missed too much. If they took their time driving back, rather than sticking to their plan of going straight across the country, they could detour into so many places they'd eliminated on the way out. It made sense. They could stay in New England a week, two weeks after Labor Day. After long days in the van and the intense work they'd both put in, they deserved some time off. It was reasonable.

They should work their way back, rather than rush.

If they weren't preoccupied with making time, making miles, how many pictures would come out of it? If one of them was special, it would be worth it. That was professional.

When they returned to L.A., perhaps Bryan could move in with him, share his apartment as they'd shared the van. It was impossible. Wasn't it?

She didn't want to complicate their relationship. Hadn't she said so? He didn't want the responsibility of committing himself to one person. Hadn't he made himself clear? Perhaps he'd come to need her companionship on some level. And it was true he'd learned to appreciate the way she could look at anything and see the fun and the beauty of it. That didn't equal promises, commitments or complications.

With a little time, a little distance, the need was bound to fade. The only thing he was sure of was that he wanted to put off that point for as long as possible.

Bryan spotted a convertible—red, flashy. Its driver had one arm thrown over the white leather seat while her short blond hair flew in the wind. Grabbing her camera, Bryan leaned out the open window. Half kneeling, half crouching, on the seat, she adjusted for depth.

She wanted to catch it from the rear, elongating the car into a blur of color. But she didn't want to lose the arrogant angle of the driver's arm, or the negligent way her hair streamed back. Already she knew she would dodge the plain gray highway and the other cars in the darkroom. Just the red convertible, she thought as she set her camera.

"Try to keep just this distance," she called to Shade. She took one shot and, dissatisfied, leaned out farther for the next. Though Shade swore at her, Bryan got her shot before she laughed and flopped back on her seat.

He was guilty of the same thing, he knew. Once the camera was in place, you tended to think of it as a shield. Nothing could happen to you—you simply weren't part of what was happening. Though he'd known better, it had happened to him often enough, even after his first stint overseas. Perhaps it was the understanding that made his voice mild, though he was annoyed.

"Don't you have more sense than to climb out the window of a moving car?"

"Couldn't resist. There's nothing like a convertible on an open highway in August. I'm always toying with the idea of getting one myself."

"Why don't you?"

"Buying a new car is hard work." She looked at the green-and-white road signs as she'd looked at so many others that summer. There were cities, roads and routes she'd never heard of. "I can hardly believe we're in Maryland. We've come so far and yet, I don't know, it doesn't seem like two months."

"Two years?"

She laughed. "Sometimes. Other times it seems like days. Not enough time," she said, half to herself. "Never enough."

Shade didn't give himself the chance to think before he took the opening. "We've had to leave out a lot."

"I know."

"We went through Kansas, but not Nebraska, Mississippi, and not the Carolinas. We didn't go to Michigan or Wisconsin."

"Or Florida, Washington State, the Dakotas." She

shrugged, trying not to think of what was left behind. Just today, Bryan told herself. Just take today.

"I've been thinking about tying them in on the way back."

"On the way back?" Bryan turned to him as he reached for a cigarette.

"We'd be on our own time." The van's lighter glowed red against the tip. "But I think we could both take a month or so and finish the job."

More time. Bryan felt the quick surge of hope, then ruthlessly toned it down. He wanted to finish the job his way. It was his way, she reminded herself, to do things thoroughly. But did the reason really matter? They'd have more time. Yes, she realized as she stared out the side window. The reason mattered a great deal too much.

"The job's finished in New England," she said lightly. "Summer's over, and it's back to business. My work at the studio will be backed up for a month. Still…" She felt herself weakening, though he said nothing, did nothing, to persuade her. "I wouldn't mind a few detours on the trip back."

Shade kept his hands easy on the wheel, his voice casual. "We'll think about it," he said, and let the subject they both wanted to pursue drop.

Weary of the highway, they took to the back roads. Bryan took her pictures of kids squirting each other with garden hoses, of laundry drying in the breeze, of an elderly couple sitting on a porch glider. Shade took his of sweating construction workers spreading tar on roofs, of laborers harvesting peaches and, surprisingly, of two ten-year-old businessmen hawking lemonade in their front yard.

Touched, Bryan accepted the paper cup Shade handed her. "That was sweet."

"You haven't tasted it yet," he commented, and climbed into the passenger's seat. "To keep down the overhead, they used a light hand on the sugar."

"I meant you." On impulse, she leaned over and kissed him, lightly, comfortably. "You can be a very sweet man."

As always, she moved him, and he couldn't stop it. "I can give you a list of people who'd disagree."

"What do they know?" With a smile, she touched her lips to his again. She drove down the neat, shady street appreciating the trim lawns, flower gardens and dogs barking in the yards. "I like the suburbs," she said idly. "To look at, anyway. I've never lived in one. They're so orderly." With a sigh, she turned right at the corner. "If I had a house here, I'd probably forget to fertilize the lawn and end up with crab grass and dandelions. My neighbors would take up a petition. I'd end up selling my house and moving into a condo."

"So ends Bryan Mitchell's career as a suburbanite."

She made a face at him. "Some people aren't cut out for picket fences."

"True enough."

She waited, but he said nothing that made her feel inadequate—nothing that made her feel as though she should be. She laughed delightedly, then grabbed his hand and squeezed. "You're good for me, Shade. You really are."

He didn't want to let her hand go, and released it reluctantly. Good for her. She said it so easily, laughing. Because she did, he knew she had no idea just what it meant to him to hear it. Maybe it was time he told her. "Bryan—"

"What's that?" she said abruptly, and swung toward the curb. Excited, she inched the car forward until she could read the colorful cardboard poster tacked to a telephone pole. "Nightingale's Traveling Carnival." Pulling on the brake, she nearly climbed over Shade to see it more clearly. "Voltara, the Electric Woman." With a half whoop, she nudged closer to Shade. "Terrific, just terrific. Sampson, the Dancing Elephant. Madame Zoltar, Mystic. Shade, look, it's their last night in town. We can't miss it. What's summer without a carny? Thrilling rides, games of skill and chance."

"And Dr. Wren, the Fire Eater."

It was easy to ignore the dry tone. "Fate." She scrambled back to her own seat. "It has to be fate that we turned down this road. Otherwise, we might've missed it."

Shade glanced back at the sign as Bryan pulled away from the curb. "Think of it," he murmured. "We might've gotten all the way to the coast without seeing a dancing elephant."

A half hour later, Shade leaned back in his seat, calmly smoking, his feet on the dash. Frazzled, Bryan swung the van around the next turn.

"I'm not lost."

Shade blew out a lazy stream of smoke. "I didn't say a word."

"I know what you're thinking."

"That's Madame Zoltar's line."

"And you can stop looking so smug."

"Was I?"

"You always look smug when I get lost."

"You said you weren't."

Bryan gritted her teeth and sent him a killing look. "Why don't you just pick up that map and tell me where we are?"

"I started to pick it up ten minutes ago and you snarled at me."

Bryan let out a long breath. "It was the *way* you picked it up. You were smirking, and I could hear you thinking—"

"You're stepping into Madame Zoltar's territory again."

"Damn it, Shade." But she had to choke back a laugh as she drove down the long, unlit country road. "I don't mind making a fool of myself, but I hate it when someone lifts an eyebrow over it."

"Did I?"

"You know you did. Now, if you'd just—"

Then she caught the first glimmer of red, blue, green lights flickering. A Ferris wheel, she thought. It had to be. The sound of tinny music came faintly through the summer dusk. A calliope. This time it was Bryan who looked smug. "I knew I'd find it."

"I never had a doubt."

She might've had something withering to say to that, but the lights glowing in the early-evening dusk, and the foolish piping music held her attention. "It's been years," she murmured. "Just years since I've seen anything like this. I've got to watch the fire eater."

"And your wallet."

She shook her head as she turned off the road onto the bumpy field where cars were parked. "Cynic."

"Realist." He waited until she maneuvered the van next to a late-model pickup. "Lock the van." Shade gathered his bag and waited outside the van until Bryan had hers. "Where first?"

She thought of pink cotton candy but restrained herself. "Why don't we just wander around a bit? We might want some shots now, but at night they'd have more punch."

Without the dark, without the bright glow of colored lights, the carnival looked too much like what it was—a little weary, more than a little tawdry. Its illusions were too easily unmasked now, and that wasn't why Bryan had come. Carnivals, like Santa Claus, had a right to their mystique. In another hour, when the sun had completely set behind those rolling, blue-tinted hills to the west, the carnival would come into its own. Peeling paint wouldn't be noticed.

"Look, there's Voltara." Bryan grabbed Shade's arm and swung him around to see a life-size poster that gave her lavish curves and scant cover as she was being strapped into what looked like a homemade electric chair.

Shade looked at the painted spangles over generous cleavage. "Might be worth watching after all."

With a quick snort, Bryan pulled him toward the Ferris wheel. "Let's take a ride. From the top we'll be able to see the whole layout."

Shade pulled a bill out of his wallet. "That's the only reason you want to ride."

"Don't be ridiculous." They walked over, waiting

while the attendant let a couple off. "It's a good way of covering ground and sitting down at the same time," she began as she took the vacated seat. "It's sure to be an excellent angle for some aerial pictures, and..." She slipped a hand into his as they started the slow swing up. "It's the very best place to neck at a carnival."

When he laughed, she wrapped her arms around him and silenced his lips with hers. They reached the top where the evening breeze flowed clean and hung there one moment—two—aware only of each other. On the descent, the speed picked up and the drop had her stomach shivering, her mind swimming. It was no different from the sensation of being held by him, loved by him. They held tight and close through two revolutions.

Gathering her against his shoulder, Shade watched the carnival rush up toward them. It'd been years since he'd held someone soft and feminine on a Ferris wheel. High school? he wondered. He could hardly remember. Now he realized he'd let his youth slip by him because so many other things had seemed important at the time. He'd let it go freely, and though he wouldn't, couldn't, ask for the whole of it back, perhaps Bryan was showing him how to recapture pieces of it.

"I love the way this feels," she murmured. She could watch the sun go down in a last splashy explosion of arrogance, hear the music, the voices, ebb and fade as the wheel spun around. She could look down and be just removed enough from the scene to enjoy it, just separate enough to understand it. "A ride on a Ferris wheel should be required once a year, like a routine physical."

With her head against Shade's shoulder, she examined the scene below, the midway, the concessions, the booths set up for games of skill. She wanted to see it all, close up. She could smell popcorn, grilling meat, sweat, the heavy-handed after-shave of the attendant as their car swung by him. It gave her the overall view. This was life, a sidelong glance at it. This was the little corner of life where children could see wonders and adults could pretend for just a little while.

Taking her camera, she angled down through the cars and wires to focus in on the attendant. He looked a bit bored as he lifted the safety bar for one couple and lowered it for the next. A job for him, Bryan thought, a small thrill for the rest. She sat back, content to ride.

When it was dark, they went to work. There were people gathered around the wheel of fortune, plopping down a dollar for a chance at more. Teenagers showed off for their girls or their peers by hurling softballs at stacked bottles. Toddlers hung over the rope and tossed Ping-Pong balls at fishbowls, hoping to win a goldfish whose life expectancy was short at best. Young girls squealed on the fast-spinning Octopus, while young boys goggled at the posters along the midway.

Bryan took one telling shot of a woman carrying a baby on one hip while a three-year-old dragged her mercilessly along. Shade took another of a trio of boys in muscle shirts standing apart and doing their best to look tough and aloof.

They ate slices of pizza with rubber crusts as they watched with the rest of the crowd as Dr. Wren, Fire Eater, came out of his tent to give a quick, teasing demonstration of his art. Like the ten-year-old boy who watched beside her, Bryan was sold.

With an agreement to meet back at the entrance to

the midway in thirty minutes, they separated. Caught up, Bryan wandered. She wasn't able to resist Voltara, and slipped into part of the show to see the somewhat weary, glossy-faced woman strapped into a chair that promised to zap her with two thousand volts.

She pulled it off well enough, Bryan thought, closing her eyes and giving a regal nod before the lever was pulled. The special effects weren't top-notch, but they worked. Blue light shimmered up the chair and around Voltara's head. It turned her skin to the color of summer lightning. At fifty cents a shot, Bryan decided as she stepped back out, the audience got their money's worth.

Intrigued, she wandered around in back of the midway to where the carnival workers parked their trailers. No colorful lights here, she mused as she glanced over the small caravan. No pretty illusions. Tonight, they'd pack up the equipment, take down the posters and drive on.

The moonlight hit the metal of a trailer and showed the scratches and dents. The shades were drawn at the little windows, but there was faded lettering on the side. Nightingale's.

Bryan found it touching and crouched to shoot.

"Lost, little lady?"

Surprised, Bryan sprang up and nearly collided with a short, husky man in T-shirt and work pants. If he worked for the carnival, Bryan thought quickly, he'd been taking a long break. If he'd come to watch, the lights and sideshows hadn't held his interest. The smell of beer, warm and stale, clung to him.

"No." She gave him a careful smile and kept a careful distance. Fear hadn't entered into it. The move had been automatic and mild. There were lights and people only a few yards away. And she thought he might give her another angle for her photographs. "Do you work here?"

"Woman shouldn't wander around in the dark alone. 'Less she's looking for something."

No, fear hadn't been her first reaction, nor did it come now. Annoyance did. It was that that showed in her eyes before she turned away. "Excuse me."

Then he had her arm, and it occurred to her that the lights were a great deal farther away than she'd have liked. Brazen it out, she told herself. "Look, I've people waiting for me."

"You're a tall one, ain't you?" His fingers were very firm, if his stance wasn't. He weaved slightly as he looked Bryan over. "Don't mind looking eye to eye with a woman. Let's have a drink."

"Some other time." Bryan put her hand on his arm to push it away and found it solid as a concrete block. That's when the fear began. "I came back here to take some pictures," she said as calmly as she could. "My partner's waiting for me." She pushed at his arm again. "You're hurting me."

"Got some more beer in my truck," he mumbled as he began to drag her farther away from the lights.

"No." Her voice rose on the first wave of panic. "I don't want any beer."

He stopped a moment, swaying. As Bryan took a good look in his eyes, she realized he was as drunk as a man could get and still stand. Fear bubbled hot in her throat. "Maybe you want something else." He skimmed down her thin summer top and brief shorts.

"Woman usually wants something when she wanders around half naked."

Her fear ebbed as cold fury rushed in. Bryan glared. He grinned.

"You ignorant ass," she hissed just before she brought her knee up, hard. His breath came out in a whoosh as he dropped his hand. Bryan didn't wait to see him crouch over. She ran.

She was still running when she rammed straight into Shade.

"You're ten minutes late," he began, "but I've never seen you move that fast."

"I was just— I had to…" She trailed off, breathless, and leaned against him. Solid, dependable, safe. She could have stayed just like that until the sun rose again.

"What is it?" He could feel the tension before he drew her away and saw it on her face. "What happened?"

"Nothing really." Disgusted with herself, Bryan dragged her hair back from her face. "I just ran into some jerk who wanted to buy me a drink whether I was thirsty or not."

His fingers tightened on her arms, and she winced as they covered the same area that was already tender. "Where?"

"It was nothing," she said again, furious with herself that she hadn't taken the time to regain her composure before she ran into him. "I went around back to get a look at the trailers."

"Alone?" He shook her once, quickly. "What kind of idiot are you? Don't you know carnivals aren't just cotton candy and colored lights? Did he hurt you?"

It wasn't concern she heard in his voice, but anger. Her spine straightened. "No, but you are."

Ignoring her, Shade began to drag her through the crowds toward the parking section. "If you'd stop looking at everything through rose-colored glasses, you'd see a lot more clearly. Do you have any idea what might've happened?"

"I can take care of myself. I did take care of myself." When they reached the van, she swung away from him. "I'll look at life any way I like. I don't need you to lecture me, Shade."

"You need something." Grabbing the keys from her, he unlocked the van. "It's brainless to go wandering around alone in the dark in a place like this. Looking for trouble," he muttered as he climbed into the driver's seat.

"You sound remarkably like the idiot I left sprawled on the grass with his hands between his legs."

He shot her a look. Later, when he was calm, he might admire the way she'd dealt with an obnoxious drunk, but now he couldn't see beyond her carelessness. Independence aside, a woman was vulnerable. "I should've known better than to let you go off alone."

"Now just a minute." She whirled around in her seat. "You don't *let* me do anything, Colby. If you've got it in your head that you're my keeper or anything of the sort, then you'd better get it right out again. I answer to myself. Only myself."

"For the next few weeks, you answer to me as well."

She tried to control the temper that pushed at her, but it wasn't possible. "I may work with you," she said,

pacing her words. "I may sleep with you. But I don'
answer to you. Not now. Not ever."

Shade punched in the van's lighter. "We'll see abou
that."

"Just remember the contract." Shaking with fury
she turned away again. "We're partners on this job
fifty-fifty."

He gave his opinion of what she could do with the
contract. Bryan folded her arms, shut her eyes and
willed herself to sleep.

He drove for hours. She might sleep, but there was
too much churning inside him to allow him the same
release. So he drove, east toward the Atlantic.

She'd been right when she'd said she didn't answer
to him. That was one of the first rules they'd laid down
He was damned sick of rules. She was her own woman
His strings weren't on her any more than hers were on
him. They were two intelligent, independent people
who wanted it that way.

But he'd wanted to protect her. When everything
else was stripped away, he'd wanted to protect her. Was
she so dense that she couldn't see he'd been furious
not with her but with himself for not being there when
she'd needed him?

She'd tossed that back in his face, Shade thought
grimly as he ran a hand over his gritty eyes. She'd put
him very clearly, very concisely, in his place. And his
place, he reminded himself, no matter how intimate
they'd become, was still at arm's length. It was best for
both of them.

With his window open, he could just smell the

ing of the ocean. They'd crossed the country. They'd crossed more lines than he'd bargained for. But they were a long way from crossing the final one.

How did he feel about her? He'd asked himself that question time after time, but he'd always managed to block out the answer. Did he really want to hear it? But it was three o'clock in the morning, that hour he knew well. Defenses crumbled easily at three o'clock in the morning. Truth had a way of easing its way in.

He was in love with her. It was too late to take a step back and say no thanks. He was in love with her in a way that was completely foreign to him. Unselfishly. Unlimitedly.

Looking back, he could almost pinpoint the moment when it had happened to him, though he'd called it something else. When he'd stood on the rock island in the Arizona lake, he'd desired her, desired her more intensely than he'd desired anything or anyone. When he'd woken from the nightmare and had found her warm and solid beside him, he'd needed her, again more than anything or anyone.

But when he'd looked across the dusty road on the Oklahoma border and seen her standing in front of a sad little house with a plot of pansies, he'd fallen in love.

They were a long way from Oklahoma now, a long way from that moment. Love had grown, overwhelming him. He hadn't known how to deal with it then. He hadn't a clue what to do about it now.

He drove toward the ocean where the air was moist. When he pulled the van between two low-rising dunes, he could just see the water, a shadow with sound in the distance. Watching it, listening to it, he slept.

Bryan woke when she heard the gulls. Stiff, disori-
ented, she opened her eyes. She saw the ocean, blu
and quiet in the early light that wasn't quite dawn. A
the horizon, the sky was pink and serene. Misty. Wak
ing slowly, she watched gulls swoop over the shorelin
and soar to sea again.

Shade slept in the seat beside her, turned slightly ir
his seat, his head resting against the door. He'd driver
for hours, she realized. But what had driven him?

She thought of their argument with a kind of weary
tolerance. Quietly, she slipped from the van. She wantec
the scent of the sea.

Had it only been two months since they'd stood or
the shore of the Pacific? Was this really so different
she wondered as she stepped out of her shoes and fel
the sand, cool and rough under her feet. He'd driver
through the night to get here, she mused. To get here
one step closer to the end. They had only to drive up th
coast now, winding their way through New England
A quick stop in New York for pictures and darkroom
work, then on to Cape Cod, where summer would enc
for both of them.

It might be best, she thought, if they broke there
completely. Driving back together, touching on some
of the places they'd discovered as a team, might be toc
much to handle. Perhaps when the time came, she'c
make some excuse and fly back to L.A. It might be
best, she reflected, to start back to those separate lives
when summer ended.

They'd come full circle. Through the tension and annoyance of the beginning, into the cautious friendship
the frenzied passion, and right back to the tension again

Bending, Bryan picked up a shell small enough to fit into the palm of her hand, but whole.

Tension broke things, didn't it? Cracked the whole until pressure crumbled it into pieces. Then whatever you'd had was lost. She didn't want that for Shade. With a sigh, she looked out over the ocean, where the water was green, then blue. The mist was rising.

No, she didn't want that for him. When they turned from each other, they should do so as they'd turned to each other. As whole, separate people, standing independently.

She kept the shell in her hand as she walked back toward the van. The weariness was gone. When she saw him standing beside the van watching her, with his hair ruffled by the wind, his face shadowed, eyes heavy, her heart turned over.

The break would come soon enough, she told herself. For now, there should be no pressure.

Smiling, she went to him. She took his hand and pressed the shell into it. "You can hear the ocean if you listen for it."

He said nothing, but put his arm around her and held her. Together they watched the sun rise over the east.

Chapter 12

On a street corner in Chelsea, five enterprising kids loosened the bolts on a fire hydrant and sent water swooshing. Bryan liked the way they dived through the stream, soaking their sneakers, plastering their hair. It wasn't necessary to think long about her feelings toward the scene. As she lifted her camera and focused, her one predominant emotion was envy, pure and simple.

Not only were they cool and delightfully wet while she was limp from the heat, but they hadn't a care in the world. They didn't have to worry if their lives were heading in the right direction, or any direction at all. It was their privilege in these last breathless weeks of summer to enjoy—their youth, their freedom and a cool splash in city water.

If she was envious, there were others who felt the same way. As it happened, Bryan's best shot came from incorporating one passerby in the scene. The middle-aged deliveryman in the sweaty blue shirt and dusty work shoes looked over his shoulder as one of the children lifted his arms up to catch a stream. On one face was pleasure, pure and giddy. On the other was amusement, laced with regret for something that couldn't be recaptured.

Bryan walked on, down streets packed with bad-tempered traffic, over sidewalks that tossed up heat like insults. New York didn't always weather summer with a smile and a wave.

Shade was in the darkroom they'd rented, while she'd opted to take the field first. She was putting it off, she admitted, as she skirted around a sidewalk salesman and his array of bright-lensed plastic sunglasses. Putting off coping with the last darkroom session she'd have before they returned to California. After this brief stop in New York, they'd head north for the final weekend of summer in Cape Cod.

And she and Shade had gone back to being almost unbearably careful with each other. Since that morning when they'd woken at the beach, Bryan had taken a step back. Deliberately, she admitted. She'd discovered all too forcibly that he could hurt her. Perhaps it was true that she'd left herself wide open. Bryan wouldn't deny that somewhere along the way she'd lost her determination to maintain a certain distance. But it wasn't too late to pull back just enough to keep from getting battered. She had to accept that the season was nearly over, and when it was, her relationship with Shade ended with it.

With this in mind, she took a slow, meandering route back toward midtown and the rented darkroom.

Shade already had ten rows of proofs. Sliding a strip under the enlarger, he methodically began to select and eliminate. As always, he was more ruthless, more critical with his own work than he'd have been with anyone else's. He knew Bryan would be back shortly, so any printing he did would have to wait until the following day. Still, he wanted to see one now, for himself.

He remembered the little motel room they'd taken that rainy night just outside of Louisville. He remembered the way he'd felt then—involved, a little reckless. That night had been preying on his mind, more and more often, as he and Bryan seemed to put up fences again. There'd been no boundaries between them that night.

Finding the print he was looking for, he brought the magnifier closer. She was sitting on the bed, her dress falling off her shoulders, raindrops clinging to her hair. Soft, passionate, hesitant. All those things were there in the way she held herself, in the way she looked at the camera. But her eyes...

Frustrated, he narrowed his own. What was in her eyes? He wanted to enlarge the proof now, to blow it up so that he could see and study and understand.

She was holding back now. Every day he could feel it, sense it. Just a little bit more distance every day. But what had been in her eyes on that rainy night? He had to know. Until he did, he couldn't take a step, either toward her or away.

When the knock came on the door, he cursed it. He wanted another hour. With another hour, he could have the print, and perhaps his answer. He found it a simple matter to ignore the knock.

"Shade, come on. Time for the next shift."

"Come back in an hour."

"An hour!" On the other side of the door, Bryan pounded again. "Look, I'm melting out there. Besides, I've already given you twenty minutes more than your share."

The moment he yanked open the door, Bryan felt the waves of impatience. Because she wasn't in the mood to wrestle with it, she merely lifted a brow and skirted around him. If he wanted to be in a foul mood, fine. As long as he took it outside with him. Casually she set down her camera and a paper cup filled with soft drink and ice.

"So how'd it go?"

"I'm not finished."

With a shrug, she began to set out the capsules of undeveloped film she'd stored in her bag. "You've tomorrow for that."

He didn't want to wait until tomorrow, not, he discovered, for another minute. "If you'd give me the rest of the time I want, I wouldn't need tomorrow."

Bryan began to run water in a shallow plastic tub. "Sorry, Shade. I've run out of steam outside. If I don't get started in here, the best I'll do is go back to the hotel and sleep the rest of the afternoon. Then I'll be behind. What's so important?"

He stuffed his hands in his pockets. "Nothing. I just want to finish."

"And I've got to start," she murmured absently as she checked the temperature of the water.

He watched her a moment, the competent way she set up, arranging bottles of chemicals to her preference. Little tendrils of her hair curled damply around her face from the humidity. Even as she set up to work, she slipped out of her shoes. He felt a wave of love, of need, of confusion, and reached out to touch her shoulder. "Bryan—"

"Hmm?"

He started to move closer, then stopped himself. "What time will you be finished?"

There were touches of amusement and annoyance in her voice. "Shade, will you stop trying to push me out?"

"I want to come back for you."

She stopped long enough to look over her shoulder. "Why?"

"Because I don't want you walking around outside after it's dark."

"For heaven's sake." Exasperated, she turned completely around. "Do you have any idea how many times I've been to New York alone? Do I look stupid?"

"No."

Something in the way he said it had her narrowing her eyes. "Look—"

"I want to come back for you," he repeated, and this time touched her cheek. "Humor me."

She let out a long breath, tried to be annoyed and ended by lifting her hand to his. "Eight, eight-thirty."

"Okay. We can grab something to eat on the way back."

"There's something we can agree on." She smiled and lowered her hand before she could give in to the urge to move closer. "Now go take some pictures, will you? I've got to get to work."

He lifted his camera bag and started out. "Any longer than eight-thirty and you buy dinner."

Bryan locked the door behind him with a decisive click.

She didn't lose track of time while she worked. Time was too essential. In the dark she worked briskly. In the amber light, her movements flowed with the same rhythm. As one set of negatives was developed and hung to dry, she went on to the next, then the next. When at length she could switch on the overhead light, Bryan arched her back, stretched her shoulders and relaxed.

An idle glance around showed her that she'd forgotten the carryout drink she'd picked up on the way. Unconcerned, she took a long gulp of lukewarm, watered-down soda.

The work satisfied her—the precision it required. Now her thoughts were skipping ahead to the prints. Only then would the creativity be fully satisfied. She had time, she noticed as she took a quick glance at her watch, to fuss with the negatives a bit before he came back. But then she'd end up putting herself in the same position she'd put him in—leaving something half done. Instead, mildly curious, she walked over to study his proofs.

Impressive, she decided, but then she'd expected no less. She might just be inclined to beg for a blowup of the old man in the baseball cap. Not Shade's usual style, she mused as she bent over the strip. It was so rare that he focused in on one person and let the emotions flow. The man who'd taken it had once told her he had no compassion. Bryan shook her head as she skimmed over other proofs. Did Shade believe that, or did he simply want the rest of the world to?

Then she saw herself and stopped with a kind of dazed wonder. Of course she remembered Shade setting up that picture, amusing, then arousing her while he changed angles and f-stops. The way he'd touched her… It wasn't something she'd forget, so it shouldn't surprise her to see the proof. Yet it did more than surprise her.

Not quite steady, Bryan picked up a magnifying glass and held it over one tiny square. She looked…pliant. She heard her own nervous swallow as she looked deeper. She looked…soft. It could be her imagination or, more likely, the skill of the photographer. She looked…in love.

Slowly, Bryan set down the glass and straightened. The skill of the photographer, she repeated, fighting to believe it. A trick of the angle, of the light and shadows. What a photographer captured on film wasn't always the truth. It was often illusion, often that vague blur between truth and illusion.

A woman knew when she loved. That's what Bryan told herself. A woman knew when she'd given her heart. It wasn't something that could happen and not be felt.

She closed her eyes a moment and listened to the quiet. Was there anything she hadn't felt when it came to Shade? How much longer was she going to pretend that passion, needs, longings, stood on their own? Love had bound them together. Love had cemented them into something solid and strong and undeniable.

She turned to where her negatives hung. There was one she'd managed to ignore. There was one tiny slice of film she'd taken on impulse and then buried because she'd come to be afraid of the answer she'd find. Now, when she had the answer already, Bryan stared at it.

It was reversed, so that his hair was light, his face dark. The little sliver of river in the corner was white, like the oars in his hands. But she saw him clearly.

His eyes were too intense, though his body seemed relaxed. Would he ever allow his mind true rest? His face was hard, lean, with the only tangible sensitivity around his mouth. He was a man, Bryan knew, who'd have little patience with mistakes—his own or others'. He was a man with a rigid sense of what was important. And he was a man who was capable of harnessing his own emotions and denying them to another. What he gave, when he gave, would be on his terms.

She knew, and understood, and loved regardless.

She'd loved before, and love had made more sense then. At least it had seemed to. Still, in the end, love hadn't been enough. What did she know about making love work? Could she possibly believe that when she'd failed once, she could succeed with a man like Shade?

She loved now, and told herself she was wise enough, strong enough, to let him go.

Rule number one, Bryan reminded herself as she put the darkroom in order. No complications. It was a litany she had running through her head until Shade knocked on the door. When she opened it for him, she nearly believed it.

They'd reached the last stop, the last day. Summer was not, as some would wish it, endless. Perhaps the weather would stay balmy for weeks longer. Flowers might still bloom defiantly, but just as Bryan had considered the last day of school summer's conception, so did she consider the Labor Day weekend its demise.

Clambakes, beach parties, bonfires. Hot beaches and cool water. That was Cape Cod. There were volleyball games in the sand and blasting portable radios. Teenagers perfected the tans they'd show off during those first few weeks of school. Families took to the water in a last, frantic rush before autumn signaled the end. Backyard barbecues smoked. Baseball hung on gamely before football could push its way through. As if it knew its time was limited, summer poured on the heat.

Bryan didn't mind. She wanted this last weekend to be everything summer could be—hot, hazy, torrid. She wanted her last weekend with Shade to reflect it. Love could be disguised with passion. She could let herself flow with it. Long, steamy days led to long, steamy nights, and Bryan held on to them.

If her lovemaking was a little frantic, if her desires were a little desperate, she could blame it on the heat. While Bryan became more aggressive, Shade became more gentle.

He'd noticed the change. Though he'd said nothing, Shade had noticed it the night he'd come back to meet her at the darkroom. Perhaps because she rarely had nerves, Bryan thought she hid them well. Shade could almost see them jump every time he looked at her.

Bryan had made a decision in the darkroom—a decision she felt would be best for both herself and for Shade. Shade had made a decision in the darkroom as well, the day after, when he'd watched the print of Bryan slowly come to life.

On the ride east, they'd become lovers. Now he had

to find a way on the ride west to court her, as a man does the woman he wants to spend his life with.

Gentleness came first, though he wasn't an expert at it. Pressure, if it came to that, could be applied later. He was more experienced there.

"What a day." After long hours walking, watching and shooting, Bryan dropped down on the back of the van where the doors were open wide to let in the breeze. "I can't believe how many half-naked people I've seen." Grinning at Shade, she arched her back. She wore nothing but her sleek red bathing suit and a loose white cover-up that drooped over one shoulder.

"You seem to fit right in."

Lazily, she lifted one leg and examined it. "Well, it's nice to know that this assignment hasn't ruined my tan." Yawning, she stretched. "We've got a couple more hours of sun. Why don't you put on something indecent and walk down to the beach with me?" She rose, lifting her arms so they could wind easily around his neck. "We could cool off in the water." She touched her lips to his, teasing, taunting. "Then we could come back and heat up again."

"I like the second part." He turned the kiss into something staggering with an increase of pressure and change of angle. Beneath his hands, he felt her sigh. "Why don't you go ahead down, do the cooling-off? I've got some things to do."

With her head resting against his shoulder, Bryan struggled not to ask again. She wanted him to go with her, be with her every second they had left. Tomorrow she'd have to tell him that she'd made arrangements

to fly back to the Coast. This was their last night, but
only she knew it.

"All right." She managed to smile as she drew away.
"I can't resist the beach when we're camped so close.
I'll be back in a couple hours."

"Have fun." He gave her a quick, absent kiss and
didn't watch as she walked away. If he had, he might've
seen her hesitate and start back once, only to turn
around again and walk on.

The air had cooled by the time Bryan started back
to the van. It chilled her skin, a sure sign that summer
was on its last legs. Bonfires were set and ready to light
down on the beach. In the distance, Bryan heard a few
hesitant, amateur guitar chords. It wouldn't be a quiet
night, she decided as she passed two other campsites
on the way to the van.

She paused a moment to look toward the water, tossing her hair back. It was loose from its braid and slightly
damp from her dip in the Atlantic. Idly she considered
grabbing her shampoo out of the van and taking a quick
trip to the showers. She could do that before she threw
together a cold sandwich. In an hour or two, when the
bonfires were going steadily, and the music was at its
peak, she and Shade would go back down and work.

For the last time, she thought as she reached for the
door of the van.

At first, she stood blinking, confused by the low,
flickering light. Candles, she saw, baffled. Candles and
white linen. There on the little collapsible table they
sometimes set between the bunks were a fresh, snowy
cloth and two red tapers in glass holders. There were

red linen napkins folded at angles. A rosebud stood in a narrow, clear glass vase. On the little radio in the back was low, soft music.

At the narrow makeshift counter was Shade, legs spread as he added a sprinkling of alfalfa to a salad.

"Have a nice swim?" he said casually, as if she'd climbed into the van every evening to just such a scene.

"Yeah, I... Shade, where did you get all this?"

"Took a quick trip into town. Hope you like your shrimp spicy. I made it to my taste."

She could smell it. Over the scent of candle wax, under the fragrance of the single rose, was the rich, ripe aroma of spiced shrimp. With a laugh, Bryan moved to the table and ran a finger down one of the tapers. "How did you manage all this?"

"I've been called adept occasionally." She looked up from the candle to him. Her face was lovely, clean-lined. In the soft light, her eyes were dark, mysterious. But above all he saw her lips curve hesitantly as she reached out for him.

"You did this for me."

He touched her, lightly, just a hand to her hair. Both of them felt something shimmer. "I intend to eat, too."

"I don't know what to say." She felt her eyes fill and didn't bother to blink the tears back. "I really don't."

He lifted her hand and, with a simplicity he'd never shown, kissed her fingers, one by one. "Try thanks."

She swallowed and whispered. "Thanks."

"Hungry?"

"Always. But..." In a gesture that always moved him, she lifted her hands to his face. "Some things are more important."

Bryan brought her lips to his. It was a taste he could drown in—a taste he could now admit he wanted to drown in. Moving slowly, gently, he brought her into his arms.

Their bodies fit. Bryan knew it was so, and ached from the knowledge. Even their breathing seemed to merge until she was certain their hearts beat at precisely the same rhythm. He ran his hands under her shirt, along her back, where the skin was still damp from the sea.

Touch me. She drew him closer, as if her body could shout the words to him.

Savor me. Her mouth was suddenly avid, hot and open, as if with lips alone she could draw what she needed from him.

Love me. Her hands moved over him as if she could touch the emotion she wanted. Touch it, hold it, keep it—if only for one night.

He could smell the sea on her, and the summer and the evening. He could feel the passion as her body pressed against his. Needs, demands, desires—they could be tasted as his mouth drew from hers. But tonight he found he needed to hear the words. Too soon, his mind warned as he began to lose himself. It was too soon to ask, too soon to tell. She'd need time, he thought, time and more finesse than he was accustomed to employing.

But even when he drew her away, he wasn't able to let go. Looking down at her, he saw his own beginning. Whatever he'd seen and done in the past, whatever memories he had, were unimportant. There was only one vital thing in his life, and he held it in his arms.

"I want to make love with you."

Her breath was already unsteady, her body trembling. "Yes."

His hands tightened on her as he tried to be logical. "Room's at a premium."

This time she smiled and drew him closer. "We have the floor." She pulled him down with her.

Later, when her mind was clearer and her blood cooler, Bryan would remember only the tumult of feeling, only the flood of sensation. She wouldn't be able to separate the dizzying feel of his mouth on her skin from the heady taste of his under hers.

She'd know that his passion had never been more intense, more relentless, but she wouldn't be able to say how she'd known. Had it been the frantic way he'd said her name? Had it been the desperate way he'd pulled the snug suit down her body, exploiting, ravishing, as he went?

She understood that her own feelings had reached an apex she could never express with words. Words were inadequate. She could only show him. Love, regrets, desires, wishes, had all culminated to whirl inside her until she'd clung to him. And when they'd given each other all they could, she clung still, holding the moment to her as she might a photograph faded after years of looking.

As she lay against him, her head on his chest, she smiled. They had given each other all they could. What more could anyone ask? With her eyes still closed, she pressed her lips against his chest. Nothing would spoil the night. Tonight they'd have candlelight and laughter. She'd never forget it.

"I hope you bought plenty of shrimp," she murmured. "I'm starving."

"I bought enough to feed an average person and a greedy one."

Grinning, she sat up. "Good." With a rare show of energy, she struggled back into the bulky cover-up and sprang up. Bending over the pot of shrimp, she breathed deep. "Wonderful. I didn't know you were so talented."

"I decided it was time I let you in on some of my more admirable qualities."

With a half smile, she looked back to see him slipping on his shorts. "Oh?"

"Yeah. After all, we've got to travel a long way together yet." He sent her a quiet, enigmatic look. "A long way."

"I don't—" She stopped herself and turned to toy with the salad. "This looks good," she began, too brightly.

"Bryan." He stopped her before she could reach in the cupboard above for bowls. "What is it?"

"Nothing." Did he always have to see? she demanded. Couldn't she hide anything from him?

He stepped over, took her arms and held her face to face. "What?"

"Let's talk about it tomorrow, all right?" The brightness was still there, straining. "I'm really hungry. The shrimp's cool by now, so—"

"Now." With a quick shake, he reminded both of them that his patience only stretched so far.

"I've decided to fly back," she blurted out. "I can get a flight out tomorrow afternoon."

He went very still, but she was too busy working out

her explanation to notice just how dangerously still. "Why?"

"I've had to reschedule like crazy to fit in this assignment. The extra time I'd get would ease things." It sounded weak. It was weak.

"Why?"

She opened her mouth, prepared to give him a variation on the same theme. One look from him stopped her. "I just want to get back," she managed. "I know you'd like company on the drive, but the assignment's finished. Odds are you'll make better time without me."

He fought back the anger. Anger wasn't the way. If he'd given in to it, he'd have shouted, raged, threatened. That wasn't the way. "No," he said simply, and left it at that.

"No?"

"You're not flying back tomorrow." His voice was calm, but his eyes said a great deal more. "We go together, Bryan."

She braced herself. An argument, she decided, would be easy. "Now look—"

"Sit down."

Haughtiness came to her rarely, but when it did, it was exceptional. "I beg your pardon?"

For an answer, Shade gave her a quick shove onto the bench. Without speaking, he pulled open a drawer and took out the manila envelope that held his most recently developed prints. Tossing them onto the table, he pulled out the one of Bryan.

"What do you see?" he demanded.

"Myself." She cleared her throat. "I see myself, of course."

"Not good enough."

"That's what I see," she tossed back, but she didn't look down at the print again. "That's all there is."

Perhaps fear played a part in his actions. He didn't want to admit it. But it was fear, fear that he'd imagined something that wasn't there. "You see yourself, yes. A beautiful woman, a desirable woman. A woman," he continued slowly, "looking at the man she loves."

He'd stripped her. Bryan felt it as though he'd actually peeled off layer after layer of pretense, defense, disguise. She'd seen the same thing in the image he'd frozen on film. She'd seen it, but what gave him the right to strip her?

"You take too much," she said in a quiet voice. Rising, she turned away from him. "Too damned much."

Relief poured through him. He had to close his eyes on it for a moment. Not imagination, not illusion, but truth. Love was there, and with it, his beginning. "You've already given it."

"No." Bryan turned back, holding on to what she had left. "I haven't given it. What I feel is my responsibility. I haven't asked you for anything, and I won't." She took a deep breath. "We agreed, Shade. No complications."

"Then it looks like we both reneged, doesn't it?" He grabbed her hand before she could move out of reach. "Look at me." His face was close, candlelight flickering over it. Somehow the soft light illuminated what he'd seen, what he'd lived through, what he'd overcome. "Don't you see anything when you look at me? Can you see more in a stranger on the beach, a woman in a crowd, a kid on a street corner, than you do when you look at me?"

"Don't—" she began, only to be cut off.

"What do you see?"

"I see a man," she said, speaking quickly, passionately. "A man who's had to see more than he should. I see a man who's learned to keep his feelings carefully controlled because he isn't quite sure what would happen if he let loose. I see a cynic who hasn't been able to completely stamp out his own sensitivity, his own empathy."

"True enough," he returned evenly, though it was both more and less than he'd wanted to hear. "What else?"

"Nothing," she told him, close to panic. "Nothing."

It wasn't enough. The frustration came through; she could feel it in his hands. "Where's your perception now? Where's the insight that takes you under the glitter of some temperamental leading man to the core? I want you to see into me, Bryan."

"I can't." The words came out on a shudder. "I'm afraid to."

Afraid? He'd never considered it. She took emotions in stride, sought them, dug for them. He loosened his grip on her and said the words that were the most difficult for him to speak. "I love you."

She felt the words slam into her, knocking her breathless. If he said them, he meant them, of that she could be sure. Had she been so caught up in her own feelings that she hadn't seen his? It was tempting, it would be easy, to simply go into his arms and take the risk. But she remembered that they'd both risked before, and failed.

"Shade..." She tried to think calmly, but his words of love still rang in her head. "I don't—you can't—"

"I want to hear you say it." He held her close again. There was no place to go. "I want you to look at me, knowing everything you've said about me is true, and tell me."

"It couldn't work," she began quickly, because her knees were shaking. "It couldn't, don't you see? I'd want it all because I'm just idiot enough to think maybe this time—with you… Marriage, children, that's not what you want, and I understand. I didn't think I wanted them either, until everything got so out of control."

He was calmer now, as she became more frazzled. "You haven't told me yet."

"All right." She nearly shouted it. "All right then, I love you, but I—"

He closed his mouth over hers so there could be no excuses. For now, he could simply drink in the words and all they meant to him. Salvation. He could believe in it.

"You've a hell of a nerve," he said against her mouth, "telling me what I want."

"Shade, please." Giving in to the weakness, she dropped her head on his shoulder. "I didn't want to complicate things. I don't want to now. If I fly back, it'll give us both time to put things back in perspective. My work, your work—"

"Are important," he finished. "But not as important as this." He waited until her eyes slowly lifted to his. Now his voice was calm again. His grip eased, still holding her but without the desperation. "Nothing is, Bryan. You didn't want it, maybe I thought I didn't, but I know better now. Everything started with you. Everything important. You make me clean." He ran a hand through her hair. "God, you make me hope again, believe again. Do you think I'm going to let you take all that away from me?"

The doubts began to fade, quietly, slowly. Second chances? Hadn't she always believed in them? Long shots, she remembered. You only had to want to win badly enough.

"No," she murmured. "But I need a promise. I need the promise, Shade, and then I think we could do anything."

So did he. "I promise to love you, to respect you. To care for you whether you like it or not. And I promise that what I am is yours." Reaching up, he flipped open the cupboard door. Speechless, Bryan watched him draw out a tiny cardboard pot of pansies. Their scent was light and sweet and lasting.

"Plant them with me, Bryan."

Her hands closed over his. Hadn't she always believed life was as simple as you made it? "As soon as we're home."

Epilogue

"Cooperate, will you?"

"No." Amused, but not altogether pleased, Shade watched Bryan adjust the umbrellas beside and behind him. It seemed to him she'd been fiddling with the lighting a great deal longer than necessary.

"You said I could have anything I wanted for Christmas," she reminded him as she held the light meter up to his face. "I want this picture."

"It was a weak moment," he mumbled.

"Tough." Unsympathetic, Bryan stepped back to study the angles. There, the lighting was perfect, the shadows just where they should be. But... A long-suffering sigh came out. "Shade, stop glowering, will you?"

"I said you could take the picture. I didn't say it'd be pretty."

"No chance of that," she said under her breath.

Exasperated, she brushed at her hair, and the thin gold band on her left hand caught the light. Shade watched it glimmer with the same sort of odd pleasure he always felt when it hit him that they were a team, in every way. With a grin, he joined his left hand with hers, so that the twin rings they wore touched lightly.

"Sure you want this picture for Christmas? I'd thought of buying you ten pounds of French chocolate."

She narrowed her eyes, but her fingers laced with his. "A low blow, Colby. Dead low." Refusing to be distracted, she backed off. "I'll have my picture," she told him. "And if you want to be nasty, I'll buy my own chocolate. Some husbands," she continued as she walked back to the camera set on a tripod, "would cater to their wife's every whim when she's in my delicate condition."

He glanced down at the flat stomach under baggy overalls. It still dazed him that there was life growing there. Their life. When summer came again, they'd hold their first child. It wouldn't do to let her know he had to fight the urge to pamper her, to coddle her every moment. Instead, Shade shrugged and dipped his hands in his pockets.

"Not this one," he said lightly. "You knew what you were getting when you married me."

She looked at him through the viewfinder. His hands were in his pockets, but he wasn't relaxed. As always, his body was ready to move, his mind moving already. But in his eyes she saw the pleasure, the kindness and the love. Together they were making it work. He didn't smile, but Bryan did as she clicked the shutter.

"So I did," she murmured.

* * * * *

TEMPTATION

This book is dedicated with gratitude and affection to Nancy Jackson.

Chapter 1

"If there's one thing I hate," Eden mumbled, "it's six o'clock in the morning."

Sunlight poured through the thinly screened windows of the cabin and fell on the wooden floor, the metal bars of her bunk, and her face. The sound of the morning bell echoed dully in her head. Though she'd known that long, clanging ring for only three days, Eden already hated it.

For one fanciful moment, she buried her face under the pillow, imagining herself cuddled in her big four-poster. The Irish-linen sheets would smell ever-so-slightly of lemon. In her airy pastel bedroom, the curtains would be drawn against the morning, the scent of fresh flowers sweetening the air.

The pillowcase smelled of feathers and detergent.

With a grunt, Eden tossed the pillow to the floor,

then struggled to sit up. Now that the morning bell had stopped, she could hear the cries of a couple of excited crows. From the cabin directly across the compound came a happy blast of rock music. With glazed eyes, she watched Candice Bartholomew bound out of the adjoining bunk. Her sharp-featured pixie's face was split by a grin.

"Morning." Candy's long, clever fingers ran through her thatch of red hair like scoops, causing it to bounce into further disarray. Candy was, Eden had always thought, all bounce. "It's a beautiful day," she announced, in a voice as cheerful as the rest of her. Watching her friend stretch in frilly baby-doll pajamas, Eden gave another noncommittal grunt. She swung her bare legs off the mattress and contemplated the accomplishment of putting her feet on the floor.

"I could grow to hate you." Eden's voice, still husky with sleep, carried the rounded tones of her finishing-school education. Eyes shut, she pushed her own tousled blond hair away from her face.

Grinning, Candy tossed open the cabin door so that she could breathe in the fresh morning air while she studied her friend. The strong summer sunlight shot through Eden's pale hair, making it look fragile where it lay against her forehead and cheeks. Her eyes remained shut. Her slender shoulders slumped, she let out an enormous yawn. Candy wisely said nothing, knowing Eden didn't share her enthusiasm for sunrise.

"It can't be morning," Eden grumbled. "I swear I only lay down five minutes ago." Resting her elbows on her knees, she dropped her face into her hands. Her complexion was creamy, with just a suggestion of rose on the crest of her cheekbones. Her nose was small, with a hint of an upward tilt at the tip. What might have been a coolly aristocratic face was gentled by a full, generous mouth.

Candy took in one last breath of air, then shut the door. "All you need is a shower and some coffee. The first week of camp's the toughest, remember?"

Eden opened wide, lake-blue eyes. "Easy for you to say. You're not the one who fell in the poison ivy."

"Still itching?"

"A little." Because her own foul mood was making her feel guilty, Eden managed a smile. Everything softened, eyes, mouth, voice. "In any case, this is the first time we're the campees instead of the campers." Letting out another fierce yawn, she rose and tugged on a robe. The air coming through the screens was fresh as a daisy, and chilly enough to make Eden's toes curl. She wished she could remember what she'd done with her slippers.

"Try under the bunk," Candy suggested.

Eden bent down and found them. They were embroidered pink silk, hardly practical, but it hadn't seemed worthwhile to invest in another pair. Putting them on gave her an excuse to sit down again. "Do you really think five consecutive summers at Camp Forden for Girls prepared us for this?"

Haunted by her own doubts, Candy clasped her hands together. "Eden, are you having second thoughts?"

Because she recognized distress in the bubbly voice, Eden buried her own doubts. She had both a financial and emotional interest in the newly formed Camp Liberty. Complaining wasn't going to put her on the road to success. With a shake of her head, she walked over to squeeze Candy's shoulder. "What I have is a terminal case of morning crankiness. Let me get that shower, then I'll be ready to face our twenty-seven tenants."

"Eden." Candy stopped her before she closed the bathroom door. "It's going to work, for both of us. I know it."

"I know it, too." Eden closed the bathroom door and leaned against it. She could admit it now, while she was alone. She was scared to death. Her last dime, and her last ray of hope, were tied up in the six cabins, the stables and the cafeteria that were Camp Liberty. What did Eden Carlbough, former Philadelphia socialite, know about managing a girls' summer camp? Just enough to terrify her.

If she failed now, with this, could she pick up the pieces and go on? Would there be any pieces left? Confidence was what was needed, she told herself as she turned the taps on. Once inside the narrow shower stall, she gave the tap optimistically marked HOT another twist. Water, lukewarm, dripped out halfheartedly. Confidence, Eden thought again as she shivered under the miserly spray. Plus some cold hard cash and a whole barrel of luck.

She found the soap and began to lather with the soft-scented French milled she still allowed herself to indulge in. A year ago she would never have considered something as lowly as soap an indulgence.

A year ago.

Eden turned so that the rapidly cooling water hit her back. A year ago she would have risen at eight, had a leisurely, steaming shower, then breakfasted on toast

and coffee, perhaps some shirred eggs. Sometime before ten, she would have driven to the library for her
volunteer morning. There would have been lunch with
Eric, perhaps at the Deux Cheminées before she gave
her afternoon to the museum or one of Aunt Dottie's
charities.

The biggest decision she might have made was
whether to wear her rose silk suit or her ivory linen.
Her evening might have been spent quietly at home, or
at one of Philadelphia's elegant dinner parties.

No pressure. No problems. But then, Papa had been
alive.

Eden sighed as she rinsed away the last of the lather.
The light French scent clung to her even as she dried her
skin with the serviceable camp-issue towel. When her
father had been alive, she had thought that money was
simply something to spend and that time was forever.
She had been raised to plan a menu, but not to cook; to
run a home, but not to clean it.

Throughout her childhood, she had been carelessly
happy with her widowed father in the ageless elegance
of their Philadelphia home. There had always been party
dresses and cotillions, afternoon teas and riding lessons.
The Carlbough name was an old and respected one. The
Carlbough money had been a simple fact of life.

How quickly and finally things could change.

Now she was giving riding instructions and juggling
columns in a ledger with the vain hope that one and one
didn't always make two.

Because the tiny mirror over the tiny sink was dripping with condensation, Eden rubbed it with the towel.
She took a miserly dab of the half pot of imported

face cream she had left. She was going to make it last through the summer. If *she* lasted through the summer herself, another pot would be her reward.

Eden found the cabin empty when she opened the bathroom door. If she knew Candy, and after twenty years she certainly did, the redhead would be down with the girls already. How easily she became acclimatized, Eden thought; then she reminded herself it was time she did the same. She took her jeans and her red T-shirt with CAMP LIBERTY emblazoned on the chest, and began to dress. Even as a teenager, Eden had rarely dressed so casually.

She had enjoyed her social life—the parties, the well-chaperoned ski trips to Vermont, the trips to New York for shopping or the theater, the vacations in Europe. The prospect of earning a living had never been considered, by her, or her father. Carlbough women didn't work, they chaired committees.

College years had been spent with the idea of rounding out her education rather than focusing on a career. At twenty-three, Eden was forced to admit she was qualified to do absolutely nothing.

She could have blamed her father. But how could she blame a man who had been so indulgent and loving? She had adored him. She could blame herself for being naive and shortsighted, but she could never blame her father. Even now, a year after his sudden death, she still felt pangs of grief.

She could deal with that. The one thing she had been taught to do, the one thing she felt herself fully qualified to accomplish, was to cover emotion with poise, with control, or with disdain. She could go day after day, week after week through the summer, surrounded by the girls at camp and the counselors Candy had hired, and none of them would know she still mourned her father. Or that her pride had been shattered by Eric Keeton.

Eric, the promising young banker with her father's firm. Eric, always so charming, so attentive, so suitable. It had been during her last year of college that she had accepted his ring and made her promises to him. And he had made promises to her.

When she discovered the hurt was still there, Eden coated it, layer by layer, with anger. Facing the mirror, she tugged her hair back in a short ponytail, a style her hairdresser would have shuddered at.

It was more practical, Eden told her reflection. She was a practical woman now, and hair waving softly to the shoulders would just have got in the way during the riding lessons she was to give that morning.

For a moment, she pressed her fingers against her eyes. Why were the mornings always the worst? She would wake, expecting to come out of some bad dream and find herself at home again. But it wasn't her home any longer. There were strangers living in it now. Brian Carlbough's death had not been a bad dream, but a horrible, horrible reality.

A sudden heart attack had taken him overnight, leaving Eden stunned with shock and grief. Even before the grief could fade, Eden had been struck with another shock.

There had been lawyers, black-vested lawyers with long, technical monologues. They had had offices that had smelled of old leather and fresh polish. With solemn faces and politely folded hands, they had shattered her world.

Poor investments, she had been told, bad market trends, mortgages, second mortgages, short-term loans. The simple fact had been, once the details had been sifted through, there had been no money.

Brian Carlbough had been a gambler. At the time of his death, his luck had turned, and he hadn't had time to recoup his losses. His daughter had been forced to liquidate his assets in order to pay off the debts. The house she had grown up in and loved was gone. She had still been numbed by grief when she had found herself without a home or an income. Crashing down on top of that had been Eric's betrayal.

Eden yanked open the cabin door and was met by the balmy morning air of the mountains. The breathtaking view of greening hills and blue sky didn't affect her. She was back in Philadelphia, hearing Eric's calm, reasonable voice.

The scandal, she remembered and began marching toward the big cabin where mess would be served. *His* reputation. *His* career. Everything she had loved had been taken away, but he had only been concerned with how he might be affected.

He had never loved her. Eden jammed her hands into her pockets and kept walking. She'd been a fool not to see it from the beginning. But she'd learned, Eden reminded herself. How she'd learned. It had simply been a merger to Eric, the Carlbough name, the Carlbough money and reputation. When they had been destroyed, he had cut his losses.

Eden slowed her quick pace, realizing she was out

of breath, not from exertion but from temper. It would never do to walk into breakfast with her face flushed and her eyes gleaming. Giving herself a moment, she took a few deep breaths and looked around her.

The air was still cool, but by midmorning the sun would be warm and strong. Summer had barely begun.

And it was beautiful. Lining the compound were a half-dozen small cabins with their window flaps open to the morning. The sound of girlish laughter floated through the windows. Along the pathway between cabins four and five was a scattering of anemones. A dogwood, with a few stubborn blooms clinging to it, stood nearby. Above cabin two, a mockingbird chattered.

Beyond the main camp to the west were rolling hills, deeply green. Grazing horses and trees dotted them. There was an openness here, a sense of space which Eden found incredible. Her life had always been focused on the city. Streets, buildings, traffic, people, those had been the familiar. There were times when she felt a quick pang of need for what had been. It was still possible for her to have all that. Aunt Dottie had offered her home and her love. No one would ever know how long and hard Eden had wrestled with the temptation to accept the invitation and let her life drift.

Perhaps gambling was in Eden's blood, too. Why else would she have sunk what ready cash she had had left into a fledgling camp for girls in the hills?

Because she had had to try, Eden reminded herself. She had had to take the risk on her own. She could never go back into the shell of the fragile porcelain doll she had been. Here, centered in such open space, she would take the time to learn about herself. What was inside

Eden Carlbough? Maybe, just maybe, by expanding her horizons, she would find her place.

Candy was right. Eden took a long last breath. It was going to work. They were going to make it work.

"Hungry?" Her hair damp from whatever shower she'd popped into, Candy cut across Eden's path.

"Starved." Content, Eden swung a friendly arm around Candy's shoulder. "Where did you run off to?"

"You know me, I can't let any part of this place run by itself." Like Eden, Candy swept her gaze over the camp. Her expression reflected everything inside her— the love, the fear, the fierce pride. "I was worried about you."

"Candy, I told you, I was just cranky this morning." Eden watched a group of girls rush out of a cabin and head for breakfast.

"Eden, we've been friends since we were six months old. No one knows better than I what you're going through."

No, no one did, and since Candy was the person she loved best, Eden determined to do a better job of concealing the wounds that were still open. "I've put it behind me, Candy."

"Maybe. But I know that the camp was initially my venture, and that I roped you in."

"You didn't rope me in. I wanted to invest. We both know it was a pitifully small amount."

"Not to me. The extra money made it possible for me to include the equestrian program. Then, when you agreed to come in and give riding lessons…"

"Just keeping a close eye on my investment," Eden said lightly. "Next year I won't be a part-time riding instructor and bookkeeper. I'll be a full-fledged counselor. No regrets, Candy." This time she meant it. "It's ours."

"And the bank's."

Eden shrugged that away. "We need this place. You, because it's what you've always wanted to do, always worked and studied toward. Me..." She hesitated, then sighed. "Let's face it, I haven't got anything else. The camp's putting a roof over my head, giving me three meals a day and a goal. I need to prove I can make it."

"People think we're crazy."

The pride came back, with a feeling of recklessness Eden was just learning to savor. "Let them."

With a laugh, Candy tugged at Eden's hair. "Let's eat."

Two hours later, Eden was winding up the day's first riding lesson. This was her specialty, her contribution to the partnership she and Candy had made. It had also been decided to trust Eden with the books, mainly because no one could have been more inept with figures than Candice Bartholomew.

Candy had interviewed and hired a staff of counselors, a nutritionist and a nurse. They hoped to have a pool and a swimming instructor one day, but for now there was supervised swimming and rowing on the lake, arts and crafts, hiking and archery. Candy had spent months refining a program for the summer, while Eden had juggled the profit-and-loss statements. She prayed the money would hold out while Candy ordered supplies.

Unlike Candy, Eden wasn't certain the first week of camp would be the toughest. Her partner had all the training, all the qualifications for running the camp, but Candy also had an optimist's flair for overlooking details like red ink on the books.

Pushing those thoughts aside, Eden signaled from the center of the corral. "That's all for today." She scanned the six young faces under their black riding hats. "You're doing very well."

"When can we gallop, Miss Carlbough?"

"After you learn to trot." She patted one of the horses' flanks. Wouldn't it be lovely, she thought, to gallop off into the hills, riding so fast even memories couldn't follow? Foolish, Eden told herself; she gave her attention back to the girls. "Dismount, then cool down your horses. Remember, they depend on you." The breeze tossed her bangs, and she brushed at them absently. "Remember to put all the tack in its proper place for the next class."

This caused the groans she expected. Riding and playing with the horses was one thing, tidying up afterward was another. Eden considered exerting discipline without causing resentment another accomplishment. Over the past week, she'd learned to link the girls' faces and names. The eleven-and twelve-year-olds in her group had an enthusiasm that kept her on her toes. She'd already separated in her mind the two or three she instructed who had the kind of horse fever she recognized from her own adolescence. It was rewarding, after an hour on her feet in the sun, to answer the rapid-fire questions. Ultimately, one by one, she nudged them toward the stables.

"Eden!" Turning, she spotted Candy hustling toward her. Even from a distance, Eden recognized concern.

"What's happened?"

"We're missing three kids."

"What?" Panic came first, and quickly. Years of training had her pulling it back. "What do you mean, missing?"

"I mean they're nowhere in camp. Roberta Snow, Linda Hopkins and Marcie Jamison." Candy dragged a hand through her hair, a habitual gesture of tension. "Barbara was lining up her group for rowing, and they didn't show. We've looked everywhere."

"We can't panic," Eden said, as much to warn herself as Candy. "Roberta Snow? Isn't she the little brunette who stuck a lizard down one of the other girls' shirts? And the one who set off the morning bell at 3:00 a.m.?"

"Yes, that's her." Candy set her teeth. "The little darling. Judge Harper Snow's granddaughter. If she's skinned her knee, we'll probably face a lawsuit." With a shake of her head, Candy switched to an undertone. "The last anyone saw of her this morning, she was walking east." She pointed a finger, paint-spattered from her early art class. "No one noticed the other girls, but my bet is that they're with her. Darling Roberta is an inveterate leader."

"If she's walking that way, wouldn't she run into that apple orchard?"

"Yeah." Candy shut her eyes. "Oh, yeah. I'm going to have six girls up to their wrists in modeling clay in ten minutes, or I'd go off myself. Eden, I'm almost sure they headed for the orchard. One of the other girls admitted she heard Roberta planning to sneak over there for a few samples. We don't want any trouble with the owner. He's letting us use his lake only because I begged, shamelessly. He wasn't thrilled about having a girls' summer camp for a neighbor."

"Well, he has one," Eden pointed out. "So we'll all have to deal with it. I'm the one most easily spared around here, so I'll go after them."

"I was hoping you'd say that. Seriously, Eden, if they've snuck into that orchard, which I'd bet my last dime they have, we could be in for it. The man made no bones about how he feels about his land and his privacy."

"Three little girls are hardly going to do any damage to a bunch of apple trees." Eden began to walk, with Candy scurrying to keep pace.

"He's Chase Elliot. You know, Elliot Apples? Juice, cider, sauce, jelly, chocolate-covered apple seeds, whatever can be made from an apple, they do it. He made it abundantly clear that he didn't want to find any little girls climbing his trees."

"He won't find them, I will." Leaving Candy behind, Eden swung over a fence.

"Put Roberta on a leash when you catch up to her." Candy watched her disappear through the trees.

Eden followed the path from the camp, pleased when she found a crumpled candy wrapper. Roberta. With a grim smile, Eden picked it up and stuffed it in her pocket. Judge Snow's granddaughter had already earned a reputation for her stash of sweets.

It was warm now, but the path veered through a cool grove of aspens. Sunlight dappled the ground, making the walk, if not her errand, pleasant. Squirrels dashed here and there, confident enough in their own speed not to be alarmed at Eden's intrusion. Once a rabbit darted across her path, and disappeared into the brush with a frantic rustle. Overhead a woodpecker drummed, sending out an echo.

It occurred to Eden that she was more completely alone than she had ever been before. No civilization here. She bent down for another candy wrapper. Well, very little of it.

There were new scents here, earth, animal, vegetation, to be discovered. Wildflowers sprang up, tougher and more resilient than hothouse roses. It pleased her that she was even beginning to be able to recognize a few. They came back, year after year, without pampering, taking what came and thriving on it. They gave her hope. She could find a place here. Had found a place, she corrected herself. Her friends in Philadelphia might think her mad, but she was beginning to enjoy it.

The grove of aspens thinned abruptly, and the sunlight was strong again. She blinked against it, then shielded her eyes as she scanned the Elliot orchards.

Apple trees stretched ahead of her as far as she could see, to the north, south and east. Row after row after row of trees lined the slopes. Some of them were old and gnarled, some young and straight. Instantly she thought of early spring and the overwhelming scent of apple blossoms.

It would be magnificent, she thought as she stepped up to the fence that separated the properties. The fragrance, the pretty white-and-pink blossoms, the freshly green leaves, would be a marvelous sight. Now the leaves were dark and thick, and instead of blossoms, she could see fruit in the trees closest to her. Small, shiny, and green they hung, waiting for the sun to ripen them.

How many times had she eaten applesauce that had begun right here? The idea made her smile as she began to climb the fence. Her vision of an orchard had been a lazy little grove guarded by an old man in overalls. A quaint picture, but nothing as huge and impressive as the reality.

The sound of giggling took her by surprise. Shifting toward the direction of the sound, Eden watched an apple fall from a tree and roll toward her feet. Bending, she picked it up, tossing it away as she walked closer. When she looked up, she spotted three pairs of sneakers beneath the cover of leaves and branches.

"Ladies." Eden spoke coolly and was rewarded by three startled gasps. "Apparently you took a wrong turn on your way to the lake."

Roberta's triangular, freckled face appeared through the leaves. "Hi, Miss Carlbough. Would you like an apple?"

The devil. But even as she thought it, Eden had to tighten her lips against a smile. "Down," she said simply, then stepped closer to the trunk to assist.

They didn't need her. Three agile little bodies scrambled down and dropped lightly onto the ground. In a gesture she knew could be intimidating, Eden lifted her left eyebrow.

"I'm sure you're aware that leaving camp property unsupervised and without permission is against the rules."

"Yes, Miss Carlbough." The response would have been humble if it hadn't been for the gleam in Roberta's eye.

"Since none of you seem interested in rowing today,

Mrs. Petrie has a great deal of washing up to be done in the kitchen." Pleased by her own inspiration, Eden decided Candy would approve. "You're to report to Miss Bartholomew, then to Mrs. Petrie for kitchen detail."

Only two of the girls dropped their heads and looked down at the ground.

"Miss Carlbough, do you think it's fair to give us extra kitchen detail?" Roberta, one half-eaten apple still in hand, tilted her pointed chin. "After all, our parents are paying for the camp."

Eden felt her palms grow damp. Judge Snow was a wealthy and powerful man with a reputation for indulging his granddaughter. If the little monster complained... No. Eden took a deep breath and not by a flicker showed her anxiety. She wouldn't be intimidated or blackmailed by a pint-size con artist with apple juice on her chin.

"Yes, your parents are paying for you to be entertained, instructed and disciplined. When they signed you up for Camp Liberty, it was with the understanding that you would obey the rules. But if you prefer, I'd be glad to call your parents and discuss this incident with them."

"No, ma'am." Knowing when to retreat, Roberta smiled charmingly. "We'll be glad to help Mrs. Petrie, and we're sorry for breaking the rules."

And I'm sure you have a bridge I could buy, Eden thought, but she kept her face impassive. "Fine. It's time to start back."

"My hat!" Roberta would have darted back up the tree if Eden hadn't made a lucky grab for her. "I left my hat up there. Please, Miss Carlbough, it's my Phillies cap, and it's autographed and everything."

"You start back. I'll get it. I don't want Miss Bartholomew to worry any longer than necessary."

"We'll apologize."

"See that you do." Eden watched them scramble over the fence. "And no detours," she called out. "Or I keep the cap." One look at Roberta assured her that that bit of blackmail was all that was needed. "Monsters," she murmured as they jogged back into the grove, but the smile finally escaped. Turning back, she studied the tree.

All she had to do was climb up. It had looked simple enough when Roberta and her partners-in-crime had done it. Somehow, it didn't look as simple now. Squaring her shoulders, Eden stepped forward to grab a low-hanging branch. She'd done a little mountain-climbing in Switzerland; how much harder could this be? Pulling herself up, she hooked her foot in the first vee she found. The bark was rough against her palm. Concentrating on her goal, she ignored the scrapes. With both feet secured, she reached for the next branch and began to work her way up. Leaves brushed her cheeks.

She spotted the cap hanging on a short branch, two arms' lengths out of reach. When she made the mistake of looking down, her stomach clenched. So don't look, Eden ordered herself. What you can't see can't hurt you. She hoped.

Eden cautiously inched her way out to the cap. When her fingers made contact with it, she let out a low breath of relief. After setting it on her own head, she found herself looking out, beyond the tree, over the orchard.

Now it was the symmetry that caught her admiration. From her bird's height, she could see the order as well as the beauty. She could just barely glimpse a slice of the lake beyond the aspens. It winked blue in the distance. There were barnlike buildings, and what appeared to be a greenhouse, far off to the right. About a quarter of a mile away, there was a truck, apparently abandoned, on a wide dirt path. In the quiet, birds began to sing again. Turning her head, she saw the bright yellow flash of a butterfly.

The scent of leaves and fruit and earth was tangy, basic. Unable to resist, Eden reached out and plucked a sun-warmed apple.

He'd never miss it, she decided as she bit into the skin. The tart flavor, not quite ripe, shot into her mouth. She shivered at the shock of it, the sensual appeal, then bit again. Delicious, she thought. Exciting. Forbidden fruit usually was, she remembered, but she grinned as she took a third bite.

"What in the devil are you doing?"

She started, almost unseating herself, as the voice boomed up from below. She swallowed the bite of apple quickly before peering down through the leaves.

He stood with his hands on his hips, narrow, lean, spare. A faded denim workshirt was rolled up past the elbows to show tan and muscle. Warily, Eden brought her eyes to his face. It was tanned like his arms, with the skin drawn tight over bone. His nose was long and not quite straight, his mouth full and firm and frowning. Jet-black and unruly, his hair fell over his brow and curled just beyond the collar of his shirt. Pale, almost translucent green eyes scowled up at her.

An apple, Eden, and now the serpent. The idea ran through her head before she drew herself back.

Wonderful, she thought. She'd been caught pinching apples by the foreman. Since disappearing wasn't an option, she opened her mouth to start a plausible explanation.

"Young lady, do you belong at the camp next door?"

The tone brought on a frown. She might be penniless, she might be scrambling to make a living, but she was still a Carlbough. And a Carlbough could certainly handle an apple foreman. "Yes, that's right. I'd like to—"

"Are you aware that this is private property, and that you're trespassing?"

The color of her eyes deepened, the only outward sign of her embarrassed fury. "Yes, but I—"

"These trees weren't planted for little girls to climb."

"I hardly think—"

"Come down." There was absolute command in his tone. "I'll have to take you back to the camp director."

The temper she had always gently controlled bubbled up until she gave serious consideration to throwing what was left of the apple down on his head. No one, absolutely no one, gave her orders. "That won't be necessary."

"I'll decide what's necessary. Come down here."

She'd come down all right, Eden thought. Then, with a few well-chosen words, he'd be put precisely in his place. Annoyance carried her from branch to branch, leaving no room for thoughts of height or inexperience. The two scrapes she picked up on the trip were hardly felt. Her back was to him as she lowered herself into a vee of the trunk. The pleasure of demolishing him with icy manners would be well worth the embarrassment of having been caught in the wrong place at the wrong time. She imagined him cringing and babbling an incoherent apology.

Then her foot slipped, and her frantic grab for a limb was an inch short of the mark. With a shriek that was equal parts surprise and dismay, she fell backward into space.

The breath whooshed back out of her as she connected with something solid. The tanned, muscled arms she'd seen from above wrapped around her. Momentum carried them both to the ground and, like the apple, they rolled. When the world stopped spinning, Eden found herself beneath a very firm, very long body.

Roberta's cap had flown off and Eden's face, no longer shadowed by the brim, was left unguarded in the sunlight. Chase stared down at her and felt soft breasts yield under him.

"You're not twelve years old," he murmured.

"Certainly not."

Amused now, he shifted his weight, but didn't remove it. "I didn't get a good look at you when you were in the tree." He had time to make up for that now, he decided, and he looked his fill. "You're quite a windfall." Carelessly, he brushed stray strands of hair away from her face. His fingertips were as rough against her skin as the bark had been to her palms. "What are you doing in a girls' summer camp?"

"Running it," she said coldly. It wasn't a complete lie. Because it would have bruised her dignity even more to squirm, she settled on sending him an icy look. "Would you mind?"

"Running it?" Since she had dropped out of one of his trees, he had no qualms about ignoring her request. "I met someone. Bartholomew—red hair, appealing face." He scanned Eden's classic features. "You're not her."

"Obviously not." Because his body was too warm, too male, and too close, she sacrificed some dignity by putting her hands to his shoulders. He didn't budge. "I'm her partner. Eden Carlbough."

"Ah, of the Philadelphia Carlboughs."

The humor in his voice was another blow to her pride. Eden combated it with a withering stare. "That's correct."

Intriguing little package, he thought. All manners and breeding. "A pleasure, Miss Carlbough. I'm Chase Elliot of the South Mountain Elliots."

Chapter 2

Perfect, just perfect, Eden thought as she stared up at him. Not the foreman, but the bloody owner. Caught stealing apples by, falling out of trees on and pinned to the ground under, the owner. She took a deep breath.

"How do you do, Mr. Elliot."

She might have been in the front parlor pouring tea, Chase thought; he had to admire her. Then he burst out laughing. "I do just fine, Miss Carlbough. And you?"

He was laughing at her. Even after the scandal and shame she had faced, no one had dared laugh at her. Not to her face. Her lips trembled once before she managed to control them. She wouldn't give the oaf the pleasure of knowing how much he infuriated her.

"I'm quite well, thank you, or will be when you let me up."

City manners, he thought. Socially correct and absolutely meaningless. His own were a bit cruder, but more honest. "In a minute. I'm finding this conversation fascinating."

"Then perhaps we could continue it standing up."

"I'm very comfortable." That wasn't precisely true. The soft, slender lines of her body were causing him some problems. Rather than alleviate them, Chase decided to enjoy them. And her. "So, how are you finding life in the rough?"

He was still laughing at her, without troubling to pretend otherwise. Eden tasted the fury bubbling up in her throat. She swallowed it. "Mr. Elliot—"

"Chase," he interrupted. "I think, under the circumstances, we should dispense with formalities."

Control teetered long enough for her to shove against his shoulders again. It was like pushing rock. "This is ridiculous. You *have* to let me up."

"I rarely have to do anything." His voice was a drawl now, and insolent, but no less imposing than the bellow that had first greeted her. "I've heard a lot about you, Eden Carlbough." And he'd seen the newspaper pictures that he now realized had been just shy of the mark. It was difficult to capture that cool sexuality in two dimensions. "I never expected a Carlbough of Philadelphia to fall out of one of my trees."

Her breathing became unsteady. All the training, the years she'd spent being taught how to coat every emotion with politeness, began to crack. "It was hardly my intention to fall out of one of your trees."

"Wouldn't have fallen out if you hadn't climbed up." He smiled, realizing how glad he was that he'd decided to check this section of the orchard himself.

This couldn't be happening. Eden closed her eyes a moment and waited for things to fall back into their proper places. She couldn't be lying flat on her back under a stranger. "Mr. Elliot." Her voice was calm and reasonable when she tried it again. "I'd be more than happy to give you a complete explanation if you'd let me up."

"Explanation first."

Her mouth quite simply fell open. "You are the most unbelievably rude and boorish man I have ever met."

"My property," he said simply. "My rules. Let's hear your explanation."

She almost shuddered with the effort to hold back the torrent of abuse that leaped to her tongue. Because of her position, she had to squint up at him. Already a headache was collecting behind her eyes. "Three of my girls wandered away from camp. Unfortunately, they climbed over the fence and onto your property. I found them, ordered them down and sent them back to the camp, where they are being properly disciplined."

"Tar and feathers?"

"I'm sure you'd prefer that, but we settled on extra kitchen detail."

"Seems fair. But that doesn't explain you falling out of my tree and into my arms. Though I've about decided not to complain about that. You smell like Paris." To Eden's amazement, he leaned down and buried his face in her hair. "Wicked nights in Paris."

"Stop it." Now her voice wasn't calm, wasn't disciplined.

Chase felt her heart begin to thud against his own. It ran through his mind that he wanted to do more than sample her scent. But when he lifted his head, her eyes were wide. Along with the awareness in them was a trace of fear.

"Explanation," he said lightly. "That's all I intend to take at the moment."

She could hear her own pulse hammering in her throat. Of its own accord, her gaze fell upon his mouth. Was she mad, or could she almost taste the surge of masculine flavor that would certainly be on his lips? She felt her muscles softening, then instantly stiffened. She might very well be mad. If an explanation was what it took, she'd give it to him and get away. Far away.

"One of the girls…" Her mind veered vengefully to Roberta. "One of them left her cap in the tree."

"So you went up after it." He nodded, accepting her explanation. "That doesn't explain why you were helping yourself to one of my apples."

"It was mealy."

Grinning again, he ran a hand along her jawline. "I doubt that. I'd imagine it was hard and tart and delicious. I had my share of stomachaches from green apples years ago. The pleasure's usually worth the pain."

Something uncomfortably like need was spreading through her. The fear of it chilled both her eyes and voice. "You have your explanation, and your apology."

"I never heard an apology."

She'd be damned, she'd be twice damned if she'd give him one now. Glaring at him, she nearly managed to look regal. "I want you to let me up this instant. You're perfectly free to prosecute if you feel the need for compensation for a couple of worm-filled apples, but for now, I'm tired of your ridiculous backwoods arrogance."

His apples were the best in the state, the best in the country. But at the moment, he relished the idea of her sinking her pretty white teeth into a worm. "You haven't had a taste of backwoods arrogance yet. Maybe you should."

"You wouldn't dare," she began, only to have the last word muffled by his mouth.

The kiss caught her completely off guard. It was rough and demanding and as tart as the apple had been. Forbidden fruit. To a woman accustomed to coaxing, to requesting, the hard demand left her limp, unable to respond or protest. Then his hands were on her face, his thumbs tracing her jawline. Like the kiss, his palms were hard and thrilling.

He didn't regret it. Though he wasn't a man used to taking from a woman what wasn't offered, he didn't regret it. Not when the fruit was this sweet. Even though she lay very still, he could taste the panicked excitement on her lips. Yes, very sweet, he thought. Very innocent. Very dangerous. He lifted his head the moment she began to struggle.

"Easy," he murmured, still stroking her chin with his thumb. Her eyes were more frantic than furious. "It seems you're not the woman of the world you're reputed to be."

"Let me up." Her voice was shaking now, but she was beyond caring.

Getting to his feet, Chase brought her with him. "Want some help brushing off?"

"You are the most offensive man I've ever met."

"I can believe it. A pity you've been spoiled and pampered for so long." She started to turn away, but he caught her shoulders for one last look. "It should be interesting to see how long you last here without the basics—like hairdressers and butlers."

He's just like everyone else, she thought; she coated her hurt and doubt with disdain. "I'm very late for my next class, Mr. Elliot. If you'll excuse me?"

He lifted his hands from her shoulders, holding the palms out a moment before dropping them. "Try to keep the kids out of the trees," he warned. "A fall can be dangerous."

His smile had insults trembling on her lips. Clamping her tongue between her teeth, Eden scrambled over the fence.

He watched her, enjoying the view until she was swallowed up by the aspens. Glimpsing the cap at his feet, he bent down for it. As good as a calling card, he decided, tucking it into his back pocket.

Eden went through the rest of the day struggling not to think. About anything. She had deliberately avoided telling Candy about her meeting with Chase. In telling of it, she would have to think about it.

The humiliation of being caught up a tree was hard enough to swallow. Still, under other circumstances, she and Candy might have shared a laugh over it. Under any other circumstances.

But more than the humiliation, even more than the anger, were the sensations. She wasn't sure what they were, but each separate sensation she had experienced in the orchard remained fresh and vibrant throughout the day. She couldn't shake them off or cover them over, and she certainly couldn't ignore them. If she understood anything, she understood how important it was for her to close off her feelings before they could grow.

Ridiculous. Eden interrupted her own thoughts. She didn't know Chase Elliot. Moreover, she didn't want to know him. It was true that she couldn't block out what had happened, but she could certainly see that it never happened again.

Over the past year, she had taken control of the reins for the first time in her life. She knew what it was to fumble, what it was to fail, but she also knew she would never fully release those reins again. Disillusionment had toughened her. Perhaps that was the one snatch of silver lining in the cloud.

Because of it, she recognized Chase Elliot as a man who held his own reins, and tightly. She had found him rude and overbearing, but she had also seen his power and authority. She'd had her fill of dominating men. Rough-edged or polished, they were all the same underneath. Since her experience with Eric, Eden's opinion of men in general had reached a low ebb. Her encounter with Chase had done nothing to raise it.

It was annoying that she had to remind herself continually to forget about him.

Learning the camp's routine was enough to occupy her mind. Since she didn't have Candy's years of training and experience in counseling, her responsibilities were relatively few and often mundane, but at least she had the satisfaction of knowing she was more than a spectator. Ambition had become a new vice. If her role as apprentice meant she mucked out stalls and groomed horses, then Eden was determined to have the cleanest stables and the glossiest horses in Pennsylvania. She considered her first blister a badge of accomplishment.

The rush after the dinner bell still intimidated Eden. Twenty-seven girls aged ten to fourteen swarmed the cafeteria. It was one of Eden's new duties to help keep order. Voices were raised on topics that usually ranged from boys to rock stars, then back to boys. With a little luck, there was no jostling or shoving in line. But luck usually required an eagle eye.

Camp Liberty's glossy brochures had promised wholesome food. Tonight's menu included crispy chicken, whipped potatoes and steamed broccoli. Flatware rattled on trays as the girls shuffled, cafeteria-style, down the serving line.

"It's been a good day." Candy stood beside Eden, her eyes shifting back and forth as she managed to watch the entire room at once.

"And nearly over." Even as she said it, Eden realized her back didn't ache quite as much as it had the first couple of days. "I've got two girls in the morning riding session who show real promise. I was hoping I could give them a little extra time a couple of days a week."

"Great, we'll check the schedule." Candy watched one of the counselors convince a camper to put a stem of broccoli on her plate. "I wanted to tell you that you handled Roberta and company beautifully. Kitchen detail was an inspiration."

"Thanks." Eden realized how low her pride had fallen when such a small thing made her glow. "I did have a twinge of guilt about dumping them on Mrs. Petrie."

"The report is they behaved like troopers."

"Roberta?"

"I know." Candy's smile was wry. Both women turned to see the girl in question, already seated and eating daintily. "It's like waiting for the other shoe to drop. Eden, do you remember Marcia Delacroix from Camp Forden?"

"How could I forget?" With the bulk of the campers seated, Eden and Candy joined the line. "She was the one who put the garter snake in Miss Forden's lingerie drawer."

"Yeah." She turned to give Roberta another look. "Do you believe in reincarnation?"

With a laugh, Eden accepted a scoop of potatoes. "Let's just say I'll be checking my underwear." Hefting the tray, she started forward. "You know, Candy, I—" She saw it as if in slow motion. Roberta, the devil's own gleam in her eyes, held her fork vertically, a thick blob of potatoes clinging to the tines. Aim was taken as Roberta pulled back the business end of the fork with an expert flick. Even as Eden opened her mouth, Roberta sent the blob sailing into the hair of the girl across from her. Pandemonium.

Globs of potatoes flew. Girls screamed. More retaliated. In a matter of seconds, floors, tables, chairs and adolescents were coated in a messy layer of white. Like a general leading the way into battle, Candy stepped into the chaos and lifted her whistle. Before she had the chance to blow it, she was hit, right between the eyes.

A shocked silence fell.

With her tray still in her hands, Eden stood, afraid to breathe. One breath, one little breath, she thought, and she would dissolve into helpless laughter. She felt the pressure of a giggle in her lungs as Candy slowly wiped the dollop of potato from the bridge of her nose.

"Young ladies." The two words, delivered in Candy's most ferocious voice, had Eden's breath catching in her throat. "You will finish your meal in silence. Absolute silence. As you finish, you will line up against this wall. When the dinner hour is over, you will be issued rags, mops and buckets. The mess area will shine tonight."

"Yes, Miss Bartholomew." The acknowledgment came in murmured unison. Only Roberta, her hands folded neatly, her face a picture of innocence, responded in clear tones.

After a long ten seconds of silent staring, Candy walked back to Eden and picked up her tray. "If you laugh," she said in an undertone, "I'll tie your tongue into a square knot."

"Who's laughing?" Eden desperately cleared her throat. "I'm not laughing."

"Yes, you are." Candy sailed, like a steamship, to the head table. "You're just clever enough to do it discreetly."

Eden sat, then carefully smoothed her napkin on her lap. "You've got mashed potatoes in your eyebrows." Candy glared at her, and she lifted her coffee cup to hide a grin behind it. "Actually, it's very becoming. You may have found an alternative to hair gel."

Candy glanced down at the cooling potatoes on her own plate. "Would you like to try some?"

"Now, darling, you're the one who's always telling me we have to set an example." Eden took a satisfying bite of her chicken. "Mrs. Petrie's a gem, isn't she?"

* * *

It took the better part of two hours to clean the mess area and to mop up the puddles of water spilled by the inexperienced janitorial crew. By lights-out most of the girls were too tired to loiter. A pleasant late-evening hush covered the camp.

If the mornings were the worst for Eden, the evenings were invariably the best. A long day of physical activity left her comfortably tired and relaxed. The sounds of night birds and insects were becoming familiar. More and more, she looked forward to an hour of solitude with a sky full of stars. There was no theater to dress for, no party to attend. The longer she was away from her former lifestyle, the less she missed it.

She was growing up, she reflected, and she liked the idea. She supposed maturity meant recognizing what was really important. The camp was important, her friendship with Candy vital. The girls under their care for the summer, even the dastardly Roberta Snow, were what really mattered. She came to realize that even if everything she had once had was handed back to her, she would no longer be able to treat it in the same way.

She had changed. And even though she was certain there were still more changes to come, she liked the new Eden Carlbough. This Eden was independent, not financially, but internally. She'd never realized how dependent she had been on her father, her fiancé, the servants. The new Eden could cope with problems, large ones, small ones. Her hands were no longer elegantly manicured. The nails were neat, but short and rounded, unpainted. Practical, Eden thought as she held one up for inspection. Useful. She liked what she saw.

She continued her nightly ritual by walking to the stables. Inside it was cool and dark, smelling of leather, hay and horses. Just stepping inside helped to cement her confidence. This was her contribution. In most other areas, she still relied on pride and nerve, but here she had skill and knowledge.

She would check each of the six horses, then the tack, before she would consider her duties over for the day. Candy might be able to build a cathedral out of papier-mâché, but she knew nothing about strained tendons or split hooves.

Eden stopped at the first stall to stroke the roan gelding she called Courage. In her hand was a paper bag with six apple halves. It was a nightly ritual the horses had caught on to quickly. Courage leaned his head over the stall door and nuzzled her palm.

"Such a good boy," she murmured as she reached into the bag. "Some of the girls still don't know a bit from a stirrup, but we're going to change that." She held the apple in her palm and let him take it. While he chewed contentedly, Eden stepped into the stall to check him over. He'd been a bargain because of his age and his slight swayback. She hadn't been looking for Thoroughbreds, but for dependability and gentleness. Satisfied that his grooming had been thorough, she latched the stall door behind her and went to the next.

Next summer they'd have at least three more mounts. Eden smiled as she worked her way from stall to stall. She wasn't going to question whether there would be a Camp Liberty next summer. There would be, and she'd be part of it. A real part.

She realized that she'd brought little with her other

than money and a flair for horses. It was Candy who had the training, Candy who had had the three younger sisters and a family that had possessed more tradition than money. Unlike Eden, Candy had always known she would have to earn her own way and had prepared for it. But Eden was a quick learner. By Camp Liberty's second season, she would be a partner in more than name.

Her ambition was already spiraling upward. In a few years, Camp Liberty would be renowned for its equestrian program. The name Carlbough would be respected again. There might even come a time when her Philadelphia contemporaries would send their children to her. The irony of it pleased her.

After the fifth apple had been devoured, Eden moved to the last stall. Here was Patience, a sweet-tempered, aging mare who would tolerate any kind of ineptitude in a rider as long as she received affection. Sympathetic to old bones and muscles, Eden often spent an extra hour rubbing the mare down with liniment.

"Here you are, sweetheart." As the horse gnawed the apple, Eden lifted each hoof for inspection. "A pretty sketchy job," she mumbled before drawing a hoof pick out of her back pocket. "Let's see, wasn't it little Marcie who rode you last? I suppose this means we have to have a discussion on responsibility." With a sigh, Eden switched to another hoof. "I hate discussions on responsibility. Especially when I'm giving them." Patience snorted sympathetically. "Well, I can't leave all the dirty work to Candy, can I? In any case, I don't think Marcie meant to be inconsiderate. She's still a bit nervous around horses. We'll have to show her what a nice lady you are. There. Want a rubdown?" After sticking the pick back in her pocket, Eden rested her cheek against the mare's neck. "Oh, me too, Patience. A nice long massage with some scented oil. You can just lie there with your eyes closed while all the kinks are worked out, then your skin feels so soft, your muscles so supple." With a quick laugh, Eden drew away. "Well, since you can't oblige me, I'll oblige you. Just let me get the liniment."

Giving the mare a final pat, she turned. Her breath caught on a gasp.

Chase Elliot leaned against the open stall door. Shadows fell across his face, deepening its hollows. In the dim light, his eyes were like sea foam. She would have taken a step backward in retreat, but the mare blocked her way. He smiled at her predicament.

That triggered her pride. She could be grateful for that. It had thrown her that, in the shadowed light, he was even more attractive, more...compelling than he had been in the sun. Not handsome, she amended quickly. Certainly not in the smooth, conventional sense, the sense she had always gauged men's looks by before. Everything about him was fundamental. Not simple, she thought. No, not simple, but basic. Basic, like his kiss that morning. Warmth prickled along her skin.

"I'd be happy to help you with the massage." He smiled again. "Yours, or the mare's."

"No, thank you." She became aware that she was even more disheveled than she had been at their first meeting, and that she smelled, all too obviously, of horse. "Is there something I can do for you, Mr. Elliot?"

He liked her style, Chase decided. She might be

standing in a stall that could use a bit of cleaning, but she was still the lady of the drawing room. "You've got a good stock here. A bit on the mature side, but solid."

Eden had to ward off a surge of pleasure. His opinion hardly mattered. "Thank you. I'm sure you didn't come to look over the horses."

"No." But he stepped inside the stall. The mare shifted to accommodate him. "Apparently you know your way around them." He lifted a hand to run it down the mare's neck. There was a simple gold ring on his right hand. Eden recognized its age and value, as well as the strength of the man who wore it.

"Apparently." There was no way past him, so she linked her fingers together and waited. "Mr. Elliot, you haven't told me what you're doing here."

Chase's lips twitched as he continued to stroke the mare. Miss Philadelphia was nervous, he thought. She covered it well enough with frigid manners, but her nerves were jumping. It pleased him to know that she hadn't been able to brush off that quick, impulsive kiss any more than he had. "No, I haven't." Before she could avoid it, he reached down for her hand. An opal gleamed dully in the shadowed light, nestled in a circle of diamond chips that promised to catch heat and fire.

"Wrong hand for an engagement ring." He discovered that the fact pleased him, perhaps more than it should have. "I'd heard you and Eric Keeton were to be married last spring. Apparently it didn't come off."

She would like to have sworn, shouted, yelled. That's what *he* wanted, Eden told herself, letting her hand lie passive in his. "No, it didn't. Mr. Elliot, for a, let's say, country squire, you have boundless curiosity about

Philadelphia gossip. Don't your apples keep you busy enough?"

He had to admire anyone who could shoot straight and smile. "I manage to eke out a bit of free time. Actually, I was interested because Keeton's a family connection."

"He is not."

There, he'd ruffled her. For the first time since her initial surprise, she was really looking at him. Take a good look, Chase thought. You won't see any resemblance. "Distant, certainly." Capturing her other hand, he turned the palms up. "My grandmother was a Winthrop, and a cousin of his grandmother. Your Philadelphia hands have a couple of blisters. You should take care."

"A Winthrop?" Eden was surprised enough at the name to forget her hands.

"We've thinned the blood a bit in the last few generations." She should be wearing gloves, he thought, as he touched a blister with his thumb. "Still, I'd expected an invitation and was curious why you dumped him."

"I didn't dump him." The words came out like poisoned honey. "But to satisfy your curiosity, and to use your own crude phrase, he dumped me. Now if you'd give me back my hands, I could finish for the day."

Chase obliged, but continued to block her way out of the stall. "I'd never considered Eric bright, but I'd never thought him stupid."

"What a delightful compliment. Please excuse me, Mr. Elliot."

"Not a compliment." Chase brushed at the bangs over her forehead. "Just an observation."

"Stop touching me."

"Touching's a habit of mine. I like your hair, Eden. It's soft, but it goes its own way."

"A veritable bouquet of compliments." She managed one small step backward. He had her pulse thudding again. She didn't want to be touched, not physically, not emotionally, not by anyone. Instinct warned her how easily he could do both. "Mr. Elliot—"

"Chase."

"Chase." She acknowledged this with a regal nod. "The morning bell goes off at six. I still have several things to do tonight, so if there's a purpose in your being here, could we get to it?"

"I came to bring you back your hat." Reaching into his back pocket, he pulled out the Phillies cap.

"I see." One more black mark against Roberta. "It's not mine, but I'd be happy to return it to its owner. Thank you for troubling."

"You were wearing it when you fell out of my tree." Chase ignored her outstretched hand and dropped the cap on her head. "Fits, too."

"As I've already explained—"

Eden's frigid retort was interrupted by the sound of running feet. "Miss Carlbough! Miss Carlbough!" Roberta, in an angelic pink nightgown and bare feet, skidded to a halt at the open stall. Beaming, she stared up at Chase. Her adolescent heart melted. "Hi."

"Hi."

"Roberta." Voice stern, teeth nearly clenched, Eden stepped forward. "It's almost an hour past lights-out."

"I know, Miss Carlbough. I'm sorry." When she smiled, Eden thought you could almost believe it. "I just couldn't get to sleep because I kept thinking about my cap. You promised I could have it back, but you never gave it to me. I helped Mrs. Petrie. Honest, you can ask. There were millions of pans, too. I even peeled potatoes, and—"

"Roberta!" The sharp tone was enough for the moment. "Mr. Elliot was kind enough to return your hat." Whipping it off her own head, Eden thrust it into the girl's hands. "I believe you should thank him, as well as apologize for trespassing."

"Gee, thanks." She treated him to a dazzling smile. "Are those your trees, really?"

"Yeah." With a fingertip, Chase adjusted the brim of her hat. He had a weakness for black sheep and recognized a kindred soul in Roberta.

"I think they're great. Your apples tasted a whole lot better than the ones we get at home."

"Roberta."

The quiet warning had the girl rolling her eyes, which only Chase could see. "I'm sorry I didn't show the proper respect for your property." Roberta turned her head to see whether Eden approved of the apology.

"Very nice, Roberta. Now straight back to bed."

"Yes, ma'am." She shot a last look at Chase. Her little heart fluttered. Crushing the cap down on her head, she raced to the door.

"Roberta." She whipped back around at the sound of Chase's voice. He grinned at her. "See you around."

"Yeah, see you." In love, Roberta floated off to her cabin. When the stable door slammed at her back, all Eden could manage was a sigh.

"It's no use," Chase commented.

"What isn't?"

"Pretending you don't get a kick out of her. A kid like that makes you feel good."

"You wouldn't be so sure of that if you'd seen what she can do with mashed potatoes." But Eden gave in enough to smile. "She's a monster, but an appealing one. Still, I have to admit, if we had twenty-seven Robertas in camp this summer, I'd end up in a padded room."

"Certain people just breed excitement."

Eden remembered the dinner hour. "Some call it chaos."

"Life flattens out quickly without a little chaos."

She looked at him, realizing she'd dropped her guard enough to have an actual conversation. And realizing as well that they'd stopped talking about Roberta. The stables suddenly seemed very quiet. "Well, now that we've gotten that settled, I think—"

He took a step forward. She took a step back. A smile played around his lips again as he reached for her hand. Eden bumped solidly into the mare before she managed to raise her free hand to his chest.

"What do you want?" Why was she whispering, and why was the whisper so tremulous?

He wasn't sure what he wanted. Once, quickly, he scanned her face before bringing his gaze back to hers with a jolt. Or perhaps he was. "To walk with you in the moonlight, I think. To listen to the owls hoot and wait for the nightingale."

The shadows had merged. The mare stood quietly, breathing softly. His hand was in Eden's hair now, as if it belonged there. "I have to go in." But she didn't move.

"Eden and the apple," he murmured. "I can't tell you

how tempting I've found that combination. Come with me. We'll walk."

"No." Something was building inside her, too quickly. She knew he was touching more than her hand, more than her hair. He was reaching for something he should not have known existed.

"Sooner or later." He'd always been a patient man. He could wait for her the way he waited for a new tree to bear fruit. His fingers slid down to her throat, stroking once. He felt her quick shudder, heard the unsteady indrawn breath. "I'll be back, Eden."

"It won't make any difference."

Smiling, he brought her hand to his lips, turning it palm up. "I'll still be back."

She listened to his footsteps, to the creak of the door as he opened it, then shut it again.

Chapter 3

The camp was developing its own routine. Eden adjusted hers to it. Early hours, long, physical days and basic food were both a solace and a challenge. The confidence she'd once had to work at became real.

There were nights during the first month of summer that she fell into her bunk certain she would never be able to get up in the morning. Her muscles ached from rowing, riding and endless hiking. Her head spun from weekly encounters with ledgers and account books. But in the morning the sun would rise, and so would she.

Every day it became easier. She was young and healthy. The daily regimented exercise hardened muscles only touched on by occasional games of tennis. The weight she had lost over the months since her father's death gradually came back, so that her look of fragility faded.

To her surprise, she developed a genuine affection for the girls. They became individuals, not simply a group to be coped with or income on the books. It surprised her more to find that same affection returned.

Right from the start, Eden had been certain the girls would love Candy. Everyone did. She was warm, funny, talented. The most Eden had hoped for, for herself, was to be tolerated and respected. The day Marcie had brought her a clutch of wildflowers, Eden had been too stunned to do more than stammer a thank-you. Then there had been the afternoon she had given Linda Hopkins an extra half hour in the corral. After her first gallop, Linda had thrown herself into Eden's arms for a fierce and delightful hug.

So the camp had changed her life, in so many more ways than she'd expected.

The summer grew hot with July. Girls darted around the compound in shorts. Dips in the lake became a glorious luxury. Doors and windows stayed open at night to catch even the slightest breeze. Roberta found a garter snake and terrorized her cabin mates. Bees buzzed around the wildflowers and stings became common.

Days merged together, content, but never dull, so that it seemed possible that summer could last forever. As the time passed, Eden began to believe that Chase had forgotten his promise, or threat, to come back. She'd been careful to stay well within the borders of the camp herself. Though once or twice she'd been tempted to wander toward the orchards, she stayed away.

It didn't make sense for her to still be tense and uneasy. She could tell herself he'd only been a brief annoyance. Yet every time she went into the stables in the evening, she caught herself listening. And waiting.

Late in the evening, with the heat still shimmering, Eden stretched out on her bunk, fully dressed. Bribed by the promise of a bonfire the following night, the campers had quieted down early. Relaxed and pleasantly weary, Eden pictured it. Hot dogs flaming on sharpened sticks, marshmallows toasting, the blaze flickering heat over her face and sending smoke billowing skyward. Eden found herself looking forward to the evening every bit as much as the youngest camper. With her head pillowed on her folded arms, she stared up at the ceiling while Candy paced.

"I'm sure we could do it, Eden."

"Hmm?"

"The dance." Gesturing with the clipboard she was carrying, Candy stopped at the foot of the bunk. "The dance I've been talking about having for the girls. Remember?"

"Of course." Eden forced her mind back to business. "What about it?"

"I think we should go ahead with it. In fact, if it works out, I think it should be an annual event." Even after she plopped herself down on Eden's bed, her enthusiasm continued to bounce around the room. "The boys' camp is only twenty miles from here. I'm sure they'd go for it."

"Probably." A dance. That would mean refreshments for somewhere close to a hundred, not to mention music, decorations. She thought first of the red ink in the ledger, then about how much the girls would enjoy it. There had to be a way around the red ink. "I guess there'd be room in the mess area if we moved the tables."

"Exactly. And most of the girls have records with them. We could have the boys bring some, too." She began to scrawl on her clipboard. "We can make the decorations ourselves."

"We'd have to keep the refreshments simple," Eden put in before Candy's enthusiasm could run away with her. "Cookies, punch, that sort of thing."

"We can plan it for the last week of camp. Kind of a celebrational send-off."

The last week of camp. How strange, when the first week had been so wearing, that the thought of it ending brought on both panic and regret. No, summer wouldn't last forever. In September there would be the challenge of finding a new job, a new goal. She wouldn't be going back to a teaching job as Candy was, but to want ads and résumés.

"Eden? Eden, what do you think?"

"About what?"

"About planning the dance for the last week of camp?"

"I think we'd better clear it with the boys' camp first."

"Honey, are you okay?" Leaning forward, Candy took Eden's hand. "Are you worried about going back home in a few weeks?"

"No. Concerned." She gave Candy's hand a squeeze. "Just concerned."

"I meant it when I told you not to worry about a job right away. My salary takes care of the rent on the apartment, and I still have a little piece of the nest egg my grandmother left me."

"I love you, Candy. You're the best friend I've ever had."

"The reverse holds true, Eden."

"For that reason, there's no way I'm going to sit around while you work to pay the rent and put dinner on the table. It's enough that you've let me move in with you."

"Eden, you know I'm a lot happier sharing my apartment with you than I was living alone. If you look at it as a favor, you're going to feel pressured, and that's ridiculous. Besides, for the past few months, you were taking care of fixing all the meals."

"Only a small portion of which were edible."

"True." Candy grinned. "But I didn't have to cook. Listen, give yourself a little space. You'll need some time to find out what it is you want to do."

"What I want to do is work." With a laugh, Eden lay back on the bed again. "Surprise. I really want to work, to keep busy, to earn a living. The past few weeks have shown me how much I enjoy taking care of myself. I'm banking on getting a job at a riding stable. Maybe even the one I used to board my horse at. And if that doesn't pan out—" She shrugged her shoulders. "I'll find something else."

"You will." Candy set the clipboard aside. "And next year, we'll have more girls, a bigger staff and maybe even a profit."

"Next year, I'm going to know how to make a hurricane lamp out of a tuna can."

"And a pillow out of two washcloths."

"And pot holders."

Candy remembered Eden's one mangled attempt. "Well, maybe you should take it slow."

"There's going to be no stopping me. In the meantime, I'll contact the camp director over at—what's the name, Hawk's Nest?"

"Eagle Rock," Candy corrected her, laughing. "It'll be fun for us, too, Eden. They have counselors. *Male* counselors." Sighing, she stretched her arms to the ceiling. "Do you know how long it's been since I've spoken with a man?"

"You talked to the electrician just last week."

"He was a hundred and two. I'm talking about a man who still has all his hair and teeth." She touched her tongue to her upper lip. "Not all of us have passed the time holding hands with a man in the stables."

Eden plumped up her excuse for a pillow. "I wasn't holding hands. I explained to you."

"Roberta Snow, master spy, gave an entirely different story. With her, it appears to be love at first sight."

Eden examined the pad of callus on the ridge of her palm. "I'm sure she'll survive."

"Well, what about you?"

"I'll survive, too."

"No, I mean, aren't you interested?" After folding her legs under her, Candy leaned forward. "Remember, darling, I got a good look at the man when I was negotiating for the use of his lake. I don't think there's a woman alive who wouldn't sweat a bit after a look at those spooky green eyes."

"I never sweat."

Chuckling, Candy leaned back. "Eden, you're talking to the one who loves you best. The man was interested enough to track you down in the stables. Think of the possibilities."

"It's possible that he was returning Roberta's cap."

"And it's possible that pigs fly. Haven't you been tempted to wander over by the orchard, just once?"

"No." Only a hundred times. "Seen one apple tree, you've seen them all."

"The same doesn't hold true for an apple grower who's about six-two, with a hundred and ninety well-placed pounds and one of the most fascinating faces this side of the Mississippi." Concern edged into her voice. She had watched her friend suffer and had been helpless to do more than offer emotional support. "Have fun, Eden. You deserve it."

"I don't think Chase Elliot falls into the category of fun." Danger, she thought. Excitement, sexuality and, oh yes, temptation. Tossing her legs over the bunk, Eden walked to the window. Moths were flapping at the screen.

"You're gun-shy."

"Maybe."

"Honey, you can't use Eric as a yardstick."

"I'm not." With a sigh, she turned back. "I'm not pining or brooding over him, either."

The quick shrug was Candy's way of dismissing someone she considered a weasel. "That's because you were never really in love with him."

"I was going to marry him."

"Because it seemed the proper thing to do. I know you, Eden, like no one else. Everything was very simple and easy with Eric. It all fit—click, click, click."

Amused, Eden shook her head. "Is something wrong with that?"

"Everything's wrong with that. Love makes you giddy and foolish and achy. You never felt any of that with Eric." She spoke from the experience of a woman who'd fallen in love, and out again, a dozen times before she'd hit twenty. "You would have married him, and maybe you would even have been content. His tastes were compatible with yours. His family mixed well with yours."

Amusement fled. "You make it sound so cold."

"It was. But you're not." Candy raised her hands, hoping she hadn't gone too far. "Eden, you were raised a certain way, to be a certain way; then the roof collapsed. I can only guess at how traumatic that was. You've picked yourself up, but still you've closed pieces of yourself off. Isn't it time you put the past behind you, really behind you?"

"I've been trying."

"I know, and you've made a good start, with the camp, with your outlook. Maybe it's time you started looking for a little more, just for yourself."

"A man?"

"Some companionship, some sharing, some affection. You're too smart to think that you need a man to make things work, but to cut them off because one acted like a weasel isn't the answer, either." She rubbed at a streak of red paint on her fingernail. "I guess I still believe that everyone needs someone."

"Maybe you're right. Right now I'm too busy pasting myself back together and enjoying the results. I'm not ready for complications. Especially when they're six foot two."

"You were always the romantic one, Eden. Remember the poetry you used to write?"

"We were children." Restless, Eden moved her shoulders. "I had to grow up."

"Growing up doesn't mean you have to stop dreaming." Candy rose. "We've started one dream here, together. I want to see you have other dreams."

"When the time's right." Touched, Eden kissed Candy's cheek. "We'll have your dance and charm your counselors."

"We could invite some neighbors, just to round things out."

"Don't press your luck." Laughing, Eden turned toward the door. "I'm going for a walk before I check on the horses. Leave the light on low, will you?"

The air was still, but not quiet. The first nights Eden had spent in the hills, the country quiet had disturbed her. Now, she could hear and appreciate the night music. The chorus of crickets in soprano, the tenor crying of an owl, the occasional bass lowing of the cows on a farm half a mile away all merged into a symphony accompanied by the rustling of small animals in the brush. The three-quarter moon and a galaxy of stars added soft light and dramatic shadows. The erratic yellow beams of an army of fireflies was a nightly light show.

As she strolled toward the lake, she heard the rushing song of peepers over the softer sound of lapping water. The air smelled as steamy as it felt, so she rounded the edge of the lake toward the cooler cover of trees.

With her mind on her conversation with Candy, Eden

bent to pluck a black-eyed Susan. Twisting the stem between her fingers, she watched the petals revolve around the dark center.

Had she been a romantic? There had been poetry, dreamy, optimistic poetry, often revolving around love. Troubadour love, she thought now. The sort that meant long, wistful glances, sterling sacrifices and purity. Romantic, but unrealistic, Eden admitted. She hadn't written any poetry in a long time.

Not since she had met Eric, Eden realized. She had gone from dreamy young girl to proper young woman, exchanging verses for silver patterns. Now both the dreamy girl and the proper woman were gone.

That was for the best, Eden decided, and she tossed her flower onto the surface of the lake. She watched it float lazily.

Candy had been right. It had not been a matter of love with Eric, but of fulfilling expectations. When he had turned his back on her, he had broken not her heart, but her pride. She was still repairing it.

Eric had given her a suitable diamond, sent her roses at the proper times and had never been at a loss for a clever compliment. That wasn't romance, Eden mused, and it certainly wasn't love. Perhaps she'd never really understood either.

Was romance white knights and pure maidens? Was it Chopin and soft lights? Was it the top of the Ferris wheel? Maybe she'd prefer the last after all. With a quiet laugh, Eden wrapped her arms around herself and held her face up to the stars.

"You should do that more often."

She whirled, one hand pressing against her throat. Chase stood a few feet away at the edge of the trees, the edge of the shadows. It flashed through her mind that this was the third time she had seen him and the third time he had taken her by surprise. It was a habit she wanted to break.

"Do you practice startling people, or is it a natural gift?"

"I can't remember it happening much before you." The fact was, he hadn't come up on her, but she on him. He'd been walking since dusk, and had stopped on the banks of the lake to watch the water and to think of her. "You've been getting some sun." Her hair seemed lighter, more fragile against the honeyed tone of her skin. He wanted to touch it, to see if it was still as soft and fragrant.

"Most of the work is outdoors." It amazed her that she had to fight the urge to turn and run. There was something mystical, even fanciful, about meeting him here in the moonlight, by the water. Almost as if it had been fated.

"You should wear a hat." He said it absently, distracted by the pounding of his own heart. She might have been an illusion, long slender arms and legs gleaming in the moonlight, her hair loose and drenched with it. She wore white. Even the simple shorts and shirt seemed to glimmer. "I'd wondered if you walked here."

He stepped out of the shadows. The monotonous song of the crickets seemed to reach a crescendo. "I thought it might be cooler."

"Some." He moved closer. "I've always been fond of hot nights."

"The cabins tend to get stuffy." Uneasy, she glanced back and discovered she had walked farther than she'd intended. The camp, with its comforting lights and company, was very far away. "I didn't realize I'd crossed over onto your property."

"I'm only a tyrant about my trees." She was less of an illusion up close, more of a woman. "You were laughing before. What were you thinking of?"

Her mouth was dry. Even as she backed away, he seemed to be closer. "Ferris wheels."

"Ferris wheels? Do you like the drop?" Satisfying his own need, he reached for her hair. "Or the climb?"

At his touch, her stomach shot down to her knees. "I have to get back."

"Let's walk."

To walk with you in the moonlight. Eden thought of his words, and of fate. "No, I can't. It's late."

"Must be all of nine-thirty." Amused, he took her hand, then immediately turned it over. There was a hardening ridge of calluses on the pad beneath her fingers. "You've been working."

"Some people make a living that way."

"Don't get testy." He turned her hand back to run a thumb over her knuckles. Was it a talent of his, Eden wondered, to touch a woman in the most casual of ways and send her blood pounding? "You could wear gloves," Chase went on, "and keep your Philadelphia hands."

"I'm not in Philadelphia." She drew her hand away. Chase simply took her other one. "And since I'm pitching hay rather than serving tea, it hardly seems to matter."

"You'll be serving tea again." He could see her, seated in some fussy parlor, wearing pink silk and holding a china pot. But, for the moment, her hand was warm in his. "The moon's on the water. Look."

Compelled, she turned her head. There were such

things as moonbeams. They gilded the dark water of the lake and silvered the trees. She remembered some old legend about three women, the moonspinners, who spun the moon on spindles. More romance. But even the new, practical Eden couldn't resist.

"It's lovely. The moon seems so close."

"Some things aren't as close as they seem; others aren't so far away."

He began to walk. Because he still had her hand, and because he intrigued her, Eden walked with him. "I suppose you've always lived here." Just small talk, she told herself. She didn't really care.

"For the most part. This has always been headquarters for the business." He turned to look down at her. "The house is over a hundred years old. You might find it interesting."

She thought of her home and of the generations of Carlboughs who had lived there. And of the strangers who lived there now. "I like old houses."

"Are things going well at camp?"

She wouldn't think of the books. "The girls keep us busy." Her laugh came again, low and easy. "That's an understatement. We'll just say their energy level is amazing."

"How's Roberta?"

"Incorrigible."

"I'm glad to hear it."

"Last night she painted one of the girls while the girl was asleep."

"Painted?"

Eden's laugh came again, low and easy. "The little darling must have copped a couple of pots of paint from the art area. When Marcie woke up, she looked like an Indian preparing to attack a wagon train."

"Our Roberta's inventive."

"To say the least. She told me she thought it might be interesting to be the first woman chief justice."

He smiled at that. Imagination and ambition were the qualities he most admired. "She'll probably do it."

"I know. It's terrifying."

"Let's sit. You can see the stars better."

Stars? She'd nearly forgotten who she was with and why she had wanted to avoid being with him. "I don't think I—" Before she'd gotten the sentence out, he'd tugged her down on a soft, grassy rise. "One wonders why you bother to ask."

"Manners," he said easily as he slipped an arm around her shoulders. Even as she stiffened, he relaxed. "Look at the sky. How often do you notice it in the city?"

Unable to resist, she tilted her face up. The sky was an inky black backdrop for countless pinpoints of lights. They spread, winking, shivering, overhead with a glory that made Eden's throat ache just in the looking. "It isn't the same sky that's over the city."

"Same sky, Eden. It's people who change." He stretched out on his back, crossing his legs. "There's Cassiopeia."

"Where?" Curious, Eden searched, but saw only stars without pattern.

"You can see her better from here." He pulled her closer to him, and before she could protest, he was pointing. "There she is. Looks like a W this time of year."

"Yes!" Delighted, she reached for his wrist and outlined the constellation herself. "I've never been able to find anything in the sky."

"You have to look first. There's Pegasus." Chase shifted his arm. "He has a hundred and sixty-six stars you can view with the naked eye. See? He's flying straight up."

Eyes narrowed, she concentrated on finding the pattern. Moonlight splashed on her face. "Oh yes, I see." She shifted a bit closer to guide his hand again. "I named my first pony Pegasus. Sometimes I'd imagine he sprouted wings and flew. Show me another."

He was looking at her, at the way the stars reflected in her eyes, at the way her mouth softened so generously with a smile. "Orion," he murmured.

"Where?"

"He stands with his sword behind him and his shield lifted in front. And a red star, thousands of times brighter than the sun, is the shoulder of his sword arm."

"Where is he? I—" Eden turned her head and looked directly into Chase's eyes. She forgot the stars and the moonlight and the soft, sweet grass beneath her. The hand on his wrist tightened until the rhythm of his pulse was the rhythm of hers.

Her muscles contracted and held as she braced for the kiss. But his lips merely brushed against her temple. Warmth spread through her as softly as the scent of honeysuckle spread through the air. She heard an owl call out to the night, to the stars, or to a lover.

"What are we doing here?" she managed.

"Enjoying each other." Without rushing, his lips moved over her face.

Enjoying? That was much too mild a word for what

was burning through her. No one had ever made her feel like this, so weak and hot, so strong and desperate. His lips were soft, the hand that rested on the side of her face was hard. Beneath his, her heart began to gallop uncontrolled. Eden's fingers slipped off the reins.

She turned her head with a moan and found his mouth with hers. Her arms went around him, holding him close as her lips parted in demand. In all her life she had never known true hunger, not until now. This was breathless, painful, glorious.

He'd never expected such unchecked passion. He'd been prepared to go slowly, gently, as the innocence he'd felt in her required. Now she was moving under him, her fingers pressing and kneading the muscles of his back, her mouth hot and willing on his. The patience that was so much a part of him drowned in need.

Such new, such exciting sensations. Her body gave as his pressed hard against it. Gods and goddesses of the sky guarded them. He smelled of the grass and the earth, and he tasted of fire. Night sounds roared in her head, and her own sigh was only a dim echo when his lips slid down to her throat.

Murmuring his name, Eden combed her fingers through his hair. He wanted to touch her, all of her. He wanted to take her now. When her hand came to rest on his face, he covered it with his own and felt the smooth stone of her ring.

There was so much more he needed to know. So little he was sure of. Desire, for the moment, couldn't be enough. Who was she? He lifted his head to look down at her. Who the hell was she, and why was she driving him mad?

Pulling himself back, he tried to find solid ground. "You're full of surprises, Eden Carlbough of the Philadelphia Carlboughs."

For a moment, she could only stare. She'd had her ride on the Ferris wheel, a wild, dizzying ride. Somewhere along the line, she'd been tossed off to spiral madly in the air. Now she'd hit the ground, hard. "Let me up."

"I can't figure you, Eden."

"You aren't required to." She wanted to weep, to curl up into a ball and weep, but she couldn't focus on the reason. Anger was clearer. "I asked you to let me up."

He rose, holding out a hand to help her. Ignoring it, Eden got to her feet. "I've always felt it was more constructive to shout when you're angry."

She shot him one glittering look. Humiliation. It was something she'd sworn she would never feel again. "I'm sure you do. If you'll excuse me."

"Damn it." He caught her arm and swung her back to face him. "Something was happening here tonight. I'm not fool enough to deny that, but I want to know what I'm getting into."

"We were enjoying each other. Wasn't that your term?" Nothing more, Eden repeated over and over in her head. Nothing more than a moment's enjoyment. "We've finished now, so good night."

"We're far from finished. That's what worries me."

"I'd say that's your problem, Chase." But a ripple of fear—of anticipation—raced through her, because she knew he was right.

"Yeah, it's my problem." My God, how had he passed so quickly from curiosity to attraction to blazing need?

"And because it is, I've got a question. I want to know why Eden Carlbough is playing at camp for the summer rather than cruising the Greek Isles. I want to know why she's cleaning out stables instead of matching silver patterns and planning dinner parties as Mrs. Eric Keeton."

"My business." Her voice rose. The new Eden wasn't as good as the old one at controlling emotion. "But if you're so curious, why don't you call one of your family connections? I'm sure any of them would be delighted to give you all the details."

"I'm asking you."

"I don't owe you any explanations." She jerked her arm away and stood trembling with rage. "I don't owe you a damn thing."

"Maybe not." His temper had cooled his passion and cleared his head. "But I want to know who I'm making love with."

"That won't be an issue, I promise you."

"We're going to finish what we started here, Eden." Without stepping closer, he had her arm again. The touch was far from gentle, far from patient. "That I promise you."

"Consider it finished."

To her surprise and fury, he only smiled. His hand eased on her arm to one lingering caress. Helpless against her response, she shivered. "We both know better than that." He touched a finger to her lips, as if reminding her what tastes he'd left there. "Think of me."

He slipped back into the shadows.

Chapter 4

It was a perfect night for a bonfire. Only a few wispy clouds dragged across the moon, shadowing it, then freeing it. The heat of the day eased with sunset, and the air was balmy, freshened by a calm, steady breeze.

The pile of twigs and sticks that had been gathered throughout the day had been stacked, tepeelike, in a field to the east of the main compound. In the clearing, it rose from a wide base to the height of a man. Every one of the girls had contributed to the making of it, just as every one of them circled around the bonfire now, waiting for the fire to catch and blaze. An army of hot dogs and marshmallows was laid out on a picnic table. Stacked like swords were dozens of cleaned and sharpened sticks. Nearby was the garden hose with a tub full of water, for safety's sake.

Candy held up a long kitchen match, drawing out

the drama as the girls began to cheer. "The first annual bonfire at Camp Liberty is about to begin. Secure your hot dogs to your sticks, ladies, and prepare to roast."

Amid the giggles and gasps, Candy struck the match, then held it to the dry kindling at the base. Wood crackled. Flames licked, searched for more fuel, and spread around and around, following the circle of starter fluid. As they watched, fire began its journey up and up. Eden applauded with the rest.

"Fabulous!" Even as she watched, smoke began to billow. Its scent was the scent of autumn, and that was still a summer away. "I was terrified we wouldn't get it started."

"You're looking at an expert." Catching her tongue between her teeth, Candy speared a hot dog with a sharpened stick. Behind her, the bonfire glowed red at the center. "The only thing I was worried about was rain. But just look at those stars. It's perfect."

Eden tilted her head back. Without effort, without thought, she found Pegasus. He was riding the night sky just as he'd been riding it twenty-four hours before. One day, one night. How could so much have happened? Standing with her face lifted to the breeze and her hands growing warm from the fire, she wondered if she had really experienced that wild, turbulent moment with Chase.

She had. The memories were too ripe, too real for dreams. The moment had happened, and all the feelings and sensations that had grown from it. Deliberately she turned her gaze to a riot of patternless stars.

It didn't change what she remembered, or what she still felt. The moment had happened, she thought again, and it had passed. Yet, somehow, she wasn't certain it was over.

"Why does everything seem different here, Candy?"

"Everything *is* different here." Candy took a deep breath, drawing in the scents of smoke, drying grass and roasting meat. "Isn't it marvelous? No stuffy parlors, no boring dinner parties, no endless piano recitals. Want a hot dog?"

Because her mouth was watering, Eden accepted the partially blackened wiener. "You simplify things, Candy." Eden ran a thin line of ketchup along the meat and stuck it in a bun. "I wish I could."

"You will once you stop thinking you're letting down the Carlbough name by enjoying a hot dog by a bonfire." When Eden's mouth dropped open, Candy gave her a friendly pat. "You ought to try the marshmallows," she advised before she wandered off to find another stick.

Is that what she was doing? Eden wondered, chewing automatically. Maybe, in a way that wasn't quite as basic as Candy had said, it was. After all, she had been the one who had sold the house that had been in the family for four generations. In the end, it had been she who had inventoried the silver and china, the paintings and the jewelry for auction. So, in the end, it had been she who had liquidated the Carlbough tradition to pay off debts and to start a new life.

Necessary. No matter how the practical Eden accepted the necessity, the grieving Eden still felt the loss, and the guilt.

With a sigh, Eden stepped back. The scene that played out in front of her was like a memory from her own childhood. She could see the column of gray smoke rising toward the sky, twirling and curling. At the core of the tower of wood, the fire was fiercely gold and greedy. The smell of outdoor cooking was strong and summery, as it had been during her own weeks at Camp Forden for Girls. For a moment, there was regret that she couldn't step back into those memories of a time when life was simple and problems were things for parents to fix.

"Miss Carlbough."

Brought out of a half-formed dream, Eden glanced down at Roberta. "Hello, Roberta. Are you having fun?"

"It's super!" Roberta's enthusiasm was evident from the smear of ketchup on her chin. "Don't you like bonfires?"

"Yes, I do." Smiling, she looked back at the crackling wood, one hand dropping automatically to Roberta's shoulder. "I like them a lot."

"I thought you looked sort of sad, so I made you a marshmallow."

The offering dripped, black and shriveled, from the end of a stick. Eden felt her throat close up the same way it had when another girl had offered her a clutch of wildflowers. "Thanks, Roberta. I wasn't sad really, I was just remembering." Gingerly, Eden pulled the melted, mangled marshmallow from the stick. Half of it plopped to the ground on the way to her mouth.

"They're tricky," Roberta observed. "I'll make you another one."

Left with the charred outer hull, Eden swallowed valiantly. "You don't have to bother, Roberta."

"Oh, I don't mind." She looked up at Eden with a

glowing, generous grin. Somehow, all her past crimes didn't seem so important. "I like to do it. I thought camp was going to be boring, but it's not. Especially the horses. Miss Carlbough..." Roberta looked down at the ground and seemed to draw her courage out of her toes. "I guess I'm not as good as Linda with the horses, but I wondered if maybe you could—well, if I could spend some more time at the stables."

"Of course you can, Roberta." Eden rubbed her thumb and forefinger together, trying fruitlessly to rid herself of the goo. "And you don't even have to bribe me with marshmallows."

"Really?"

"Yes, really." Attracted despite herself, Eden ruffled Roberta's hair. "Miss Bartholomew and I will work it into your schedule."

"Gee, thanks, Miss Carlbough."

"But you'll have to work on your posting."

Roberta's nose wrinkled only a little. "Okay. But I wish we could do stuff like barrel racing. I've seen it on TV."

"Well, I don't know about that, but you might progress to small jumps before the end of camp."

Eden had the pleasure of seeing Roberta's eyes saucer with pleasure. "No fooling?"

"No fooling. As long as you work on your posting."

"I will. And I'll be better than Linda, too. Wow, jumps." She spun in an awkward pirouette. "Thanks a lot, Miss Carlbough. Thanks a lot."

She was off in a streak, undoubtedly to spread the word. If Eden knew Roberta, and she was beginning to, she was certain the girl would soon have talked herself into a gold medal for equestrian prowess at the next Olympic Games.

But, as she watched Roberta spin from group to group, Eden realized she wasn't thinking of the past any longer; nor was she regretting. She was smiling. As one of the counselors began to strum a guitar, Eden licked marshmallow goop from her fingers.

"Need some help with that?"

With her fingers still in her mouth, Eden turned. She should have known he'd come. Perhaps, in her secret thoughts, she had hoped he would. Now she found herself thrusting her still-sticky fingers behind her back.

He wondered if she knew how lovely she looked, with the fire at her back and her hair loose on her shoulders. There was a frown on her face now, but he hadn't missed that one quick flash of pleasure. If he kissed her now, would he taste that sweet, sugary flavor she had been licking from her fingers? Through it would he find that simmering, waiting heat he'd tasted once before? The muscles in his stomach tightened, even as he dipped his thumbs into his pockets and looked away from her toward the fire.

"Nice night for a bonfire."

"Candy claims she arranged it that way." Confident there was enough distance between them, and that there were enough people around them, Eden allowed herself to relax. "We weren't expecting any company."

"I spotted your smoke."

That made her glance up and realize how far the smoke might travel. "I hope it didn't worry you. We notified the fire department." Three girls streaked by behind them. Chase glanced their way and had them lapsing into giggles. Eden caught her tongue in her cheek. "How long did it take you to perfect it?"

With a half smile, Chase turned back to her. "What?"

"The deadly charm that has females crumpling at your feet?"

"Oh, that." He grinned at her. "I was born with it."

The laugh came out before she could stop it. To cover her lapse, Eden crossed her arms and took a step backward. "It's getting warm."

"We used to have a bonfire on the farm every Halloween. My father would carve the biggest pumpkin in the patch and stuff some overalls and a flannel shirt with straw. One year he dressed himself up as the Headless Horseman and gave every kid in the neighborhood a thrill." Watching the fire, he remembered and wondered why until tonight he hadn't thought of continuing the tradition. "My mother would give each of the kids a caramel apple, then we'd sit around the fire and tell ghost stories until we'd scared ourselves silly. Looking back, I think my father got a bigger kick out of it than any of us kids."

She could see it, just as he described, and had to smile again. For her, Halloween had been tidy costume parties where she'd dressed as a princess or ballerina. Though the memories were still lovely, she couldn't help wishing she'd seen one of the bonfires and the Headless Horseman.

"When we were planning tonight, I was as excited as any of the girls. I guess that sounds foolish."

"No, it sounds promising." He put a hand to her cheek, turning her slightly toward him. Though she stiffened, her skin was warm and soft. "Did you think of me?"

There it was again—that feeling of drowning, of floating, of going under for the third time. "I've been busy." She told herself to move away, but her legs didn't respond. The sound of singing and strumming seemed to be coming from off in the distance, with melody and lyrics she couldn't quite remember. The only thing that was close and real was his hand on her cheek.

"I-it was nice of you to drop by," she began, struggling to find solid ground again.

"Am I being dismissed?" He moved his hand casually from her cheek to her hair.

"I'm sure you have better things to do." His fingertip skimmed the back of her neck and set every nerve end trembling. "Stop."

The smoke billowed up over her head. Light and shadow created by the fire danced over her face and in her eyes. He'd thought of her, Chase reminded himself. Too much. Now he could only think what it would be like to make love with her near the heat of the fire, with the scent of smoke, and night closing in.

"You haven't walked by the lake."

"I told you, I've been busy." Why couldn't she make her voice firm and cool? "I have a responsibility to the girls, and the camp, and—"

"Yourself?" How badly he wanted to walk with her again, to study the stars and talk. How badly he wanted to taste that passion and that innocence again. "I'm a very patient man, Eden. You can only avoid me for so long."

"Longer than you think," she murmured, letting out

a sigh of relief as she spotted Roberta making a bee-line for them.

"Hi!" Delighted with the quick fluttering of her heart, Roberta beamed up at Chase.

"Hi, Roberta," he said. She was thrilled that he'd remembered her name. He gave her a smile, and his attention, without releasing Eden's hair. "You're taking better care of your cap, I see."

She laughed and pushed up the brim. "Miss Carlbough said if I wandered into your orchard again, she'd hold my cap for ransom. But if you invited us to come on a tour, that would be educational, wouldn't it?"

"Roberta." Why was it the child was always one step ahead of everyone else? Eden lifted her brow in a quelling look.

"Well, Miss Bartholomew said we should think of interesting things." Roberta put her most innocent look to good use. "And I think the apple trees are interesting."

"Thanks." Chase thought he heard Eden's teeth clench. "We'll give it some thought."

"Okay." Satisfied, Roberta stuck out a wrinkled black tube. "I made you a hot dog. You have to have a hot dog at a bonfire."

"Looks terrific." Accepting it, he pleased Roberta by taking a generous bite. "Thanks." Only Chase and his stomach knew that the meat was still cold on the inside.

"I got some marshmallows and sticks, too." She handed them over. "It's more fun to do it yourself, I guess." Because she was on the border between childhood and womanhood, Roberta picked up easily on the vibrations around her. "If you two want to be alone, you know, to kiss and stuff, no one's in the stables."

"Roberta!" Eden pulled out her best camp director's voice. "That will do."

"Well, my parents like to be alone sometimes." Undaunted, she grinned at Chase. "Maybe I'll see you around."

"You can count on it, kid." As Roberta danced off toward a group of girls, Chase turned back. The moment he took a step toward her, Eden extended her skewered marshmallow toward the fire. "Want to go kiss and stuff?"

It was the heat of the fire that stung her cheeks with color, Eden assured herself. "I suppose you think it would be terribly amusing for Roberta to go home and report that one of the camp directors spent her time in the stables with a man. That would do a lot for Camp Liberty's reputation."

"You're right. You should come to my place."

"Go away, Chase."

"I haven't finished my hot dog. Have dinner with me."

"I've had a hot dog already, thank you."

"I'll make sure hot dogs aren't on the menu. We can talk about it tomorrow."

"We will not talk about it tomorrow." It was anger that made her breathless, just as it was anger that made her unwise enough to turn toward him. "We will not talk about anything tomorrow."

"Okay. We won't talk." To show how reasonable he was, he bent down and closed the conversation, his mouth covering hers. He wasn't holding her, but it took her brain several long, lazy seconds before it accepted the order to back away.

"Don't you have any sense of propriety?" she managed in a strangled voice.

"Not much." He made up his mind, looking down at her eyes, dazed and as blue as his lake, that he wasn't going to take no for an answer—to any question. "We'll make it about nine tomorrow morning at the entrance to the orchard."

"Make what?"

"The tour." He grinned and handed her his stick. "It'll be educational."

Though she was in an open field, Eden felt her back press into a corner. "We have no intention of disrupting your routine."

"No problem. I'll pass it on to your co-director before I go back. That way, you'll be sure to be coordinated."

Eden took a long breath. "You think you're very clever, don't you?"

"Thorough, just thorough, Eden. By the way, your marshmallow's on fire."

With his hands in his pockets, he strolled off while she blew furiously on the flaming ball.

She'd hoped for rain but was disappointed. The morning dawned warm and sunny. She'd hoped for support but was faced with Candy's enthusiasm for a field trip through one of the most prestigious apple orchards in the country. The girls were naturally delighted with any shift in schedule, so as they walked as a group the short distance to the Elliot farm, Eden found herself separated from the excitement.

"You could try not to look as though you're walking to the guillotine." Candy plucked a scrawny blue flower from the side of the road and stuck it in her hair. "This is a wonderful opportunity—for the girls," she added quickly.

"You managed to convince me of that, or else I wouldn't be here."

"Grumpy."

"I'm not grumpy," Eden countered. "I'm annoyed at being manipulated."

"Just a small piece of advice." Picking another flower, Candy twirled it. "If I'd been manipulated by a man, I'd make certain he believed it was my idea in the first place. Don't you think it would throw him off if you walked up to the gates with a cheery smile and boundless enthusiasm?"

"Maybe." Eden mulled the idea over until her lips began to curve. "Yes, maybe."

"There now. With a little practice, you'll find out that deviousness is much better in some cases than dignity."

"I wouldn't have needed either if you'd let me stay behind."

"Darling, unless I miss my guess, a certain apple baron would have plucked you up from whatever corner you'd chosen to hide in, tossed you over his wonderfully broad shoulder and dragged you along on our little tour, like it or not." Pausing, Candy let a sigh escape. "Now that I think about it, that would have been more exciting."

Because she was well able to picture it herself, Eden's mood hardened again. "At least I thought I could count on support from my best friend."

"And you can. Absolutely." With easy affection, Candy draped an arm over Eden's shoulder. "Though why you think you need my support when you have a gorgeous man giving you smoldering kisses, I can't imagine."

"That's just it!" Because several young heads turned when she raised her voice, Eden fought for calm again. "He had no business pulling something like that in front of everyone."

"I suppose it is more fun in private."

"Keep this up, and you may find that garter snake in your underwear yet."

"Just ask him if he's got a brother, or a cousin. Even an uncle. Ah, here we are," she continued before Eden could reply. "Now smile and be charming, just like you were taught."

"You're going to pay for this," Eden promised her in an undertone. "I don't know how, I don't know when, but you'll pay."

They brought the group to a halt when the road forked. On the left were stone pillars topped with an arching wrought-iron sign that read ELLIOT. Sloping away from the pillars was a wall a foot thick and high as a man. It was old and sturdy, proving to Eden that the penchant for privacy hadn't begun with Chase.

The entrance road, smooth and well-maintained, ribboned back over the crest of a hill before it disappeared. Along the road were trees, not apple but oak, older and sturdier than the wall.

It was the continuity that drew her, the same symmetry she had seen and admired in the groves. The stone, the trees, even the road, had been there for generations. Looking, Eden understood his pride in them. She, too, had once had a legacy.

Then he strode from behind the wall and she fought back even that small sense of a common ground.

In a T-shirt and jeans, he looked lean and capable. There was a faint sheen of sweat on his arms that made her realize he'd already been working that morning. Drawn against her will, she dropped her gaze to his hands, hands that were hard and competent and unbearably gentle on a woman's skin.

"Morning, ladies." He swung the gates open for them.

"Oh Lord, he's something," Eden heard one of the counselors mumble. Remembering Candy's advice, she straightened her shoulders and fixed on her most cheerful smile.

"This is Mr. Elliot, girls. He owns the orchards we'll tour today. Thank you for inviting us, Mr. Elliot."

"My pleasure—Miss Carlbough."

The girlish murmurs of agreement became babbles of excitement as a dog sauntered to Chase's side. His fur was the color of apricots and glistened as though it had been polished in the sunlight. The big, sad eyes studied the group of girls before the dog pressed against Chase's leg. Eden had time to think that a smaller man might have been toppled. The dog was no less than three feet high at the shoulder. More of a young lion than a house pet, she thought. When he settled to sit at Chase's feet, Chase didn't have to bend to lay a hand on the dog's head.

"This is Squat. Believe it or not, he was the runt of his litter. He's a little shy."

Candy gave a sigh of relief when she saw the enormous tail thump the ground. "But friendly, right?"

"Squat's a pushover for females." His gaze circled the group. "Especially so many pretty ones. He was hoping he could join the tour."

"He's neat." Roberta made up her mind instantly. Walking forward, she gave the dog's head a casual pat. "I'll walk with you, Squat."

Agreeable, the dog rose to lead the way.

There was more to the business of apples than Eden had imagined. It wasn't all trees and plump fruit to be plucked and piled into baskets for market. Harvesting wasn't limited to autumn with the variety of types that were planted. The season, Chase explained, had been extended into months, from early summer to late fall.

They weren't just used for eating and baking. Even cores and peelings were put to use for cider, or dried and shipped to Europe for certain champagnes. As they walked, the scent of ripening fruit filled the air, making more than one mouth water.

The Tree of Life, Eden thought as the scent tempted her. Forbidden fruit. She kept herself surrounded by girls and tried to remember that the tour was educational.

He explained that the quick-maturing trees were planted in the forty-foot spaces between the slow growers, then cut out when the space was needed. A practical business, she remembered, organized, with a high level of utility and little waste. Still, it had the romance of apple blossoms in spring.

Masses of laborers harvested the summer fruit. While they watched the men and machines at work, Chase answered questions.

"They don't look ripe," Roberta commented.

"They're full-size." Chase rested a hand on her shoulder as he chose an apple. "The changes that take place after the fruit's reached maturity are mainly chemical. It goes on without the tree. The fruit's hard, but the seeds are brown. Look." Using a pocketknife with casual skill, he cut the fruit in half. "The apples we harvest now are superior to the ones that hang longer." Reading Roberta's expression correctly, Chase tossed her half the fruit. The other half Squat took in one yawning bite.

"Maybe you'd like to pick some yourself." The reaction was positive, and Chase reached up to demonstrate. "Twist the fruit off the stem. You don't want to break the twig and lose bearing wood."

Before Eden could react, the girls had scattered to nearby trees. She was facing Chase. Perhaps it was the way his lips curved. Perhaps it was the way his eyes seemed so content to rest on hers, but her mind went instantly and completely blank.

"You have a fascinating business." She could have kicked herself for the inanity of it.

"I like it."

"I, ah…" There must be a question, an intelligent question, she could ask. "I suppose you ship the fruit quickly to avoid spoilage."

He doubted that either of them gave two hoots about apples at the moment, but he was willing to play the game. "It's stored right after picking at thirty-two degrees Fahrenheit. I like your hair pulled back like that. It makes me want to tug on the string and watch it fall all over your shoulders."

Her pulse began to sing, but she pretended she hadn't

heard. "I'm sure you have various tests to determine quality."

"We look for richness." Slowly, he turned the fruit over in his hand, but his gaze roamed to her mouth. "Flavor." He watched her lips part as if to taste. "Firmness," he murmured, as he circled her throat with his free hand. "Tenderness."

Her breath seemed to concentrate, to sweeten into the sound of a sigh. It was almost too late when she bit it off. "It would be best if we stuck to the subject at hand."

"Which subject?" His thumb traced along her jawline.

"Apples."

"I'd like to make love with you in the orchards, Eden, with the sun warm on your face and the grass soft at your back."

It terrified her that she could almost taste what it would be like, to be with him, alone. "If you'll excuse me."

"Eden." He took her hand, knowing he was pushing too hard, too fast, but unable to stop himself. "I want you. Maybe too much."

Though his voice was low, hardly more than a whisper, she felt her nerves jangling. "You should know you can't say those things to me here, now. If the children—"

"Have dinner with me."

"No." On this, she told herself she would stand firm. She would not be manipulated. She would not be maneuvered. "I have a job, Chase, one that runs virtually twenty-four hours a day for the next few weeks. Even if I wanted to have dinner with you, which I don't, it would be impossible."

He considered all this reasonable. But then, a great many smoke screens were. "Are you afraid to be alone with me? Really alone."

The truth was plain and simple. She ignored it. "You flatter yourself."

"I doubt a couple hours out of an evening would disrupt the camp's routine, or yours."

"You don't know anything about the camp's routine."

"I know that between your partner and the counselors, the girls are more than adequately supervised. And I know that your last riding lesson is at four o'clock."

"How did you—"

"I asked Roberta," he said easily. "She told me you have supper at six, then a planned activity or free time from seven to nine. Lights-out is at ten. You usually spend your time after supper with the horses. And sometimes you ride out at night when you think everyone's asleep."

She opened her mouth, then shut it again, having no idea what to say. She had thought those rides exclusively hers, exclusively private.

"Why do you ride out alone at night, Eden?"

"Because I enjoy it."

"Then tonight you can enjoy having dinner with me."

She tried to remember there were girls beneath the trees around them. She tried to remember that a display of temper was most embarrassing for the person who lost control. "Perhaps you have some difficulty understanding a polite refusal. Why don't we try this? The last place I want to be tonight, or at any other time, is with you."

He moved his shoulders before he took a step closer. "I guess we can just settle all this now. Here."

"You wouldn't…" She didn't bother to finish the thought. By now she knew very well what he would dare. One quick look around showed her that Roberta and Marcie were leaning against the trunk of a tree, happily munching apples and enjoying the show. "All right, stop it." So much for not being manipulated. "I have no idea why you insist on having dinner with someone who finds you so annoying."

"Me, either. We'll discuss it tonight. Seven-thirty." Tossing Eden the apple, he strolled over toward Roberta.

Eden hefted the fruit. She even went so far as to draw a mental bull's-eye on the back of his head. With a sound of disgust, she took a hefty bite instead.

Chapter 5

Vengefully, Eden dragged a brush through her hair. Despite the harsh treatment, it sprang back softly to wisp around her face and wave to her shoulders. She wouldn't go to any trouble as she had for other dates and dinners, but leave it loose and unstyled. Though he was undoubtedly too hardheaded to notice that sort of female subtlety.

She didn't bother with jewelry, except for the simple pearl studs she often wore around camp. In an effort to look cool, even prim, she wore a high-necked white blouse, regretting only the lace at the cuffs. Matching it with a white skirt, she tried for an icy look. The result was an innocent fragility she couldn't detect in the one small mirror on the wall.

Intending on making it plain that she had gone to no trouble for Chase's benefit, she almost ignored makeup.

Grumbling to herself, Eden picked up her blusher. Basic feminine vanity, she admitted; then she added a touch of clear gloss to her lips. There was, after all, a giant step between not fussing and looking like a hag. She was reaching for her bottle of perfume before she stopped herself. No, that was definitely fussing. He would get soap, and soap only. She turned away from the mirror just as Candy swung through the cabin door.

"Wow." Stopping in the doorway, Candy took a long, critical look. "You look terrific."

"I do?" Brow creased, Eden turned back to the mirror. "Terrific wasn't exactly what I was shooting for. I wanted something along the lines of prim."

"You couldn't look prim if you wore sackcloth and ashes, any more than I could look delicate even with lace at my wrists."

With a sound of disgust, Eden tugged at the offending lace. "I knew it. I just knew it was a mistake. Maybe I can rip it off."

"Don't you dare." Laughing, Candy bounded into the room to stop Eden from destroying her blouse. "Besides, it isn't the clothes that are important. It's the attitude, right?"

Eden gave the lace a last tug. "Right. Candy, are you sure everything's going to be under control here? I could still make excuses."

"Everything's already under control." Candy flopped down on her bunk, then began to peel the banana she held. "In fact, things are great. I've just taken a five-minute break to see you off and stuff my face." She took a big bite to prove her point. "Then," she continued over a mouthful of banana, "we're getting together in the mess area to take an inventory of our record collection for the dance. The girls want some practice time before the big night."

"You could probably use extra supervision."

Candy waved her half-eaten banana. "Everyone's going to be in the same four walls for the next couple of hours. You go enjoy your dinner and stop worrying. Where are you going?"

"I don't know." She stuffed some tissue in her bag. "And I really don't care."

"Come on, after nearly six weeks of wholesome but god-awful boring food, aren't you just a little excited about the prospect of oysters Rockefeller or escargots?"

"No." She began to clasp and unclasp her bag. "I'm only going because it was simpler than creating a scene."

Candy broke off a last bite of banana. "Certainly knows how to get his own way, doesn't he?"

"That's about to end." Eden closed her purse with a snap. "Tonight."

At the sound of an approaching car, Candy propped herself up on an elbow. She noticed Eden nervously biting her lower lip, but she only gestured toward the door with her banana peel. "Well, good luck."

Eden caught the grin and paused, her hand on the screen door. "Whose side are you on, anyway?"

"Yours, Eden." Candy stretched, and prepared to go rock and roll. "Always."

"I'll be back early."

Candy grinned, wisely saying nothing as the screen door slammed shut.

However hard Eden might have tried to look remote,

icy, disinterested, the breath clogged up in Chase's lungs the moment she stepped outside. They were still an hour from twilight, and the sun's last rays shot through her hair. Her skirt swirled around bare legs honey-toned after long days outdoors. Her chin was lifted, perhaps in anger, perhaps in defiance. He could only see the elegant line of her throat.

The same slowly drumming need rose up inside him the moment she stepped onto the grass.

She'd expected him to look less...dangerous in more formal attire. Eden discovered she had underestimated him again. The muscles in his arms and shoulders weren't so much restricted as enhanced by the sports jacket. The shirt, either by design or good fortune, matched his eyes and was left open at the throat. Slowly and easily he smiled at her, and her lips curved in automatic response.

"I imagined you looking like this." In truth, he hadn't been sure she would come, or what he might have done if she had locked herself away in one of the cabins and refused to see him. "I'm glad you didn't disappoint me."

Feeling her resolve weaken, Eden made an effort to draw back. "I made a bargain," she began, only to fall silent when he handed her a bunch of anemones freshly picked from the side of the road. He wasn't supposed to be sweet, she reminded herself. She wasn't supposed to be vulnerable to sweetness. Still, unable to resist, she buried her face in the flowers.

That was a picture he would carry with him forever, Chase realized. Eden, with wildflowers clutched in both hands; her eyes, touched with both pleasure and confusion, watching him over the petals.

"Thank you."

"You're welcome." Taking one of her hands, he brought it to his lips. She should have pulled away. She knew she should. Yet there was something so simple, so right in the moment—as if she recognized it from some long-ago dream. Bemused, Eden took a step closer, but the sound of giggling brought her out of the spell.

Immediately she tried to pull her hand away. "The girls." She glanced around quickly enough to catch the fielder's cap as it disappeared around the corner of the building.

"Well, then, we wouldn't want to disappoint them?" Turning her hand over, Chase pressed a kiss to her palm. Eden felt the heat spread.

"You're being deliberately difficult." But she closed her hand as if to capture the sensation and hold it.

"Yes." He smiled, but resisted the impulse to draw her into his arms and enjoy the promise he'd seen so briefly in her eyes.

"If you'd let me go, I'd like to put the flowers in water."

"I'll do it." Candy left her post by the door and came outside. Even Eden's glare didn't wipe the smile from her face. "They're lovely, aren't they? Have a good time."

"We'll do that." Chase linked his fingers with Eden's and drew her toward his car. She told herself the sun had been in her eyes. Why else would she have missed the low-slung white Lamborghini parked beside the cabin. She settled herself in the passenger's seat with a warning to herself not to relax.

The moment the engine sprang to life, there was

a chorus of goodbyes. Every girl and counselor had lined up to wave them off. Eden disguised a chuckle with a cough.

"It seems this is one of the camp's highlights this summer."

Chase lifted a hand out of the open window to wave back. "Let's see if we can make it one of ours."

Something in his tone made her glance over just long enough to catch that devil of a smile. Eden made up her mind then and there. No, she wouldn't relax, but she'd be damned if she'd be intimidated either. "All right." She leaned back in her seat, prepared to make the best of a bad deal. "I haven't had a meal that wasn't served on a tray in weeks."

"I'll cancel the trays."

"I'd appreciate it." She laughed, then assured herself that laughing wasn't really relaxing. "Stop me if I start stacking the silverware." The breeze blowing in the open window was warm and as fresh as the flowers Chase had brought her. Eden allowed herself the pleasure of lifting her face to it. "This is nice, especially when I was expecting a pickup truck."

"Even country bumpkins can appreciate a well-made machine."

"That's not what I meant." Ready with an apology, she turned, but saw he was smiling. "I suppose you wouldn't care if it was."

"I know what I am, what I want and what I can do." As he took a curve he slowed. His eyes met hers briefly. "But the opinions of certain people always matter. In any case, I prefer the mountains to traffic jams. What do you prefer, Eden?"

"I haven't decided." That was true, she realized with a jolt. In a matter of weeks her priorities, and her hopes, had changed direction. Musing on that, she almost missed the arching ELLIOT sign when Chase turned between the columns. "Where are we going?"

"To dinner."

"In the orchard?"

"In my house." With that he changed gears and had the car cruising up the gravel drive.

Eden tried to ignore the little twist of apprehension she felt. True, this wasn't the crowded, and safe, restaurant she had imagined. She'd shared private dinners before, hadn't she? She'd been raised from the cradle to know how to handle any social situation. But the apprehension remained. Dinner alone with Chase wouldn't be, couldn't possibly be, like any other experience.

Even as she was working out a polite protest, the car crested the hill. The house rose into view.

It was stone. She couldn't know it was local stone, quarried from the mountains. She saw only that it was old, beautifully weathered. At first glance, it gave the appearance of being gray, but on a closer look colors glimmered through. Amber, russet, tints of green and umber. The sun was still high enough to make the chips of mica and quartz glisten. There were three stories, with the second overhanging the first by a skirting balcony. Eden could see flashes of red and buttercup yellow from the pots of geraniums and marigolds. She caught the scent of lavender even before she saw the rock garden.

A wide, sweeping stone stairway, worn slightly in the center, led to double glass doors of diamond panes.

A redwood barrel was filled with pansies that nodded in the early evening breeze.

It was nothing like what she had expected, and yet… the house, and everything about it, was instantly recognizable.

His own nervousness caught Chase off guard. Eden said nothing when he stopped the car, still nothing when he got out to round the hood and open her door. It mattered, more than he had ever imagined it could, what she thought, what she said, what she felt about his home.

She held her hand out for his in a gesture he knew was automatic. Then she stood beside him, looking at what was his, what had been his even before his birth. Tension lodged in the back of his neck.

"Oh, Chase, it's beautiful." She lifted her free hand to shield her eyes from the sun behind the house. "No wonder you love it."

"My great-grandfather built it." The tension had dissolved without his being aware of it. "He even helped quarry the stone. He wanted something that would last and that would carry a piece of him as long as it did."

She thought of the home that had been her family's for generations, feeling the too-familiar burning behind her eyes. She'd lost that. Sold it. The need to tell him was almost stronger than pride, because in that moment she thought he might understand.

He felt her change in mood even before he glanced down and saw the glint of tears in her eyes. "What is it, Eden?"

"Nothing." No, she couldn't tell him. Some wounds were best left hidden. Private. "I was just thinking how important some traditions are."

"You still miss your father."

"Yes." Her eyes were dry now, the moment past. "I'd love to see inside."

He hesitated a moment, knowing there had been more and that she'd been close to sharing it with him. He could wait, Chase told himself, though his patience was beginning to fray. He would have to wait until she took that step toward him rather than away from him.

With her hand still in his, he climbed the steps to the door. On the other side lay a mountain of apricot fur known as Squat. Even after Chase opened the door, the mound continued to snore.

"Are you sure you should have such a vicious watch-dog unchained?"

"My theory is most burglars wouldn't have the nerve to step over him." Catching Eden around the waist, Chase lifted her up and over.

The stone insulated well against the heat, so the hall was cool and comfortable. High, beamed ceilings gave the illusion of unlimited space. A Monet landscape caught her eye, but before she could comment on it, Chase was leading her through a set of mahogany doors.

The room was cozily square, with window seats recessed into the east and west walls. Instantly Eden could imagine the charm of watching the sun rise or set. Comfort was the theme of the room, with its range of blues from the palest aqua to the deepest indigo. Hand-hooked rugs set off the American antiques. There were fresh flowers here, too, spilling out of a Revere Ware bowl. It was a touch she hadn't expected from a bachelor, particularly one who worked with his hands.

Thoughtful, she crossed the room to the west window. The slanting sun cast long shadows over the buildings he had taken them through that morning. She remembered the conveyor belts, the busy sorters and packers, the noise. Behind her was a small, elegant room with pewter bowls and wild roses.

Peace and challenge, she realized, and she sighed without knowing why. "I imagine it's lovely when the sun starts to drop."

"It's my favorite view." His voice came from directly behind her, but for once she didn't stiffen when he rested his hands on her shoulders. He tried to tell himself it was just coincidence that she had chosen to look out that window, but he could almost believe that his own need for her to see and understand had guided her there. It wouldn't be wise to forget who she was and how she chose to live. "There's no Symphony Hall or Rodin Museum."

His fingers gently massaged the curve of her shoulders. But his voice wasn't as patient. Curious, she turned. His hands shifted to let her slide through, then settled on her shoulders again. "I don't imagine they're missed. If they were, you could visit, then come back to this." Without thinking, she lifted her hand to brush the hair from his forehead. Even as she caught herself, his hand closed around her wrist. "Chase, I—"

"Too late," he murmured; then he kissed each of her fingers, one by one. "Too late for you. Too late for me."

She couldn't allow herself to believe that. She couldn't accept the softening and opening of her emotions. How badly she wanted to let him in, to trust again, to need again. How terrifying it was to be vulnerable. "Please don't do this. It's a mistake for both of us."

"You're probably right." He was almost sure of it himself. But he brushed his lips over the pulse that hammered in her wrist. He didn't give a damn. "Everyone's entitled to one enormous mistake."

"Don't kiss me now." She lifted a hand but only curled her fingers into his shirt. "I can't think."

"One has nothing to do with the other."

When his mouth touched hers, it was soft, seeking. *Too late.* The words echoed in her head even as she lifted her hands to his face and let herself go. This is what she had wanted, no matter how many arguments she had posed, no matter how many defenses she had built. She wanted to be held against him, to sink into a dream that had no end.

He felt her fingers stream through his hair and had to force himself not to rush her. Desire, tensed and hungry, had to be held back until it was tempered with acceptance and trust. In his heart he had already acknowledged that she was more than the challenge he had first considered her. She was more than the summer fling he might have preferred. But as her slim, soft body pressed against his, as her warm, willing mouth opened for him, he could only think of how he wanted her, now, when the sun was beginning to sink toward the distant peaks to the west.

"Chase." It was the wild, drumming beat of her heart that frightened her most. She was trembling. Eden could feel it start somewhere deep inside and spread out until it became a stunning combination of panic and excitement. How could she fight the first and give in to the second? "Chase, please."

He had to draw himself back, inch by painful inch.

He hadn't meant to take either of them so far, so fast. Yet perhaps he had, he thought as he ran a hand down her hair. Perhaps he had wanted to push them both toward an answer that still seemed just out of reach.

"The sun's going down." His hands weren't quite steady when he turned her toward the window again. "Before long, the light will change."

She could only be grateful that he was giving her time to regain her composure. Later she would realize how much it probably had cost him.

They stood a moment in silence, watching the first tints of rose spread above the mountains. A loud, rasping cough had her already-tense nerves jolting.

"S'cuze me."

The man in the doorway had a grizzled beard that trailed down to the first button of his red checked shirt. Though he was hardly taller than Eden, his bulk gave the impression of power. The folds and lines in his face all but obscured his dark eyes. Then he grinned, and she caught the glint of a gold tooth.

So this was the little lady who had the boss running around in circles. Deciding she was prettier than a barrelful of prime apples, he nodded to her by way of greeting. "Supper's ready. Unless you want to eat it cold, you best be moving along."

"Eden Carlbough, Delaney." Chase only lifted a brow, knowing Delaney had already sized up the situation. "He cooks and I don't, which is why I haven't fired him yet."

This brought on a cackle. "He hasn't fired me because I wiped his nose and tied his shoes."

"We could add that that was close to thirty years ago."

She recognized both affection and exasperation. It pleased her to know someone could exasperate Chase Elliot. "It's nice to meet you, Mr. Delaney."

"Delaney, ma'am. Just Delaney." Still grinning, he pulled on his beard. "Mighty pretty," he said to Chase. "It's smarter to think of settling down with someone who isn't an eyesore at breakfast. Supper's going to get cold," he added. Then he was gone.

Though Eden had remained politely silent during Delaney's statement, it took only one look at Chase's face to engender a stream of laughter. The sound made Chase think more seriously about gagging Delaney with his own beard.

"I'm glad you're amused."

"Delighted. It's the first time I've ever seen you speechless. And I can't help being pleased not to be considered an eyesore." Then she disarmed him by offering him her hand. "Supper's going to get cold."

Instead of the dining room, Chase led her out to a jalousied porch. Two paddle fans circled overhead, making the most of the breeze that crept in the slanted windows. A wind chime jingled cheerfully between baskets of fuchsia.

"Your home is one surprise after another," Eden commented as she studied the plump love seats and the glass-and-wicker table. "Every room seems fashioned for relaxation and stunning views."

The table was set with colorful stoneware. Though the sun had yet to drop behind the peaks, two tapers were already burning. There was a single wild rose beside her plate.

Romance, she thought. This was the romance she

had once dreamed of. This was the romance she must now be very wary of. But, wary or not, she picked up the flower and smiled at him. "Thank you."

"Did you want one, too?" As she laughed, Chase drew back her chair.

"Sit down. Sit down. Eat while it's hot." Despite his bulk, Delaney bustled into the room. In his large hands was an enormous tray. Because she realized how easily she could be mowed down, Eden obeyed. "Hope you got an appetite. You could use a little plumping up, missy. Then, I've always preferred a bit of healthy meat on female bones."

As he spoke, he began to serve an exquisite seafood salad. "Made my special, Chicken Delaney. It'll keep under the covers if you two don't dawdle over the salad. Apple pie's on the hot plate, biscuits in the warmer." He stuck a bottle of wine unceremoniously in an ice bucket. "That's the fancy wine you wanted." Standing back, he took a narrowed-eyed glance around before snorting with satisfaction. "I'm going home. Don't let my chicken get cold." Wiping his hands on his jeans, he marched to the door and let it swing shut behind him.

"Delaney has amazing style, doesn't he?" Chase took the wine from the bucket to pour two glasses.

"Amazing," Eden agreed, finding it amazing enough that those gnarled hands had created anything as lovely as the salad in front of her.

"He makes the best biscuits in Pennsylvania." Chase lifted his glass and toasted her. "And I'd put his Beef Wellington up against anyone's."

"Beef Wellington?" With a shake of her head, Eden sipped her wine. It was cool, just a shade tart. "I hope you'll take it the right way when I say he looks more like the type who could charcoal a steak over a backyard grill." She dipped her fork in the salad and sampled it. "But..."

"Appearances can be deceiving," Chase finished for her, pleased with the way her eyes half shut as she tasted. "Delaney's been cooking here as long as I can remember. He lives in a little cottage my grandfather helped him build about forty years ago. Nose-wiping and shoe-tying aside, he's part of the family."

She only nodded, looking down at her plate for a moment as she remembered how difficult it had been to tell her longtime servants she was selling out. Perhaps they had never been as familiar or as informal as Chase's Delaney, but they, too, had been part of the family.

It was there again, that dim candle glow of grief he'd seen in her eyes before. Wanting only to help, he reached over to touch her hand. "Eden?"

Quickly, almost too quickly, she moved her hand and began to eat again. "This is wonderful. I have an aunt back home who would shanghai your Delaney after the first forkful."

Home, he thought, backing off automatically. Philadelphia was still home.

The Chicken Delaney lived up to its name. As the sun set, the meal passed easily, even though they disagreed on almost every subject.

She read Keats and he read Christie. She preferred Bach and he Haggard, but it didn't seem to matter as the glass walls filtered the rosy light of approaching twilight. The candles burned lower. The wine shimmered in crystal, inviting one more sip. Close and clear and quick came the two-tone call of a quail.

"That's a lovely sound." Her sigh was easy and content. "If things are quiet at camp, we can hear the birds in the evening. There's a whippoorwill who's taken to singing right outside the cabin window. You can almost set your watch by her."

"Most of us are creatures of habit," he murmured. He wondered about her, what habits she had, what habits she had changed. Taking her hand, he turned it up. The ridge of callus had hardened. "You didn't take my advice."

"About what?"

"Wearing gloves."

"It didn't seem worth it. Besides…" Letting the words trail off, she lifted her wine.

"Besides?"·

"Having calluses means I did something to earn them." She blurted it out, then sat swearing at herself and waiting for him to laugh.

He didn't. Instead he sat silently, passing his thumb over the toughened skin and watching her. "Will you go back?"

"Go back?"

"To Philadelphia."

It was foolish to tell him how hard she'd tried not to think about that. Instead, she answered as the practical Eden was supposed to. "The camp closes down the last week in August. Where else would I go?"

"Where else?" he agreed, but when he released her hand she felt a sense of loss rather than relief. "Maybe there comes a time in everyone's life when they have to take a hard look at the options." He rose, and her hands balled into fists. He took a step toward her, and her heart rose up to her throat. "I'll be back."

Alone, she let out a long, shaky breath. What had she been expecting? she asked herself. What had she been hoping for? Her legs weren't quite steady when she rose, but it could have been the wine. But wine would have made her warm, and she felt a chill. To ward it off, she rubbed her arms with her hands. The sky was a quiet, deepening blue but for a halo of scarlet along the horizon. She concentrated on that, trying not to imagine how it would look when the stars came out.

Maybe they would look at the stars together again. They could look, picking out the patterns, and she would again feel that click that meant her needs and dreams were meshing. With his.

Pressing a hand to her lips, she struggled to block off that train of thought. It was only that the evening had been lovelier than she had imagined. It was only that they had more in common than she had believed possible. It was only that he had a gentleness inside him that softened parts of her when she least expected it. And when he kissed her, she felt as though she had the world pulsing in the palm of her hand.

No. Uneasy, she wrapped her hands around her forearms and squeezed. She was romanticizing again, spinning daydreams when she had no business dreaming at all. She was just beginning to sort out her life, to make her own place. It wasn't possible that she was looking to him to be any part of it.

She heard the music then, something low and unfamiliar that nonetheless had tiny shivers working their way up her spine. She had to leave, she thought quickly. And right away. She had let the atmosphere get to her. The house, the sunset, the wine. Him. Hearing his foot-steps, she turned. She would tell him she had to get back. She would thank him for the evening, and…es-cape.

When he came back into the room, she was stand-ing beside the table so that the candlelight flickered over her skin. Dusk swirled behind her with its smoky magic. The scent of wild roses from the bush outside the window seemed to sigh into the room. He won-dered, if he touched her now, if she would simply dis-solve in his hands.

"Chase, I think I'd better—"

"Shh." She wouldn't dissolve, he told himself as he went to her. She was real, and so was he. One hand cap-tured hers, the other slipping around her waist. After one moment of resistance, she began to move with him. "One of the pleasures of country music is dancing to it."

"I, ah, I don't know the song." But it felt so good, so very good, to sway with him while darkness fell.

"It's about a man, a woman and passion. The best songs are."

She shut her eyes. She could feel the brush of his jacket against her cheek, the firm press of his hand at her waist. He smelled of soap, but nothing a woman would use. This had a tang that was essentially mascu-line. Wanting to taste, she moved her head so that her lips rested against his neck.

His pulse beat there, quick, surprising her. Forget-ting caution, she nestled closer and felt its sudden rise in speed. As her own raced to match it, she gave a murmur of pleasure and traced it with the tip of her tongue.

He started to draw her away. He meant to. When he'd left her, he'd promised himself that he would slow the pace to one they could both handle. But now she was cuddled against him, her body swaying, her fingers straying to his neck, and her mouth… With an oath, Chase dragged her closer and gave in to hunger.

The kiss was instantly torrid, instantly urgent. And somehow, though she had never experienced anything like it, instantly familiar. Her head tilted back in surrender. Her lips parted. Here and now, she wanted the fire and passion that had only been hinted at.

Perhaps he lowered her to the love seat, perhaps she drew him to it, but they were wrapped together, pressed against the cushions. An owl hooted once, then twice, then gave them silence.

He'd wanted to believe she could be this generous. He'd wanted to believe his lips would touch hers and find unrestricted sweetness. Now his mind spun with it. Whatever he had wanted, whatever he had dreamed of, was less, so much less than what he now held in his arms.

He stroked a hand down her body and met trembling response. With a moan, she arched against him. Through the sheer fabric of her blouse, he could feel the heat rising to her skin, enticing him to touch again and yet again.

He released the first button of her blouse, then the second, following the course with his lips. She shivered with anticipation. Her lace cuffs brushed against his cheeks as she lifted her hands to his hair. It seemed her body was filling, flooding with sensations she'd once only imagined. Now they were so real and so clear that she could feel each one as it layered over the next.

The pillows at her back were soft. His body was hard and hot. The breeze that jingled the wind chime overhead was freshened with flowers. Behind her closed eyes came the flicker and glow of candlelight. In teams of thousands, the cicadas began to sing. But more thrilling, more intense, was the sound of her name whispering from him as he pressed his lips against her skin.

Suddenly, searing, his mouth took hers again. In the kiss she could taste everything, his need, his desire, the passion that teetered on the edge of sanity. As her own madness hovered, she felt her senses swimming with him. And she moaned with the ecstasy of falling in love.

For one brief moment, she rose on it, thrilled with the knowledge that she had found him. The dream and the reality were both here. She had only to close them both in her arms and watch them become one.

Then the terror of it fell on her. She couldn't let it be real. How could she risk it? Once she had given her trust and her promise, if not her heart. And she had been betrayed. If it happened again, she would never recover. If it happened with Chase, she wouldn't want to.

"Chase, no more." She turned her face away and tried to clear her head. "Please, this has to stop."

Her taste was still exploding in his mouth. Beneath his, her body was trembling with a need he knew matched his own. "Eden, for God's sake." With an effort that all but drained him, he lifted his head to look down at her. She was afraid. He recognized her fear immediately and struggled to hold back his own needs. "I won't hurt you."

That almost undid her. He meant it, she was sure, but that didn't mean it wouldn't happen. "Chase, this isn't right for me. For either of us."

"Isn't it?" Tension knotted in his stomach as he drew her toward him. "Can you tell me you didn't feel how right it was a minute ago?"

"No." It was both confusion and fear that had her dragging her hands through her hair. "But this isn't what I want. I need you to understand that this can't be what I want. Not now."

"You're asking a hell of a lot."

"Maybe. But there isn't any choice."

That infuriated him. She was the one who had taken his choice away, simply by existing. He hadn't asked her to fall into his life. He hadn't asked her to become the focus of it before he had a chance for a second breath. She'd given in to him to the point where he was half-mad for her. Now she was drawing away. And asking him to understand.

"We'll play it your way." His tone chilled as he drew away from her.

She shuddered, recognizing instantly that his anger could be lethal. "It's not a game."

"No? Well, in any case, you play it well."

She pressed her lips together, understanding that she deserved at least a part of the lash. "Please, don't spoil what happened."

He walked to the table and, lifting his glass, studied the wine. "What did happen?"

I fell in love with you. Rather than answer him, she began to button her blouse with nerveless fingers.

"I'll tell you." He tossed back the remaining wine, but it didn't soothe him. "Not for the first time in our fascinating relationship, you blew hot and cold without any apparent reason. It makes me wonder if Eric backed out of the marriage out of self-defense."

He saw her fingers freeze on the top button of her blouse. Even in the dim light, he could watch the color wash out of her face. Very carefully, he set his glass down again. "I'm sorry, Eden. That was uncalled-for."

The fight for control and composure was a hard war, but she won. She made her fingers move until the button was in place, then, slowly, she rose. "Since you're so interested, I'll tell you that Eric jilted me for more practical reasons. I appreciate the meal, Chase. It was lovely. Please thank Delaney for me."

"Damn it, Eden."

When he started forward, her body tightened like a bow. "If you could do one thing for me, it would be to take me back now and say nothing. Absolutely nothing."

Turning, she walked away from the candlelight.

Chapter 6

During the first weeks of August, the camp was plagued with one calamity after another. The first was an epidemic of poison ivy. Within twenty-four hours, ten of the girls and three of the counselors were coated with calamine lotion. The sticky heat did nothing to make the itching more bearable.

Just as the rashes started to fade came three solid days of rain. As the camp was transformed into a muddy mire, outdoor activities were canceled. Tempers soared. Eden broke up two hair-pulling battles in one day. Then, as luck would have it, lightning hit one of the trees and distracted the girls from their boredom.

By the time the sun came out, they had enough pot holders, key chains, wallets and pillows to open their own craft shop.

Men with Jeeps and chain saws came to clear away

the debris from the tree. Eden wrote out a check and prayed the last crisis was over.

It was doubtful the check had even been cashed when the secondhand restaurant stove she and Candy had bought stopped working. In the three days the parts were on order, cooking was done in true camp style— around an open fire.

The gelding, Courage, developed an infection that settled in his lungs. Everyone in camp worried about him and fussed over him and pampered him. The vet dosed him with penicillin. Eden spent three sleepless nights in the stables, nursing him and waiting for the crisis to pass.

Eventually the horse's appetite improved, the mud in the compound dried and the stove was back in working order. Eden told herself that the worst had to be over as the camp's routine picked up again.

Yet oddly, the lull brought out a restlessness she'd been able to ignore while the worst was happening. At dusk, she wandered to the stables with her sackful of apples. It wasn't hard to give a little extra attention to Courage. He'd gotten used to being pampered during his illness. Eden slipped him a carrot to go with the apple.

Still, as she worked her way down the stalls, she found the old routine didn't keep her mind occupied. The emergencies over the past couple of weeks had kept her too busy to take a second breath, much less think. Now, with calm settling again, thinking was unavoidable.

She could remember her evening with Chase as if it had been the night before. Every word spoken, every touch, every gesture, was locked in her mind as it had been when it had been happening. The rushing, tumbling sensation of falling in love was just as vital now, and just as frightening.

She hadn't been prepared for it. Her life had always been a series of preparations and resulting actions. Even her engagement had been a quiet step along a well-paved road. Since then, she'd learned to handle the detours and the roadblocks. But Chase was a sudden one-way street that hadn't been on any map.

It didn't matter, she told herself as she finished Patience's rubdown. She would navigate this and swing herself back in the proper direction. Having her choices taken away at this point in her life wasn't something she would tolerate. Not even when the lack of choice seemed so alluring and so right.

"I thought I'd find you here." Candy leaned against the stall door to give the mare a pat. "How was Courage tonight?"

"Good." Eden walked to the little sink in the corner to wash liniment from her hands. "I don't think we have to worry about him anymore."

"I'm glad to know that you'll be using your bunk instead of a pile of hay."

Eden pressed both hands to the small of her back and stretched. No demanding set of tennis had ever brought on this kind of ache. Strangely enough, she liked it. "I never thought I'd actually look forward to sleeping in that bunk."

"Well, now that you're not worried about the gelding, I can tell you I'm worried about you."

"Me?" Eden looked for a towel and, not finding one, dried her hands on her jeans. "Why?"

"You're pushing yourself too hard."

"Don't be silly. I'm barely pulling my weight."

"That stopped being even close to the truth the second week of camp." Now that she'd decided to speak up, Candy took a deep breath. "Damn it, Eden, you're exhausted."

"Tired," Eden corrected her. "Which is nothing a few hours on that miserable bunk won't cure."

"Look, it's okay if you want to avoid the issue with everyone else, even with yourself. But don't do it with me."

It wasn't often Candy's voice took on that firm, no-nonsense tone. Eden lifted a brow and nodded. "All right, what is the issue?"

"Chase Elliot," Candy stated, and she saw Eden freeze up. "I didn't hound you with questions the night you came back from dinner."

"And I appreciate that."

"Well, don't, because I'm asking now."

"We had dinner, talked a bit about books and music, then he brought me back."

Candy closed the stall door with a creak. "I thought I was your friend."

"Oh, Candy, you know you are." With a sigh, Eden closed her eyes a moment. "All right, we did exactly what I said we did, but somewhere between the talk and the ride home, things got a little out of hand."

"What sort of things?"

Eden found she didn't even have the energy to laugh. "I've never known you to pry."

"I've never known you to settle comfortably into depression."

"Am I?" Eden blew her bangs out of her eyes. "God, maybe I am."

"Let's just say that you've jumped from one problem to the next in order to avoid fixing one of your own." Taking a step closer, Candy drew Eden down on a small bench. "So let's talk."

"I'm not sure I can." Linking her hands, Eden looked down at them. The opal ring that had once been her mother's winked back at her. "I promised myself after Papa died and everything was in such a mess that I would handle things and find the best way to solve the problems. I've needed to solve them myself."

"That doesn't mean you can't lean on a friend."

"I've leaned on you so much I'm surprised you can walk upright."

"I'll let you know when I start limping. Eden, unless my memory's faulty, we've taken turns leaning on each other since before either of us could walk. Tell me about Chase."

"He scares me." With a long breath, Eden leaned back against the wall. "Everything's happening so fast, and everything I feel seems so intense." Dropping the last of her guard, she turned her face to Candy's. "If things had worked out differently, I'd be married to another man right now. How can I even think I might be in love with someone else so soon?"

"You're not going to tell me you think you're fickle." The last thing Eden had expected was Candy's bright, bubbling laughter, but that was what echoed off the stable walls. "Eden, I'm the fickle one, remember? You've always been loyal to a fault. Wait, I can see you're getting annoyed, so let's take this logically." Candy crossed her ankles and began to count off on her fingers.

"First, you were engaged to Eric—the slime— because of all the reasons we've discussed before. It seemed the proper thing to do. Were you in love with him?"

"No, but I thought—"

"Irrelevant. No is the answer. Second, he showed his true colors, the engagement's been off for months, and you've met a fascinating, attractive man. Now, let's even take it a step further." Warming up to the subject, Candy shifted on the bench. "Suppose—God forbid—that you had actually been madly in love with Eric. After he had shown himself to be a snake, your heart would have been broken. With time and effort, you would have pulled yourself back together. Right?"

"I certainly like to think so."

"So we agree."

"Marginally."

That was enough for Candy. "Then, heart restored, if you'd met a fascinating and attractive man, you would have been equally free to fall for him. Either way, you're in the clear." Satisfied, Candy rose and dusted her palms on her jeans. "So what's the problem?"

Not certain she could explain, or even make sense of it herself, Eden looked down at her hands. "Because I've learned something. Love is a commitment, it's total involvement, promises, compromises. I'm not sure I can give those things to anyone yet. And if I were, I don't know if Chase feels at all the same way."

"Eden, your instincts must tell you he does."

With a shake of her head, she rose. She did feel better having said it all out loud, but that didn't change the bottom line. "I've learned not to trust my instincts, but to be realistic. Which is why I'm going to go hit the account books."

"Oh, Eden, give it a break."

"Unfortunately, I had to give it a break during the poison ivy, the lightning, the stove breakdown and the vet visits." Hooking her arm through Candy's, she started to walk toward the door. "You were right, and talking it out helped, but practicality is still the order of the day."

"Meaning checks and balances."

"Right. I'd really like to get to it. The advantage is I can frazzle my brain until the bunk really does feel like a feather bed."

Candy pushed open the door, then squared her shoulders. "I'll help."

"Thanks, but I'd like to finish them before Christmas."

"Oh, low blow, Eden."

"But true." She latched the door behind them. "Don't worry about me, Candy. Talking about it cleared my head a bit."

"Doing something about it would be better, but it's a start. Don't work too late."

"A couple of hours," Eden promised.

The office, as Eden arrogantly called it, was a small side room off the kitchen. After switching on the gooseneck lamp on the metal army-surplus desk, she adjusted the screen, flap up. As an afterthought, she switched the transistor radio on the corner of the desk to a classical station. The quiet, familiar melodies would go a long way toward calming her.

Still, as always, she drew in a deep breath as she took her seat behind the desk. Here, she knew too well, things were black-and-white. There were no multiple choices, no softening the rules as there could be in other areas of the camp. Figures were figures and facts were facts. It was up to her to tally them.

Opening the drawers, she pulled out invoices, the business checkbook and the ledger. She began systematically sorting and entering as the tape spilled out of the adding machine at her elbow.

Within twenty minutes, she knew the worst. The additional expenses of the past two weeks had stretched their capital to the limit. No matter how many ways Eden worked the numbers, the answer was the same. They weren't dead broke, but painfully close to it. Wearily, she rubbed the bridge of her nose between her thumb and forefinger.

They could still make it, she told herself. She pressed her hand down on the pile of papers, letting her palm cover the checks and balances. By the skin of their teeth, she thought, but they could still make it. If there were no more unexpected expenses. And if, she continued, the pile seeming to grow under her hand, she and Candy lived frugally over the winter. She imagined the pile growing another six inches under her restraining hand. If they got the necessary enrollments for the next season, everything would turn around.

Curling her fingers around the papers, she let out a long breath. If one of those *if*s fell through, she still had some jewelry that could be sold.

The lamplight fell across her opal-and-diamond ring, but she looked away, feeling guilty at even considering selling it. But she would. If her other choices were taken away, she would. What she wouldn't do was give up.

The tears began so unexpectedly that they fell onto the blotter before she knew she had shed them. Even as she wiped them away, new ones formed. There was no one to see, no one to hear. Giving in, Eden laid her head on the piles of bills and let the tears come.

They wouldn't change anything. With tears would come no fresh ideas or brilliant answers, but she let them come anyway. Quite simply, her strength had run out.

He found her like that, weeping almost soundlessly over the neat stacks of paper. At first Chase only stood there, with the door not quite shut at his back. She looked so helpless, so utterly spent. He wanted to go to her, but held himself back. He understood that the tears would be private. She wouldn't want to share them, particularly not with him. And yet, even as he told himself to step back, he moved toward her.

"Eden."

Her head shot up at the sound of her name. Her eyes were drenched, but he saw both shock and humiliation in them before she began to dry her cheeks with the backs of her hands.

"What are you doing here?"

"I wanted to see you." It sounded simple enough, but didn't come close to what was moving inside him. He wanted to go to her, to gather her close and fix whatever was wrong. He stuck his hands in his pockets and remained standing just inside the door. "I just heard about the gelding this morning. Is he worse?"

She shook her head, then struggled to keep her voice calm. "No, he's better. It wasn't as serious as we thought it might be."

"That's good." Frustrated by his inability to think of something less inane, he began to pace. How could he offer comfort when she wouldn't share the problem? Her eyes were dry now, but he knew it was pride, and pride alone, that held her together. The hell with her pride, he thought. He needed to help.

When he turned back, he saw she had risen from the desk. "Why don't you tell me about it?"

The need to confide in him was so painfully strong that she automatically threw up the customary shield. "There's nothing to tell. It's been a rough couple of weeks. I suppose I'm overtired."

It was more than that, he thought, though she did look exhausted. "The girls getting to you?"

"No, really, the girls are fine."

Frustrated, he looked for another answer. The radio was playing something slow and romantic. Glancing toward it, Chase noticed the open ledger. The tail of adding-machine tape was spilling onto the floor. "Is it money? I could help."

Eden closed the book with a snap. Humiliation was a bitter taste at the back of her throat. At least it dried the last of her tears. "We're fine," she told him in a voice that was even and cool. "If you'd excuse me, I still have some work to do."

Rejection was something Chase had never fully understood until he'd met her. He didn't care for it. Nodding slowly, he searched for patience. "It was meant as an offer, not an insult." He would have turned and left her then, but the marks of weeping and sleeplessness gave her a pale, wounded look. "I'm sorry about the trouble you've been having the past year, Eden. I knew you'd lost your father, but I didn't know about the estate."

She wanted, oh so badly, to reach out, to let him gather her close and give her all the comfort she needed. She wanted to ask him what she should do, and have him give her the answers. But wouldn't that mean that all the months of struggling for self-sufficiency had been for nothing? She straightened her shoulders. "It isn't necessary to be sorry."

"If you had told me yourself, it would have been simpler."

"It didn't concern you."

He didn't so much ignore the stab of hurt as turn it into annoyance. "Didn't it? I felt differently—feel differently. Are you going to stand there and tell me there's nothing between us, Eden?"

She couldn't deny it, but she was far too confused, far too afraid, to try to define the truth. "I don't know how I feel about you, except that I don't want to feel anything. Most of all, I don't want your pity."

The hands in his pockets curled into fists. He didn't know how to handle his own feelings, his own needs. Now she was treating them as though they didn't matter. He could leave, or he could beg. At the moment, Chase saw no choice between the two. "Understanding and pity are different things, Eden. If you don't know that, there's nothing else to say."

Turning, he left her. The screen door swished quietly behind him.

* * *

For the next two days, Eden functioned. She gave riding instructions, supervised meals and hiked the hills with groups of girls. She talked and laughed and listened, but the hollowness that had spread inside her when the door had closed at Chase's back remained.

Guilt and regret. Those were the feelings she couldn't shake, no matter how enthusiastically she threw herself into her routine. She'd been wrong. She'd known it even as it was happening, but pride had boxed her in. He had offered to help. He had offered to care, and she'd refused him. If there was a worse kind of selfishness, she couldn't name it.

She'd started to phone him, but hadn't been able to dial the number. It hadn't been pride that had held her back this time. Every apology that formed in her mind was neat and tidy and meaningless. She couldn't bear to give him a stilted apology, nor could she bear the possibility that he wouldn't care.

Whatever had started to grow between them, she had squashed. Whatever might have been, she had cut off before it had begun to flower. How could she explain to Chase that she'd been afraid of being hurt again? How could she tell him that when he'd offered help and understanding she'd been afraid to accept it because it was so easy to be dependent?

She began to ride out alone at night again. Solitude didn't soothe her as it once had; it only reminded her that she had taken steps to insure that she would remain alone. The nights were warm, with the lingering scent of honeysuckle bringing back memories of a night where there had been pictures in the sky. She couldn't look at the stars without thinking of him.

Perhaps that was why she rode to the lake, where the grass was soft and thick. Here she could smell the water and wild blossoms. The horse's hooves were muffled, and she could just hear the rustle of wings in flight— some unseen bird in search of prey or a mate.

Then she saw him.

The moon was on the wane, so he was only a shadow, but she knew he was watching her. Just as she had known, somehow, that she would find him there to-night. Reining in, she let the magic take her. For the moment, even if it were only a moment, she would forget everything but that she loved him. Tomorrow would take care of itself.

She slid from the horse and went to him.

He said nothing. Until she touched him, he wasn't sure she wasn't a dream. In silence, she framed his face in her hands and pressed her lips to his. No dream had ever tasted so warm. No illusion had ever felt so soft.

"Eden—"

With a shake of her head, she cut off his words. There were weeks of emptiness to fill, and no questions that needed answering. Rising on her toes, she kissed him again. The only sound was her sigh as his arms finally came around her. She discovered a bottomless well of giving inside her. Something beyond passion, something beyond desire. Here was comfort, strength and the un-derstanding she had been afraid to accept.

His fingers trailed up to her hair, as if each touch reassured him she was indeed real. When he opened his eyes again, his arms wouldn't be empty, but filled with her. Her cheek rubbed his, smooth skin against a day's growth of beard. With her head nestled in a curve

of his shoulder, she watched the wink and blink of fireflies and thought of stars.

They stood in silence while an owl hooted and the
horse whinnied in response.

"Why did you come?" He needed an answer, one he
could take back with him when she had left him again.

"To see you." She drew away, wanting to see his
face. "To be with you."

"Why?"

The magic shimmered and began to dim. With a
sigh, she drew back. Dreams were for sleeping, Eden
reminded herself. And questions had to be answered.
"I wanted to apologize for the way I behaved before.
You were being kind." Searching for words, she turned
to pluck a leaf from the tree that shadowed them. "I
know how I must have seemed, how I sounded, and I
am sorry. It's difficult, still difficult for me to…" Restless, she moved her shoulders. "We were able to muf-
fle most of the publicity after my father died, but there
was a great deal of gossip, of speculation and not-so-
quiet murmurs."

When he said nothing, she shifted again, uncomfortable. "I suppose I resented all of that more than anything else. It became very important to me to prove
myself, that I could manage, even succeed. I realize
that I've become sensitive about handling things myself and that when you offered to help, I reacted badly.
I apologize for that."

Silence hung another moment before he took a step
toward her. Eden thought he moved the way the shadows did. Silently. "That's a nice apology, Eden. Before
I accept it, I'd like to ask if the kiss was part of it."

So he wasn't going to make it easy for her. Her chin lifted. She didn't need an easy road any longer. "No."

Then he smiled and circled her throat with his hand. "What was it for then?"

The smile disturbed her more than the touch, though it was the touch she backed away from. Strange how you could take one step and find yourself sunk to the hips. "Does there have to be a reason?" When she walked toward the edge of the lake, she saw an owl swoop low over the water. That was the way she felt, she realized. As if she were skimming along the surface of something that could take her in over her head. "I wanted to kiss you, so I did."

The tension he'd lived with for weeks had vanished, leaving him almost light-headed. He had to resist the urge to scoop her up and carry her home, where he'd begun to understand she belonged. "Do you always do what you want?"

She turned back with a toss of her head. She'd apologized, but the pride remained. "Always."

He grinned, nudging a smile from her. "So do I."

"Then we should understand each other."

He trailed a finger down her cheek. "Remember that."

"I will." Steady again, she moved past him to the gelding. "We're having a dance a week from Saturday. Would you like to come?"

His hand closed over hers on the reins. "Are you asking me for a date?"

Amused, she swung her hair back before settling a foot in the stirrup. "Certainly not. We're short of chaperons."

She bent her leg to give herself a boost into the saddle, but found herself caught at the waist. She dangled in midair for a moment before Chase set her on the ground again, turning her to face him. "Will you dance with me?"

She remembered the last time they had danced and saw from the look in his eyes that he did as well. Her heart fluttered in the back of her dry throat, but she lifted a brow and smiled. "Maybe."

His lips curved, then descended slowly to brush against hers. She felt the world tilt, then steady at an angle only lovers understand. "A week from Saturday," he murmured, then lifted her easily into the saddle. His hand remained over hers another moment. "Miss me."

He stayed by the water until she was gone and the night was silent again.

Chapter 7

The last weeks of summer were hot and long. At night, there was invariably heat lightning and rumbling thunder, but little rain. Eden pushed herself through the days, blocking out the uncertainty of life after September.

She wasn't escaping, she told herself. She was coping with one day at a time. If she had learned one important lesson over the summer, it was that she could indeed make changes, in herself and in her life.

The frightened and defeated woman who had come to Camp Liberty almost as if it were a sanctuary would leave a confident, successful woman who could face the world on her own terms.

Standing in the center of the compound, she ran her hands down her narrow hips before dipping them into the pockets of her shorts. Next summer would be even better, now that they'd faced the pitfalls and learned how to maneuver around them. She knew she was skipping over months of her life, but found she didn't want to dwell on the winter. She didn't want to think of Philadelphia and snowy sidewalks, but of the mountains and what she had made of her life there.

If it had been possible, she would have found a way to stay behind during the off-season. Eden had begun to understand that only necessity and the need for employment were taking her back east. It wasn't her home any longer.

With a shake of her head, Eden pushed away thoughts of December. The sun was hot and bright. She could watch it shimmer on the surface of Chase's lake and think of him.

She wondered what would have happened if she had met him two years earlier when her life had been so ordered and set and mapped-out. Would she have fallen in love with him then? Perhaps it was all a matter of timing; perhaps she would have given him a polite how-do-you-do and forgotten him.

No. Closing her eyes, she could recall vividly every sensation, every emotion he'd brought into her life. Timing had nothing to do with something so overwhelming. No matter when, no matter where, she would have fallen in love with him. Hadn't she fought it all along, only to find her feelings deepening?

But she'd thought herself in love with Eric, too.

She shivered in the bright sun and watched a jay race overhead. Was she so shallow, so cold, that her feelings could shift and change in the blink of an eye? That was what held her back and warned her to be cautious. If

Eric hadn't turned his back on her, she would have married him. His ring would be on her finger even now. Eden glanced down at her bare left hand.

But that hadn't been love, she reassured herself. Now she knew what love felt like, what it did to heart and mind and body. And yet... How did he feel? He cared, and he wanted, but she knew enough of love now to understand that wasn't enough. She, too, had once cared and wanted. If Chase was in love with her, there wouldn't be any *before*. Time would begin now.

Don't be a fool, she told herself with a flash of annoyance. That kind of thinking would only make her drift back to dependence. There was a before for both of them, and a future. There was no way of being sure that the future would merge with what she felt today.

But she wanted to be a fool, she realized with a quick, delicious shudder. Even if only for a few weeks, she wanted to absorb and concentrate all those mad feelings. She'd be sensible again. Sensible was for January, when the wind was sharp and the rent had to be paid. In a few days she would dance with him, smile up at him. She would have that one night of the summer to be a fool.

Kicking off her shoes, Eden plucked them up in one hand and ran the rest of the way to the dock. Girls, already separated into groups, were waiting for the signal to row out into the lake.

"Miss Carlbough!" In her camp uniform and her familiar cap, Roberta hopped up and down on the grass near the rowboats. "Watch this." With a quick flurry of motion, she bent over, kicked up her feet and stood on her head. "What do you think?" she demanded through teeth clenched with effort. Her triangular face reddened.

"Incredible."

"I've been practicing." With a grunt, Roberta tumbled onto the grass. "Now, when my mom asks what I did at camp, I can stand on my head and show her."

Eden lifted a brow, hoping Mrs. Snow got a few more details. "I'm sure she'll be impressed."

Still sprawled on the grass, arms splayed out to the sides, Roberta stared up at Eden. She was just old enough to wish that her hair was blond and wavy. "You look real pretty today, Miss Carlbough."

Touched, and more than a little surprised, Eden held out a hand to help Roberta up. "Why, thank you, Roberta. So do you."

"Oh, I'm not pretty, but I'm going to be once I can wear makeup and cover my freckles."

Eden rubbed a thumb over Roberta's cheek. "Lots of boys fall for freckles."

"Maybe." Roberta tucked that away to consider later. "I guess you're soft on Mr. Elliot."

Eden dropped her hand back in her pocket. "Soft on?"

"You know." To demonstrate, Roberta sighed and fluttered her eyes. Eden wasn't sure whether to laugh or give the little monster a shove into the lake.

"That's ridiculous."

"Are you getting married?"

"I haven't the vaguest idea where you come up with such nonsense. Now into the boat. Everyone's ready to go."

"My mom told me people sometimes get married when they're soft on each other."

"I'm sure your mother's quite right." Hoping to close the subject, Eden helped Roberta into their assigned rowboat, where Marcie and Linda were already waiting. "However, in this case, Mr. Elliot and I barely know each other. Everyone hook their life jackets, please."

"Mom said she and Daddy fell in love at first sight." Roberta hooked on the preserver, though she thought it was a pain when she swam so well. "They kiss all the time."

"I'm sure that's nice. Now—"

"I used to think it was kind of gross, but I guess it's okay." Roberta settled into her seat and smiled. "Well, if you decide not to marry Mr. Elliot, maybe I will."

Eden was busy locking in the oars, but she glanced up. "Oh?"

"Yeah. He's got a neat dog and all those apple trees." Roberta adjusted the brim of her cap over her eyes. "And he's kind of pretty." The two girls beside her giggled in agreement.

"That's certainly something to think about." Eden began to row. "Maybe you can discuss the idea with your mother when you get home."

"'Kay. Can I row first?"

Eden could only be grateful that the girl's interest span was as fast-moving as the rest of her. "Fine. You and I will row out. Marcie and Linda can row back."

After a bit of drag and a few grunts, Roberta matched her rhythm to Eden's. As the boat began to glide, it occurred to Eden that she was rowing with the same three girls who had started the adventure in the apple orchard.

With a silent chuckle, she settled into sync with Roberta and let her mind drift.

What if she had never gone up in that tree? Absently, she touched her lower lip with her tongue, recalling the taste and feel of Chase. If she had it to do over, would she run in the opposite direction?

Smiling, Eden closed her eyes a moment, so that the sun glowed red under her lids. No, she wouldn't run. Being able to admit it, being able to be sure of it, strengthened her confidence. She wouldn't run from Chase, or from anything else in life.

Perhaps she was soft on him, as Roberta had termed it. Perhaps she could hug that secret to herself for a little while. It would be wonderful if things could be as simple and uncomplicated as Roberta made them. Love equaled marriage, marriage equaled happiness. Sighing, Eden opened her eyes and watched the surface of the lake. For a little while she could believe in poetry and dreams.

Daydreams... They were softer and even more mystical than dreams by night. It had been a long time since Eden had indulged in them. Now the girls were chattering and calling to their friends in the other boats. Someone was singing, deliberately off-key. Eden's arms moved in a steady rhythm as the oars cut smoothly into the water and up into the air again.

So she was floating...dreaming with her eyes open... silk and ivory and lace. The glitter of the sun on water was like candlelight. The call of crows was music to dance by.

She was riding on Pegasus. High in a night sky, his white wings effortlessly cut through the air. She could taste the cool, thin wind that took them through clouds. Her hair was free, flying behind her, twined with flowers. More clouds, castle-like, rose up in the distance, filmy and gray and secret. Their secrets were nothing to her. She had freedom for the first time, full, unlimited freedom.

And he was with her, riding the sky through snatches of light and dark. Higher, still higher they rose, until the earth was only mist beneath them. And the stars were flowers, the white petals of anemones that she could reach out and pick as the whim struck her.

When she turned in his arms, she was his without boundaries. All restrictions, all doubts, had been left behind in the climb.

"Hey, look. It's Squat!"

Eden blinked. The daydream disintegrated. She was in a rowboat, with muscles that were just beginning to ache from exertion. There were no flowers, no stars, only water and sky.

They'd rowed nearly the width of the lake. A portion of Chase's orchard spread back from the shore, and visible was one of the greenhouses he had taken the camp through on the day of the tour. Delighted with the company, Squat dashed back and forth in the shallow water near the lake's edge. His massive paws scattered a flurry of water that coated him until he was a sopping, shaggy mess.

Smiling as the girls called out greetings to the dog, Eden wondered if Chase was home. What did he do with his Sundays? she thought. Did he laze around the house with the paper and cups of coffee? Did he switch on the ball game, or go out for long, solitary drives?

Just then, as if to answer her questions, he and Delaney joined the dog on the shore. Across the water, Eden felt the jolt as their eyes met.

Would it always be like that? Always stunning, always fresh? Always immediate? Inhaling slowly, she coaxed her pulse back to a normal rate.

"Hey, Mr. Elliot!" Without a thought for the consequences, Roberta dropped her oar and jumped up. Excitement had her bouncing up and down as the boat teetered.

"Roberta." Acting by instinct, Eden locked her oars. "Sit down, you'll turn us over." Eden started to grab for her hand as the other girls took Roberta's lead and jumped to their feet.

"Hi, Mr. Elliot!"

The greeting rang out in unison, just before the boat tipped over.

Eden hit the water headfirst. After the heat of the sun it seemed shockingly cold, and she surfaced sputtering with fury. With one hand, she dragged the hair out of her eyes and focused on the three bobbing heads. The girls, buoyed by their life jackets, waved unrepentantly at the trio on shore.

Eden grabbed the edge of the upended boat. "Roberta!"

"Look, Miss Carlbough." Apparently the tone, said through gritted teeth, passed over the girl's head. "Squat's coming out."

"Terrific." Treading water, Eden plucked Roberta by the arm and tried to drag her back to the capsized boat. "Remember the rules of boating safety. Stay here." Eden went for the next girl, but twisted her head to see the dog paddling toward them. Uneasy with his progress, she looked back toward shore.

Her request that Chase call back his dog caught in her throat as she spotted his grin. Though she couldn't hear the words, she saw Delaney turn to him with some remark. It was enough to see Chase throw back his head and laugh. That sound carried.

"Want some help?" he called out.

Eden pulled at the next giggling girl. "Don't put yourself out," she began, then shrieked when Squat laid a wet, friendly nose on her shoulder. Her reaction seemed to amuse everyone, dog included. Squat began to bark enthusiastically in her ear.

Fresh pandemonium broke out as the girls began to splash water at each other and the dog. Eden found herself caught in the crossfire. In the other boats, campers and counselors looked on, grinning or calling out encouraging words. Squat paddled circles around her as she struggled to restore some kind of order.

"All right, ladies. Enough." That earned her a mouthful of lake. "It's time to right the boat."

"Can Squat take a ride with us?" Roberta giggled as he licked water from her face.

"No."

"That hardly seems fair."

Eden nearly submerged before Chase gripped her arm. She'd been too busy trying to restore order and her own dignity to notice that he'd swum the few yards from shore. "He came out to help."

His hair was barely damp, while hers was plastered to her head. Chase hooked an arm around her waist to ease her effort to tread water.

"You'd better right the boat," he said to the girls, who immediately fell to doing so with a vengeance. "Apparently you do better with horses." His voice was soft and amused in Eden's ear.

She started to draw away, but her legs tangled with his. "If you and that monster hadn't been on shore—"

"Delaney?"

"No, not Delaney." Frustrated, Eden pushed at her hair.

"You're beautiful when you're wet. Makes me wonder why I haven't thought of swimming with you before."

"We're not supposed to be swimming, we're supposed to be boating."

"Either way, you're beautiful."

She wouldn't be moved. Even though the girls had already righted the boat, Eden knew she was in over her head. "It's that dog," she began. Even as she said it, the girls were climbing back into the boat and urging Squat to join them.

"Roberta, I said—" Chase gently dunked her. Surfacing, she heard him striking the bargain.

"We'll swim back. You bring Squat. He likes boats."

"I said—" Again, she found herself under water. This time when she came up for air, she gave Chase her full attention. The swing she took at him was slow and sluggish because of the need to tread water.

He caught her fist and kissed it. "Beat you back."

Narrowing her eyes, Eden gave him a shove before striking out after the boat. The water around her ears muffled the sound of Squat's deep barking and the girls'

excited cheering. With strong, even strokes, she kept a
foot behind the boat and made certain the girls behaved.

Less than twenty feet from shore, Chase caught her
by the ankle. Laughing and kicking, Eden found herself tangled in his arms.

"You cheat." As he rose, he swept her off her feet so
that her accusation ended in another laugh. His bare
chest was cool and wet under her palms. His hair was
dripping so that the sunlight was caught in each separate drop of water. "I won."

"Wrong." She should have seen it coming. Without
effort, he pitched her back in the lake. Eden landed bottom first. "I won."

Eden stood to shake herself off. Managing to sup-
press a smile, she nodded toward the whooping girls.
"And that, ladies, is a classic example of poor sports-
manship." She reached up to squeeze the water out of
her hair, unaware that her shirt clung to every curve.
Chase felt his heart stop. She waded toward shore, with
the clear lake water clinging to her tanned legs. "Good
afternoon, Delaney."

"Ma'am." He gave her a gold, flashing grin. "Nice
day for a swim."

"Apparently."

"I was about to pick me some blackberries for jam."
He cast his gaze over the three dripping girls. "If I had
some help, could be I'd have a jar or so extra for some
neighbors."

Before Eden could consent or refuse, all the girls
and Squat were jumping circles around her. She had to
admit that a ten-or fifteen-minute break would make
the row back to camp a little more appealing. "Ten min-

utes," she told them before turning back to signal to the
other boats.

Delaney toddled off, sandwiched between girls who
were already barraging him with questions. As they
disappeared into a cluster of trees, a startled flock of
birds whizzed out. She laughed, turning back to see
Chase staring at her.

"You're a strong swimmer."

She had to clear her throat. "I think I've just become
more competitive. Maybe I should keep an eye on the
girls so—"

"Delaney can handle them." He reached out to brush
a bead of water from her jawline. Beneath his gentle
touch, she shivered. "Cold?"

More than the sun had taken the lake's chill from
her skin. Eden managed to shake her head. "No." But
when his hands came to her shoulders, she stepped back.

He wore only cutoffs, faded soft from wear. The shirt
he had peeled off before diving into the lake had been
tossed carelessly to the ground. "You don't feel cold,"
he murmured as he stroked his hands down her arms.

"I'm not." She heard the laughter beyond the trees. "I
really can't let them stay long. They'll have to change."

Patient, Chase took her hand. "Eden, you're going
to end up in the lake again if you keep backing up."
He was frightening her. Frustrated, he struggled not to
push. It seemed that every time he thought he'd gained
her trust, he saw that quick flash of anxiety in her eyes
again. He smiled, hoping the need that was roiling inside him didn't show. "Where are your shoes?"

Off-balance, she looked down and stared at her own
bare feet. Slowly, her muscles began to relax again. "At

the bottom of your lake." Laughing, she shook her wet hair back, nearly destroying him. "Roberta always manages to keep things exciting. Why don't we give them a hand with the berry-picking."

His arm came across her body to take her shoulder before she could move past him. "You're still backing away, Eden." Lifting a hand, he combed his fingers through her sleek, wet hair until they rested at the base of her neck. "It's hard to resist you this way, with your face glowing and your eyes aware and just a bit frightened."

"Chase, don't." She put her hand to his.

"I want to touch you." He shifted so that the full length of her body was against his. "I need to touch you." Through the wet cotton, she could feel the texture of his skin on hers. "Look at me, Eden." The slightest pressure of his fingers brought her face up to his. "How close are you going to let me get?"

She could only shake her head. There weren't any words to describe what she was feeling, what she wanted, what she was still too afraid to need. "Chase, don't do this. Not here, not now." Then she could only moan, as his mouth traveled with a light, lazy touch over her face.

"When?" He had to fight the desire to demand rather than to ask, to take rather than to wait. "Where?" This time the kiss wasn't lazy, but hard, bruising. Eden felt rational thought spiral away even as she groped for an answer. "Don't you think I know what happens to you when we're like this?" His voice thickened as his patience stretched thinner and thinner. "Good God, Eden, I need you. Come with me tonight. Stay with me."

Yes, yes. Oh, yes. How easy it would be to say it, to give in, to give everything without a thought for tomorrow. She clung to him a moment, wanting to believe dreams were possible. He was so solid, so real. But so were her responsibilities.

"Chase, you know I can't." Fighting for rationality, she drew away. "I have to stay at camp."

Before she could move away again, he caught her face in his hands. She thought his eyes had darkened, a stormier green now, with splashes of gold from the sun. "And when summer's over, Eden? What then?"

What then? How could she have the answer, when the answer was so cold, so final? It wasn't what she wanted, but what had to be. If she was to keep her promise to herself, to make her life work, there was only one answer. "Then I'll go back, back to Philadelphia, until next summer."

Only summers? Was that all she was willing to give? It was the panic that surprised him and kept the fury at bay. When she left, his life would be empty. He took her shoulders again, fighting back the panic.

"You'll come to me before you go." It wasn't a question. It wasn't a demand. It was a simple statement. The demand she could have rebelled against; the question she could have refused.

"Chase, what good would it do either of us?"

"You'll come to me before you go," he repeated. Because if she didn't, he'd follow her. There would be no choice.

Chapter 8

Red and white crepe paper streamed from corner to corner, twined together in elongated snakes of color. Balloons, bulging with air from energetic young lungs, were crowded into every available space. Stacked in three uneven towers were all the records deemed fit to play.

Dance night was only a matter of hours away.

Under Candy's eagle eye, tables were carried outside, while others were grouped strategically around the mess area. This simple chore took twice as long as it should have, as girls had to stop every few feet to discuss the most important aspect of the evening: boys.

Although her skills with paint and glue were slim at best, Eden had volunteered for the decorating committee—on the understanding that her duties were limited to hanging and tacking what was already made. In addition to the crepe paper and balloons, there were banners and paper flowers that the more talented members of campers and staff had put together by hand. The best of these was a ten-foot banner dyed Camp Liberty red and splashed with bold letters that spelled out WELCOME TO CAMP LIBERTY'S ANNUAL SUMMER DANCE.

Candy had already taken it for granted that it would be the first of many. In her better moods, Eden hoped she was right. In her crankier ones, she wondered if they could swing a deal with the boys' camp to split the cost of refreshments. For the moment, she pushed both ideas aside, determined to make this dance the best-decorated one in Pennsylvania.

Eden let an argument over which records had priority run its course below her as she climbed a stepladder to secure more streamers. Already, the record player at the far end of the room was blaring music.

It was silly. She told herself that yet again as she realized she was as excited about the evening as any of the girls. She was an adult, here only to plan, supervise and chaperon. Even as she reminded herself of this, her thoughts ran forward to the evening, when the mess area would be filled with people and noise and laughter. Like the girls below her, her thoughts kept circling back to vital matters—like what she should wear.

It was fascinating to realize that this simple end-of-the-summer dance in the mountains was more exciting for her than her own debutante ball. That she had taken lightly, as the next step along the path that had been cleared for her before she was born. This was new, untried and full of possibilities.

It all centered on Chase. Eden was nearly ready to

accept that as a new song blared into life. Since it was one she'd heard dozens of times before, she began to hum along with it. Her ponytail swayed with the movement as she attached another streamer.

"We'll ask Miss Carlbough." Eden heard the voices below, but paid little attention, as she had a tack in her mouth and five feet of crepe paper held together by her thumb. "She always knows, and if she doesn't, she finds out."

She had started to secure the tack, but as the statement drifted up to her, she stopped pushing. Was that really the way the girls saw her? Dependable? With a half laugh, she sent the tack home. To her, the statement was the highest of compliments, a sign of faith.

She'd done what she had set out to do. In three short months, she had accomplished something she had never done in all her years of living. She had made something of herself, by herself. And, perhaps more importantly, for herself.

It wasn't going to stop here. Eden dropped the rest of the tacks into her pocket. The summer might be nearly over, but the challenge wasn't. Whether she was in South Mountain or Philadelphia, she wasn't going to forget what it meant to grow. Twisting on the ladder, she started down to find out what it was the girls had wanted to ask her. On the second rung, she stopped, staring.

The tall, striking woman strode into the mess. The tail of her Hermès scarf crossed the neck of a cerise suit and trailed on behind. Her bone-white hair was perfect, as was the double strand of pearls that lay on her bosom. Tucked in the crook of one arm was a small piece of white fluff known as BooBoo.

"Aunt Dottie!" Delighted, Eden scrambled down from the ladder. In seconds she was enveloped by Dottie's personal scent, an elusive combination of Paris and success. "Oh, it's wonderful to see you." Drawing back from the hug, Eden studied the lovely, strong-boned face. Even now, she could see shadows of her father in the eyes and around the mouth. "You're the last person I expected to see here."

"Darling, have you grown thorns in the country?"

"Thorns? I—oh." Laughing, Eden reached in her pocket. "Thumbtacks. Sorry."

"The hug was worth a few holes." Taking Eden's hand, she stepped back to make her own study. Though her face remained passive, she let out a quiet sigh of relief. No one knew how many restless nights she'd spent worrying over her brother's only child. "You look beautiful. A little thin, but with marvelous color." With Eden's hand still in hers, she glanced around the room. "But darling, what an odd place you've chosen to spend the summer."

"Aunt Dottie." Eden just shook her head. Throughout the weeks and months after her father's death, Dottie had stubbornly refused to accept Eden's decision not to use Dottie's money as a buffer, her home as a refuge. "If I have marvelous color, credit the country air."

"Hmm." Far from convinced, Dottie continued to look around as a new record plopped down to continue the unbroken cycle of music. "I've always considered the south of France country enough."

"Aunt Dottie, tell me what you're doing here. I'm amazed you could even find the place."

"It wasn't difficult. The chauffeur reads a map very well." Dottie gave the fluff in her arms a light pat. "Boo-Boo and I felt an urge for a drive to the country."

"I see." And she did. Like everyone else she had left behind, Eden knew that her aunt considered her camp venture an impulse. It would take more than one summer to convince Dottie, or anyone else, that she was serious. After all, it had taken her most of the summer to convince herself.

"Yes, and since I was in the neighborhood…" Dottie let that trail off. "What a chic outfit," she commented, taking in Eden's paint-spattered smock and tattered sneakers. "Then, perhaps bohemian's coming back. What do you have there?"

"Crepe paper. It goes with the thumbtacks." Eden extended her hand. BooBoo regally allowed her head to be patted.

"Well, give them both to one of these charming young ladies and come see what I've brought you."

"Brought me?" Obeying automatically, Eden handed over the streamers. "Start these around the tables, will you, Lisa?"

"Do you know," Dottie began as she linked her arm through Eden's, "the nearest town is at least twenty miles from here? That is if one could stretch credibility and call what we passed through a town. There, there, BooBoo, I won't set you down on the nasty ground." She cuddled the dog as they stepped outside. "BooBoo's a bit skittish out of the city, you understand."

"Perfectly."

"Where was I? Oh yes, the town. It had one traffic light and a place called Earl's Lunch. I was almost curious enough to stop and see what one did at Earl's Lunch."

Eden laughed, and leaned over to kiss Dottie's cheek. "One eats a small variety of sandwiches and stale potato chips and coffee while exchanging town gossip."

"Marvelous. Do you go often?"

"Unfortunately, my social life's been a bit limited."

"Well, your surprise might just change all that." Turning, Dottie gestured toward the canary-yellow Rolls parked in the main compound. Eden felt every muscle, every emotion freeze as the man straightened from his easy slouch against the hood.

"Eric."

He smiled, and in a familiar gesture, ran one hand lightly over his hair. Around him, a group of girls had gathered to admire the classic lines of the Rolls and the classic looks of Eric Keeton.

His smile was perfectly angled as he walked toward her. His walk was confident, just a shade too conservative for a swagger. As she watched him, Eden saw him in the clear light of disinterest. His hair, several shades darker than her own, was perfectly styled for the boardroom or the country club. Casual attire, which included pleated slacks and a polo shirt, fit neatly over his rather narrow frame. Hazel eyes, which had a tendency to look bored easily, smiled and warmed now. Though she hadn't offered them, he took both her hands.

"Eden, how marvelous you look."

His hands were soft. Strange, she had forgotten that.

Though she didn't bother to remove hers, her voice was cool. "Hello, Eric."

"Lovelier than ever, isn't she, Dottie?" Her stiff greeting didn't seem to disturb him. He gave her hands an intimate little squeeze. "Your aunt was worried about you. She expected you to be thin and wan."

"Fortunately, I'm neither." Now, carefully, deliberately, Eden removed her hands. She would have been greatly pleased, though she had no way of knowing it, that her eyes were as cold as her voice. It was so easy to turn away from him. "Whatever possessed you to drive all this way, Aunt Dottie? You weren't really worried?"

"A tad." Concerned with the ice in her niece's voice, Dottie touched Eden's cheek "And I did want to see the—the place where you spent the summer."

"I'll give you a tour."

A thin left brow arched in a manner identical to Eden's. "How charming."

"Aunt Dottie!" Red curls bouncing, Candy raced around the side of the building. "I knew it had to be you." Out of breath and grinning broadly, Candy accepted Dottie's embrace. "The girls were talking about a yellow Rolls in the compound. Who else could it have been?"

"As enthusiastic as ever." Dottie's smile was all affection. She might not have always understood Candice Bartholomew, but she had always been fond of her. "I hope you don't mind a surprise visit."

"I love it." Candy bent down to the puff of fur. "Hi, BooBoo." Straightening, she let her gaze drift over Eric. "Hello, Eric." Her voice dropped an easy twenty-five degrees. "Long way from home."

"Candy." Unlike Dottie, he had no fondness for Eden's closest friend. "You seem to have paint all over your hands."

"It's dry," she said, carelessly, and somewhat regretfully. If the paint had been wet, she would have greeted him more personally.

"Eden's offered to take us on a tour." Dottie was well aware of the hostility. She'd driven hundreds of miles from Philadelphia for one purpose. To help her niece find happiness. If it meant she had to manipulate...so much the better. "I know Eric's dying to look around, but if I could impose on you—" She laid her hand on Candy's. "I'd really love to sit down with a nice cup of tea. BooBoo, too. The drive was a bit tiring."

"Of course." Manners were their own kind of trap. Candy sent Eden a look meant to fortify her. "We'll use the kitchen, if you don't mind the confusion."

"My dear, I thrive on it." With that she turned to smile at Eden and was surprised by the hard, knowing look in Eden's eyes.

"Go right ahead, Aunt Dottie. I'll show Eric what the camp has to offer."

"Eden, I—"

"Go have your tea, darling." She kissed Dottie's cheek. "We'll talk later." She turned, leaving Eric to follow or not. When he fell into step beside her, she began. "We've six sleeping cabins this season, with plans to add two more for next summer. Each cabin has an Indian name to keep it distinct."

As they passed the cabins, she saw that the anemones were still stubbornly blooming. They gave her strength. "Each week, we have a contest for the neatest cabin. The reward is extra riding time, or swimming time, or whatever the girls prefer. Candy and I have a small shower in our cabin. The girls share facilities at the west end of the compound."

"Eden." Eric cupped her elbow in his palm in the same manner he had used when strolling down Broad Street. She gritted her teeth, but didn't protest.

"Yes?" The cool, impersonal look threw him off. It took him only a moment to decide it meant she was hiding a broken heart.

"What have you been doing with yourself?" He waved his hand in a gesture that took in the compound and the surrounding hills. "Here?"

Holding on to her temper, Eden decided to take the question literally. "We've tried to keep the camp regimented, while still allowing for creativity and fun. Over the past few weeks, we've found that we can adhere fairly tightly to the schedule as long as we make room for fresh ideas and individual needs." Pleased with herself, she dipped her hands into the pockets of her smock. "We're up at six-thirty. Breakfast is at seven sharp. Daily inspection begins at seven-thirty and activities at eight. For the most part, I deal with the horses and stables, but when necessary, I can pitch in and help in other areas."

"Eden." Eric stopped her by gently tightening his fingers on her elbow. Turning to him, she watched the faint breeze ruffle his smooth, fair hair. She thought of the dark confusion of Chase's hair. "It's difficult to believe you've spent your summer camping out in a cabin and overseeing a parade of girls on horseback."

"Is it?" She merely smiled. Of course it was difficult for him. He owned a stable, but he'd never lifted a pitchfork. Rather than resentment, Eden felt a stirring of pity. "Well, there's that, among a few other things such as hiking, smoothing over cases of homesickness and poison ivy, rowing, giving advice on teenage romance and fashion, identifying fifteen different varieties of local wildflowers and seeing that a group of girls has fun. Would you like to see the stables?" She headed off without waiting for his answer.

"Eden." He caught her elbow again. It took all her willpower not to jab it back into his soft stomach. "You're angry. Of course you are, but I—"

"You've always had a fondness for good horseflesh." She swung the stable door open so that he had to back off or get a faceful of wood. "We've two mares and four geldings. One of the mares is past her prime, but I'm thinking of breeding the other. The foals would interest the girls and eventually become part of the riding stock. This is Courage."

"Eden, please. We have to talk."

She stiffened when his hands touched her shoulders. But she was calm, very calm, when she turned and removed them. "I thought we were talking."

He'd heard the ice in her voice before, and he understood it. She was a proud, logical woman. He'd approach her on that level. "We have to talk about us, darling."

"In what context?"

He reached for her hand, giving a small shrug when she drew it away. If she had accepted him without a murmur, he would have been a great deal more surprised. For days now, he'd been planning exactly the proper way to smooth things over. He'd decided on regretful, with a hint of humble thrown in.

"You've every right to be furious with me, every right to want me to suffer."

His tone, soft, quiet, understanding, had her swallowing a ball of heat. Indifference, she reminded herself, disinterest, was the greatest insult she could hand him. "It doesn't really concern me if you suffer or not." That wasn't quite true, she admitted. She wouldn't be averse to seeing him writhe a bit. That was because he had come, she realized. Because he had had the gall to come and assume she'd be waiting.

"Eden, you have to know that I have suffered, suffered a great deal. I would have come before, but I wasn't sure you'd see me."

This was the man she had planned to spend her life with. This was the man she had hoped to have children with. She stared at him now, unsure whether she was in the midst of a comedy or a tragedy. "I'm sorry to hear that, Eric. I don't see any reason why you should have suffered. You were only being practical, after all."

Soothed by her placid attitude, he stepped toward her. "I admit that, rightly or wrongly, I was practical." His hands slid up her arms in an old gesture that made her jaw clench. "These past few months have shown me that there are times when practical matters have to take second place."

"Is that so?" She smiled at him, surprised that he couldn't feel the heat. "What would go first?"

"Personal…" He stroked a finger over her cheek. "Much more personal matters."

"Such as?"

His lips were curved as his mouth lowered. She felt the heat of anger freeze into icy disdain. Did he think her a fool? Could he believe himself so irresistible? Then she nearly did laugh, as she realized the answer to both questions was yes.

She let him kiss her. The touch of his lips left her totally unmoved. It fascinated her that, only a few short months before, his kisses had warmed her. It had been nothing like the volcanic heat she experienced with Chase, but there had been a comfort and an easy pleasure. That was all she had thought there was meant to be.

Now there was nothing. The absence of feeling in itself dulled the edge of her fury. She was in control. Here, as in other areas of her life, she was in control. Though his lips coaxed, she simply stood, waiting for him to finish.

When he lifted his head, Eden put her hands on his arms to draw herself away. It was then she saw Chase just inside the open stable door.

The sun was at his back, silhouetting him, blinding her to the expression on his face. Even so, her mouth was dry as she stared, trying to see through shadow and sun. When he stepped forward, his eyes were on hers.

Explanations sprang to her tongue, but she could only shake her head as his gaze slid over her and onto Eric.

"Keeton." Chase nodded, but didn't extend his hand. He knew if he had the other man's fingers in his he would take pleasure in breaking them, one by one.

"Elliot." Eric returned the nod. "I'd forgotten. You have land around here, don't you?"

"A bit." Chase wanted to murder him, right there in

the stables, while Eden watched. Then he would find it just as satisfying to murder her.

"You must know Eden, then." Eric placed a hand on her shoulder in a casually possessive movement. Chase followed the gesture before looking at her again. Her instinctive move to shrug away Eric's hand was stopped by the look. Was it anger she saw there, or was it disgust?

"Yes. Eden and I have run into each other a few times." He dipped his hands into his pockets as they balled into fists.

"Chase was generous enough to allow us to use his lake." Her right hand groped for her left until they were clasped together. "We had a tour of his orchards." Though pride suffered, her eyes pleaded with him.

"Your land must be very near here." Eric hadn't missed the exchange of looks. His hand leaned more heavily on Eden's shoulder.

"Near enough."

Then they were looking at each other, not at her. Somehow that, more than anything, made her feel as though she'd been shifted to the middle. If there was tension and she was the cause of it, she wanted to be able to speak on her own behalf. But the expression in Chase's eyes only brought confusion. The weight of Eric's hand only brought annoyance. Moving away from Eric, she stepped toward Chase.

"Did you want to see me?"

"Yes." But he'd wanted more than that, a great deal more. Seeing her in Eric's arms had left him feeling both murderous and empty. He wasn't ready to deal with either yet. "It wasn't important."

"Chase—"

"Oh, hello." The warmth in Candy's voice came almost as a shock. She stepped through the doorway with Dottie at her side. "Aunt Dottie, I want you to meet our neighbor, Chase Elliot."

Even as Dottie extended her hand, her eyes were narrowed speculatively. "Elliot? I'm sure I know that name. Yes, yes, didn't we meet several years ago? You're Jessie Winthrop's grandson."

Eden watched his lips curve, his eyes warm, but he wasn't looking at her. "Yes, I am, and I remember you very well, Mrs. Norfolk. You haven't changed."

Dottie's laugh was low and quick. "It's been fifteen years if it's been a day. I'd say there's been a change or two. You were about a foot shorter at the time." She sized him up approvingly in a matter of ten seconds. "It's apples, isn't it? Yes, of course, it is. Elliot's."

And, oh my God, she realized almost as quickly, I've brought Eric along and jammed up the works. A person would have to have a three-inch layer of steel coating not to feel the shock waves bouncing around the stables.

What could be done, she told herself, could be undone. Smiling, she looked at her niece. "Candy's been telling me about the social event of the season. Are we all invited?"

"Invited?" Eden struggled to gather her scattered wits. "You mean the dance?" She had to laugh. Her aunt was standing in the stables in Italian shoes and a suit that had cost more than any one of the horses. "Aunt Dottie, you don't intend to stay here?"

"Stay here?" The white brows shot up. "I should say not." She twisted the pearls at her neck as she began to calculate. She didn't intend to bunk down in a cabin, but neither was she about to miss the impending fireworks. "Eric and I are staying at a hotel some miles away, but I'd be heartbroken if you didn't ask us to the party tonight." She put a friendly hand on Chase's arm. "You're coming, aren't you?"

He knew a manipulator when he saw one. "Wouldn't miss it."

"Wonderful." Dottie slid Candy's hand back into the crook of her arm, then patted it. "We're all invited then."

Fumbling, Candy looked from Eric to Eden. "Well, yes, of course, but——"

"Isn't this sweet?" Dottie patted her hand again. "We'll have a delightful time. Don't you think so, Eden?"

"Delightful," Eden agreed, wondering if she could hitch a ride out of town.

Chapter 9

Eden had problems—big problems. But not the least of them were the sixty adolescents in the mess hall. However she handled Eric, however she managed to explain herself to Chase, sixty young bodies couldn't be put on hold.

The boys arrived in vans at eight o'clock. Unless Eden missed her guess, they were every bit as nervous as the girls. Eden remembered her own cotillion days, the uncertainty and the damp palms. The blaring music helped cover some of the awkwardness as the boys' counselors trooped them in.

The refreshment table was loaded. There was enough punch stored in the kitchen to bathe in. Candy gave a brief welcoming speech to set the tone, the banners and the paper flowers waving at her back. A fresh record was set spinning on the turntable. Girls stood on one side of the room, boys on the other.

The biggest problem, naturally, was that no one wanted to go first. Eden had worked that out by making up two bowls of corresponding numbers. Boys picked from one, girls from another. You matched, you danced. It wasn't imaginative, but it was expedient.

When the first dance was half over, she slipped into the kitchen to check on backup refreshments, leaving Candy to supervise and to mingle with the male counselors.

When she returned, the dance floor wasn't as crowded, but this time the partners had chosen for themselves.

"Miss Carlbough?"

Eden turned her head as she bent to place a bowl of chips in an empty space on the long crowded table. Roberta's face was spotless. Her thatch of wild hair had been tamed into a bushy ponytail and tied with a ribbon. She had little turquoise stars in her ears to match a ruffled and not-too-badly-wrinkled blouse. The dusting of freckles over her face had been partially hidden by a layer of powder. Eden imagined she had conned it out of one of the older girls, but let it pass.

"Hi, Roberta." Plucking two pretzels from a bowl, she handed one over. "Aren't you going to dance?"

"Sure." She glanced over her shoulder, confident and patient. "I wanted to talk to you first."

"Oh?" It didn't appear that she needed a pep talk. Eden had already seen the skinny, dark-haired boy Roberta had set her sights on. If Eden was any judge, he didn't stand a chance. "What about?"

"I saw that guy in the Rolls."

Eden's automatic warning not to speak with her mouth full was postponed. "You mean Mr. Keeton?"

"Some of the girls think he's cute."

"Hmm." Eden nibbled on her own pretzel.

"A couple of them said you were soft on him. They think you had a lovers' quarrel, you know, like Romeo and Juliet or something. Now he's come to beg you to forgive him, and you're going to realize that you can't live without him and go off and get married."

The pretzel hung between two fingers as Eden listened. After a moment, she managed to clear her throat. "Well, that's quite a scenario."

"I said it was baloney."

Trying not to laugh, she bit into the pretzel. "Did you?"

"You're smart, all the girls say so." Reaching behind Eden, she took a handful of chips. "I said you were too smart to be soft on the guy in the Rolls, because he's not nearly as neat as Mr. Elliot." Roberta glanced over her shoulder as if in confirmation. "He's shorter, too."

"Yes." Eden had to bite her lip. "Yes, he is."

"He doesn't look like he'd jump in the lake to fool around."

The last statement had Eden trying to imagine Eric diving into the cool waters of the lake half-dressed. Or bringing her a clutch of wildflowers. Or finding pictures in the sky. Her lips curved dreamily. "No, Eric would never do that."

"That's why I knew it was all baloney." Roberta devoured the chips. "When Mr. Elliot comes, I'm going to dance with him, but now I'm going to dance with

Bobby." Shooting Eden a smile, she walked across the room and grabbed the hand of the lanky, dark-haired boy. As Eden had thought, he didn't have a chance.

She watched the dancing, but thought of Chase. It came to her all at once that he was the only man she knew whom she hadn't measured against her father. Comparisons had never occurred to her. She hadn't measured Chase against anyone but had fallen in love with him for himself. Now all she needed was the courage to tell him.

"So this is how young people entertain themselves these days."

Eden turned to find Dottie beside her. For Camp Liberty's summer dance, she had chosen mauve lace. The pearls had been exchanged for a single, sensational ruby. BooBoo had a clip of rhinestones—Eden sincerely hoped they were only rhinestones—secured on top of her head. Feeling a wave of affection, Eden kissed her aunt. "Are you settled into your hotel?"

"So to speak." Accepting a potato chip, Dottie took her own survey. The powder-blue voile was the essence of simplicity with its cap sleeves and high neck, but Dottie approved the way it depended on the wearer for its style. "Thank God you haven't lost your taste."

Laughing, Eden kissed her again. "I've missed you. I'm so glad you came."

"Are you?" Always discreet, Dottie led her toward the screen door. "I was afraid you weren't exactly thrilled to see me here." She let the screen whoosh shut as they stepped onto the porch. "Particularly with the surprise I brought you."

"I was glad to see you, Aunt Dottie."

"But not Eric."

Eden leaned back on the rail. "Did you think I would be?"

"Yes." She sighed, and brushed at the bodice of her lace. "I suppose I did. It only took five minutes to realize what a mistake I'd made. Darling, I hope you understand I was trying to help."

"Of course I do, and I love you for it."

"I thought that whatever had gone wrong between you would have had time to heal over." Forgetting herself, Dottie offered BooBoo the rest of the chip. "To be honest, the way he's been talking to me, I was sure by bringing him to you I'd be doing the next-best thing to saving your life."

"I can imagine," Eden murmured.

"So much for grand gestures." Dottie moved her shoulders so that the ruby winked. "Eden, you never told me why you two called off the wedding. It was so sudden."

Eden opened her mouth, then closed it again. There was no reason to hurt and infuriate her aunt after all these months. If she told her now, it would be for spite or, worse, for sympathy. Eric was worth neither. "We just realized we weren't suited."

"I always thought differently." There was a loud blast of music and a chorus of laughter. Dottie cast a glance over her shoulder. "Eric seems to think differently, too. He's been to see me several times in recent weeks."

Pushing the heavy fall of hair from her shoulders, Eden walked to the edge of the porch. Perhaps Eric had discovered that the Carlbough name wasn't so badly tarnished after all. It gave her no pleasure to be cynical, but it was the only answer that seemed right. It wouldn't have taken him long to realize that eventually she would come into money again, through inheritances. She swallowed her bitterness as she turned back to her aunt.

"He's mistaken, Aunt Dottie. Believe me when I say he doesn't have any genuine feelings for me. Perhaps he thinks he does," she added, when she saw the frown centered between Dottie's brows. "I'd say it's a matter of habit. I didn't love Eric." Her hands outstretched, she went to take her aunt's. "I never did. It's taken me some time to understand that I was going to marry him for all the wrong reasons—because it was expected, because it was easy. And…" She drew in her breath. "Because I mistakenly thought he was like Papa."

"Oh, darling."

"It was my mistake, so most of it was my fault." Now that it was said, and said aloud, she could accept it. "I always compared the men I dated with Papa. He was the kindest, most caring man I've ever known, but even though I loved and admired him, it was wrong of me to judge other men by him."

"We all loved him, Eden." Dottie drew Eden into her arms. "He was a good man, a loving man. A gambler, but—"

"I don't mind that he was a gambler." Now, when she drew back, Eden could smile. "I know if he hadn't died so suddenly, he'd have come out on top again. But it doesn't matter, Aunt Dottie, because I'm a gambler, too." She turned so that her gesture took in the camp. "I've learned how to make my own stake."

"How like him you are." Dottie was forced to draw a tissue out of her bag. "When you insisted on doing this, even when I first came here today, I could only think my poor little Eden's gone mad. Then I looked, really looked, at your camp, at the girls, at you, and I could see you'd made it work." After one inelegant sniff, she stuffed the tissue back in her bag. "I'm proud of you, Eden. Your father would have been proud of you."

Now it was Eden's eyes that dampened. "Aunt Dottie, I can't tell you how much that means to me. After he died and I had to sell everything, I felt I'd betrayed him, you, everyone."

"No." Dottie cupped Eden's chin in her hand. "What you did took tremendous courage, more than I had. You know how badly I wanted to spare you all of that."

"I know, and I appreciate it, but it had to be this way."

"I think I understand that now. I want you to know that I hurt for you, Eden, but I was never ashamed. Even now, knowing you don't need it, I'll tell you that my house is yours whenever you like."

"Knowing that is enough."

"And I expect this to be the finest camp in the east within five years."

Eden laughed again, and all the weight she'd carried with her since her father's death slipped off her shoulders. "It will be."

With a nod, Dottie took a step along the rail and looked out at the compound. "I do believe you should have a pool. Girls should have regulated, regimented swimming lessons. Splashing in the lake doesn't meet those standards. I'm going to donate one."

Eden's back went up immediately. "Aunt Dottie—"

"In your father's name." Dottie paused and cocked a brow. "Yes, I can see you won't argue with that. If I can donate a wing to a hospital, I can certainly donate a swimming pool in my brother's name to my favorite niece's camp. In fact, my accountant's going to be thrilled. Now, would you like Eric and me to go?"

Barely recovered from being so neatly maneuvered, Eden only sighed. "Having Eric here means nothing now. I want you to stay as long as you like."

"Good. BooBoo and I are enjoying ourselves." Dottie bent down to nuzzle in the dog's fur. "The delightful thing about BooBoo is that she's so much more tractable than any of my children were. Eden, one more thing before I go inside and absorb culture. I would swear that I felt, well, how to put it? One might almost say earth tremors when I walked into the stables this afternoon. Are you in love with someone else?"

"Aunt Dottie—"

"Answer enough. I'll just add my complete approval, not that it matters. BooBoo was quite charmed."

"Are you trying to be eccentric?"

With a smile, Dottie shifted the bundle in her arms. "When you can't rely on beauty any longer, you have to fall back on something. Ah, look here." She stepped aside as the Lamborghini cruised up. Lips pursed, Dottie watched Chase climb out. "Hello again," she called. "I admire your taste." She gave Eden a quick pat. "Yes, I do. I think I'll just pop inside and try some punch. It isn't too dreadful, is it?"

"I made it myself."

"Oh." Dottie rolled her eyes. "Well, I've some gambler in me as well."

Bracing herself, Eden turned toward Chase. "Hello. I'm glad you could—"

His mouth covered hers so quickly, so completely, that there wasn't even time for surprise. She might think of the hard possessiveness of the kiss later, but for now she just slid her hands up his back so that she could grip his shoulders. Instantly intense, instantly real, instantly right.

She hadn't felt this with Eric. That was what Chase told himself as she melted against him. She'd never felt this with anyone else. And he was going to be damn sure she didn't. Torn between anger and need, he drew her away.

"What—" She had to stop and try again. "What was that for?"

He gathered her hair in his hand to bring her close again. His lips tarried a breath from hers. "As someone once said to me, I wanted to kiss you. Any objections?"

He was daring her. Her chin angled in acceptance. "I can't think of any."

"Mull it over. Get back to me." With that, he propelled her toward the lights and music.

She didn't like to admit that cowardice might be part of the reason she carefully divided her time between the girls and the visiting counselors. Eden told herself it was a matter of courtesy and responsibility. But she knew she needed to have her thoughts well in hand before she spoke privately with Chase again.

She watched him dance with Roberta and wanted to throw herself into his arms and tell him how much she loved him. How big a fool would that make her? He hadn't asked about Eric, so how could she explain? It hummed through her mind that if he hadn't asked, it didn't matter to him. If it didn't matter, he wasn't nearly as involved as she was. Still, she told herself that before the evening was over she would find the time to talk it through with him, whether he wanted to hear it or not. She just wanted to wait until she was sure she could do a good job of it.

There was no such confusion about the evening in general. The summer dance was a hit. Plans between the camp coordinators were already under way to make it an annual event. Already Candy was bubbling with ideas for more joint ventures.

As always, Eden would let Candy plan and organize; then she would tidy up the details.

By keeping constantly on the move, Eden avoided any direct confrontation with Eric or Chase. Of course they spoke, even danced, but all in the sanctuary of the crowded mess hall. Eric's conversation had been as mild as hers, but there had been something dangerous in Chase's eyes. It was that, and the memory of that rocketing kiss, that had her postponing the inevitable.

"I guess you like her a lot," Roberta ventured as she saw Chase's gaze wander toward Eden yet again.

"What?" Distracted, Chase looked back at his dance partner.

"Miss Carlbough. You're soft on her. She's so pretty," Roberta added with only the slightest touch of envy. "We voted her the prettiest counselor, even though Miss Allison has more—" She caught herself, realizing suddenly that you didn't discuss certain parts of a woman's anatomy with a man, even with Mr. Elliot. "More, ah…"

"I get the picture." Charmed, as always, Chase swung her in a quick circle.

"Some of the other girls think Mr. Keeton's a honey."

"Oh?" Chase's smile turned into a sneer as he glanced at the man in question.

"I think his nose is skinny."

"It was almost broken," Chase muttered.

"And his eyes are too close together," Roberta added for good measure. "I like you a lot better."

Touched, and remembering his first crush, Chase tugged on her ponytail to tilt her face to his. "I'm pretty soft on you, too."

From her corner, Eden watched the exchange. She saw Chase bend down and saw Roberta's face explode into smiles. A sigh nearly escaped her before she realized she was allowing herself to be envious of a twelve-year-old. With a shake of her head, she told herself that it was the strain of keeping herself unavailable that was beginning to wear on her. The music never played below loud. Uncountable trips to the kitchen kept the refreshment table full. Boys and girls shouted over the music to make themselves heard.

Five minutes, she told herself. She would steal just five quiet, wonderful minutes by herself.

This time, when she slipped back into the kitchen, she kept going. The moist summer air soothed her the moment she stepped outside. It smelled of grass and honeysuckle. Grateful for the fresh air after the cloying scent of fruit punch, Eden breathed deeply.

Tonight, the moon was only a sliver in the sky. She realized she had seen it change, had watched its waning and waxing more in the past three months than she had in all of her life. This was true of more than the moon. She would never look at anything else exactly the same way again.

She stood for a moment, finding the pictures in the sky that Chase had shown her. With the air warm on her face, she wondered if there would ever be a time when he would show her more.

As she crossed the grass, the light was silvery. From behind her came the steady murmur of music and voices. She found an old hickory tree and leaned against it, enjoying the solitude and the distance.

This was what warm summer nights were for, she thought. For dreams and wishes. No matter how cold it got during the winter, no matter how far away summer seemed, she would be able to take this night out of her memory and live it again.

The creak and swish of the back door cut through her concentration.

"Eric." She straightened, not bothering to disguise the irritation in her voice.

He came to her until he, too, stood under the hickory. Starlight filtered through the leaves to mix with the shadows. "I've never known you to leave a party."

"I've changed."

"Yes." Her eyes were calm and direct. He shifted uncomfortably. "I've noticed." When he reached out to touch her, she didn't step back. She didn't even feel his touch. "We never finished talking."

"Yes, we did. A long time ago."

"Eden." Moving cautiously, he lifted a finger to trace her jawline. "I've come a long way to see you, to make things right between us."

Eden merely tilted her head to the side. "I'm sorry

you were inconvenienced, but there's nothing to make right." Oddly, the anger, even the bitterness, had become diluted. It had started weakening, she knew, when he had kissed her that afternoon. Looking at him now, she felt detached, as if he were someone she'd known only vaguely. "Eric, it's foolish for either of us to drag this out. Let's just leave things alone."

"I admit I was a fool." He blocked her exit, as if by simply continuing in the same vein he could put things back in the order he wanted. "Eden, I hurt you, and I'm sorry, but I was thinking of you as well as myself."

She wanted to laugh, but found she didn't even have the energy to give him that much. "Of me, Eric? All right, have it your way. Thank you and goodbye."

"Don't be difficult," he said, displaying a first trace of impatience. "You know how difficult it would have been for you to go through with the wedding while the scandal was still fresh in everyone's mind."

That stopped her, more than his hand had. She leaned back against the tree and waited. Yes, there was still a trace of anger, she discovered. It was mild, and buried quite deep, but it was still there. Perhaps it would be best to purge everything from her system. "Scandal. By that I assume you mean my father's poor investments."

"Eden." He moved closer again to put a comforting hand on her arm. "Your position changed so dramatically, so abruptly, when your father died and left you..."

"To earn my own way," she finished for him. "Yes, we can agree on that. My position changed. Over the past few months I've become grateful for that." There was annoyance now, but only as if he were a pesky fly she had to swat away. "I've learned to expect things from myself and to realize money had very little to do with the way I was living."

She saw by his frown that he didn't understand, would never understand the person who had grown up from the ashes of that old life. "You might find this amazing, Eric, but I don't care what anyone thinks about my altered circumstances. For the first time in my life, I have what I want, and I earned it myself."

"You can't expect me to believe that this little camp is what you want. I know you, Eden." He twined a lock of hair around his finger. "The woman I know would never choose something like this over the life we could have together in Philadelphia."

"You might be right again." Slowly, she reached up to untangle his hand from her hair. "But I'm no longer the woman you knew."

"Don't be ridiculous." For the first time he felt a twinge of panic. The one thing he had never considered was driving hundreds of miles to be humiliated. "Come back to the hotel with me tonight. Tomorrow we can go back to Philadelphia and be married, just as we always planned."

She studied him for a moment, trying to see if there was some lingering affection for her there, some true emotion. No, she decided almost at once. She wished it had been true, for then she could have had some kind of respect for him.

"Why are you doing this? You don't love me. You never did, or you couldn't have turned your back on me when I needed you."

"Eden—"

"No, let me finish. Let's finish this once and for all."

She pushed him back a foot with an impatient movement of her hands. "I'm not interested in your apologies or your excuses, Eric. The simple truth is you don't matter to me."

It was said so calmly, so bluntly, that he very nearly believed it. "You know you don't mean that, Eden. We were going to be married."

"Because it was convenient for both of us. For that much, Eric, I'll share the blame with you."

"Let's forget blame, Eden. Let me show you what we can have."

She held him off with a look. "I'm not angry anymore, and I'm not hurt. The simple fact is, Eric, I don't love you, and I don't want you."

For a moment, he was completely silent. When he did speak, Eden was surprised to hear genuine emotion in his voice. "Find someone to replace me so soon, Eden?"

She could almost laugh. He had jilted her almost two steps from the altar, but now he could act out the role of betrayed lover. "This grows more and more absurd, but no, Eric, it wasn't a matter of replacing you, it was a matter of seeing you for what you are. Don't make me explain to you what that is."

"Just how much does Chase Elliot have to do with all of this?"

"How dare you question me?" She started past him, but this time he grabbed her arm, and his grip wasn't gentle. Surprised by his refusal to release her, she stepped back and looked at him again. He was a child, she thought, who had thrown away a toy and was ready to stamp his feet now that he wanted it back and couldn't have it. Because her temper was rising, she fell back on her attitude of icy detachment. "Whatever is or isn't between Chase and me is none of your concern."

This cool, haughty woman was one he recognized. His tone softened. "Everything about you concerns me."

Weary, she could only sigh. "Eric, you're embarrassing yourself."

Before she could rid herself of him again, the screen door opened for a second time.

"Apparently I'm interrupting again." Hands in pockets, Chase stepped down from the porch.

"You seem to be making a habit of it." Eric released Eden, only to step between her and Chase. "You should be able to see that Eden and I are having a private conversation. They do teach manners, even here in the hills, don't they?"

Chase wondered if Eric would appreciate his style of manners. No, he doubted the tidy Philadelphian would appreciate a bloody nose. But then, he didn't give a damn what Eric appreciated. He'd taken two steps forward before Eden realized his intent.

"The conversation's over," she said quickly, stepping between them. She might as well have been invisible. As she had felt herself being shifted to the middle that afternoon, now she felt herself being nudged aside.

"Seems you've had considerable time to say what's on your mind." Chase rocked back on his heels, keeping his eyes on Eric.

"I don't see what business it is of yours how long I speak with my fiancée."

"Fiancée!" Eden's outraged exclamation was also ignored.

"You've let some months slip past you, Keeton."

Chase's voice remained mild. His hands remained in his pockets. "Some changes have been made."

"Changes?" This time Eden turned to Chase, with no better results. "What are you talking about?"

Calmly, without giving her a glance, he took her hand. "You promised me a dance."

Instantly, Eric had her other arm. "We haven't finished."

Chase turned back, and for the first time the danger in his eyes was as clear as glass. "Yes, you have. The lady's with me."

Infuriated, Eden yanked herself free of both of them. "Stop it!" She'd had enough of being pulled in two directions without being asked if she wanted to move in either. For the first time in her life, she forgot manners, courtesy and control and did what Chase had once advised. When you're mad, he'd said, yell.

"You are both so *stupid*!" A toss of her head had the hair flying into her eyes to be dragged back impatiently. "How dare you stand here like two half-witted dogs snarling over the same bone? Don't either of you think I'm capable of speaking my own mind, making my own decisions? Well, I've got news for both of you. I can speak my own mind just fine. You." She turned to face Eric. "I meant every word I said to you. Understand? *Every single word.* I tried to phrase things as politely as possible, but if you push, let me warn you, you won't receive the same courtesy again."

"Eden, darling—"

"No, no, no!" She slapped away the hand he held out to her. "You dumped me the moment things got rough. If you think I'll take you back now, after you've shown yourself to be a weak, callous, insensitive—" oh, what was Candy's word? "—weasel," she remembered with relish, "you're crazy. And if you dare, if you *dare* touch me again, I'll knock your caps loose."

God, what a woman, Chase thought. He wondered how soon he could take her into his arms and show her how much he loved her. He'd always thought her beautiful, almost ethereal; now she was a Viking. More than he'd wanted anything in his life, he wanted to hold that passion in his arms and devour it. He was smiling at her when she whirled on him.

"And you." Taking a step closer to Chase, she began to stab him in the chest with her finger. "You go find someone else to start a common brawl over. I'm not flattered by your Neanderthal attempts at playing at the white knight."

It wasn't quite what he'd had in mind. "For God's sake, Eden, I was—"

"Shut up." She gave him another quick jab. "I can take care of myself, Mr. Macho. And if you think I appreciate your interference in my affairs, you're mistaken. If I wanted some—some muscle-flexing he-man to clean up after me, I'd rent one."

Sucking in a deep breath, she turned to face both of them. "The two of you have behaved with less common sense than those children in there. Just for future reference, I don't find it amusing that two grown men should feel it necessary for their egos to use me as a Ping-Pong ball. I make my own choices, and I've got one for you, so listen carefully. I don't want either one of you."

Turning on her heel, she left them standing under the hickory, staring after her.

Chapter 10

The last day of the session was pandemonium. There was packing and tears and missing shoes. Each cabin gave birth to its own personal crisis. Gear had to be stored until the following summer, and an inventory had to be made of kitchen supplies.

Beds were stripped. Linen was laundered and folded. Eden caught herself sniffling over a pillowcase. Somehow, during the first inventory, they came up short by two blankets and counted five towels more than they'd started with.

Eden decided to leave her personal packing until after the confusion had died down. It even crossed her mind to spend one last night in camp and leave fresh the following morning. She told herself it was more practical, even more responsible, for one of them to stay behind so that a last check could be made of the empty cabins. In truth, she just couldn't let go.

She wasn't ready to admit that. Leaving the laundry area for the stables, she began counting bridles. The only reason she was considering staying behind, she lectured herself, was to make certain all the loose ends were tied up. As she marked numbers on her clipboard, she struggled to block out thoughts of Chase. He certainly had nothing to do with her decision to remain behind. She counted snaffle bits twice, got two different totals, then counted again.

Impossible man. She slashed the pencil over the paper, marking and totaling until she was satisfied. Without pausing, she started a critical study of reins, checking for wear. A good rubbing with saddle soap was in order, she decided. That was one more reason to stay over one more night. But, as it often had during the past week, her confrontation with Chase and Eric ran through her mind.

She had meant everything she'd said. Just reaffirming that satisfied her. Every single word, even though she had shouted it, had come straight from the heart. Even after seven days her indignation, and her resolve, were as fresh as ever.

She had simply been a prize to be fought over, she remembered, as indignation began to simmer toward rage. Is that all a woman was to a man, something to yank against his side and stretch his ego on? Well, that wasn't something she would accept. She had only truly forged her own identity in recent months. That wasn't something she was going to give up, or even dilute, for anyone, for any man.

Fury bubbling, Eden crossed over to inspect the saddles. Eric had never loved her. Now, more than ever, that was crystal clear. Even without love, without caring, he'd wanted to lay some sort of claim. My woman. My property. My *fiancée*! She made a sound, somewhere between disgust and derision, that had one of the horses blowing in response.

If her aunt hadn't taken him away, Eden wasn't sure what she might have done. And, at this point, she was equally unsure she wouldn't have enjoyed it immensely.

But worse, a hundred times worse, was Chase. As she stared into space, her pencil drummed a rapid rat-a-tat-tat on the clipboard. He'd never once spoken of love or affection. There had been no promises asked or given, and yet he'd behaved just as abominably as Eric.

That was where the comparison ended, she admitted, as she pressed the heel of her hand to her brows. She was in love with Chase. Desperately in love. If he'd said a word, if he'd given her a chance to speak, how different things might have been. But now she was discovering that leaving him was infinitely more difficult than it had been to leave Philadelphia.

He hadn't spoken; he hadn't asked. The compromises she might have made for him, and only him, would never be needed now. Whatever might have been was over, she told herself, straightening her shoulders. It was time for new adjustments, new plans and, again, a new life. She had done it once, and she could do it again.

"Plans," she muttered to herself as she studied the clipboard again. There were so many plans to make for the following season. It would be summer again before she knew it.

Her fingers clutched the pencil convulsively. Was that how she would live her life, from summer to summer? Would there only be emptiness in between, emptiness and waiting? How many times would she come back and walk along the lake hoping to see him?

No. This was the mourning period. Eden closed her eyes for a moment and waited for the strength to return. You couldn't adjust and go on unless you'd grieved first. That was something else she had learned. So she would grieve for Chase. Then she would build her life.

"Eden. Eden, are you in there?"

"Right here." Eden turned as Candy rushed into the tack room.

"Oh, thank God."

"What now?"

Candy pressed a hand to her heart as if to push her breath back. "Roberta."

"Roberta?" Her stomach muscles balled like a fist. "Is she hurt?"

"She's gone."

"What do you mean, gone? Did her parents come early?"

"I mean gone." Pacing, Candy began to tug on her hair. "Her bags are all packed and stacked in her cabin. She's nowhere in camp."

"Not again." More annoyed than worried now, Eden tossed the clipboard aside. "Hasn't that child learned anything this summer? Every time I turn around she's off on a little field trip of her own."

"Marcie and Linda claim that she said she had something important to take care of before she left." Candy lifted her hands, then let them fall. "She didn't tell them what she was up to, that I'm sure of. You and I both know that she might only have gone to pick some flowers for her mother, but—"

"We can't take any chances," Eden finished.

"I've got three of the counselors out looking, but I thought you might have some idea where she could have gone before we call out the marines." She paused to catch her breath. "What a way to round out the summer."

Eden closed her eyes a minute to concentrate. Conversations with Roberta scattered through her memory until she focused on one in particular. "Oh, no." Her eyes shot open. "I think I know where she's gone." She was already rushing out of the tack room as Candy loped to keep up.

"Where?"

"I'll need to take the car. It'll be quicker." Thinking fast, Eden dashed to the rear of their cabin, where the secondhand compact was parked under a gnarled pear tree. "I'd swear she's gone to say goodbye to Chase, but make sure the orchard gets checked."

"Already done, but—"

"I'll be back in twenty minutes."

"Eden—"

The gunning of the motor drowned out Candy's words. "Don't worry, I'll bring the little darling back." She set her teeth. "If I have to drag her by her hair."

"Okay, but—" Candy stepped back as the compact shot forward. "Gas," she said with a sigh as Eden drove away. "I don't think there's much gas in the tank."

Eden noticed that the sky was darkening and decided to blame Roberta for that as well. She would have sworn an oath that Roberta had gone to see Chase one last time. A three-mile hike would never have deterred a girl of Roberta's determination.

Eden drove under the arching sign, thinking grimly of what she would say to Roberta once she had her. The pleasure she got from that slid away as the car bucked and sputtered. Eden looked down helplessly as it jolted again, then stopped dead. The needle of the gas gauge registered a flat *E*.

"Damn!" She slapped a hand on the steering wheel, then let out a yelp. Padded steering wheels weren't part of the amenities on cars as old as this one. Nursing her aching wrist, she stepped out of the car just as the first blast of thunder shook the air. As if on cue, a torrent of rain poured down.

For a moment, Eden merely stood beside the stalled car, her throbbing hand at her mouth, while water streamed over her. Her clothes were soaked through in seconds. "Perfect," she mumbled; then, on the heels of that: "Roberta." Casting one furious look skyward, she set off at a jogging run.

Lightning cracked across the sky like a whip. Thunder bellowed in response. Each time, Eden's heart leaped toward her throat. As each step brought her closer to Chase's home, her fear mounted.

What if she'd been wrong? What if Roberta wasn't there, but was caught somewhere in the storm, wet and frightened? What if she was lost or hurt? Her breath began to hitch as anxiety ballooned inside her.

She reached Chase's door, soaked to the skin and terrified.

Her pounding at the door sounded weak against the cannoning thunder. Looking back over her shoulder,

Eden could see nothing but a solid wall of rain. If Roberta was out there, somewhere… Whirling back, she pounded with both fists, shouting for good measure.

When Chase opened the door, she nearly tumbled over his feet. He took one look at her soaked, bedraggled figure and knew he'd never seen anything more beautiful in his life. "Well, this is a surprise. Get you a towel?"

Eden grabbed his shirt with both hands. "Roberta," she managed, trying to convey everything with one word.

"She's in the front room." Gently, he pushed the hair out of her eyes. "Relax, Eden, she's fine."

"Oh, thank God." Near tears, Eden pressed her fingers to her eyes. But when she lowered them, her eyes were dry and furious. "I'll murder her. Right here, right now. Quickly."

Before she could carry through with her threat, Chase stepped in front of her. Now that he'd had a good taste of her temper, he no longer underestimated it. "I think I have an idea how you feel, but don't be too rough on her. She came by to propose."

"Just move aside, or I'll take you down with her." She shoved him aside and strode past him. The moment she stood in the doorway, Eden drew a breath. "Roberta." Each syllable was bitten off. The girl on the floor stopped playing with the dog and looked up.

"Oh, hi, Miss Carlbough." She grinned, apparently pleased with the company. After a moment her teeth dropped down to her lower lip. Though perhaps an optimist, Roberta was no fool. "You're all wet, Miss Carlbough."

The low sound deep in Eden's throat had Squat's ears pricking. "Roberta," she said again as she started forward. Squat moved simultaneously. Drawing up short, Eden gave the dog a wary glance. He sat now, his tail thumping, directly between Eden and Roberta. "Call off your dog," she ordered without bothering to look at Chase.

"Oh, Squat wouldn't hurt you." Roberta scurried across the floor to leap lovingly on his neck. Squat's tail thumped even harder. Eden thought for a moment that he was smiling. She was certain she'd gotten a good view of his large white teeth. "He's real friendly," Roberta assured her. "Just hold your hand out and he'll sniff it."

And take it off at the wrist—which was giving her enough trouble as it was. "Roberta," Eden began again, staying where she was. "After all these weeks, aren't you aware of the rules about leaving camp?"

"Yes, ma'am." Roberta hooked an arm around Squat's neck. "But it was important."

"That isn't the point." Eden folded her hands. She was aware of how she looked, how she sounded, and she knew that if she turned her head she would see Chase grinning at her. "Rules have a purpose, Roberta. They aren't made up just to spoil your fun, but to see to order and safety. You've broken one of the most important ones today, and not for the first time. Miss Bartholomew and I are responsible for you. Your parents expect, and rightfully so, that we'll…"

Eden trailed off as Roberta listened, solemn-eyed. She opened her mouth again, prepared to complete the lecture, but only a shuddering breath came out. "Roberta, you scared me to death."

"Gee, I'm sorry, Miss Carlbough." To Eden's surprise, Roberta jumped up and dashed across the room to throw her arms around Eden's waist. "I didn't mean to, really. I guess I didn't think anyone would miss me before I got back."

"Not miss you?" A laugh, a little shaky, whispered out as Eden pressed a kiss to the top of Roberta's head. "You monster, don't you know I've developed radar where you're concerned?"

"Yeah?" Roberta squeezed hard.

"Yeah."

"I am sorry, Miss Carlbough, really I am." She drew back so that her freckled, triangular face was tilted to Eden's. "I just had to see Chase for a minute." She sent Eden an intimate, feminine glance that had Eden looking quickly over at Chase.

"Chase?" Eden repeated, knowing her emphasis on Roberta's use of the first name would get her nowhere.

"We had a personal matter to discuss." Chase dropped down onto the arm of a chair. He wondered if Eden had any idea how protectively she was holding Roberta.

Though it was difficult, Eden managed to display some dignity in her dripping clothes. "I realize it's too much to expect a twelve-year-old to show a consistent sense of responsibility, but I would have expected more from you."

"I called the camp," he said, taking the wind out of her sails. "Apparently I just missed catching you. They know Roberta's safe." Rising, he walked over and grabbed the tail of her T-shirt. A flick of the wrist had water dripping out. "Did you walk over?"

"No." Annoyed that he had done exactly what he should have done, Eden smacked his hand away. "The car..." She hesitated, then decided to lie. "Broke down." She turned to frown at Roberta again. "Right before the storm."

"I'm sorry you got wet," Roberta said again.

"And so you should be."

"Didn't you put gas in the car? It was out, you know."

Before Eden could decide to murder her after all, they were interrupted by the blast of a horn.

"That'll be Delaney." Chase walked to the window to confirm it. "He's going to run Roberta back to camp."

"That's very kind of him." Eden held her hand out for Roberta's. "I appreciate all the trouble."

"Just Roberta." Chase caught Eden's hand before she could get away from him again. Ready and willing, or kicking and screaming, he was holding on to what he needed. "You'd better get out of those wet clothes before you come down with something."

"As soon as I get back to camp."

"My mother says you catch a chill if your feet stay wet." Roberta gave Squat a parting hug. "See you next year," she said to Chase, and for the first time Eden saw a hint of shyness. "You really will write?"

"Yeah." Chase bent down, tilted her head and kissed both cheeks. "I really will write."

Her freckles all but vanished under her blush. Turning, she threw herself into Eden's arms again. "I'll miss you, Miss Carlbough."

"Oh, Roberta, I'll miss you, too."

"I'm coming back next year and bringing my cousin. Everyone says we're so much alike we should be sisters."

"Oh," Eden managed weakly. "Wonderful." She hoped one winter was enough time to recharge.

"This was the best summer ever." Roberta gave one last squeeze as tears began to cloud Eden's eyes. "Bye!"

The front door was slamming behind her before Eden had taken the first step. "Roberta—"

"It was my best summer ever, too." Chase took her free hand before she could try for the door.

"Chase, let me go. I have to get back."

"Dry clothes. Though, as I may have mentioned before, you look wonderful wet and dripping."

"I'm not staying," she said, even as he tugged her toward the stairs.

"Since I just heard Delaney pull off, and your car's out of gas, I'd say you are." Because she was shivering now, he hurried her up. "And you're leaving puddles on the floor."

"Sorry." He propelled her through his bedroom. Eden had a fleeting impression of quiet colors and a brass bed before she was nudged into the adjoining bath. "Chase, this is very nice of you, but if you could just drive me back—"

"After you've had a hot shower and changed."

A hot shower. He could have offered her sable and emeralds and not tempted her half so much. Eden hadn't had a hot shower since the first week of June. "No, I really think I should get back."

But the door was already closing behind him.

Eden stared at it; then, her lower lip caught between

her teeth, she looked back at the tub. Nothing she'd ever seen in her life had seemed so beautiful, so desirable. It took her less than ten seconds to give in.

"Since I'm here anyway..." she mumbled, and began to peel out of her clothes.

The first sizzle of hot spray stole her breath. Then, with a sigh of pure greed, she luxuriated in it. It was sinful, she thought as the water sluiced over her head. It was heaven.

Fifteen minutes later, she turned the taps off, but not without regret. On the rack beside the tub was a thick, thirsty bath towel. She wrapped herself in it and decided it was nearly as good as the shower. Then she noticed her clothes were gone.

For a moment, she only frowned at the empty rail where she'd hung them. Then she gripped the towel tighter. He must have come in and taken them while she was in the shower. Lips pursed, Eden studied the frosted glass doors and wondered how opaque they really were.

Be practical, she told herself. Chase had come in and taken her clothes because they needed to be dried. He was simply being a considerate host. Still, her nerves drummed a bit as she lifted the navy-blue robe from the hook on the back of the door.

It was his, of course. His scent clung to the material so that she felt he was all but in the room with her as she drew it on. It was warm and thick, but she shivered once as she secured the belt.

It was practical, she reminded herself. The robe was nothing more than an adequate covering until her clothes were dry again. But she tilted her head so that her chin rubbed along the collar.

Fighting off the mood, she took the towel and rubbed the mist away from the mirror. What she saw was enough to erase any romantic fantasies from her mind. True, the hot water from the shower had brought some color to her cheeks, but she hadn't even a trace of mascara left to darken her lashes. With the color of the robe to enhance them, her eyes dominated her face. She looked as though she'd been saved just before going under for the third time. Her hair was wet, curling in little tendrils around her face. Eden dragged a hand through it a few times, but couldn't bring it to order without a brush.

Charming, she thought before she pulled the door open. In Chase's bedroom she paused, wanting to look, wanting even more to touch something that belonged to him. With a shake of her head, she hurried through the bedroom and down the stairs. It was only when she stopped in the doorway of the front room and saw him that her nerves returned in full force.

He looked so right, so at ease in his workshirt and jeans as he stood in front of a nineteenth-century cabinet pouring brandy from a crystal decanter. She'd come to realize that it was his contradictions, as much as anything else, that appealed to her. At the moment, reasons didn't matter. She loved him. Now she had to get through this last encounter before burying herself in the winter months.

He turned and saw her. He'd known she was there, had felt her there, but had needed a moment. When he'd come into the bath to take her wet clothes, she'd been humming. He'd only seen a shadow of her behind the glass but had wanted, more than he could remember wanting anything, to push the barrier aside and take her. To hold her with her skin wet and warm, her eyes huge and aware.

He wanted her as much, as sharply, now as she stood in the doorway dwarfed by his robe.

So he'd taken a moment, for the simple reason that he had to be sure he could speak.

"Better?"

"Yes, thanks." Her hand reached automatically for the lapels of the robe and fidgeted there. He crossed the room to offer her a snifter.

"Drink. This should ward off the danger of wet feet."

As she took the glass, Chase closed the doors at her back. Eden found herself gripping the snifter with both hands. She lifted it slowly, hoping the brandy would clear her head.

"I'm sorry about all this." She made certain her tone was as polite and as distant as she could manage. She kept her back to the doors.

"No trouble." He wanted to shake her. "Why don't you sit down?"

"No, I'm fine." But when he continued to stand in front of her, she felt it necessary to move. She walked to the window, where the rain was still pouring from the sky. "I don't suppose this can keep up for long."

"No, it can't." The amusement he was beginning to feel came out in his voice. Wary, Eden turned back to him. "In fact, I'm amazed it's gone on this long." Setting his brandy aside, he went to her. "It's time we stopped it, Eden. Time you stopped backing away."

She gave a quick shake of her head and skirted around him. "I don't know what you mean."

"The hell you don't." He was behind her quickly, and there was nowhere to run. He took the snifter from her nerveless fingers before turning her to face him again. Slowly, deliberately, he gathered her hair in his hands, drawing it back until her face was unframed. There was a flash of fear in her eyes, but beneath it, waiting, was the need he'd wanted to see.

"We stood here once before, and I told you then it was too late."

The sun had been streaming through the glass then. Now the rain was lashing against it. As she stood there, Eden felt past and present overlap. "We stood here once before, and you kissed me."

His mouth found hers. Like the storm, the kiss was fierce and urgent. He'd expected hesitation and found demand. He'd expected fear and found passion. Drawing her closer, he found hunger and need and shimmering desire. What he had yet to find, what he discovered he needed most, was acceptance.

Trust me. He wanted to shout it at her, but her hands were in his hair, entangling him and pulling him to her.

The rain beat against the windowpanes. Thunder walked across the sky. Eden was whirling in her own private storm. She wanted him, wanted to feel him peeling the robe from her shoulders and touching her. She wanted that first delirious sensation of skin meeting skin. She wanted to give her love to him where it could be alive and free, but knew she had to keep it locked inside, secret, lonely.

"Chase. We can't go on like this." She turned her head away. "I can't go on like this. I have to leave. People are waiting for me."

"You're not going anywhere. Not this time." He slid a hand up her throat. His patience was at an end.

She sensed it and backed away. "Candy will be wondering where I am. I'd like to have my clothes now."

"No."

"No?"

"No," he said again as he lifted his brandy. "Candy won't be wondering where you are, because I phoned her and told her you weren't coming back. She said you weren't to worry, that things were under control. And no—" he sipped his brandy "—you can't have your clothes. Can I get you something else?"

"You phoned her?" All the fear, all the anxiety, drained away to make room for temper. Her eyes darkened, losing their fragility. Chase almost smiled. He loved the cool woman, the nervous one, the determined one, but he adored the Viking.

"Yeah. Got a problem with that?"

"Where did you possibly get the idea that you had a right to make my decisions for me?" She pushed a hand, covered by the cuff of his robe, against his chest. "You had no business calling Candy, or anyone else. More, you had no business assuming that I'd stay here with you."

"I'm not assuming anything. You are staying here. With me."

"Guess again." This time, when she shoved, there was enough power behind it to take him back a step. He knew that if he hadn't already been mad about her, he would have fallen in love at that moment. "God, but I'm sick to death of dealing with overbearing, dictatorial men who think all they have to do is want something to have it."

"You're not dealing with Eric now, Eden." His voice was soft, perhaps a shade too soft. "You're not dealing with other men, but with me. Only me."

"Wrong again, because I'm through dealing with you. Give me my clothes."

He set the snifter down very carefully. "No."

Her mouth would have fallen open if her jaw hadn't been clenched so tightly. "All right, I'll walk back in this." Ready to carry out her threat, she marched to the door and yanked it open. Squat lay across the threshold. As they spotted each other, he rose on his haunches with what Eden was certain was a leer. She took one more step, then, cursing herself for a coward, turned back.

"Are you going to call off that beast?"

Chase looked down at Squat, knowing the dog would do nothing more dangerous than slobber on her bare feet. Hooking his thumb in his pocket, he smiled. "He's had his shots."

"Terrific." With her mind set on one purpose, she strode to the window. "I'll go out this way then." Kneeling on the window seat, she began to struggle with the sash. When Chase caught her around the waist, she turned on him.

"Take your hands off me. I said I was leaving, and I meant it." She took a swing, surprising them both when it landed hard in his gut. "Here, you want your robe back. I don't need it. I'll walk the three miles naked." To prove her point, she began fighting the knot at the belt.

"I wouldn't do that." As much for his sake as hers,

he caught her hands. "If you do, we won't spend much time talking this through."

"I'm not spending any time at all." She squirmed until they both went down on the cushions of the window seat. "I don't have anything else to say to you." She managed to kick until the robe was hitched up to her thighs. "Except that you have the manners of a pig, and I can't wait until I'm hundreds of miles away from you. I decided the other night, when I was given the choice between a boring fool and a hardheaded clod, that I'd rather join a convent. Now take your hands off me, or I swear, I'll hurt you. No one, but no one, pushes me around."

With that, she put all her energy into one last shove. It sent them both tumbling off the cushions and onto the floor. As he had done once before, Chase rolled with her until he had her pinned beneath him. He stared at her now as he had then, while she fought to get her breath back.

"Oh God, Eden, I love you." Laughing at them both, he crushed his lips to hers.

She didn't fight the kiss. She didn't even move, though her fingers stiffened under his. Each breath took such an effort that she thought her heart had slowed down to nothing. When she could speak again, she did so carefully.

"I'd appreciate it if you'd say that again."

"I love you." He watched her eyes close and felt that quick twinge of panic. "Listen to me, Eden. I know you've been hurt, but you have to trust me. I've watched you take charge of your life this summer. It hasn't been the easiest thing I've ever done to stand back and give you the space you needed to do that."

She opened her eyes again. Her heart wasn't beating at a slow rhythm now, but seemed capable of bursting out of her chest. "Was that what you were doing?"

"I understood that you needed to prove something to yourself. And I think I knew that until you had, you wouldn't be ready to share whatever that was with me."

"Chase—"

"Don't say anything yet." He brought her hand to his lips. "Eden, I know you're used to certain things, a certain way of life. If that's what you need, I'll find a way to give it to you. But if you give me a chance, I can make you happy here."

She swallowed, afraid of misunderstanding. "Chase, are you saying you'd move back to Philadelphia if I asked you to?"

"I'm saying I'd move anywhere if it was important to you, but I'm not letting you go back alone, Eden. Summers aren't enough."

Her breath came out quietly. "What do you want from me?"

"Everything." He pressed his lips to her hand again, but his eyes were no longer calm. "A lifetime, starting now. Love, arguments, children. Marry me, Eden. Give me six months to make you happy here. If I can't, we'll go anywhere you like. Just don't back away."

"I'm not backing away." Her fingers entwined with his. "And I don't want to be anyplace but here."

She saw the change in his eyes even as his fingers tightened on hers. "If I touch you now, there's no going back."

"You've already told me it was too late." She drew him down to her. Passion and promises merged as they strained closer. She felt again that she had the world in the palm of her hand and held it tightly. "Don't ever let me go. Oh, Chase, I could feel my heart breaking when I thought of leaving here today, leaving you when I loved you so much."

"You wouldn't have gotten far."

Her lips curved at that. Perhaps, in some areas, she could accept a trace of arrogance. "You'd have come after me?"

"I'd have come after you so fast I'd have been there before you."

She felt pleasure grow, and glow. "And begged?"

His brow lifted at the glint in her eyes. "Let's just say I'd have left little doubt as to how much I wanted you."

"And crawled," she said, twining her arms around his neck. "I'm almost sorry I missed that. Maybe you could do it now."

He took a quick nip at her ear. "Don't press your luck."

Laughing, she held on. "One day this will be gray," she murmured as she trailed her fingers through his hair. "And I still won't be able to keep my hands out of it." She drew his head back to look at him, and this time there was no laughter, only love. "I've waited for you all my life."

He buried his face in her throat, fighting back the need to make her his, then and there. With Eden it would be perfect, it would be everything dreams were made of. He drew away to trace the line of her cheekbone. "You know, I wanted to murder Eric when I saw him with his hands on you."

"I didn't know how to explain when I saw you there. Then, later…" Her brow arched. "Well, you behaved very badly."

"You were magnificent. You scared Eric to death."

"And you?"

"You only made me want you more." He tasted her again, feeling the wild, sweet thrill only she had ever brought to him. "I had plans to kidnap you from camp. Bless Roberta for making it easy."

"I hope she's not upset you're going to marry me instead. You have a neat dog, and you're kind of cute." She pressed her lips to the sensitive area just below his ear.

"She understood perfectly. In fact, she approves."

Eden stopped her lazy exploration of his throat. "Approves? You mean you told her you were going to marry me?"

"Sure I did."

"Before you asked me?"

Grinning, Chase leaned down to nip at her bottom lip. "I figured Squat and I could convince you."

"And if I'd said no?"

"You didn't."

"There's still time to change my mind." He touched his lips to hers again, letting them linger and warm. "Well," she said with a sigh, "maybe just this once I'll let you get away with it."

* * * * *

Celebrate the holidays with a brand-new McKettrick
tale by beloved #1 *New York Times* bestselling author

LINDA LAEL MILLER

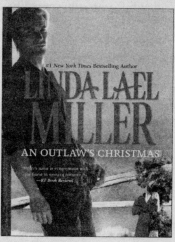

With his wild heart, Sawyer McKettrick isn't ready to settle down on the
Triple M family ranch in Arizona. So he heads to Blue River, Texas, to seek
a job as marshal. But in a blinding snowstorm he's injured—and collapses
into the arms of a prim and proper lady in calico.

The shirtless, bandaged stranger recuperating in teacher Piper St. James's
room behind the schoolhouse says he's a McKettrick, but he looks like
an outlaw. As they wait out the storm, the handsome loner has Piper
remembering long-ago dreams of marriage and motherhood.
But how long is Sawyer willing to call Blue River home?

AN OUTLAW'S CHRISTMAS

Available in hardcover today!

REQUEST YOUR FREE BOOKS!

2 FREE NOVELS
FROM THE ROMANCE COLLECTION
PLUS 2 FREE GIFTS!

YES! Please send me 2 FREE novels from the Romance Collection and my 2 FREE gifts (gifts are worth about $10). After receiving them, if I don't wish to receive any more books, I can return the shipping statement marked "cancel." If I don't cancel, I will receive 4 brand-new novels every month and be billed just $5.99 per book in the U.S. or $6.49 per book in Canada. That's a saving of at least 25% off the cover price. It's quite a bargain! Shipping and handling is just 50¢ per book in the U.S. and 75¢ per book in Canada.* I understand that accepting the 2 free books and gifts places me under no obligation to buy anything. I can always return a shipment and cancel at any time. Even if I never buy another book, the two free books and gifts are mine to keep forever.

194/394 MDN FELQ

Name _____ (PLEASE PRINT) _____

Address _____ Apt. #

City _____ State/Prov. _____ Zip/Postal Code

Signature (if under 18, a parent or guardian must sign)

Mail to the **Reader Service**:
IN U.S.A.: P.O. Box 1867, Buffalo, NY 14240-1867
IN CANADA: P.O. Box 609, Fort Erie, Ontario L2A 5X3

Not valid for current subscribers to the Romance Collection
or the Romance/Suspense Collection.

Want to try two free books from another line?
Call 1-800-873-8635 or visit www.ReaderService.com.

* Terms and prices subject to change without notice. Prices do not include applicable taxes. Sales tax applicable in N.Y. Canadian residents will be charged applicable taxes. Offer not valid in Quebec. This offer is limited to one order per household. All orders subject to credit approval. Credit or debit balances in a customer's account(s) may be offset by any other outstanding balance owed by or to the customer. Please allow 4 to 6 weeks for delivery. Offer available while quantities last.

Your Privacy—The Reader Service is committed to protecting your privacy. Our Privacy Policy is available online at www.ReaderService.com or upon request from the Reader Service.

We make a portion of our mailing list available to reputable third parties that offer products we believe may interest you. If you prefer that we not exchange your name with third parties, or if you wish to clarify or modify your communication preferences, please visit us at www.ReaderService.com/consumerschoice or write to us at Reader Service Preference Service, P.O. Box 9062, Buffalo, NY 14269. Include your complete name and address.

ROM11

NORA ROBERTS

(limited quantities available)

TOTAL AMOUNT	$	_____
POSTAGE & HANDLING	$	_____
($1.00 FOR 1 BOOK, 50¢ for each additional)		
APPLICABLE TAXES*	$	_____
TOTAL PAYABLE	$	_____

(check or money order—please do not send cash)

To order, complete this form and send it, along with a check or money order for the total above, payable to Harlequin Books, to: **In the U.S.:** 3010 Walden Avenue, P.O. Box 9077, Buffalo, NY 14269-9077; **In Canada:** P.O. Box 636, Fort Erie, Ontario, L2A 5X3.

Name: _____

Address: _____ City: _____

State/Prov.: _____ Zip/Postal Code: _____

Account Number (if applicable): _____

075 CSAS

*New York residents remit applicable sales taxes.
*Canadian residents remit applicable GST and provincial taxes.

Silhouette®

Where love comes alive™

PSNR1012BL